# CHAINED
# TO MY
# *Heart*

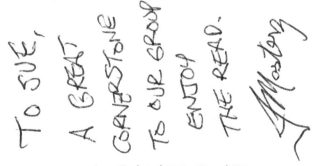

TO SUE,
A GREAT
CORNERSTONE
TO OUR GROUP
ENJOY
THE READ.

J Mastory

## JEFFREY MASTERZ

PAGE PUBLISHING, INC.
Conneaut Lake, PA

First originally published by Page Publishing 2021

ISBN 978-1-6624-2655-1 (pbk)
ISBN 978-1-6624-2656-8 (digital)

Printed in the United States of America

With my wife's unwavering love and never-ending belief, she has proved to me that anything and everything is possible.

And without her help, I can honestly say that there would be one less storyteller in the world. Thank you dear, for all you've done!

I would also like to give a very special thanks to Donna, Sue, Pam, Joe & Donna, the incredible team of proofreaders. Thank you all.

# CHAPTER 1

Lucas modestly turned up the volume on one of his favorite songs. Adjusting the chrome dial in his friend's SUV, he befittingly leveled it for a thirty-something-year-old man instead of that of a mind-numbing, bass-demanding teenager, who wanted the whole world to hear.

Through the soft glow of the console's instrumentation, Luke lip-synced the lyrics to the endearing Beach Boys tune, "Surfer Girl." He never sang or whispered the compilation of note perfection, knowing it would only dilute or contaminate such a flawless classic. And the second reason was he couldn't carry a tune in a bucket.

This tune may have graced the airwaves and of course vinyl, some twenty years before he was born, but he thoroughly savored its timeless harmonies and overall low-keyed melody. And yet he would say that of any of their hits on his old CD that undoubtedly had more mileage on it than he did as of late.

Lucas guided the Toyota SUV following the zigzagged road, even though the music had him veering in a completely different direction. From early this morning, he opened his eyes to the day thinking about his long upcoming furlough.

Since dawn he had concocted a mirage-like image of white-sand beaches and a pristine blue sea as it ebbed and flowed to the heartbeat of nature, down along a virtually endless shoreline. His mind's eye even combined that with a bevy of palms trees that swayed harmoniously to a breeze that kept them forever in motion.

This tropical scene had all the makings of a wonderous couple of weeks! The problem is, the vacation Luke had artfully puzzled together in his head was not the one he was about to take. With glimpses of Luke's truth materializing before his eyes, his landscape of paradise quickly dissolved. And with that the contrast of ground to sky brought him back to a tangible but true black-and-white reality.

The snow-packed channels crunched below as the red utility vehicle wound around the wintry perimeter to the rear of the vacant Seaview Inn. Pounded by an abrupt squall, the wind peppered the SUV that now sat dormant between the lodge and its freestanding carport.

After the hurricane-force blast ceased, he exited to lift the painted white wooden overhead door of the garage, only to expediently climb back in. Frantic were the flurries, scattering into the stall's cavity as if they too were trying to escape the cold.

With a firm grip on his luggage, Luke followed the gleam of the buildings rear light, using it to lead him to the lodge, through the bleakness of an ordinary Alaskan December afternoon.

Inside, he closed the kitchen door, leaving the wind to trail off, producing a dreadfully eerie sound that changed in both pitch and volume up until its full closure. It reminded him of when he once lived here, leaving him to shiver.

From the narrowed entryway of the kitchen, Luke flipped on a light before ridding himself of his worn brown bomber jacket and gray knit hat. In his blue flannel check shirt and jeans, he informally placed the flag with this being the official start of his vacation. And he was okay with that even if it wasn't the one he had envisioned earlier.

Getting his bearings, he focused on the oh so familiar faded 1960s wallpaper that displayed a worn and weathered tricolor grouping of time-honored cookware and utensils. The sight for him pleasingly called up some of his best recollections from the past, prompting him to grin.

Lucas flipped aside his untamed wavy raven locks that fell just into his field of vision. Then he ditched his bulky boots, for a pair of not-made-for-winter-use shoes. Lacing them, he lugged his bags up to what his best friend Kyle the innkeeper suggested, to room seven, as the time-worn pine boards beneath him creaked, replicating his every step.

The man eyeballed the room, or suite in this case, where he was to lie his head for the next two weeks. And being a builder by trade, he was immediately drawn to the massive coffee-colored rough-cut beams that spanned the width of the vanilla tinted walls, where a vaulted roofline ceiling flared above.

Rounding out its overall coziness, he viewed the beautiful array of early American furniture that included a king-size bed, a long waist-high bureau, a table with chairs, plus a loveseat and coffee table, with each piece hued in a gratifying milky golden oak.

He set his bags upon the white-based floral pattern of the thick cotton quilt as a booming gust rattled the windows and shutters, forcing his attention. A discernible aftershock in the form of exhaustion followed, making him dip into his second wind. But trying not to dwell on it or give in to it either, the man retreated for sustenance, to help extinguish and make the long travel day of his disappear.

Descending the banister, he thought back to his inbound flight from Anchorage that had been deemed unsuitable for flying. But the hopper pilot, who made that same run almost daily, gave him a second option. The man mentioned that he could get him there safely by using another route, with it adding only an extra hour or so. Luke, who wanted to be here and in one piece, took only a minute before he okayed the idea.

Although it wasn't turbulent-free by any means, his outcome changed as the two of them made it safely to Alaska's northernmost coast. And because of that, Lucas was very thankful that he had said yes and that he wasn't stuck seven hundred miles away on his very first night.

In the kitchen, Lucas pulled on the chrome handle of the dated white Westinghouse refrigerator, where he paused to read a note that Kyle penned, most likely on his way out the door. With some ingredients, a dab of inspiration and mayo, he crafted a sandwich of turkey, onion, and tomato on rye that roughly matched his hadn't-eaten-since-morning appetite.

Performing a quick cleanup, he left with plate in hand, to discover his favorite part of the inn, the pub. Luke was desperately in need of some whiskey, preferably a scotch, to wash down the sandwich, along with a comfy chair to enjoy them both.

A plethora of incredible memories peppered his brain as he inched his way to the bar that he hadn't saw in more than a decade. And because of that alone, he was looking forward to some new ones, even if he was to be alone for the first week.

Luke crept over the threshold into the pitch-black taproom, pushing at a heavy groaning hinged door that was in need of oil. With an outreached hand he flipped the first switch, turning on a light, if you could call it that. Its low-wattage incandescence barely lit the multiple glass tiers where the alcohol was stored or scarcely any of the service area. But not needing much for illumination this evening, he closed the thick rustic barrier behind him.

Lucas slid into the business side of the bar like he was slipping into a brand-new automobile, with both forbidden reluctance and undeserving anticipation. Gazing at what he could see of it, he placed the porcelain dish down upon its wooden surface so to extend his palm across the smooth, glasslike top. And that brought a flashback of when he and his father had built this spectacular piece.

His thoughts returned all the way back to the time when Kyle's grandfather Michael had told them how he had first acquired a stash of rough-cut Alaskan birch. Stacking the lumber neatly in the garage and basement in the 1950s, the man vowed that someday he would use it on something big, in some part of the inn.

After deciding that the yellowed stock be used for a bar that all would want to sit around, he chose to hire Luke and his father, from the town's mill yard. Michael said his choice was simple since Luke had been a long-time friend of his grandson's, and his father was known about town for his craftsmanship and dedication to perfection.

With only one stipulation, Michael asked if he could have the center round located directly in front of the fireplace. Finding out that it could be done, the man gave a resounding thumbs-up on the bar's design,

With that in mind, the two set out to turn the unfinished wood into a masterpiece. They milled, then cut and spliced the pieces, before immaculately finishing its patterned grain off, with eight coats of yellow shellac. The completed appearance was like glass then and still is to this day.

The memory for him might have concluded fifteen years ago, with Lucas experiencing his first beer, but it wasn't until the completion of the bar and the sixteen small tabletops. That is when his dad allowed him to partake of a draft, offered by the innkeeper. Touching the counter once more, he thought about all the memories that remained intact within its fabricated core.

Distraction over, he reached for a rocks glass and dipped into the cooler for a few cubes of ice, before pouring three fingers of Johnnie Walker Black. Then lighting a candle that he found from under the bar, Lucas meandered to the far end of the room, where he stopped in front of the colossal gray granite fireplace. Starving, the man took a bite of the deli sandwich, followed by a long draw on the full-bodied scotch.

Another powerful although muffled blast blew at the front of the lodge bringing on a chill. Combatting a sense of urgency, Lucas stacked and lit a match under the assemblage of dried kindling that he carefully piled atop of the black wrought iron rack.

With the wood ignited, he finally took the time to answer the text from Kyle that had been sitting there idly on his phone. He typed out, "Made it here. No problems. See you next week!" followed by "Thanks for the food."

It didn't dawn on him back at the fridge, but it truly was a blessing with him not having to run into town to get something to eat, when all he wanted to do was kick back and pacify himself.

With a second bite and another sip, he ventured out along the outskirts of the room to inflame only the closest wall lamps. When he was satisfied, he plunked himself down a few feet out from the welcoming hearth. It was there that Luke took in the tranquility of the pub that might have been weathered through the years, and yet still maintained that homey feel.

Lucas felt enveloped in the pine from the walls and floor as the flames grew, exposing more and more of the room as the seconds passed. Michael finished it with a light stain and polyurethane, which Lucas knew he had used to lighten the room for those long dark winter months. This place was bringing back so many memories, with him recalling his favorite hiding spot, over there in the stockroom. Going unsaid, he missed it.

The fire yielded a steady burn, interrupting Luke's gaze of checking out all that was around him. After more sandwich and more Johnnie, he closed his eye lids to take it all in, with only an occasional pop from the wood or the wind whistling down the chimney to break his solitude.

It was then that he detected a creak from the door he just stepped through minutes ago. Opening his eyes, he thought it was strange. Nobody's here, and Kyle's not due for another week.

A clamoring of hardened heels from a pair of boots sounded behind him, followed by a woman's voice that pleasingly filled the air. "Lucas?" Thinking he recognized her voice, he turned to view what was nothing but a silhouette until it transformed moments later, with her advancing towards him.

The woman sashayed in his direction, portraying a hint of a smile, which Luke gladly cloned. Meeting her partway, he brought the woman in close for a hug. When the embrace concluded, they parted only to gather at the now semi-heated hearth. Luke grabbed a second chair before refueling the fire for his good friend and best friend's sister, Taylor.

"I didn't hear you drive up," Lucas said as he retrieved a second glass.

"No, I had a friend pick me up at the airport. I didn't want to put her out any longer, so I walked the service road down to the garage. Plus, with that wind out there, you wouldn't have heard me anyway."

"Well, I'm glad you're here!" he exclaimed as he repeated his finger pour into the cubed glass of Taylor's. "Your brother said you're still in Fairbanks?" Lucas asked.

"Yes, I am. I bartend and wait tables," she answered while Luke held out his plate, graciously offering her half his meal. "Thank you," she said as she delicately accepted the diagonally cut sandwich.

During her silence, Luke stared down the profile of the long brown-haired five-foot, nine-inch beauty as she became entranced by the fires glow. He viewed Taylor, who sat on the edge of her seat, most likely for the warmth, wearing an eye-appealing cream knit sweater and gray wool pants, along with a pair of stylish black buckle boots.

Finally feeling the heat, Taylor leaned back in her seat and took a bite. She watched intently as the flames danced about. Realizing its distraction, she turned herself more in the direction of Lucas. "So are you still a contractor?" Taylor queried. It was the best she could come up with, with her already knowing the answer, speaking with Kyle about it many times in the past months.

"Yes, in Seattle. I have been doing that for about nine years now."

Taylor nodded. "And what brings you back to the Point?"

"Well, Kyle wanted me to watch the place and help him for New Year's Eve. He must have known that I needed a break, but it was my turn to come see him as he visited me the last two times. But what about you?" Lucas said, redirecting the question back to her.

"Actually, it is for the same reason. My brother called me to cover for him while he was off visiting Isla in Nome. I just couldn't give him a definite yes because of work, so I guess he asked you next," Taylor replied.

The man simply nodded before inquiring. "I am starting to hear a lot more about Isla. Are things getting serious?" Luke asked as he admired her high cheekbones along with her full set of perfectly defined lips from a few feet away.

"I think so. It's hard to tell what's going on in Kyle's head. I did see them together this past summer, and it appeared that there is much more than he leads on," Taylor answered, following it up with a taste of the Walker Black.

"I've got to apologize. I didn't know of your grandfather's passing until a month after! And I was very sorry to hear it," Lucas said, remembering the man's death just now.

"Thank you! Yeah, Kyle was really busy trying to find someone who could fill in for him at the inn since it was peak season. I know he would have told you if he had the time. It wasn't fun, but in the end, we were all together to help grandma Tilly, just like a family should do."

After more than an hour of conversation, and with it being mostly about Kyle, the two slowed in what they had to say. Taylor and Luke both enjoyed the light of the fire until it died off, allowing for the fatigue of their travels to consume them. Standing, they slowly departed in the direction of their rooms, snuffing out the kerosene lamps as they passed.

Taylor, who knew the history of the place backward and forward, gladly gave Luke the three-dollar tour as they walked. He was rightly surprised that so much had happened here, not having heard any of it before.

"The inn once had a guest known as Clay Wesner, a renowned area poet. Then there was a painter who stayed here for two weeks. The town council brought her in to capture the true feel of Point Hope while paying for her lodging. She loved it so much that she extended it to a month."

"So now her paintings hang in the town hall, with two that were personally earmarked for my grandparents. One hangs there behind the front desk. And the second, which was originally for my grandparents' room, is now hanging on the wall of room four, where the artist stayed."

He studied the portrait of her grandparents sitting proudly in the summery forefront of the inn as Luke toted Taylor's backpack over his shoulder, following her as they casually climbed the squeaky staircase. "From that sprung a strong relationship. I still hear from Katy Orenstein, who still asks about her!" she concluded.

The end of the tour was a slow stroll down her grandmother's hall of history, where Taylor pointed out pictures of her ancestors, explaining how the Cheesh-Na tribe had lived back then. Luke appreciated the images, with the first few captured on a tin plate, having learned they date back to the late 1800s. He never thought to ask when he saw the pictures as a youth. He honestly thought they represented the many tribes of Native Americans that resided here in Alaska.

Luke placed Taylor's blue denim bag on the bed and turned to leave, but not before she reached out for a hug. With Lucas closing the door following his exit, she juggled happy thoughts of being there with a dear friend.

Lucas stirred to the aroma of a home-cooked breakfast. Noticing he was famished, he dressed and allowed that same smell to lead him nose-first down to where he viewed one singular decorated table in the middle of the dining room.

While all the others remained as he remembered them in the offseason, the next nearest tabletop held a large oval metal cover. But before he could go and search for the cook, the early bird marched in with a pot of piping hot coffee. "Oh, I was just about to call you!" she exclaimed as she retracted the stainless cover to present an array of eggs, bacon, home fries, and toast, which was enough for at least four people.

When they finished and neither could ingest another bite, Taylor spoke. "So how are Mom and Dad doing?"

"They are good, really good. They are in St. Petersburg now."

"That's quite a change from living here. Talk about going from one extreme to another," Taylor stated with her coffee in hand.

"That's for sure," Lucas agreed. "But it hasn't changed Mom much, as she is still a homebody, keeping Dad well fed and the rest of the place neat and tidy. And Dad, who is retired, never embraced the concept, but he fights it less now," Luke informed her. "The guy is something. If it weren't for his arthritis, I would still have trouble keeping up with him." Halting his multiple breathed rant, he asked, "And how's your family?"

"Mom and Dad are good, although they have been lightly hounding me to either get back together with Marty or get my life restarted. Outside of that, they are enjoying all the perks of the retirement village. Grandma is in the nursing home in Fairbanks, where she has been missing my grandfather, my Nonno, something terribly since he passed. But now I don't think she has much more time left," Taylor said, trailing off, noticeably saddened.

"Is it bothering you that you left home then?"

"No, because you know Tilly, when she says to do something, you better do it!" she exclaimed before adding more. "She also told me not to stay by her bedside. She insisted I go on with my life by stating that I don't need to be with her to be with her."

Scooping up the dishes, Taylor questioned an observance concerning her old-time friend. "Lucas, am I starting to see a hint of gray here and there?"

"Yeah, I'm not sure what to make of it yet. I think I am following in my dad's footsteps. His is completely salt-and-pepper now," Lucas answered. "Why, do you think I should cover it up?" Lucas inquired.

"Don't you dare. I like it. It makes a man distinguished and sexy."

"Even me?"

"Yes, even you," Taylor replied with a smirk.

Wanting to get the remainder of the leftovers in the fridge, the two hauled the food back into the kitchen when Luke's phone rang. Taylor dismissed him by saying that the dishes could wait, prompting him to excuse himself, as it was already into its fourth ring.

"Oh, hi, Kyle," he said, making sure he made eye contact with Taylor. Pacing as Lucas often did with calls, he interjected, "Oh, I had quite the surprise last night. Your sister's here!"

"Oh, really? I know she wanted to. She likes being at Point Hope for New Year's. You know her, she gets to reunite with friends, but it also gets her away from her ex! So everything else all right?" Kyle asked.

"All is fine. Hey, I know we have a lot to catch up on, but I don't want to keep you, so why don't you get back to Isla and have a great Christmas! We'll talk next week!"

"Will do, buddy," Kyle concluded.

Lucas hated to cut him short, but he wanted to help Taylor, who apparently was now off somewhere else, as she was clearly not in the kitchen. But instead of searching for her any further, he slipped out to complete his first chore of the day, that being to fill the wood rack that they nearly emptied last night.

With only the light of the sixty-watt bulb to guide him, Luke stepped carefully out to the drift-covered tarp on the edge of the yard and loaded his arms full with wood. Covering it, he worked his way back to the inn, not so much for its warmth and light but for his company inside.

Grossly misjudging the weight, he wished he had given it more thought, with maybe carrying it in in two trips. It took all of his strength to finish those last twenty feet. He hoofed it toward Taylor, who was busy hanging ornaments on a very real looking artificial Christmas tree, signifying the very late transition of the alehouse into the holiday season.

Seeing he needed help, she took the wood a couple of pieces at a time and dropped them onto the rack rather than let the man try to figure how to unload it or hurt himself in the process. Then with his two free hands he, in turn, thankfully assisted her in the co-decorating of the fake blue fir that was located along the front wall.

"How did you get all this done?" Luke queried since even though the room wasn't too well-lit last night, he knew there wasn't a tree.

"I was up very early this morning," Taylor replied as she threw a handful of her long hair back over her right shoulder.

Minutes transpired until a round of laughter erupted, as Lucas recalled one of the few Christmases they both were lucky enough to share. She grinned broadly, with it not being something she had done a lot of lately. Taylor was undeniably as content as could be with Luke managing to make her feel good about herself, at least for the time being.

While searching for the best location for a ceramic candy cane, she gazed across into his slate gray eyes. Growing curious, Taylor thought she still didn't know what his situation was. Later would be a good time to ask.

# CHAPTER 2

That evening Lucas and Taylor eased their way to the bar as it was apparently the best way to end one's day, in a private celebration of sorts, with a longtime friend of Point Hope.

Being a heterosexual male, Lucas inadvertently checked out his friend's backside as it swayed a few feet in front of him. He only broke his somewhat unintentional stare to divert to the same bottle of last night. But she cut him off by suggesting tequila, which had him searching for the Mexican firewater, on a bar he didn't know.

"No, not there," Taylor cheeked as she popped into the storage room, emerging with a sealed bottle of Casa Noble in hand. "This is the good stuff. It's a single-barrel anejo, and you will never find this tequila on my brother's rack!" she boldly proclaimed.

The two settled down in front of the blaze of the roaring fire, where only the bottle and many unused shot glasses separated them. Well, their first tequila hurriedly turned to two, which quickly became three. The effect spurred a soothing warmth that crept in, eventually taking control of their bodies and hindering their overall reasoning.

"You know, Luke, I am amazed the two of us never hooked up. I mean we had a great friendship for all those years," Taylor stated.

"We did, but the timing was never right, and there were a couple of things that stood in the way. I had that on-again, off-again relationship with Kelly, while you were dating Marty since you were like fifteen."

"Yeah, that's right!" she exclaimed, causing a verbal lapse.

Luke pryingly asked something that he couldn't ask her yesterday. "Taylor, what did happen to you and Marty?" He wasn't sure that he wanted to say it exactly that way, but the words were already out.

"Well, I knew this was going to come up, but Marty and I just grew apart," Taylor stated as her eyes deviated fractionally from his.

"Was he unfaithful?" She laughed uncontrollably, stopping in time from sipping her drink and from him ultimately wearing it.

Once she could vocalize her response, she answered, "No, Marty wasn't much of a lover. And that's hard to say since he was my only, and I had nothing to compare it to. But the truth is, we hardly ever had sex. And when we did, it was always one position. He had to look me in the eyes, and after that many years, I grew tired of looking back."

She wasn't sure why she told him this, but it didn't matter at this point. Besides, these were the conversations that she had with a younger Lucas, very open. Granted now they were much more age-appropriate. So in a way, this was no more than a continuation of what they had always done.

"Then are you seeing anyone?" he said as he wanted to slap himself for blatantly speaking, before he thought.

"No, I'm not. I need to find out who I am. This has been good for me. I'm lonely at times, but it's good just the same," Taylor stated, reassuring only herself. Lucas wanted to ask more, but she already told him that she's alone. Plus, he felt like he had gone too far as it is.

The liquor and one of his inquiries finally brought an unasked question from earlier today. Trying not to appear drunk, Taylor merely let it roll off her tongue. "So how about you? Do you have a woman in Seattle?"

"No, not for a couple of years now," he replied in full realization. "Because of work alone, it's tough to have any kind of relationship, and a lot of times I'm not around enough to even have a dog."

"You don't have a dog?" Taylor frowned, hoping he might have worded his comment improperly.

"No, there's no dog at home," Lucas replied.

Disappointed by it, Taylor uttered, "You know, I still walk through the inn from time to time thinking I can hear Chestnut in the halls or on the stairs. I miss her," Taylor said, recounting her grandparents' Bulgarian shepherd who would come running, whenever she visited the inn. She briefly smiled at the thought of the loving dark-brown-and-white dog, who was friendly to all, with her living a full, happy nineteen years.

The used shot glasses rested upside down, creating a grouping on the cork top tray between them. It sat there as a reminder as to how many they had consumed, although neither of them were counting. The two downed the next shot, making sure to flip the jiggers and leave them tight against all the other fluidic rimmed downturned glasses.

Then from the alcohol and its coursing haze, more recollections of their past surfaced. Saving his best story for last, Lucas recalled the only time they were both drunk together and on tequila to boot. Taylor maybe couldn't remember it, or she was urging him to retell the tale. Either way, she looked at him glassy-eyed, awaiting the anecdote from their past.

Searching for the story, Luke thought. He had mentioned that night, and now she wanted to hear it. With that same tequila fog surrounding him, he paused. "Well, the four of us were here. There were you and Marty, Kyle, and myself, and we were celebrating. You two were engaged, and it was your party," he said. "Being young and foolish, we hammered back more than a few tequilas." Taylor beamed as Luke continued, although her eyes alone would have shown this.

"Kyle called it quits early with him going up to bed. Then Marty passed out there on the bench next to you. Oh, I do remember that your grandparents didn't want us out drinking in town, so that is why we were at the inn." She twinkled when she heard that little tidbit.

"The two of us moved in front of the fire, leaving Marty to sleep it off, while we had some words that I still regret mentioning. I remember saying that you should not go through with it, and you should take some time to figure out what you want. Maybe even go to college, like your grandmother urged you to do. And that's when you stubbornly turned it all serious and stated that he was your future. You were so adamant about it that you said—"

"Oh my God! I said, if you were right, then you could spank me!" Taylor exclaimed, finishing his story with raised brows. "I said you could spank me? Was I twelve? Why would I say that?"

"I'm not sure. But it did change the flow of the conversation."

"I still don't know why I would say that, but…but I… I think you owe me a spanking," Taylor stammered, owning up to the vow she made through her youthfully drunken bolstering.

Luke peered over at Taylor as she contemplated her semi-harmless demise. The mood however changed in the upcoming minutes, when it appeared that this might become reality. So with no real way out, she stood on wavering legs and flirtingly turned her ass toward him.

"Well, what are you waiting for Lucas?" the woman and her tequila questioned. She stood there with a lifted hip, showing him a portion of her jean covered backside.

"Are you seriously asking to be spanked?" he countered, confused by the sudden turn of events.

Taylor took in a long inhale before declaring what it was, she needed to get out. "Let's do this! I don't like to owe anybody anything." Hearing that his mind cleared, almost to the point of immediate sobriety.

While surveying the area, he exclaimed, "Hold that thought!" Escorting Taylor by the hand to the circular section of the birch top bar, he said, "Wait here!" Lucas disappeared into the storeroom only to return a minute later, carrying nothing more than a potato sack, an empty wooden crate, and a barely visible smirk.

She stared at the six-foot man as he placed the empty beverage case on its end beside her, and the burlap sack upon the nearest vacant stool. Taylor stood befuddled as Lucas locked eyes with her, popping the question. "So how do you want it?"

With a drunken, halfhearted grin, she asked, "Want what?"

"Your spanking, of course. I owe you one, remember?"

Under the influence, Taylor finally answered, "By the bar?" Since it is there that he had led her in the first place. Her head was a whirl, and because of drinking herself into this self-induced stupor, she was leaving herself open to something she hadn't experienced since she was a child.

"Okay," Luke said, retreating to the fireside seating area to knuckle clench the neck of the somewhat lighter bottle of alcohol and the last two unused glasses. Taylor snapped her head aside, in speculation of the contents in what appeared to be an empty bag. Bringing the alcohol to the bewildered brunette, he swiftly poured them another round.

Taylor thought long and hard through the muddled mind of hers. Her eyes shown that she trusted Lucas, for whatever that meant right now. But it was here that she took this pivotal moment to plant an unexpected kiss on his lips with her deciding that this was as good a time as any. Lots of shot glasses ago, it would have been different. Well, Taylor figured he would dole out her playful punishment, and then they would have a lot to laugh at in the morning.

The two lifted their glasses again. "Here's to a great time," Luke toasted. They clinked and expediently downed the Mexican delight. When the burn subsided, Luke double-timed it to retrieve a dozen tealight candles, with their miniature glass bases from the shelf below the bar. After what felt like an endless amount of time, Lucas lit the twelve holders, with six grouped at each side of the round top in front of her.

Taylor's eyes spun erratically as Lucas reached into the cavity of the virtually endless bag, only to slowly extract a lengthy piece of white cotton rope. From the moment she saw it, she couldn't turn her eyes away or even blink for that matter. Taylor, who was too busy in thought about being spanked, knew this had never crossed her mind. Confusion set in as she theorized the possibility of being whipped.

With this train already leaving the station and a confounded Taylor left standing at the gate, he gently laid the centered length across her wrists, which he had previously gathered together. Lucas only paused to catch any form of adverse reaction.

When it appeared that Taylor was not opposed to it, he wrapped her wrists. She studied his handiwork like she was being amazed by a street magician, but by the time Taylor figured it out, the trick was over. With her arms bound tightly together, Luke completed it by adding a knot that anchored the line leaving only its two long loose lengths.

Turning the empty wooden cola crate upside down, and with the two leads still in his hand, he assisted her up onto the makeshift six-inch step. Taylor leaned against the bar's edge, searching for questions, but for the life of her, she couldn't come up with any. "Are you okay?" Luke inquired since she still stared at the ties that held her. She finally bobbed her head, showing no signs of reluctance.

Taylor never did anything like this, ever. Her husband wasn't the type, and that was just one of the reasons why they weren't still together. In her head she only questioned it, as she imagined it would be over his knee. Well, this isn't looking like that so far.

She gazed at Lucas as he one-handedly held the rope across the counter, on the rear side of the bar. With the other hand, she saw him pull the towel from the stainless-steel loop of the cooler, leaving a resounding clang, as gravity made it fall back in place. Through the round chrome ring, he unhurriedly drew the cord toward him, leading her wrists forward as he relished in her participation.

A little additional draw and her torso gradually lowered itself onto the top of the rounded wooden structure. Taylor's long brown hair that previously gathered behind her shoulders fell forward joining the rest of her body. In a state of turmoil, she was about to say something, when the Casa Noble pulled the blanket over it and called for her to relax.

With her arms extended as far as they could reach, Taylor tipped her head up to look at him, as she found herself tautly pinned into a stationary position. "You probably didn't think your spanking was going to be like this?" Luke asked. Taylor's eyes widened to the size of silver dollars, so much so that she made a mental note of no more tequila tonight!

With Taylor deep in thought, Lucas placed a towel beneath her head to make sure her face was comfortable upon its hard surface. Next, she felt her ankles as they were being strapped to the crate beneath her. Unable to keep up, she wanted to tell him again to stop. However, the liquor and her curiosity had her gagged with not a single word passing through her lips, but her pussy on the other hand, was dripping like a leaky faucet.

Right then for some reason, certain instances popped into her head of the two of them. They had a friendship that developed only because of Luke's relationship with her brother. So back when there were opportunities, they would have incredible in-depth talks. But the only time they ever kissed was on the cheek at her wedding and a couple of minutes ago.

Taylor mentally struggled to keep up with the extremely slow pace of what Lucas was doing to her, and that included the realization that he had already left her side. Because of her inebriation, too many thoughts were now engulfing her. After stoking the fire, Luke returned to position the tea lights impeccably along the outer edge of the arced top where he had Taylor softly enshrined in its amber glow.

When it was to his liking, he asked, "So where were we?" Oblivious to Luke's rhetoric, Taylor panted softly, bringing Lucas to tug on the woman's empty jean belt loops. She remained inflexible as her faded jeans were slowly being pulled from Taylor's backside. However, it wasn't until the loose material grouped at her ankles that Taylor realized that he was going to see just how aroused; she already knew she was.

Luke floated his left hand across the contour of her clothed spine, making her squirm with warranted excitement. A few passes later, he reached under her top, where he traced patterns upon the small of her back, barely grazing the edge of her thinly pantied buttocks.

Then without warning, her body bounced uncontrollably, spasming from the jolt to her backside. Taylor shuddered, panting from what Lucas had unleashed on her. "Oh my God," she let out into the cotton towel.

"Are you okay?" Lucas asked.

"Yes," she orated, breathlessly giving the muffled response. Taylor thought the pain would linger from the smack. But she guessed it hadn't because she was so severely impaired and utterly turned on.

With that, he leaned down and whispered, "So are you ready for your spanking?" Shock consumed her. What? Hadn't he done it yet? But she felt the slap, didn't she? After many seconds, Taylor did manage a nod.

Making sure she was able to continue, he slid off her panties with them piling softly atop of her already-gathered denim pants. A thin clear strand dribbled from her pussy lips, exiting down to her sheer underwear that previously held it.

The light from the candles continued its ongoing illumination of her skin as Luke moved in gradually. He could see how she lost control, and so he decided to take it slower, even as his penis now desperately wanted its time.

Taylor realized with her not having sex in over a year that this could be the time, although it's not how she would have pictured it. *What is he doing back there? Why isn't he fucking me already?* Taylor wondered as she fidgeted, testing her fixed immobility.

Placing his left palm and fingers firmly across her back, Luke's other hand roamed the territory of Taylor's smooth, soft, subtle ass, zeroing in on its fleshy target. His right hand pulled away landing itself with a smacking sound, only to have it echo vocally from her lips. It was merely a test smack, but her body let out that she liked it, even as Taylor was unable to verbalize it.

The second hit made her wince in a pleasurable sort of way. It was pain, but her body somewhat welcomed it. The next slap was again, a bit harder, as her juices continued to drip from the greatest sexual pleasure she had ever or never known. If she could have made her thoughts known while she laid there snugly secured, she wouldn't have called this sex, even though her mind was dragging her there this very minute.

Taylor didn't care that she couldn't move an inch. It finally got to the point when she was about to give in and yell out, but Lucas and his inflicted slaps to her backside ceased.

After a break with no contact to her ass, she worked to catch her breath through the white towel that still covered her mouth. A cool sensation followed, in the vicinity to where she was smacked, until she realized it was actually ice-cold.

With Luke holding nothing but a single ice cube in his fingertips, he dabbed at the pink marks that shone onto her soft tan derriere. However, it wasn't until Luke undid the last of the bonds that she asked, choosing the words that first entered her mind. "Why didn't you fuck me?"

A mute Lucas paid no attention as he safely grounded Taylor from her perch. "How come you didn't have sex with me?" she asked much louder this time while she retrieved her pants and underwear.

She appeared mad but was merely frustrated. Tucking in her light-green blouse, she grilled the man. "You know you could have had your way with me, and I couldn't have stopped you!"

Trying to be the sober one, Luke carefully chose his words before answering, "You know this was all about your spanking, and because of that, I was not going to take advantage of you while you were drunk."

Taylor was disappointed, and even though she didn't want to, she did understand. Following her recent freedom, she subconsciously reached to feel the indentations upon her joints. The moment had truly passed, and the reality of what happened was setting in, with it now being beyond uncomfortable with all the things that neither of them was ready to talk about.

The speechless pair worked their way up to their rooms, with Taylor unsure as to how she should address this form of punishment that caught her so off guard. She reminded herself of how they were both going to laugh about this in the morning. Well, that wasn't to be the case now. With nothing more than awkward silence, they each got into their own beds, thinking about what they would say when they spoke next.

Lucas opened his eyes only to let them close immediately. Then a light tap sounded seconds later. "Come in," Luke called out as he now understood why he woke in the first place.

Donning a light-blue flannel nightshirt, Taylor stepped in holding a brass chamberstick with a lit white taper projecting up from its central socket. "I can't sleep. Do you mind if we talk?"

"Sure, come in," he said as he turned on the table lamp. Taylor blew out the candle, which produced an erratic narrow billowing spire. She placed the candle on the nightstand and stepped around to the flip side of Luke's bed to join him.

She sat atop of the covers, with her back resting up against the headboard, as Luke patiently awaited Taylor who fluttered her eyes wildly, attempting to invoke her first question. However, the same ordeal that kept her from sleeping was now rendering her speechless.

"I'm not gay, Taylor!" Lucas said to get the ball rolling in comedic fashion. She cackled as Lucas verbally had broken the ice.

Once she regained her composure enough, she commented, "Luke, I have to say, I've known you for a long time and I thought I had you all figured out, but now I see there is much more to you that I didn't know. I mean it's okay if you don't want to talk about it, but if you do, I want to ask about what you did and why you didn't." Then came the pause.

Searching for an explanation, along with the fact that he was asleep just a minute ago, he gingerly spoke. "Well, your brother doesn't know this, and I would like it to stay that way, but I am telling you this, well, because you showed me your ass," Lucas said as Taylor broke a smile.

"But seriously, I have ah…had times with women, where I occasionally have softly dominated or led them." He paused to collect his thoughts and catch her expression. "In the past, I had two relationships with what others would refer to as submissive. Neither worked out for various reasons. But right from the start, they both knew upfront that this is who I am. It's not all that I am! It is just a part, you know, like a facet on a diamond."

Taylor had a little knowledge of the terms dominant and submissive, so she felt no compulsion to halt his clarification to court some stupid questions. "So under the right conditions, could I have been in trouble?"

"No! What I do and have always done is entirely for the pleasure of the one I'm with. I would never take advantage of you and definitely not after you had been drinking all night. And besides, if it weren't for the tequila, even your spanking would have gone much differently."

"What do you mean?" she inquired.

"Oh, I'm sure you would have gotten it. It just would have been over my knee, with your pants still on. So do you understand why I didn't?"

"Of course, I do! I'm over that now!" Taylor exclaimed. "Um, but back to the other two women, were they submissive when you met them?"

"Well, the first became this way by her choosing, by my hand. I guess it was the catalyst to me becoming this, acting on the thoughts

I originally had. That's when I figured out that I was, you know, dominant. The second was not a relationship and not sexual, but she was far more advanced than I was. She was a switch! Do you know what that is?" Lucas inquired. Taylor only nodded so to keep the story moving.

"Well, without my control, I found myself being pulled up to her level. It was like she was steering or leading me, and I grew very uncomfortable with that. When you do, you lose a foothold on the position you play. So, as this woman needed more, we eventually moved on, and I'll just leave it at that."

Lucas added, "In each case, neither of them were the right fit. It was hard finding the time because of my work and the travel that was involved. They were two totally different women. Celeste was too into that life and Tara; my girlfriend got a job offer in New York. I couldn't be here for her enough, so she accepted it. She made the right decision."

As he rambled, she hung to his every word trying to come up with what she was going to ask next. At some point, Lucas knew there would be an onslaught of questions, just going off his ex-girlfriend's initial reaction.

In the wonderment of the stories that flowed out of him so honestly, Taylor inquired, "So do you think I'm submissive?"

"I don't know. It's hard to say. Just because you liked it when you were drunk doesn't make you one. So I am apt to say no. And you are my best friend's sister, and I'm biased since I guess I have always wanted there to be more between us." He paused to ask her, "Hey, totally unrelated, have you had much rope time? I mean being tied up!"

"No. I have never done that before," Taylor replied.

"So I had a virgin? Then I am really sorry that we drank so much."

"Luke, don't be, because I'm not." She disclosed as she inched in closer. "However, I was shocked that I liked it so much. The feeling was so intense I thought I was going to have an orgasm."

Thoroughly astonished, Luke leaned back and chuckled while he stared her down. "Are you kidding me, Taylor? You did cum!"

In shock the woman tried to recollect when this happened. She never had an orgasm with Marty, outside of masturbating when she was young. "Wait a minute. Are you saying I came?"

"Yes, you did! Right before your spanking!" Luke professed.

Now it was all clear. Taylor thought it was the slaps that she had felt. Wow, it had been a while. "I don't get it though. I wasn't touching myself, and I don't think you were touching me either," she mentioned.

"No, for some reason, your body exploded. I found it odd. I mean it could have been the alcohol, but something set you off." Taylor sat there, shaking her head. "Look, please don't take this wrong. Basically, what it is, is occasionally I like to take the lead, like…like when a couple is on the dance floor. The only difference is that a couple moves around the floor, and the woman, in this case, can't! It's all in fun. And it's a form of foreplay, with it always leading to something sexual, with Tara anyway."

Taylor rehashed the bondage with all its raw emotion and how she always felt nothing but safe. And it was like he said, it wasn't about him. He was only there to please her, even though she felt like a deer strapped to the roof of a car. Finally, she turned in close and made it look like she needed warmth. He pushed her back to get her under the covers, with her reassuming the position, where they eventually closed their eyes.

Lucas turned on the light to see a conscious Taylor, apparently waiting for him to awake. With the questions she had racing in her head, Taylor needed answers as the new feelings she was harboring wouldn't let her mind rest. Taylor had to know more, much more. So once Luke was capable of holding a conversation, the two played a game of Q and A.

"So these two women were very different but liked the bondage?"

"Yes, and being controlled," Luke replied.

"And you did what, you tortured them?"

Lucas snickered before attempting to answer this one. "No! Sometimes I might inflict just enough pain for it to be a pleasure. That's all!"

"And they liked this?" Taylor inquired.

"Well, you were drunk, but you tell me. You left a puddle in your clothes last night. And you did that before there was even the first slap." She sat there in amazement, knowing that what he said was true.

"Have you ever blindfolded or gagged a woman?" an excited Taylor inquired as her mind ran rampant.

"Yes, sometimes! It amplifies the overall experience. The gag restricts the woman from talking and limits her air supply, turning it euphoric. And the blindfold takes away her visibility, forcing the sub to rely on her remaining senses for self-preservation. The heightened awareness stimulates and feeds off her lack of control. Occasionally, I do let the sub watch since the view gets the juices flowing too."

"Well, what happens if they try to resist?" Taylor prodded.

"If they did, I guess I would instill some form of light punishment!"

"Luke, so how exactly did this start, you know with those feelings and urges? What made you act on them?"

"That's a tough one. I'm guessing it stemmed from when I was young. However, I never let this lion out of the cage until Tara turned that key for me!"

Examples of him with other women were getting her hotter. With all the talk of bondage, as well as dominance and submission, it made her want to consider a change, even if it was just temporary. The topic for her was beyond intriguing, with it making her think about what could happen if she opened up to other avenues. With a smile that was fading and all Taylor's questions answered, she finally conked out again.

Stirring to the sound of the shower, Taylor prepared to act on what she knew she had to do. She paced, evaluating her two results, and for her, they both ended favorably. So to approach him before his shower was done, she pushed through the hardwood door.

Leaving her pajamas and panties behind in her footpath. Taylor remained still on the tile outside the enclosure, to tackle her pent-up jitters, before sliding stealthily past the partially opened opaque curtain behind Lucas. She wasn't scared, but it all derived from the excitement of the situation.

In the confines of the beige tiled stall, Taylor inched up behind Lucas, quickly checking out his medium-sized body art and then his ass, as she drew near. Feeling a pair of hands that gingerly clutched at his sides, the man handled it without so much as a flinch, as if he was expecting it.

His only reaction was when he clenched her wrists and pulled her naked body tight to his. Deep down she knew this was right, and because of it, Taylor felt boldly confident she had made the right decision.

With the embrace not being nearly enough, Lucas gradually guided her around to where the water doused the two, allowing beads of liquid to bounce off them, as their hands and lips crossed into unchartered territory for the first time.

Luke slithered downward to her enticing wet bosom, driving Taylor to throw her head back, with the sensation that went clear to her toes. He firmly anchored both hands on her buttocks, so to orally pay a tender homage to both of her slick perky breasts, with an action that made the woman pierce her nails into Luke's shoulders.

He continued with Taylor holding on, impassioned in the emotions of which she never experienced before, as they freely exuded from her body.

Luke bent her over so that she could grasp the waist-high X-shaped porcelain shower handles on the wall. For Taylor there was no backing out now. The mood was set, and there wasn't any alcohol to blame it on either. The woman closed her eyes, waiting for what she hoped was going to happen next. And her pussy didn't wait long, as Lucas slid his penis deep inside of her, forcing an enjoyable sound that lightly echoed within the shower stall.

Here Taylor was only restrained by not getting clocked by the ceramic handles, as beads of water thumped like playful nymph's, dancing across her back. Luke never got bested by his desire, as he held on dearly to her smooth, doused waist. Resounding moans intensified from Taylor as the stroke, and the speed escalated. A few minutes inside of her, and he shot making her emit echoed moans as a fanfare to his climax.

Leaving the shower, a suddenly modest Taylor brought a towel around her, poorly concealing herself and her victorious grin. Trying to distract him from her flourishing jubilation, she asked a question of the first sight of him in the shower. "What is the key tattoo on your back about?"

"Oh, I got this five years ago as a reminder to myself that in this venue, I alone hold the key." Luke lifted his shirt to give her a full view. "It is chained to another's heart." She studied the design up close this time and saw that it ended with a well-defined human heart.

Taylor nodded with a pronounced hesitation. "Luke, I… I'm very interested in trying more of this, the submissive part I mean! I want to know what it feels like; you know to have the full experience!"

With only inner elation, Luke thought about Taylor's body and how he wanted to explore it a little more thoroughly. "If that's what you want, then that's what we'll do!" Lucas said, releasing the hold on his shirt.

"So how do we do this?" Taylor asked, trying not to get too excited.

"Well, first of all, I don't give my sub any say or insight into what's going to happen. Like I told you earlier, everything I do is for your pleasure. Only it is the way that it's presented to you that will cultivate your feelings and emotions. All I am going to need from you is to be dressed in something sexy and be kneeling at my door at eight sharp and we can go from there! Are you all right with that?" Luke said blankly.

"Yes!"

"Well, since I consider this to be what I call a session, I will need you to answer me with, yes, sir! It's part of the role play. But if you don't think it's for you, we'll stop immediately, no questions asked. We don't ever have to talk about it either. So do you think you still want to do this?"

She waited seconds before she boldly replied, "Yes, sir!"

"Okay, remember, eight o'clock." The brunette nodded before sidestepping to her room. "Oh, and one last thing, Taylor! I want you to drink water. You need to hydrate. A session can be long, and I don't want you passing out. With that being said, if you still want to do this, I will see you tonight!"

"Yes, eight, sir!"

# CHAPTER 3

Taylor was determined to find something a little naughty, arousing, or even a bit risqué. Hunting, she tossed aside two entire drawers of clothes as she tried to recall what she might possibly have here at the inn in storage. What she found was none of those things.

Flinging a white bra across the end of her bed, she searched for its counterpart. The best she had was not what she considered sexy, so Luke most likely wouldn't either. Even all her nightwear was flannel! As a plan B, Taylor figured she would head down to Main Street to see what they had.

Taylor later legged it into the inn with nothing to show from the shop in town, scoring her a big fat zero and nothing but wasted time that she could have been spending with Lucas. She did walk out with one item, but she wasn't sold on it, so she left it in the car, wishing now she had decided to leave it on the store's rack, where she found it.

While the woman was out, Lucas washed the dishes but only after he scavenged for items that could be used on his sub in training. Luke knew she wanted to learn more about who he was; well, he was prepared to do that, bearing in mind that it had to be Bondage 101. And even with looking at her body earlier and seeing that she might be able to handle it, it is imperative that he introduce her to this at a level she could take.

Taylor clomped in behind Lucas with a freshly opened water bottle in hand. She reached for a lunch plate and dried it before putting it in its appropriate spot. "Any luck in town?" Lucas asked since she had made it known that she was having a little trouble with something sexy.

"No, but don't worry, I'll be ready!" she stated, viewing the clock that sat between the kitchen window and entryway. Five twenty!

Taylor never had to pay attention to time since she left Fairbanks, and since Luke had told her twice, she wasn't going to be late for her first session.

As a kid, a good part of her summers were spent here, at the inn. The place was practically a second home for her. It had always been here that Taylor remembered times, good times when she was mindfully prompted by a specific item or area of the lodge. And this was one of those moments as she was putting away dishes for Luke. Only her remembrance was of a much younger Taylor, putting them away for grandma using a step stool.

Taylor who was in a quandary over her clothing dilemma, still couldn't decide what to do about an outfit, after dismissing the sheer piece that was out in the car. She also wasn't sure what Luke had in store for her, but her mind and pussy liked the fantasies that kept her reality teetering on its edge.

In her room, she reviewed her apparel options. Having the first part figured out, Taylor chose to be barefooted. It was a start! She then rashly made a decision, hoping it would be to her new master's liking.

In front of the mirror, Taylor checked out her choice. And with only five minutes to spare, she fixed her hair, leaving it long as this clearly was the time for her to let her hair down. She poked at her long mahogany locks, primping to get her appearance just as she wanted it.

Seeing it was time Taylor clenched the neck of an opened bottle of red wine along with two stemmed wineglasses. Barefoot, the willing and excited sub made her way down the hall as only a few creaks announced her movement.

Taylor knelt in front of the off-white door of room 7. After orderly placing the wine and glasses, she bowed her head in perceptible submission. Taking a few breaths, she knuckled out three soft taps. Moments transpired until it opened to a half-dressed Lucas. He studied the beautiful woman assuming the position, robed in a knee-length canary yellow flannel nightshirt that draped loosely from her body.

Luke watched Taylor, thinking she'd most likely break one of the rules that he had told her just this morning. Head down. No talking unless asked. She clearly is into this. "Please enter!" he summoned.

"Yes, sir!" She arose, picking up the glass articles on the floor between them. He stood there, awaiting her first error. Would she hand him the wine and glasses? He found out right away, as Taylor glided past him with her eyes to the floor.

Inside, her shortsighted view was all that she allowed herself to see. If so, she would have spied the spotlight hanging from the beam in the center of the room. By design, Luke made it so Taylor would be center stage, right where a submissive should be.

Much earlier when his willing subject was out searching downtown, he strapped a gooseneck lamp to the beam above to enlighten the floor, spotlighting what it was that he wanted to see most. He studied her in anticipation of the floor show he would be getting soon.

To get her attention, he used his pointer finger to raise her head to where she was looking at him. "Listen, I need for you to understand a few things before we begin. First, I told you that we can stop at any point. Also, this never involves torture. If I do it, the way that I do it, then this will be more than enough for you. Tonight, you will be blindfolded, gagged, and bound. Are you okay with this, my sub?"

Even though Taylor's mind was soaring with what could happen to her tonight, a woman still managed to get out the answer he awaited. "Yes, sir!" she replied before dropping her head obediently.

"Then we shall proceed!" Lucas took the wine and glasses and placed it upon the dresser, before leading her to the well-lit stage. The light finally caught her eye, but not enough to see if there were any other changes to his room.

While Taylor stood there statuesquely, he walked to a small cloth-covered table that he was using for tonight's props. Picking up one item, he chose the thick red Christmas ribbon that he purposely placed atop of the cloth.

Returning to her side, he brought the ribbon across her eyes before tying it snugly over her silky straight brown hair. With her vision shut down, he retraced his steps uncovering his stash before clenching a coil of rope, three other short lengths, and two items that he stuffed into his pocket.

Lucas knew that Taylor being sightless with what could happen at any second was getting her turned on. He didn't even have to touch her, he just knew. The dominate floated like a ghost beside the blindfolded woman, where he patiently eyed his eager subject.

With ropes dangling across his left shoulder, he pulled her nightshirt up and off of her to see what she came up with. It took but a second for him to view her wardrobe selection. "Tay, I love it!" the man clarified in approval. His eyes couldn't help but ogle the well-curved, fully nude Taylor. Tripping on his thoughts and what to say, he exclaimed, "Oh… I will be calling you sub, my toy, or Tay only!"

"Yes," she said in relief that he loved her choice of nudity.

With her arms down by her side, he brought her forearms out at a ninety-degree angle, with wrists straight out, to form a pronounced cleavage of her bare breasts. Taking the first of the short ropes, he crafted a fisherman's loop tying it tightly around one wrist.

Making a fourteen-inch spacing, he mirrored the knot on her other joint. Next, handling the second and longest rope, he wound it around both wrists. Lucas tied it off separately from the two knots, creating what he had ultimately envisioned when he planned this all out earlier.

Lucas studied his handiwork before he went any further, to make sure that Taylor wasn't going to be able to slip out of her bonds or, even worse, lose circulation. When he was satisfied that it was safe, he threw the bulk of the lengthened rope over the huge dark beam above her.

The end of the cording lightly grazed across her right cheek and calf as it fell. The touch from being sightless sent a tingle up and down her spine, putting her brain into overdrive, prematurely opening the floodgates to her pussy.

Grasping a broomstick that he found in the bar, the man dropped one end of it to the floor behind Taylor. The sound reverberated loudly as her sense of hearing intensified considering that her gift of sight wasn't free to participate. This lone piece of hardwood worked just as he had imagined, with it initially being the inspiration to plot out the entire session.

He loved this part—do everything at a drawn-out pace so that she'd have time to think about what was happening to her. Clenching the last two pieces of rope, he tapped her calves to have Taylor separate her legs to about sixteen inches apart.

Then, doing what he does best, he tied off her two ankles firmly to the cylindrical rod. Not that she could figure it out at this point, but Lucas was sporting a hard-on; as a matter of fact, he was showing two.

With her ankles firmly lashed, he stood behind her and began to pull the loose rope toward him. With her arms partially raised, he leaned in close to her ear to remind Taylor of her last word. "Yes, what?"

Oh my God, Taylor frantically panicked as she believed that she had answered correctly. "Yes, sir," she said, hoping to evade any punishment. After seconds of inactivity, he tugged slowly at the rope. Her limbs that were being suspended high above her head were now as immovable as her restrained legs. Internally, Taylor was becoming so wet that she was sure there would be a spot beneath her soon.

Luke pulled the rope taut, leaving little slack before securing it to one of her tethered ankles. Reaching into his pocket, he retrieved a handkerchief with a weighted corner and tucked it deep within her left hand.

"Tay, I know that you are new to this, but if for any reason you cannot continue, I want you to drop the cloth. I will stop immediately. Since it will be hard for you to say it, I want you to do this! Do you understand me?"

"Yes, sir," she carefully stated as Luke took the second item from his pocket and placed it across the cavity of her slightly open mouth. Biting softly into the foreign object, she recognized the piece as a slender carrot that he improvised as a suitable gag.

"Tay, I do not want you to drop the cloth or break the gag! Do it only if you need or want me to stop!" She listened intently to all the words before nodding in agreement.

Circling, he beheld the sight of a nude Taylor as she awaited whatever her new master wished. Patiently he snapped off a couple of quick pictures giving her time to think about the role she was playing out tonight.

He peered at his tan-skinned tightly bound figure while another slow drip unknowingly exited, beading up at the bottom of her vaginal lips. Wanting to give her the full show, he quickly snapped another picture to be viewed by her probably tomorrow.

After a few minutes of irregular breathing on random parts of her body, he circled her neck lightly, sucking and kissing it. She twisted her head only, as that was all her body was free to do. Luke pulled her in close, working at the nape of her neck. He even yanked at the short, dangled loop of rope to force her into his already owned grasp.

While he did, his throbbing manhood nuzzled against the growing warmth of her body, with nothing more than the thin layer of flannel to separate the two. Taylor found herself in an emotional tornado, and because of this, her balance waned, with her happy that something was there to keep her upright.

Lucas nibbled at Taylor's neck and shoulders, forcing her to struggle to not break the carrot and scream out in pleasure. Breathing for her was a chore as saliva welled up within the crooks of her mouth, with it being its only possible exit. He maintained the target of her vulnerable neck, using it as his primary focus. Taylor folded as an orgasm blindsided her.

The ropes bit hard as her trembling body gave out only to have the rope catch her from dropping clear to the floor. The man stepped backward only after he felt the piece of cloth glance off his back. "Do you want me to stop my toy?" He quickly asked of the drooping rag doll before him. She swiftly straightened up to try to gain her composure, as she shook her head wildly, signifying that that was not her intention.

He retracted the piece of wet produce from her mouth. "No, sir," she articulated as she sucked in her saliva and tried to reach out for the cloth that was no longer there. "No, sir. Please!"

"Then you're okay, my toy?"

"Yes, sir!" Taylor exclaimed as she took a breath, the carrot, and the hanky with her ready to continue once more.

Lucas ventured southward to her bosom, where he treated himself to his sub's soft supple but vivacious breasts, spending minutes on them alone. He cupped them performing a soothing massage to both before his mouth moved in for a closer inspection. His past two subs were small chested, but for tonight, he welcomed the incredible sight before him.

Bringing his tongue to a point he dampened her nipples, turning them slippery to the touch. Then using his palms, he lightly massaged the tips in alternating orbital directions. Lucas, who was enjoying this beyond belief, never considered himself a boob man, but these here were true works of art.

From the story of their past, followed by a spanking, he was now viewing boobs he thought he would have never have gotten to see. Thankful, Lucas watched as she moaned in satisfaction. He knew from the sounds alone that he was creating a memorable session for her; that at least opened her eyes to the world beyond the one position.

Lucas dragged a single finger so that she knew precisely where he was. He stopped only to thump her bottom. He wouldn't have called it a slap, but he loved the sound it emitted. He continued by caressing and tenderly squeezing her ass while fondling the small of her back. Taylor was back in the game again as he lightly raked his nails across her skin, making her lunge forward from his slow intended orchestration.

Seeing that she couldn't move, he decided to inflict a little pain. He would go easy on the newbie, as he knew if it was done right, Taylor would register it as pain but process it as pleasure. Flirting with her buttocks, he individually attacked each cheek with a series of minuscule pinches.

Luke waited for it, and there it was, as Taylor went up on her toes. Attacking the other, she arched as if she was learning a demi-pointe in ballet, delivering droplets of secretion to the wooden planks and pole beneath her. The pinching kept on until he was through.

The Dom examined his sub with how well she was handling her first hang time. With the cloth in place, she looked like she was ready for more. *Well, she does deserve one more orgasm before being cut down,* he thought.

Her pussy was the last place he wished to conquer. Bringing his hand out, like a person would for a handshake, he glided his pointer finger between her vaginal folds and back between her cheeks. He ran it through the creases, softly grazing her warm, welcoming clit, releasing some of the suppressed fluid that she already couldn't contain. His hand, mainly fingers, went from damp to wet as he slid his five digits in a slow rhythmic movement. Luke toyed with her pussy as her body was again, ready to cum.

She wanted it to last longer. It felt so good, so damn good. Feeling the stirrings of a woman who was about to take off, he kept his hand in perfect time. Lucas sustained his unstoppable rhythm as Taylor appeared to fight with her bonds and inability to regain any form of control.

Tremors took hold of her body as an unknown force reached out for the fabric in her hand that she would have lost, except that it was wound around two of her fingers. Although that same force did manage to snap her gag into three pieces with two of them bouncing across the floor.

Saliva flooded down, granting the spittle to finely rain over her breasts, rendering her bosom to glisten like stars beneath the light from overhead. Her other juices fell to the floor with some taking the slower route of dripping down her inner thighs. Not being one to waste, Lucas licked the juice from his hand, to savor its contents.

He reached down to detach the rope from her right ankle as Taylor's wrists fell with little resistance to her stomach. Her arms felt weak as Lucas held his subs waist as he released the ties that locked her legs to the wooden rod.

Releasing the handle, he dropped it upon the pine planking behind her, giving him time to take the handkerchief from Taylor, with his free hand. Lucas wiped the majority of the saliva from her chest before letting it fall clear of where the two were standing.

She assumed they were done at this point. And with not having orgasms in who knows how many years, she found it much more exhausting than she had ever imagined. Luke reached in and took the remainder of the carrot from Taylor as the blindfold still impeded her vision.

"Are you all right, Tay?" Lucas inquired, undoing the knot from her wrist.

She managed a broken breath before she emotionally went to pieces. "Yes, sir!" the woman exclaimed, "I'm sorry. I didn't mean to drop the cloth, and I broke the carrot!"

"Shh," Luke said, calming the woman, as her last climax surely got the best of her.

"I wanted to be good at this, and I wasn't!"

"You did great, but now it's time to show me just how appreciative you are!" Reaching behind, Luke lifted the long pole and slid it into the crooks of her elbows. With her forearms that were still tied in the front, her limbs were now plastered to the sides of her body due to the viselike wrist ties that spanned beneath her still damp tits.

With Luke as her crutch, and some help from the handle, Taylor was assisted to her knees using a folded towel he had placed on the floor to cushion them. She awaited her next command. He stood there towering as his penis had all the visual enjoyment it could take.

"So how did you like your first session my toy?" he said as he slid his pants down, unbeknownst to her.

Taylor responded quietly, "I liked it, and thank you, sir!"

"Then show me!" With his pajamas resting upon the floor, he leaned in, touching his engorged member to her lips. She invited his swollen cock deep into her mouth. Finally, this is something that she thought she might be good at. And she was so gracious that she didn't hold anything back. She sucked it like she was trying to get to the center of a tootsie pop.

His eyes rolled as his penis would appear and disappear to his and her liking. Not able to take much more, Luke's fingertips held the handle near her elbows, where he pushed and pulled the wooden rod, giving himself full access to his own blowjob from Taylor.

She relished in the fact that she knew he was close. Their rhythm was continuous up until his body went stiff. He grasped the handle tight, so her only recourse was to take him deep as the warm salty liquid shot forcefully down her throat. As his spasms ceased, Luke released his hold on the rod as she graciously swallowed the gift her master had given her.

With her thoroughly worn out and in need of sleep, Luke undid the last of the restraints before helping a docile Taylor to bed. He slid her under the covers, then gently pulled off the ribbon blindfold with him climbing in next to her. Her satisfying smile went unnoticed.

"Merry Christmas!" he whispered as he caressed her shoulder.

"Good morning!" Taylor blurted just before a major yawn. She turned fast and kissed him hard on the lips. "Merry Christmas!" she said, thinking about the most incredible Christmas Eve she ever had. "Oh, I have a present I want you to open later," she stated as she beamed about the one hiding under the tree.

"I opened my present last night! Do you want to see it?" Taylor let out a flamboyant but hastened laugh, followed by a thrown look. He lifted his phone and called up the pictures, turning it in her direction.

"Wow, that's awesome. I tried to remember everything that was going on, but for me, it was impossible. So thank you!"

"Are you done looking at it?" Luke commented while his pointer finger hovered above the trash can icon.

"What are you doing? You're not going to delete them, are you? How are you going to remember it?" Taylor asked.

"I've got it right here," Luke answered, tapping at the side of his noggin. With no further objections besides a minor pout, he struck the icon three times. "So how did you like everything?" he asked, trying to change the subject.

"It was wild! I mean the ties, the blindfold, and the lack of control. I don't even know where to begin. I went into this to play the submissive, and I rapidly got caught up in it. I tried to do what I thought I should, and I hope I didn't disappoint you?"

"No complaints here," Lucas assuredly replied.

"It was an awesome sensation. The fact that I was so helpless and yet felt so safe at the same time was an incredible feeling. You never went beyond what you had told me in your stories. As a matter of fact, I think you went easy on me!" she said, looking Luke in the eye.

"Hey, you have to leave them wanting more. But the question is, do you?" Lucas asked as he poured some of the wine of last night.

"I think you know the answer to that already, so that would be a yes!" Taylor exclaimed before abruptly changing her mood and tone. "So where do we go from here?"

Lucas shrugged, knowing specifically what she meant, with it not being about the kink. He had no definitive answer to that. "Why don't we just enjoy ourselves until your brother shows up next week."

"No, that's not what I meant!" she said, pausing long enough to add. "Luke, I have no purpose in my life right now. I live a couple of miles from my parents. I visit my grandmother a few times a week and my brother twice a year. I feel I'm either bartending or waitressing all night or at home in a quiet apartment. I need something!"

She finished by lowering her face in palpable defeat. Luke, who just heard what his life is like each and every day, felt a stabbing to his heart as he awaited her full attention. But as she did the woman never broke a tear even though she was close.

"I do know, but can't we just go day by day and enjoy each other's company? I mean, look at how our lives changed in two days. I can't make a decision like this right now and you shouldn't either. Okay?" She gave only a halfhearted smile as she silently vowed never to bring it up again.

With the two now content in being together 24/7, Taylor decided to pick this day to show Lucas the changes to the small rural town. She drove by where Lucas had lived as a kid, as well as where Taylor had spent her entire childhood, when she wasn't at the inn, that is. She even rode by the still operating mill yard.

Since they were meeting up with Luke's friends later, they both decided to dine at the Arctic Drift Sports Bar. It was the town's watering hole where they had socialized often, although separately. It might have a new owner and a new name, but it was still the main bar in town.

Sitting, nursing their third drink, Lucas set the phone down. Taylor thought she knew but asked anyway. "Who was it?"

"Nate and Courtney! They are going to be late."

"So we are waiting, then?" Taylor asked.

"Yeah, but I think my next drink is going to be a beer. I need to slow it down if we are going to make a whole night of it," Luke replied, spinning a few degrees to survey the room, displaying his profile and quite-visible five o'clock shadow.

"I think I'll do the same."

"Dave, can I have a Guinness? And a merlot for you Taylor?" he asked, looking back to Taylor while he had the bartender's attention.

"Yes, please!" she exclaimed as she shoved her empty highball glass to the backside of the bar far from her reach.

"And a merlot, Dave!" Lucas added to complete their order.

Dave, a classmate of Luke and Kyle's, introduced them to his wife Miranda, who openly filled them in on what it took to get the business up and operational. Lucas was no stranger to this, sympathized knowing he had walked the same road years ago. But after ten minutes, the woman had to say goodbye as it was time to get back to the work.

Following a comment that Luke had brought up about his parents leaving the Point, Taylor asked, "Hey, how is it that you and your parents ended up moving here?"

"Well, I was born here, but my dad was a craftsman in a small town outside of Florence, Italy. He met my mom there in the next town over. They eventually married and came to the States before they set down roots in Seattle. He was not content with work in the city, so they traveled here. Dad had heard about the prospects of the booming lumber and fishing industry back in 1980-something, so he talked mom into Point Hope. I was born a year later."

"Wow! Do you think that is why you are in Seattle now?" Taylor asked.

"That's a good question. I never thought about it. I just moved there."

Seeing Lucas was still thinking about it, Taylor questioned, "Hey, do you want to play a game?"

"You mean pool?" he said as he looked into the other room.

"No, the game is called ask and tell. It was a game that Lauren and I made up when we were in high school."

"Sure! I don't know what that is, but if you explain it, I'm sure I'll catch on."

"The game is easy. And I am bringing it up because we will learn more about each other by playing it. The rules are simple. I ask you a question about me from when we were younger. If you are correct, then it is your turn to ask me." Taylor waited until she was sure Luke understood rule number one. "The second rule is, if you are not correct, then you must tell me something about yourself that I don't know."

"That sounds easy. So why don't you start?" Lucas offered.

"Okay, let me see…ah, okay. Who was my boyfriend before Marty? Just his first name if you can't remember!" Taylor exclaimed.

"I probably shouldn't still remember this, but I think it was Steven Leston."

"Wow, I thought I was going to stump you right away. Now it is your turn to ask me one."

Lucas downed a swig of his beer and then thought. "I had one birthday party at the inn. How old was I?"

"That one's simple. You were eleven."

"How did you know that?" Lucas said, knowing that it was over two decades ago.

"I was the one that decorated your cake," Taylor confessed.

"And I thought Grandma Tilly did it."

"No, but she baked it." She paused. "Okay, why don't you go first, this time."

Lucas, who managed to come up with the last question so rapidly, stewed. "Hmm. What was the room number where Kyle and I stayed when we slept at the inn?"

"Simple again. It was room twelve."

"Wrong!" Lucas bellowed.

"What do you mean I'm wrong?"

"It was, and I do stress was room ten. Don't you recall when your grandfather turned the storage room upstairs into two more rooms? He changed the numbers after it was finished."

Taylor, who knew that he was correct, laughed. "All right, by the way, that was a good one, and I should have remembered that. Let me see. Okay, when it came time for my parents to name me, they chose the town where they had been living and where I was conceived."

"Ah, Taylor, Alaska! I did not know that," Lucas replied.

"Now my question. What is my middle name?"

Luke's eyes bugged out. He knew this. "Oh, crap. I can't believe it. I think it's Eliza?" he answered with him not hearing it out loud since they were kids.

"No, it is Elise!"

"I knew that. So I guess it is my turn to tell you. Humm... I don't think you knew this, but when I was fourteen, I fell head over heels for a girl, two years younger. Since I didn't know what love was, I resorted to spending as much time as I could, talking and getting to know her. Do you know who that girl was?"

Taylor's eyes glistened as they became damp with his secret confession from their past. "I hope it was me!"

"It was. And by the way, they're here," Lucas replied as Taylor leaned in and dropped her head up against his bicep, savoring the emotions he had sweetly extracted from her.

The four encircled one of the tall bar tables throwing back the hard stuff. The Daltons, old classmates of Luke and Kyle's, were lit on Fireball, while Taylor and Lucas jumped back to their Casa. It wasn't long though until their laughs were the accompanying chasers to their drinks. With the place becoming busier and louder, the four retired to the back corner to play darts, far from the cacophony that all the bar regulars exuded.

Taylor and Lucas were the victors of the first game of cricket, as she clearly was the ace in darts, while Luke, who had never really played before, made it harder to win as occasionally he would miss the board altogether.

The second game placed their hash mark in the losing column since they lightly got taken by their opponents. And the final one, a marathon one at that, had them playing like they were eyeing the board through the bottom of a shot glass.

Nathan and Courtney didn't fare much better as they were just as hammered. Lucas did get a double bull to close them out, but otherwise, they weren't even in the game. And yet they still had just as much fun as in the first one when they had triumphed.

Walking to the door, neither of them realized just how much they had drank. Taylor laughed, tripping on the mat on the way out. Making sure they bundled up, they waved to Dave and a few of the townies before they tromped to the car.

With Taylor getting ready to sit, Luke called for her to wait. "Hey, Tay, I think we need to sober up a little!" Taylor, who totally missed the nickname implication, agreed since she was in no shape to drive, let alone stand.

"So what are we doing? Are we going back in?"

"No, I was thinking of something a little different," he answered as he closed the trunk and walked up to her with something tucked under his arm.

She couldn't make it out, so all she answered was, "I'm game!" Wow, he loved that term. He had never heard it from her before, but he liked the thoughts and implications he got from it. To him, that meant she was open to anything.

Lucas made sure to take her by the arm, so there was little chance of her falling unless he did too. From there, they scuffled down the snowcapped road for a block and through the alleyway, to a path that led to the cliffs on the west end of the Point.

On a clear night you can see the pier miles away. Well, tonight was one of those nights, even as the wind chill plummeted the temperature far beyond unbearable. Viewing the edge of the twenty-foot cliffs, she noticed the radiance of the stars, once they were away from the lights of Main Street. With the snow encasing the overlook, Lucas threw his arm around Taylor to keep her warm. "Are you cold?" he asked.

"Not as much as I should be. It must be the tequila!"

"Good," Lucas said, pulling out a blanket that was in hiding during their entire walk. Placing it across the snow, she tried to figure out what he was doing.

With little to no emotion, he dutifully instructed her. "I want you to get down on all fours in the center of the blanket and drop your pants because I want to fuck you while we look out at the stars!"

Taylor thought he must be joking, and yet the woman still found herself crouching to assume the position. A crunch could be heard as her knees embedded deep into the hardpacked snow. Once she was securely on all fours, the entranced Taylor reached back for her pants.

The wind caused little effect primarily because of the numbing fuel they consumed at the bar, mixed in with Luke's commanding spell he cast. With a temperature just below zero, this had to be quick. She yanked at her panties that were cold due to a damp spot that Lucas had just created.

With thoughts of it being a quickie, he knelt behind her and dropped his pants so to conclude this spontaneous and insane idea of his. This scene was kinky as hell, but he didn't want them freezing to death in the process. Luke entered her slowly making her gasp while noticing her body was already cold to the touch, even though she wasn't feeling much of its effect.

Lucas moved back and forth at a rapid pace, sliding in and out looking to get the best sounds from her. But only moments later, as she tried to stare at the star-speckled sky, she came. Those waves to her were more powerful than the ones that sounded off below.

Taylor shook violently. As her quivering ceased, he exploded, causing him to jerk her closer, with the man no longer able to continue his stride. After momentarily taking in the view and the sounds, the pair couldn't dress fast enough. Laughter filled the air as they acted like teenagers, walking away arm in arm with the blanket to shield them. The cold as intense as it had been the whole time, sobered them faster than any coffee would have.

"Hey, did you ever bring Kelly out to the overlook?" Taylor questioned as they followed their footprints back to the vehicle.

"No, but we spent some time down at the pier, although it wasn't December." Taylor let out a snort and then mentioned that they should go back to the bar to warm up. Lucas disagreed, seeing that neither were in any shape to be out in public. Taylor chuckled at what just happened and that thought too.

Well, today is the day when their quiet sanctuary was to conclude. Kyle was flying in from Nome, bringing their private time together to a close.

"What are we going to say to Kyle?" she asked, making sure they were both on the same page.

"Well, I think we should say we had a great time catching up. I mean I am leaving in another week, so let's keep it light," Luke said sadly, knowing he didn't want this to be over as much as she didn't.

Understandably, the pair were aloof as they drove to the airport. Both thought about the changes that were soon to divide them. Lucas and Taylor still had a week together, but the terms were to be different. She wasn't ready for this to be a sexless week. She had gone way too long without it before him and far too long without it being good.

Then a thought occurred to her bringing on a barely audible sound. "What was that for?" Lucas asked curiously.

"I don't know why, but I was just thinking about the overlook." The two laughed at their incredible memory that would always be and his unyielding way that he possessed in making her submit. Pulling into the lot, they waited as precious seconds ticked. Talking about nothing significant, both sat until the single propped plane landed. Nearing the building, they held hands.

Lucas threw his arms around his buddy, recalling it had been over five years since Kyle had last visited him in Seattle. Brother and sister gave each other a quick hug before they walked the short route to the SUV. During the ride, Kyle struck up a conversation.

"So what has my best friend and my sister been doing all week?" Taylor's brother asked. But neither of them wanted to be the first to disclose to Kyle, seeing he clearly was expecting nothing but an innocent answer.

"Well, your sister has been a gracious hostess. She gave me quite the tour this week," he said as he glinted into the rearview mirror, at the beautiful woman in the back seat. She beamed a cheerful look back in his direction. Luke sidestepped and purposely changed the lingering silence to a predesigned topic of Kyle and Taylor's family history.

"I never told anyone that our grandmother was a Cheesh-Na. I mean many of the people here derived from one tribe or another. It was a common thing. But I suppose she told you that!" Kyle exclaimed, waiting for a response.

"Yes, the two of us talked about everything this week!" Lucas exclaimed as Taylor worked at not laughing. She was getting wet sitting there in the fact that her brother knew nothing about what had transpired while he was gone. If he had he would freak. Or maybe try to defend his sister's honor. Well not that, but he would have thought it was strange.

During the long ten-minute drive, Taylor grew noticeably distant. She didn't have to count the days or hours, to know that Luke was leaving in a week, and that what they had started here was through. The vehicle came to a stop in the drive where Kyle hopped out to open the garage door. "Everything okay, Taylor?" Lucas questioned.

"I'm fine," was all she could spit out.

As a gust swept past, the three trudged into the rear of the inn toting Kyle's bags.

Once inside, Taylor's brother brought his luggage down to his room. During his path back, the man batted at his coarse mane that the hat and its removal paid no justice to. "You know I need a drink!" Kyle stated as he gave up on his hair.

"Sounds good. That's the first thing I did when I got here too!" Lucas exclaimed.

Luke and Taylor meandered as Kyle climbed into the pub's cockpit. "What's your liking?" he asked, referring to his modest selection of spirits. "Whiskey for you?"

"You know, I will have tequila if you have any!" Lucas answered. Saying that he hoped it would make Taylor smile, if not just on the inside.

Before Kyle could turn for the bar brand, Taylor was off to the storeroom, saying, "I'll get my Noble." She disappeared but reemerged in time to see Kyle pour his own spirit, with the first few drops skipping across the cubes, landing on the circular bar top.

Without thought, the longtime bartender reached for a towel. The stainless-steel hoop clanged against the ice chest, flipping a toggle on her newest and most favorite bar memory. And because of that, it took all she could do, just to finish the last twelve feet back to her stool.

Lucas parked himself in the center of the round with Taylor who eventually joined him to his left. Wanting to keep up with her brother, she slid the tequila bottle across, where he poured a hefty shot in both waiting glasses. After sending their drinks back, he came around to where he could join them.

"Would you rather sit in front of the fire?" Kyle asked.

"No, I love this spot right here!" Lucas said, knowing it was turning her on just being this close to it again. Taylor was squirming. *What is the man doing?* Taylor kept to herself. However, without her knowledge, he was pulling her temporarily from her pit of despondence.

The three talked for hours where they reminisced about high school, old friends, and the good times they had back then. As Taylor had not been from their class, she tried to absorb herself in their stories so to avoid her own emotional conflict with her not wanting to deal with it alone, and yet in front of others.

A couple of hours later, Taylor ran for snacks, allowing Kyle to bring up the time when Lucas had disclosed his feelings for Kyle's sister. "You know with Marty out of the picture, maybe the timing would be right for the two of you?"

Luke shrugged, having heard the same story many times from his buddy over the past year. He knew that Kyle was right, with him having the same reoccurring idea countless times, just this week.

Taylor returned to find Lucas running his hand over the smooth shine of the Alaskan birch. He knew she was in the room and yet never made eye contact. But it was this action, that straw that broke the camel's back. She giggled loudly as her knees buckled. Kyle spun around when he heard the sound and asked, "What was that for?"

She had no explanation or not one she could tell Kyle anyway. Luke watched as she shifted. "I got nothing," Taylor finally toned. Lucas somehow refrained from laughing and chose to drink only when a confused Kyle turned back toward him. He stared at Lucas until he eventually raised his glass of Johnny to his lips.

Taylor was the first to fold and call it a night, as the three had talked into the wee hours of the morning. With her exit, the other two headed to their rooms a few minutes later. She retired to room twelve, Lucas to his room and Kyle to the innkeeper's quarters on the ground floor.

On a blustery, snowflake-filled New Year's Eve at the pier, over three hundred of the town's residents gathered for one of their two annual social celebrations. The event was big since the community this time of year went into near hibernation. So with all the citizen's bundled up, wearing bright knitted party hats and toting flasks of liquid warmth, the brave stood with their noisemakers, ready to ring in the new year.

On the main piers, which were cleared of boats months ago, were two sets of townspeople with their prelaunch luminaries. The twin docks combined, yielded a hundred paper lamps along with their temporary owners who stood anxious for their celebratory release into the midnight sky. The wind, which could have had any weather vane spinning, pushed erratically at the paper bags, as a few minutes from now was to be the lighting.

The donations and the proceeds from the sale of the floating lights went toward the purchase of a short display of fireworks that they shot out over the ocean following the sky lanterns viewing. The show was not Times Square, but considering the locale, it meant just as much to these townsfolk.

Lucas stood in a huddle, trying to keep warm. It's the same every year, but the image of seeing the floating luminaries over the harbor or town was a sight to behold. "Wow, it is much colder this year!" Kyle said as steam flowed from his mouth.

"Yes, it is cold." Lucas concurred before adding, "I think being near the water only makes it colder." Kyle wasn't sure what he meant by that but agreed anyway. However, Taylor knew, as the memory of the overlook jumped to her mind's eye, as Luke was openly teasing her.

After the celebration, the bars will be open far into the morning. And Kyle's pub was no different. Soon the alcohol will be flowing, and all will be warm. A few ignited their lanterns, while the digital clock between the piers showed less than a minute, counting down each second.

More small beacons appeared on the docks like fireflies with their lights stuck on. The people grew rowdy as the seconds lapsed with the last of the wicks for the luminaries set afire. "Ten, nine, eight, seven, six, five, four, three, two, one—happy New Year," roared the crowd.

The glimmering sky lanterns floated up from the docks at a snail's pace keeping the masses soundlessly in awe. The trio made sure to wish each other a happy New Year before the crowd chorused "Auld Lang Syne" in a cappella to the scene of the hovering lights. As the fireworks began, Kyle excused himself so he could talk to a pal.

With Kyle gone, Lucas grabbed Taylor and pulled her close. "What are you doing?" she questioned, looking to see if her brother was within earshot.

"Relax, Tay," he said as Luke didn't want to be the only horny one out here tonight. He spun her around like he just didn't care what anyone thought. He passionately kissed her. "I need you," he said as the light show high above played on, with a crowd that was everywhere, still sounding their nonstop noisemakers.

Taylor, not thinking that the attention he showed in public and out in front of her brother, could possibly turn her on, and yet it did. But it was short-lived since ten minutes later the trio regrouped to drive back to the bar, with all three having to punch the clock for work.

Hours later, Taylor brought out sandwiches for the remaining hungry customers. Kyle eyed the bar, knowing it is only one night of the offseason, but it filled the cash register. They managed to pour, feed, and socialize until around three in the morning among the sounds of the few locals that weren't ready to call it quits. And that is when Taylor decided to call it a night.

Maybe it was a plea to pull Luke away, or Taylor was tired, but either way, she was heading up. Around twenty minutes later, Lucas made one last retrieval of empties before he told his friend he was heading up also. A very appreciative Kyle thanked him immensely and told him he'd see him for lunch, as a form of a joke since none of them were going to be up for breakfast.

Lucas bolted up the flight of stairs, barely touching but a few of them. Spying down the hall, he decided to check his room first, to see if he had company. Not finding Taylor, he turned to exit.

"Hey, you're not going to leave me here all alone, are you?" she softly pleaded from the opening of his bathroom. Luke immediately turned to lock the door. Taylor stepped out fashioning nothing but one of his T-shirts. And frankly, it drove him crazy, but anything would have at this point.

"I need you now!" he said in a gruff voice that told her that this was going to happen whether or not she wanted it. But of course, she did.

"Yes, sir!" Taylor responded. Luke reached for the short lengths of rope from their last session and had her turn away from him. Joining Taylor's wrists behind her, Luke tied them like he was a rodeo star tying off a calf for the best time. Next, Luke's dominant alter ego carefully assisted her to the center of the bed facedown, before he banded her ankles again with lightning speed.

Finding a hanky, he twisted it diagonally until it was long and slender with him placing it across the corners of her mouth. After creating a knot behind her head, he began to strip. But his shirt no sooner hit the floor when the phone in his room rang.

He picked up the receiver to hear Kyle talking loudly. "Luke, I am sorry to bother you, but can you help me out. One of the guys cut himself bad. I tried Taylor, but she didn't answer. I have to run him to the hospital." Taylor pouted overhearing most of the conversation.

"I'll be right down," Lucas replied. Taylor wanted to cry as she knew she was about to be reamed, but now it wasn't going to happen.

Disappointed himself, he reached for his shirt as she tried to make eye contact. "Your brother needs help downstairs. I'll be back soon."

Okay, she understood that. *But why isn't he untying me already?* she thought. Lucas finally reached over to put a stop to this night-mare ending of an evening. Grabbing a handful of the knot, he proceeded to undo her. Then with some hesitation, he bound her once more.

"Don't go anywhere, Tay, because when I get back, whether you're awake, or you're asleep, you are going to get fucked. Do you understand?" Well, she couldn't exactly say yes or no. The best she could do was nod. Handing her the ends of the cotton cordage, he tucked the quilt around her to keep her warm and make it even harder to move.

"In case of emergency you can free yourself, but otherwise, I want you right here when I get back!" he proclaimed. Exiting the room, he made sure to lock it, leaving Taylor reeling with her not knowing what she should be feeling.

Taylor wanted to be pissed about the situation, but not with him leaving her tied up, in which she found to be hot but in the fact that the call couldn't have come at a worse time. Taylor knew that Luke was going to be plenty horny because even as indifferent as she felt this very second, she was too.

In time she became drowsy as it had been a very long day. The thoughts that had kept her aroused and awake, were now disappearing as that, and her mild discomfort was no real match for her hindering exhaustion. She even tired from looking at the sheets that were up against her face. With no real chance to hold out, she closed her eyes, with the rope ends still in her hand.

Later, Taylor moved a smidge as Lucas stealthily oiled the spot that he had been thinking about for over an hour. He tried desperately not to wake the woman that was right where he had left her. He knew that Kyle just went to bed and that he was downstairs, but she was going to get what he promised.

A naked Lucas climbed covertly across Taylor's thighs before he knelt and made any motion to penetrate her. It had been minutes from when his penis toyed outside her pussy, to where full entry was finally obtained. Through it all, Taylor barely wavered.

When the time was right, and her body was taking his slow strokes and not showing any sign of waking, he let her have it. Grabbing her wrists and a handful of his shirt, he pulled them toward him with his tool ramming her, from dreamland to oblivion.

She struggled to breathe, which wasn't easy because of the gag which was still intact. Taylor was trapped, and couldn't budge, not an inch. If she hadn't been so far gone, Taylor would have feared being pushed clear through the headboard. They both came simultaneously with most of her restrained scream being caught by the cloth in her mouth and the mattress beneath her. With his eyes closed, Lucas pleasured in all the sounds she tried to let out.

He untied Taylor and laid beside her, gently massaging her arms, which had been locked in that awkward position for more than an hour. Wanting to get up when he thought she was okay, he thought that he would send her back off to her room, but in the morning, they were right where they fell asleep.

Today was a subdued one for two of the three as it was time for them to separate. It had been a great fifteen days with the three acting like friends of years ago. However, Luke was heading home to Seattle, with so many miles that were about to divide the two. She stewed sedately in the back seat with only her reoccurring memories to keep her company.

Taylor so much needed to tell him that she wanted to follow him to Washington and that she had found someone that she had so much in common with. But because she didn't, it was a hushed ride back to the airport. Inside the small building, he hugged Kyle and said that he will try to come back next winter, which made Kyle optimistically cheerful.

With the toughest part yet to come, and without showing any more emotion other than what he should, the two hugged. And as he pulled away, Luke gave her a kiss on the side of her cheek. It was a feeling she wanted to keep forever, now that she was going to be, once again alone. With her brother by her side, Taylor wiped away a single tear as Luke walked through the open doorway and out of sight.

Taylor within the confines of her room packed as it was nearly time for her to leave also. And that is when she came across a note that made her think that Lucas might not want this to be over either.

# CHAPTER 4

Luke's keys chimed a hollow echo in the glass bowl that sat upon the corner of the kitchen counter. A haunting reminder of how quiet it is with just him here. There hadn't been much noise within these walls since he moved in, nearly seven years ago. And before the past weeks with Taylor, he never remembered the quiet this much. That he could attest.

Under the light of the fridge, a thick dark stubble containing a few stray grays covered his otherwise normally well-kept jaw line. Lucas closed the door after reaching for a cold bottle of lager.

In the last week, the man had lost the battle of wanting to look good for a person who most likely may never be part of his life. But Luke wanted to get that feeling back. He figured the first week at the inn was an incredible time for the two, with him thinking that she'd move to Seattle based on that alone.

However, six weeks had passed, and still no word from Taylor. No texts, no letters, and no phone calls. The nights were getting longer for him, not in the traditional sense, but in that time seemed to move slower lately. It was so much so that the silence for him was deafening. He even chose to stay late some nights at work so not to have to be home playing host to his thoughts.

Luke had to do something. In the note he left for her at the inn, he told Taylor to give it some time. But then the man sent her back to a place where she was learning to live life on her terms. And maybe, just maybe, he wasn't going to fit into that criteria. And in the recent weeks he had even gone through the motions to call her numerous times, but never did.

An ongoing thought of her haunted him. He knew some of what a submissive went through from all the talks he had with his ex-girlfriend, Tara. She would tell him what strings he pulled or the emotions that it stirred within her each time they had those, what Tara titled "BCD moments," a thoughtful acronym for their behind closed-door moments.

But it was he, that was beginning to experience some of those same pangs. Lucas needed Taylor. She was like a drug, and he was going through withdrawal. She was playing the submissive, and yet she had him dangling from the ropes, which she right now controlled.

Lucas didn't know why she would want to change her entire life for him, when his own family had felt no compulsion to spend the rest of their days together in Alaska. Even Luke left for better work and warmth. Her family had been there for generations he understood, and yet he tried to come up with one good reason why she should be here with him.

But the truth was he missed Taylor. He missed her touch, her smell, and those brown eyes, which dug deep and engulfed his heart. He shuffled out to the deck to see the sun performing its nightly ritual over the ocean.

The waves that crashed against the shore brought on memories of the night they looked out at the stars, over the harbor. If it weren't for the alcohol, it would have been crazy to have done what they did. Well, it was still crazy, but mindfully he enjoyed replaying it over and over again.

After work some nights, he labored on a home project, a project that he hoped Taylor would eventually get to use. But this week he hardly lifted a tool. Although weeks ago, his abundant smugness made him feel as though she was going to be moving in after just a week or two of separation, and now it was a month past that.

His speed this week, in which he now worked at his extracurricular hobby, came to a crawl. Frustrated, he chugged the rest of his brew, leaving the wearied man to turn back to the house, with him deciding to call it a night.

In Fairbanks and over two thousand miles away, Taylor portered a tray, slaloming and serving alcohol to her many thirsty customers. Handing out the refills, she continued, with the barmaid dreading one particular table tonight.

Two of the regulars, Rodney and Keith, were putting on a show of trying to outdrink each other in some primitive Alaskan male ritual she was thinking. The rest of the group just looked on, maybe hoping that they would be able to catch the total transformation of these two men, as they morphed into jackasses. With each drink, the two became louder and cockier.

The owner of the bar watched with an unblinking glare. He had owned the place long enough to know when trouble was about to show its ugly head. And there were a couple of uglies just twenty feet away.

Taylor stood by the table, passing beers around while collecting the empties. Saving the worst for last, she made sure to look back to her boss, whom she knew would be peering from a distance, eagle-eyed. Putting down the first beer in front of Keith, Taylor went to retrieve his empty. She could sense something was about to happen. It was like a distant braying of a donkey.

Keith grabbed Taylor's left wrist. Struggling lightly, she tried not to alarm Greg, the owner. To put and an end to this she set the tray on the table, where she broke the man's grip with a necessary force. Rodney was the first to pipe up to Keith. "I think you should leave my future wife alone!"

A pissed Taylor quick-wittedly but snidely answered, "And I suppose we would both be living in your mom's basement?" Everyone around the table erupted with laughter. Keith never reached for her again as Rodney had been silenced by the perfect mother joke. Shortly after, the two men joined the chorus of merriment, not knowing that they were sipping their last beer of the evening. The news was delivered by Greg himself.

Taylor was getting that immersing feeling again. The kind that would blanket her, if she didn't get out from under it soon. For the first time, she thought about being anywhere else. Maybe she could work at the inn, or just get away from the bar scene altogether. Then there is always the last alternative. But it was not the kind of thought she wanted to have during a busy evening at work.

Passing another waitress, she placed the tray down on the bar. "Greg, I'm taking five!" Taylor said with her going into a full stride to the kitchen. Breathing erratically, she wedged her way into the walk-in cooler.

Inside she dragged the door closed. Lately, this was her sanctuary, where Taylor could let these moments rejuvenate her for the hours she still had left. Tonight was hard though, with her thinking about Luke again. *Why hadn't she made a decision already? And why hadn't he been in contact?* she replayed like a worn out record.

Finding a new release point, she tapped at the side of a case of jumbo shrimp. The tapping speedily turned to a rap, which then resembled pounding. She even joined in with a sound that came from a place she didn't even know existed.

Work was getting her, and she knew it, but she had no idea what to do about it. Jobs here weren't the easiest to come by. She exited the freezer, not only not feeling better about herself, but now she was even a bit depressed. At closing time, Taylor hung up her apron. It really needed to be taken home and cleaned, but this wasn't the day for it.

On dating options, Taylor in the past considered the male customers that were of course there for the alcohol first, with maybe a couple that wanted to sweep her off their feet and take her away from all this. But take her to where? There were no one-percenters in Fairbanks. Most patrons here lived week by week or day by day for that matter.

In bed, Taylor slid under the covers of her full-sized mattress. But instead of reaching to shut off the lamp, she picked up her paperback copy of *The Submissive Within*, which sat neatly on top of her twenty-year-old blue-and-white-striped journal. As soon as she got home from the inn, she ordered a used copy to fulfill her curiosities, in hope that what she had experienced might carry on again in the near future.

Taylor felt it was near impossible to squelch the memories and yearnings that often came out of nowhere. It didn't matter if she was busy, or she had nothing to do. The thoughts were there.

She decided to read about what it would be like, to hand someone else the reins. When a paragraph rang true, she thought that's me or at least it was. Taylor read until she rolled entirely on her side with the book lying in front of her, with the pages and cover that were slightly fanned.

Luke blindly reached for the alarm clock that continued to aggravate the sleeping man until his index finger finally found the button. He rolled out of bed in case, like other times, he tapped the snooze that would perform its encore annoyance in another nine minutes.

Dragging himself into the bathroom, Lucas reached blindly for the shower handle. After it was set the same as he always did, he looked at his reflection, waiting for the water to warm. Running his hand against his sandpaper scruff, he climbed in to let the water spray down over him while his alarm in the bedroom intermittently sounded.

Minutes transpired until he glanced at his watch, noticing that he was still on time to begin his day. And today his travel started with a trip to the east side of the city for the fire department renovation.

While getting ready, he pulled his phone off the charger, accidentally knocking a small box off the back of his bedside table. Placing it there two weeks ago, he hoped that he could give the piece, a bracelet, to Taylor personally, although it was beginning to look now like he might have to send it.

The box also contained a key and a worded note that he carefully penned out a few days ago urging a response. As he went to place it where it had been last, he changed his mind and dropped it into his front pocket. With nothing but a blank face the man wondered how it would go, if in fact he decided to send it out today.

Taylor swung her legs out from under the covers bearing a Cheshire cat-like grin, which consumed the lower part of her face. Today was her day off, and like most people in her profession, it was not uncommon to have it be during a weekday.

It might be Thursday, but today was her once a month get-together with her best friend Lauren, and more importantly the first time since getting back from the inn. Taylor arose to find the book she was reading on the carpet beneath her. Gliding her foot aside, she lifted the soft covered manuscript and slid it across the top of her nightstand.

A couple of hours later, Taylor hit the stop on the digital kitchen timer before carefully extracting a pan of freshly baked blueberry muffins from the oven. She no sooner placed the tin on her self-made wine cork trivet, when she heard a knock at the door of her upstairs apartment. Joyfully she ran to the door to greet her friend, the same one that she had known since the fifth grade.

"Come in!" Taylor exclaimed as she sidestepped to let the five-foot, six-inch blonde woman pass her. Lauren made sure to wipe her feet before she did. "You're early!" Taylor asked.

"Yeah, as soon as I had coverage, I was out of there," she stated as Taylor lagged a few feet behind, from her friend who pathed herself through the well-aged apartment to the 1960s-style kitchen.

Taylor got this place back when she and Marty split, and this was the best she could afford. And keeping it spotless made it only a little more visually appealing while giving her less time to think about her own situation. For her, it was either this or move back in with her parents, and she wasn't about to do that. The two sat on the high-backed stools that Taylor had acquired from work when the restaurant remodeled recently.

"So how long do I have you for?" Taylor inquired, knowing her friend's situation as both a mother of three and a wife too.

"I am all yours today! Carl decided to take the day off and work from home."

"Does Carl know what he's in for?" Taylor stated knowing just some of what her friend goes through day in and day out, with raising and teaching their three young children. Lauren let out a thunderous roar that Taylor couldn't help but join in on, as her laugh was quite infectious.

"You are right! He has no clue how rough a day he is about to have. I mean, he is a fantastic father, but let's just say, he won't be asking me to do this again anytime soon," Lauren proclaimed and then paused only long enough to ask what she had wanted to get out since she walked in the door. "So when am I going to hear about this guy from the inn?" the wavy-haired woman asked.

Taylor didn't know where to start as she had so much to say. She was definitely going to tell Lauren, but she figured it was something that she didn't want to text or say over the phone while her three children were most likely hanging off her ankles.

"Well, it was an incredible week," Taylor conveyed briefly.

"And?"

"Yes, there is a lot more to it than just that," she confessed as she retrieved the muffins and fruit. Placing it down, Taylor asked, "So you're sure you are free for the whole day?"

"Oh my God, this is going to be good!"

"Yes, it is!" Taylor exclaimed. Her girlfriend readied herself. After all these weeks she wanted to hear it all, but she was willing to settle for the best stories, if time didn't allow.

"Well, Lucas was a classmate of my brothers. So he's two years older than us. It's Lucas Calderone!" she phrased, trying to see if her classmate recalled him from school. "Well, Kyle called and asked me if I could watch the inn for the week at Christmas."

"Yes, I remember him from high school" Lauren said with heightened elation.

"Well, after telling Kyle I couldn't get the time off, he went and asked Lucas. And Lucas said yes."

"Then how did you get the time off?" Lauren prodded.

"I'm not sure why, but for some reason, Greg changed his mind and granted it." Lauren was going to be crass and ask what she had to do to get it, but she wasn't going to put a pothole in front of this ice cream truck, plus she had met the man. He wasn't her friend's type. Too old, too unattractive, and too married.

"I figured I already had it off, so I wanted to see what an older Luke looked like."

"And was he, I mean was he to your liking?" Lauren inquired.

"Oh, yes. Lucas is a dreamboat." Taylor stopped to show a selfie of the two of them at the bar in Point Hope.

Lauren took a good long look, before commenting. "If I thought he would have turned out like this, I would have gone for him myself!"

"I know, huh?" She took another look and then paused for the next part. "Well, the second night at the inn, we drank a little too much, and we were going over old times, and I reminded him of something he owed me. It was from another conversation way back, before Marty and I got married."

"I had said that Marty was the best thing that ever happened to me, and if I was wrong, then I should be spanked. I'm sure that's not exactly how the original conversation went, but with the alcohol, I... I called him on it!" Taylor murmured with eyes down, almost as if she was embarrassed by what she had just said.

"You called him on it? Does that mean he spanked you?"

"Yes, but it was the way that he did it, that makes it hard for me to tell you," Taylor explained, noticeably embarrassed.

"Hey, you better spill it, girl. I gave up precious time that I could have spent with my children, the ones that I can't quite recall their names right now and..." Lauren said, ceasing only to break into an unstoppable cackle. Taylor laughed but sat there stewing, getting wet from the notion of having to spell it out for her. "Well? What is it?" Lauren urged.

Taylor stood and pointed one finger in the air and tromped off to the bedroom, returning with the book from her nightstand. She faced it toward Lauren, knowing that she would get more out of the title than Taylor was able to say at this particular moment. Lauren read the bold heading, *The Submissive Within*. A few seconds passed before a multitude of questions clouded her brain like shots from a machine gun.

"Is this what I think it is?" said her confounded girlfriend.

"Yes!" Taylor answered timidly.

"So he what, took you over his knee, pulled down your pants, and spanked you like a little schoolgirl?"

"Well, not exactly. Lucas gave me that spanking, but not before he tied me up across the bar," Taylor said, forcing a blush-worthy smile.

"Are you kidding me? Your grandpa's bar?" Lauren replied as her eyes bugged out.

"Why is that sick?"

"Well, I would have to say that it's not normal. It's hot thinking about it, though!"

"So has Carl ever done anything like that with you?" Taylor questioned while Lauren pictured her friend hogtied to the bar, with that rocking body of hers.

"No, he would have to put thought into that, and he has always been more of a wham bam type of guy. There's nothing wrong with that. It's what turned me on about him right from the start, but what about you? I mean, a chance meeting with an old friend of your brothers. I won't even bother to ask you how that went since I've read your texts for the last few weeks. I'm surprised that you would be into that kinky shit. I mean, did he spank you, or is that what the singles are calling sex these days?"

Taylor grinned and shook her head. "Lauren, he tied my wrists across my grandpa's bar, he pulled my pants and panties down to my ankles, which were also tied, and then he proceeded to spank me!"

"Did you get wet? I know I would have been wet. Hell, I'm getting wet right now." Lauren ranted as Taylor tried hard not to laugh.

"I was very wet, but I was also very drunk."

"And did you two have sex?"

"No, not that night, but when I was over the bar, I wanted him bad."

"Wow. I can't believe you went out and found yourself a perv," Lauren cheeked, showing again that this woman didn't have a filter.

"No, it's not like that. Luke was very caring and gentle. And him being in control is all that I thought about, and still think about, even now." Taylor looked up at her other work acquisition, a neon beer clock. "Hey, we should get going. We had a full day planned!"

"Taylor, you couldn't rip me away from here, although I might need a change of underwear soon!" The two had a good laugh, followed by Lauren, who took a bite of her still-warm baked good.

On the outskirts of the city, Luke sipped the coffee that he poured from the top of his cocoa-brown thermos, as his mind again was not entirely on the job at hand. His team was into what they call stage two, now that the demolishing and clean up concluded.

Tomorrow he figured the sheetrock would go up, and then taping and the compound finishing up in a few more days, with painting at the start of next week. Everything was on schedule, and yet he still couldn't stay focused.

This morning was a good time to check out the housing project, where three of his guys were stripping a large residential roof and prepping it for shingles. Then he could go home early tonight, but to what? He knew that if work wasn't suppressing his thoughts, then the isolation of home didn't stand a chance.

"John, I'm stopping by Rockland!" Those few words told his second-in-command that he was heading to the other site, and that John was in charge during his absence. Nothing more needed to be said. Luke grabbed his stuff and climbed into the blue company F150. He slid his lunch box across to the passenger seat and his coffee mug he dropped into the console beside him. Instinctively he opened the gunmetal-gray container enough, to see that the tiny box was still there with him.

# CHAPTER 5

"Oh, crap. I was going to offer you a mimosa! I mean if you are up for one?" Taylor queried.

"Break out the good stuff girlfriend, but you better finish this story today!" Lauren exclaimed now hanging on her friend's every word. Taylor popped the cork and proceeded to pour the juice before topping it off with champagne.

"Hey, can you put more champagne in mine. Otherwise, I'll taste the orange juice," her friend wittily bantered making Taylor chuckle. As Lauren waited, she flipped the book to the back cover to see what juicy words they used to sell its contents. "This guy, Lucas, is he like this all the time?" Lauren asked as she turned it all serious, with her trying to make heads or tails of what she had heard.

"No, as a matter of fact, he has had no one for a couple of years. He just enjoys this. You know like a hobby."

"A hobby? You mean stamp collecting or crocheting wasn't cutting it?" Lauren quipped.

"No, it is hard to explain, but what he does he does to make, well, in this case, me happy."

"And did it make you happy?"

"Oh God, yes," Taylor replied without hesitation.

"So is this kid stuff or stuff from a psychopath in the making?" Lauren inquired, now thinking about her friend's safety.

"Well, it is not kid stuff, but if this were to happen again, I probably should work out more!"

Lauren choked on her mimosa, following it with a quick cough. "Are you kidding me? I don't know anyone more fit than you," she confessed. "So what are you talking about here? Listen, I don't need to know the specifics, but please give me some examples." Even though Lauren was hoping for the full blow-by-blow.

Taylor thought before vocalizing the first. "Well, one night we got hammered at the sports bar and then walked out to the overlook. It was a beautiful starlit night with it being a normal Alaskan cold, you know very cold. He laid out a blanket and then had me get on all fours with my pants down while we screwed like horny teenagers to the sound of the ocean."

"Oh, that's good, but you didn't mention rope or chains for that!"

"That was example number one. The other one was very intense. On our second night alone at the inn, Luke had me kneel at the door of his room. He answered and had me enter. I was wearing the sexiest outfit I could find."

"Wait. Wait, your outfit can I guess?" Lauren continued before Taylor even got a word out. "You were wearing nothing, right?"

"Well, I did have my long flannel shirt on until he pulled it off me. Then he blindfolded me and tied my hands and brought them up high above, tying me off to the beam in his room. Then he pleasured me, although I think that he got just as much out of it."

"And the two of you were drunk for this?" Lauren asked curiously.

"No. Not a drop. We had wine there, but let's just say Luke was all business. Then when I thought it was over, he dropped me to my knees in front of him and took control of me servicing him orally."

"And you didn't fight any of this?" Lauren probed.

"No! I didn't have a choice. Luke used a stick or handle to keep my arms pinned back while he had my hands tied in front of me. Then he used that same handle to control my every action."

Lauren stared at her friend strangely. It was almost like she didn't believe what she was hearing. "Wait a minute! I think I know enough about you to know that you are not this type of woman. You are not the type to walk three feet behind or sexually cower to any man. I'm surprised he didn't have you gagged to go along with it."

"Oh, he did. But it was a carrot. He used that and a hand-kerchief instead of a safe word. I had told him hours earlier that I wanted to find out more about it. And it was his way of showing some of what he does while giving me the right to stop at any point."

Lauren gazed at her again. Much of what Taylor said was beginning to sink in. There was no laugh, or a you got me that was displayed on her friend's solemn face. "So where is this demented dreamboat now?"

"He's back in Seattle!" Taylor answered.

"Are you two planning on getting back together anytime soon?" Lauren asked.

"Well, when he left, he said I should take some time to figure out what it is that I want."

"And what do you want?"

"I want. I think I want to be with Luke," Taylor replied.

"So what's keeping you?"

"Well, if I had decided in the first few days, I would have chosen to pack up and move there. But as time has gone by and not hearing anything from Luke, I just don't know."

"Why don't you know?" Lauren questioned.

"Well, it is complicated for me. What if I pack up everything and the man has changed his mind? I mean what if it was nothing but a good time for Lucas!"

"Do you think it was just bondage and sex for him?"

"I don't know, but I can't quit my job, move hundreds of miles, just to end up heading home with my tail between my legs," Taylor said unsurely.

Lauren leaned in close and then quietly stated, "I understand. I don't think that I would do it either. So what are you going to do next?"

"I'm not sure. I was hoping there would be a sign that would help me decide."

"Like him calling you?" Lauren blurted.

"Precisely! But I thought it would have happened already," Taylor said as her head drooped.

"Hey Taylor, are you starting to feel something for this man?"

"I don't think so, even though it was nice being in a man's arms again. But I did get sucked into the way he made me feel."

"Well, I think if he made you feel the way that you said, he will be in touch. As a matter of fact, I know he will. I have a sense about these things!"

"Thanks, Lauren. I hope you're right!"

Lauren gave her a tight hug, finished her champagne and orange juice, and said, "Hey, before we get out of here do you mind if we do a quick quiz? I think it's appropriate."

"Lauren, you didn't bring one of your mags, did you?" Taylor stated as her friend pulled it from her massive pocketbook.

"Come on, this will only take a minute!"

"Okay, but you know how I feel about those things!"

"I do," Lauren answered as she flipped the pages to get to what she was looking for. "You are going to like this, really! Okay, this one is called, does your man make you feel," Lauren said, hesitating before she began. "It is a simple one. Does your man make you feel dry like cacti, damp as a stamp, or moister than an oyster, or wet as a water jet?"

"Well, that's not appropriate because technically he is not my man."

"Come on, appease me, and answer the question!" Lauren prodded.

"Okay, then I would have to say the water jet one, and you might have to make that two," she answered displaying a full-fledged smile in her best friend's direction. "So now can we get out of here?" Taylor urged.

"Let's go," Lauren said as her grin if it were any bigger; most surely would have turned into a laugh. After bagging up the muffins for Lauren's family, the two descended the stairs to the darkened street below.

Lucas stewed, trying to reassure himself that the package he sent was truly the right thing to do. But it had to be as the situation had dragged on for far too long, and now he needed closure.

The guy was ready to get a "I will join you there," a "I'm not ready to make that decision yet," or "Look we had a great time, but this just isn't going to work out." The note, which he finally included in the hinged cover, was short and concise. Luke hoped that the

CHAINED TO MY HEART

answer would be one that he wanted, but either way, he should know soon.

His feelings for her went way back as he wanted Taylor when it wasn't even possible. He always thought she was gorgeous, but now that she was a little older, she was more beautiful than he could have ever imagined. On waiting for her reply, he expected that it might take a few weeks before he would hear anything.

A week later, Taylor marched past the downstairs delicatessen, where a boy in his midteens raised a finger trying desperately to signal the woman before she strode past their front door. Not seeing the teenager the woman went about her business ascending the stairs, toting an armload of groceries.

As she made it to the second-floor landing outside her apartment, she heard the door behind her, swing open. A young man she recognized as Zach ran up to greet her, carrying a small package in one hand. "Pardon me, Taylor, the mailman left this for you downstairs. I think he's new and didn't know you lived here!"

She didn't mind the blond-haired youth calling her by her first name since through time she had grown quite a distaste for her married one. Taylor had wanted to change it back to her maiden name, but until it became a necessity, like the rent and the car payment, it wasn't going to get done.

"Thank you. I appreciate it very much," Taylor said, staying impassive to the boy since she knew that without a doubt, he had a crush on her. "Hey, Zach, what is your special of the day?" she inquired because of her growing hunger and always weak desire to cook.

"Today is the turkey melt with Havarti, onion straws and a jalapeño spread," he replied as she casually plucked the box from his hand.

"That sounds wonderful. I think I will have that for dinner."

"Do you want me to go make you one? I can bring it to you." the vivacious kid said.

"No, I will see you and your pops later for dinner, but thanks anyway!"

"You're welcome, Taylor." Awkwardly, he turned and made his way down the staircase, happy that he would be seeing her later.

The light brown tiny box rested upon her open palm, showing no sign of an address. While keeping one eye on the packaging, Taylor reached back to grasp a serrated steak knife from its block. She carefully cut through the tape and the seal.

As the flaps were pulled away, she peered at even smaller rectangular velvet jewelry box. Taylor extracted it with her index finger and thumb, pulling it free of its packaging with her still wondering where the gift had come from.

Taylor carefully opened the blue hinged clamshell case. Inside it revealed a beautiful sterling bracelet, with a locking heart at one end, along with a key that was displayed in the center.

After studying it, she opened the note that dislodged from the inside of the top rim. Then, she finally realized that it was in fact from Luke. Taylor slowly read the words that instantaneously brought her to tears. Placing the note on the counter, she wiped away her tearful display.

The note read, "Tay, you can either return this gift or return wearing it. The decision is yours!" Taylor couldn't hold back the way that she felt, with her having no idea that the feelings she had for him were this strong. When the pools finally dried up, she reached for her phone. She hit speed dial and waited. "Hey, is this a good time to talk?"

"Sure, honey, what is it?" Lauren inquired.

"I just got a package in the mail and—"

"Is it from Luke? Are you crying? Have you been crying? Is everything okay?"

Taylor didn't know which one to answer first. "Yes, I've been crying. They're happy tears, though. It is because I just got a package with a beautiful bracelet. And I think Luke is asking if I want to join him."

"So, what are you going to do Taylor?" Lauren asked once she checked on her three boys in the next room.

"I don't know. It hasn't sunk in yet. But I don't think I can leave my family, and then I'm going to be so far from my best friend too," Taylor uttered softly.

"Hey, if you're talking about me, we're not that close!"

Taylor snorted. "See what I mean. I can't give up all this."

After moments of silence, Lauren interjected, "Seriously, I will always be just a call away, so please don't leave me as an excuse to a future regret!"

Taylor eventually confessed, "I suppose you're right."

"I know I am, and you know what, I have a feeling you have already thought this one through. You were just afraid to pull the trigger. And if this does work out, there will be no one more thrilled than me Taylor. But if it doesn't, Alaska, your family, your best friend, and your old job will be more than happy to take you back."

"Then I have to think this out. Thank you, Lauren. You're the best!"

"No, you are and don't ever forget it. Bye, girlfriend. Oh, and let me know what your decision is when you come up with one."

Taylor ended the call to reach atop of one of her cabinets for a bottle of red wine. Carrying the California Cabernet down to the BYOB deli, Taylor knew that she had a lot to contemplate, with her hoping the pros would drastically outweigh the cons.

Nine days! It had been nine days since the package left his hands. Lucas wasn't expecting to see either the box or Taylor yet, but the not knowing part was killing him. He did however receive a confirmation that it was delivered, so he now at least had the desire to get back to his project, a project that he couldn't show to anyone except for that special woman, who would appreciate it for the spirit in which it was intended. And if not for that at least the man was shaving again.

The best part of his projects, were that they're discreetly hidden and locked away, both now and after completion. In the past, he had designed a few ways to keep a sub snug, but this one by far will be his best. Since he loved working with wood and steel, this had Taylor written all over it, even though he started it before their chance encounter, he could now visualize her being part of it.

Neither of the other two restraints he built were still in the house. Lucas believed that each sub deserved items that had never been used on anyone else before. A new sub deserves new toys.

In the silence of the garage, he eyed the many pieces that he cut from two-inch steel round frame. In the last few months he bent, welded, ground, and sanded, polishing each of them off to a smooth finish, suitable for painting. Beginning with a stylish twenty-four-by-thirty-six-inch floor base, the design will have pieces, when completed, that will protrude from it that could be adjusted for that perfect fit.

Lucas for months had searched online before finally locating the restraints that he wanted, from a company in Norway. The claw manacles were the hardest to find because they needed to fit his build. And now looking at his computer print, he couldn't help thinking about Taylor.

Maybe she might be punished someday for some insignificant thing and will have to answer for it. As he couldn't contain his smirk any longer, he put the plans and pieces back in hiding in the cabinet before shutting off the light to his workshop.

The moon hung high in the sky, with him viewing its reflection as it danced across the shoreline of the never yielding ocean. And the sight made him wonder if she was looking at it at that exact moment. Luke was never a praying man, but in this case, he hoped that her destiny and his would intertwine soon to form a lifelong relationship.

If he thought he had any pull or was able to sway her with his charms, distance certainly would have stopped it. Maybe tomorrow with any luck! He reminded himself of the options he had given Taylor, with the worst one being the image of the box sitting on his doorstep. But either way, this will end, and he should finally know.

Taylor sat across from her parents, with only a bold red and white check table cover to separate them. Her chatty dad had seized the first opportunity to tell or retell in this case, the past events of the seniors. And as happy as both were to have Taylor there, Mom was detecting a deeper motive behind this particular weekly visit.

Mom lifted the tea kettle and poured the boiling water, covering the bag that lay on the bottom of her daughter's porcelain cup. After filling her own, she set it down upon the white ceramic trivet in the center of the table. That silence gave Dad an in to talk about their activities at the community center before the ladies dominated the conversation.

Taylor listened but waited for her father to pause or finish the same story she was sure that she had heard last week. She needed to speak with mom about Lucas, and it was far too important to include a third person in on.

"So how is everything at work?" her mother asked when her husband finished.

"It's the same, Mom! You know work is work." She didn't want to let on that her life was driving her to the brink of insanity. But she feared the latter which was them asking again, for her to move in.

"Have you heard from Marty lately?" her dad asked.

"No. And I won't. The divorce is final. We've moved on," Taylor said and then asked, "Dad, would it be okay if I had a talk with Mom?"

Dad gave them both a look in the eye before responding. "Sure kitten." That was the nickname he gave her as a child, and he uses it just as much to this day.

"Thanks, Dad," Taylor said as the two broke away and walked into the spare bedroom. Closing the door, she joined her mom at the foot of the bed. Studying her expression, Taylor just let it roll off her tongue. "I wanted to let you know that I am contemplating a move!"

"A move? Are you going back to the Point?"

"No, if I decide to do this, it would be Seattle!"

"But what's in Seattle?" her mom said curiously.

Even though she had thought about it during the whole ride over, she didn't know how to phrase it. "Mom, while Kyle was gone, I stayed for a week with an old friend at the inn."

"I see, and is this old friend a man?"

"Yes, it is Lucas Calderone!"

"Ah yes, he is a very nice boy, I mean, man!" Taylor kept her emotions in check, but she was pretty sure her mom could see right through it, sensing her unadulterated feelings.

"Yes, he is a good man," Taylor stated, *and a man who also has some pretty naughty thoughts*, she said to herself.

"We talked about it, but he wanted to make sure that I was okay with my life before making a decision."

"All right. And have you and Lucas done more than just talk because that could influence your decision?" her mom asked.

Taylor shamefully dropped her head a few degrees. "Yes, we have, but he has felt something for me for years, and we had a wonderful week just talking about us. I learned a lot about the man while I was there," she said, blooming a perfect Taylor smile.

"You know, all we want is for you to be happy. And from what I remember, all the Calderone's are outstanding people. You know they built the bar at the inn for your grandparents?"

"Yes, I know!" Oh God, how she knew. Her body draped across the top and tied to the other side and then her chin resting upon the wooden structure itself.

"So when would you be moving?" her mother asked, ceasing her trip down memory lane.

"Well, if I go, it will be soon. I do need a break, with Marty and all. Friends look at me differently ever since we split up. I just want to feel normal again. I need this!"

"Will you call us when you know?"

"Yes, you will be the first, but first I have to tell dad!" Leaning in, she gave her mother a big hug. Now it was time to figure out what she was going to do so to give herself one last chance to see if this was what she really wanted.

# CHAPTER 6

Luke kept his eyes on the wheel, trying to forget the extremely bad day he had at work. It began with the building inspector, who he believes has something against him, after throwing quite a few infractions from the apartment complex their way. And that alone slowed down their work, adding on at least three days to the project.

He was frustrated to put it mildly, not to mention this afternoon one of his guys somehow backed into a dumpster of all things. The man hit a large green dumpster that crunched the rear quarter panel on the company van. He didn't need this. But it was Friday, and now all he wanted to do was just go home and forget about it.

Driving below the speed limit, he rode past many of his neighbors' not-so-modest homes, the same macroscopic houses or mansions that lined the grand shore on the scenic drive where he lived.

Lucas knew that his home didn't size up or cost anywhere near, but he did like being far from the bustling city and directly on the ocean too. Looking at one of his neighbor's places he recalled when the home sold a year ago for 4.3 million dollars. He wondered how some of these people made their money, and he was shocked with what they could buy with it.

"Are you kidding me?" Luke called out when he realized that he forgot the contract that he needed to bring home. He remembered setting it on the corner of his desk where he was supposed to put it into his portfolio, which was his regular routine. Tomorrow! Tomorrow he would travel the forty-five minutes back to the fire station.

He parked a few feet from the garage of his large gray cottage-style home, making sure not to damage a second vehicle today. Lucas stepped out of the truck, grabbed his lunch pail, and gathered the mail which hung in the box outside to the right of the screen door. Thumbing through the pile, he clenched the handle. Not focusing, he was about to put the key in the door when his peripheral vision caught a glance of what he had feared most.

Placing all of what he was carrying in on the small side table, he approached the item as if he was a member of a bomb squad, closing in on an incendiary device. The sidetracked Lucas opened the door carrying the small package like it was nitroglycerin, over to the oak dining table. He knew exactly how this was supposed to play out since he was the one that had sent the package to Fairbanks. So he knew it couldn't be good news.

Taylor was instructed to send the bracelet back if she wasn't going to return with it. Well, here it is, and Lucas merely closed his eyes, not wanting to show his apparent disappointment. He carefully cut into the box and pulled the flaps back revealing the small blue velvet case that he sent her.

Shaking inside, Lucas opened it revealing nothing but the innards that once kept the bracelet in place. Confusion overwhelmed him. But it didn't last as there was a light rap at the rear sliding door. He stood in disbelief at what he saw while Taylor stood there looking back at him.

"Hey, it's a little cold out here. Can I come in?" she said, showing a big beautiful smile. Shocked he opened it to the grinning woman.

"When did you? How long have you been out there?" Lucas asked as he hugged and kissed her.

"I have been here for about an hour?" Taylor answered.

"Well, why didn't you call me?" Lucas asked.

"What and miss this?"

Luke didn't know what to say. The woman of his dreams was right here in front of him, in his house. This was the way that he had wanted it but thought it just wasn't going to be. "So does this mean you took me up on my offer?" Lucas asked in anticipation.

"Well, what do you think?" she replied, flashing the locked bracelet, which was hiding under her sleeve. Reaching into the neck hole of her shirt, she pulled the silver chain with the key attached that hung around her neck. Taylor grinned handing it over to the still-confounded man.

He gave her an appreciative full-bodied kiss. It had been a truly dreadful day, but everything was going to be much better now.

"So what were you going to do tonight?" Taylor asked.

"It doesn't matter. My plans just changed."

"You changed them for me?" Taylor stated.

"Well, I wanted to get the boat going, but the weather is still too cold. Instead, maybe we could sit around and open this," Luke said as he withdrew a bottle of tequila from one of the upper cabinets.

"Oh, my favorite! Did you have trouble finding it here?"

"No, the hardest part was not breaking it open."

"I can see that," she said as she looked at the contents, which was about 25 percent gone.

"Sorry! I missed you!"

"I missed you too, and that's why I'm here," Taylor repeated. "So you meant that I could move in with you?" she added.

"Absolutely! And how about I pour you a drink, and then I can give you a tour of our place," he stated emphasizing the, our part.

"That sounds wonderful," Taylor said while she sat at the island, fiddling with the empty box as he dowsed her ice with tequila.

"I am guessing you probably don't need a tour of the outside since you were out there that long, but do you need to freshen up?"

"Yes, please!" Taylor replied as Lucas led her down the short hall to the bathroom. She passed him as he exited to the kitchen to throw a quick plate of cheese, pepperoni, and crackers together. While he waited, he parked himself on the couch until a refreshed Taylor emerged.

"Well, thank you for deciding to do this. I mean, are you going to stay, or are you just trying this out?"

"I will stay until you can't take me anymore," Taylor answered.

"That could never happen!" he said, showing his pearly whites while handing her a plate with a few choice items. Not wanting to appear hungry, she took some, even though she was thoroughly famished.

"Later I will have Flavio's deliver us something from the restaurant. It is the best Italian we have here in Seattle!" Luke said.

"Well, Mr. Calderone, if you say it is the best, then it must be!"

The still stymied man answered once he figured it out. "Hey, I see what you did there! It's because I'm Italian right?" They both had a brief chuckle. After finishing the snacks, he made sure to call in the order before giving her the short tour.

Taking Taylor from right to left, he began at one of the spare bedrooms. Briefly showing her a catch-all bedroom upstairs and what turned out to be the only cluttered room in this very tidy house,. She viewed a laundry area and the cleanest garage she had ever saw. But in the master bedroom, she instantly fell in love with the sitting area and the four-poster king-size bed. It was finished in maple, which perfectly matched every other piece in the room.

Taylor during the showing became captivated in the ocean view from the sitting area as the sunlight through the window made her skin glow from its late afternoon rays. Still locked on the panoramic view, Taylor turned. "Oh, Luke, I left my suitcase out on the deck."

"I will get it. Do you only have the one bag?"

"For now! I wanted to make sure I didn't read your note wrong. I have the rest of my stuff over at my friend Lauren's house. She said she will ship it if it all works out."

"It will be fine! Have her send it when she can!" he exclaimed before adding, "I don't want you living out of one bag for that long."

"Okay, I will," Taylor replied. He turned and was halfway down the hall when she called out. "Is it okay if I take a shower?"

"Of course, remember, this is your place too!" he answered. Taylor, who was in the other bathroom not ten minutes ago, only partially closed the door since privacy for them went out the window a long time ago.

She was astonished to see how spacious the room was, being roughly four times the size of the one in her apartment, and this one could have been visually sold as brand new. Not wasting any time, she piled her dirty clothes on top of the hamper, only to stand nude in front of his oak mirrored vanity. Lucas brought her case in and placed it on the floor at the foot of the bed.

"Luke, can you help me with the shower!" she called out. He crept in astounded as Taylor stood naked before him, sporting a freshly shaved pussy.

"Taylor, you did that for me?" Luke asked as he started the water.

"No, Tay did. And besides, I needed to try something new!"

She playfully tugged at his shirt and said, "Are you going to join me?" Luke obliged by pulling out the key from his pocket. He unlocked and unhinged the clasp, allowing for the piece to fall upon his open palm.

Taylor, who was horny as hell, waited impatiently for the man to strip, by reaching for his belt before he even had a chance to. Lucas turned on the shower, escorting her by using one hand for her forearm and his second cupped hand that cupped her bare ass perfectly.

Water flowed down in a slow, steady stream from the ceiling showerhead, trickling down across her face and down each and every curve as Lucas moved in close to her. Then like a powerful magnet to steel, Taylor took what she wanted, pulling him in tight. If it had been any closer and he would have been inside of her.

They met in a heavy lip-lock where he whipped his tongue wildly within her agape cavity, as the tip reached deep to satisfy her.

Taylor melted as Luke took the lead and piloted her in the dance of two wet bodies. Out of the spray, he lathered her thoroughly, missing nothing. She slithered down the front of him, arising only to lather his penis and balls with her silky soapy breasts. The two concluded their back and forth foreplay by freeing themselves of the suds that ensued.

"Thanks for talking me into a shower," Luke said as he wiped down.

Moving to the master bedroom, she said, "Well, I figured you probably need it after a rough day of work."

"I did, and you know what else I need?"

"No, what?" Taylor asked.

"This!" he said as he surprised her by sprawling her across the width of the bed. Yanking her towel aside, he expediently followed her onto the mattress, dropping his head onto her freshly shaved clit.

She scooched back to give him even more comfort in the pleasures he was giving her.

It wasn't two minutes into the pussy lashing when the doorbell rang. Luke. "Oh crap, I forgot about the food. I'll be back!" he said, dragging along her towel for cover.

Lucas left to retrieve their order, even as they both knew it would get cold before they would be able to consume it. She pushed herself to the head of the bed while she tried to fix her hair. Luke set their order down on the counter and poked his head in the door. "Do you want to eat while it's hot?"

"You were eating. Now get back over here," Taylor quipped lifting her bottom half high toward the ceiling. He grinned as he double-timed it back to her aching damp pussy, where her legs stood as a beacon in case the man had lost his way.

Later the two lifted their glasses, coupling it with some outstanding microwaved Italian cuisine. With their first appetite filled, the two made sure to satisfy their other hunger while they sat naked at the kitchen island.

In the morning a smiling Taylor arose in a fleeting fog of not knowing where she was. After snapping out of it, she hunted through one of Luke's drawers until she found a T-shirt of his. Pacing, she searched for Lucas who was nowhere to be found.

She peered out the front windows and back as well. It wasn't until Taylor heard a noise coming from the laundry room that she went to investigate. She pulled the door open to view Lucas bolting some metal pieces together.

"Oh, did I wake you?" Luke commented when he noticed the scantily clad woman not ten feet away.

"No, I slept quite well, thanks to you."

"Oh, Taylor, while you are here, I would like to measure you, I mean, if you still want to be restrained every once in a while, that is."

She thought, *What an odd request for six in the morning.* But by putting on that bracelet and moving in, she knew that it was now part of the territory. This, for them, was to be a relationship with extras.

"So how do you want me?" she inquired. He grinned as he shuffled up beside her with a measuring tape in hand.

He measured her arm length extended out in front of her and then her leg when she leaned over and lastly her torso from bent leg to neck. "This isn't how you measure a woman for a dress!" She spat out sarcastically.

Lucas made a face while trying to keep her from focusing on the metal structure before ushering her briskly from his workshop. Not wanting her to return he followed her out to the kitchen, where they had breakfast before he drove to his work site to pick up the proposal he forgot.

With the sun nearly overhead, and the contract sitting on the back seat Luke asked, "Taylor, do you want to go out to lunch and then maybe do some shopping?"

"Do you have time for that? I know you have to work on your bid!"

"I will need a couple of hours later, but no more than that," Luke answered.

"Then I guess we could go shopping. It would be nice to see a different mall for a change," Taylor claimed.

"Yes, you will need different clothes. The climate is not nearly as intense here, with the cold anyway." Lucas paused before adding, "Oh, and would you mind if I have a say in what would look good on you?"

"Of course," she replied, although Taylor wondered what styling ability he had as a guy to pick out clothes for a woman. She hoped it was good as she didn't want to offend him with her just moving in yesterday. But Taylor didn't have that ability, as her clothes were often picked out by Lauren. So she thought Luke might surprise her.

Her ex had never shown any interest or complimented her on anything she wore, and that included her wedding gown, which formerly had been her mom's. It was an honor for Taylor to carry on the tradition of what her tribe did. And yet Marty never acknowledged it.

The vehicle pulled onto the highway joining the usual weekend city traffic, as vehicles traveled south like wildebeest in their typical formation, where a few joined the pack, and a few broke away.

"So your job is Monday to Friday?" Taylor inquired.

"Almost all of the time. I do have a small crew that works the weekend occasionally, so I don't have to, but if problems arise, I am the person they call."

"Then how many guys do you have working for you?"

"I have as many as fourteen when we are busy and as few as six during our slow season. Steve or John can run the day to day operation. I trust them to do everything for me. Then I have six that can do the job very well if they are told what to do."

"And the last four are the grunts. Not particularly skilled but can do the lugging, demo, and removal. Together, I have an incredible team, and I haven't had any personnel changes in two years. However, I am the only one that does the books and submits bids."

"So you are pretty busy? Is that how you can afford your home?" she questioned.

"Actually, no. The house is almost paid off. I got an incredible deal on the land after building a guesthouse for my neighbor as he was having trouble selling such a small parcel of land. We both made out in the transaction. My dad made sure that when I came out here, I had enough to start a business and a substantial deposit for a small lot and home. He said he knew what kind of worker I was, and he had no doubt that I could pull this off. So within two years, I started sending money back his way."

"I wouldn't call this a small amount of land, but that was very thoughtful of your dad," Taylor stated.

"Yes, it was! And his dad did the same for him years ago. Of course, my father was handed lira. And someday I want to do the same for mine too." She listened, astonished by his family's lowkey pact.

Taylor's eyes widened at the sight of the multistory complex that appeared down the street. She gazed at the large store signs that lined the drive as if to remind the discerning shopper that they were there for your service.

"We're going to Seattle Brewing Company for lunch. It's only a storefront and not the actual brewery. That's ten miles away. They service Idaho, Montana, and Oregon, and I heard they will be in

California soon. They have a few good specialty beers that I think you might even like."

"I can't wait!" she exclaimed, wanting to find something that will get her foot in the door to liking beer a little more.

"They also have a fantastic selection of ever-changing tapas."

"Yum," Taylor replied as she held his bicep with her cupped hand.

# CHAPTER 7

Perusing the main aisle, Taylor's eyes spied the multitude of neon strips that hung artistically from the second and third-floor glass balconies. Above that, an endless array of uniquely shaped nylon kites, many of which reflected the highlights of the city, which were all different shades of green since Seattle had been known as the Emerald City since 1982. Of course, the woman from out of town didn't know that.

Being visually awestruck, the brunette became distracted and subsequently lagged back from Luke, making her scurry up to him to hold his hand. He pointed ahead to the brewery at the far end of the food court. Nearing the restaurant, a beautiful short thin blond-haired hostess who was straightening the menus asked, "Two for lunch?"

"Yes, please!" he responded. The woman led them through the dining area to a small table to one side of an indoor waterfall.

After being seated, the woman handed them menus. The petite, woman who was adorned with a thin black rope choker, said, "Your waitress will right with you," and then turned to sway back to her station.

Lucas, who appeared as though he was about to disclose something waited, making sure she wasn't able to hear what he was about to utter. He leaned in close to Taylor to whisper, "I have seen her at meetings!"

"Meetings? What kind of meetings?"

"I have been to meetings for bondage and BDSM," he stated.

"And she was there? Did you ever want to ask her to be your sub?"

"She is a sub, but she is married, and I think they only do it, as a couple."

"It's too bad, I bet you could have taught her a few things!" Taylor stated as she mimicked the Cheshire cat.

"I wouldn't bet on that. Many are into a lot more than what we do. What I do is for fun. For others, it is a way of life. At least she didn't recognize me. And that's good. I don't want it getting weird!"

The two enjoyed three appetizers along with their beer while they sat under the nearby babbling waterfall. On their way out, the young blonde left them with a parting message. "Have a great day, and thank you for coming!" *Still nothing*, he thought. She didn't recognize him.

Walking away from the restaurant, Taylor blurted out, "Are you sure she didn't remember you? She did say thank you for cumming!" Lucas let out a thundery guffaw. The gag had caught him so off guard that he choked at the end of his jocular display. Even the hostess turned when she heard it. Taylor joined in once she knew the joke had landed.

When he finally stopped coughing, he grabbed hold of her hand and brought it up to kiss it. That is when she noticed she was already feeling quite comfortable in her brand-new Seattle life. Hunting for the first clothing outlet, they walked off holding each other.

"What do you think about this?" Lucas said, showing off another top that he had picked up in the first store.

"Well, yellow isn't really my color!" Taylor balked.

"And why not? A bright yellow with your skin tone would complement your radiance." She felt the fabric while she thought, before putting it with the other items she would try on later. Taylor was taken aback that he wasn't picking clothes that no woman would wear.

"We have a few here, but I think we should stop. My credit card is going to throw up if I abuse it this bad!" Taylor expressed.

"You're not paying for these. It's my treat, for taking a chance on me," Lucas declared.

"Luke, I couldn't!" Taylor implored.

"Don't worry, you can work it off in trade," he said, posing a cheesy grin.

"Well, if I have to get some clothes, then I have to!" she said as an associate stood two aisles over folding and eavesdropping on their entire conversation. Taylor picked up her pile of possibilities and eventually found the fitting room, where Lucas sat patiently awaiting the show.

She emerged wearing the yellow top that he had picked out with a pair of bright-white Capris showing off her figure beautifully. "I think those are just right. What do you think, Tay?"

His words rang out, taunting her, as she had trouble viewing her own reflection. She wasn't getting wet, but the door was open for it. Taylor tried on the rest of the articles, and to her astonishment, the only one that didn't look good was the one that she'd picked out. That was no surprise since Lauren has always been her personal shopper. She left the shop, beaming in front of the same associate that heard their talk earlier.

Taylor gave some words of advice to her boyfriend once they were clear of the store. Shit, she had a boyfriend. A boyfriend? That was too strange to fathom. "Luke, if you don't mind, could you refrain from calling me Tay while I am trying on clothes? It doesn't take much to get me going right now!"

"Why do you think I did it? And besides, this is your everyday clothes. Wait until later, when we are down on Bering Street. They have outfits there that will grab your fancy. And then they have an adult store next door, that is aptly named Fit to Be Tied."

So this was where Taylor had to decide if this way of life was going to work for her. But she knew that that was the pretense behind it, whether she was wearing the bracelet or not. But could she tell the hunk she was living with, no? She didn't want to, at least for now. This, after all, might be the life she was always meant to have.

"One more store and then a stop at the other place?"

"Absolutely," she stated without reservation. The store Luke mentioned sounded much better than the one they have in Fairbanks. Too bad, I am sure a place like that would have helped to keep everyone warmer.

Taylor walked in before him beneath the large bold sign that was constructed of rope letters. Upon the glass entry door was the customary "If sexually explicit material offends you, then please do not pass beyond this point." It was what she would have read if she stopped long enough to read it.

She pushed through the next blacked out door in sheer excitement. With her adrenaline in overdrive, she was having trouble containing herself. Fairbanks has a place like this, but she never had a reason to cross its threshold.

Her first sight inside was of black leather everything. Luke just looked from afar to catch her expression. She saw harnesses, whips, swings, and restraints, and things that were hanging on the wall that she couldn't figure out. Next was the sections of dildos, gags, and vibrators of every type and size. "See anything you like?" Luke inquired.

"Well, I like this blindfold. I like that feeling of not knowing what to expect next."

Lucas made a mental note. "Anything else?"

"What is all this over here?"

"It's for sadomasochism. I don't think you would ever be into that aspect, and I don't dish it out like that either."

"So what do you think I'm into then?" she asked.

"I think you are into the restraints. Is that fair to say?"

"I can see that," she agreed, looking away from the merchandise, long enough to flash him a quick smile. They concluded there, with him purchasing a small, sleek vibrator, the blindfold, and a surprise. While they checked out the entire store, she said that all she had ever used were her fingers. And with him being a gentleman, one who thought he understood a woman's needs, he bought her a second option.

"I want to take you next door to get you one article of clothing that will amplify your overall bondage experience!" Lucas exclaimed even as others were close enough to hear their not-so-private conversation.

"I'm game!"

There was that phrase that he first heard in Point Hope, a short sentence that drove him crazy. Here he was trying to be the one to drive her wild, maybe get her in a mood for later, but with two simple words, he was the one ogling and panting. They exited the toy shop only to enter the sister company next door, Leather to Lace.

The two took a few steps into the very narrow shop with endless racks that bordered its left and right walls, with Taylor spying items that ranged from outfits and role play to latex and of course leather. However, Luke was already picturing her in something leather, and something that would exude subservience.

She became fascinated by the racks of latex items that broadly covered everything from tops and bottoms to a full body suit with built-in restraints. That wasn't her, but she tried to imagine it just the same.

Lucas, who skated ahead to the last section, picked up an item, to see what it looked like. He held the hanger high, as Taylor nonchalantly worked her way toward him. "Tay, can you come here please!"

Taylor strutted to Luke, with him holding out the mostly leather outfit, placing it appropriately up to her body, like a cardboard one for his 3D paper doll. The outfit which consisted of a black corset or bustier with matching thong yielded an artful array of multiple-sized bronze grommets around the abdomen of the bodice. "This will do nicely!" Lucas said out loud and then continued, "We will need to stop at one more place quick. I mean you will need shoes to complete your ensemble." She nodded in submission. The ride was somewhat quiet all the way to the next place.

Inside the store Taylor wobbled as she strutted in the five-inch black leather heels that he thought might be the ones. "Luke, I'm not familiar with heels, and I'm not really sure I can walk in them," she replied, with not having any past experience with being up on her toes.

An accommodating older black female associate piped in before Lucas could. "Those aren't for walking, honey."

With momentary naivety and a touch of a smile, Taylor asked, "Then can I at least get them with training wheels so I don't fall?" The two finally settled for the three-inch heel, to keep her a little more grounded. After paying for the items, they walked off to the truck for the ride home. This fairy tale of a day was starting to set in, as she thought she might, in fact, turn back into a pumpkin as an inevitable question just popped out. "Lucas, I can't live here without a job. It will drive me crazy, and eventually, it will get you too!"

"Well, I have an idea, but I don't want to talk about it today, all right?"

"Okay! But soon, please."

"Soon!" he promised.

They hauled the day's purchases into their bedroom, where Lucas cleared out his short dresser and over half of the walk-in closet, while Taylor placed the stacks of designer apparel on the bed. Tops and bottoms in a broad spectrum of colors laid in neat piles, ready to be put away. The leather outfit, which she assumed she might want to try on for tonight, was placed on the other side of the bed with her two new dresses.

Later as Taylor finished putting everything away, Lucas poked his head in the door. "Hey, I made us a reservation for six o'clock!"

"Yes, sir," she replied bringing on an involuntary giggle, as she added the title when she didn't need to. Luke popped out of view, returning to his semi-private corner of the living room where his office was set up. He gracefully parked himself in the padded oak desk chair, where he went straight to work with his computer, papers, and calculator, immersing himself so to finish this proposal as rapidly as possible.

He wasn't excited at all about this one. Word was out that this was a hand to pocket. A proposal of where they were going through the formalities of taking the bids. But when all was said and done, it was still going to go to a close friend or someone that lined the palm of the one that needed the job completed.

He had to put the work in just in case, but he wasn't going to low ball and not make anything on the job. That is no way to stay afloat. Plus, his thoughts drifted thinking of Taylor in the bedroom with her wondering about what was going to happen tonight.

His mind couldn't stay on task as he leafed through the pile of papers in front of him. This one was not going to make his company any money. *Screw it*, he thought.

Another project in a couple of months was the one to go for. Lucas figured he had as good a shot as anyone else did, and it would keep them all busy until the end of summer. Yes, the new police station project in Wallington would be their golden ticket! He turned the corner and had his hand on the door to the laundry room. "Taylor, I changed my mind. I will be in the garage!" he called out loudly.

"Okay," she replied, making her feel an instant twinge. Taylor was getting turned on about the project Luke was working on, although she was entirely in the dark about it and only knew that it was for her. But as a submissive, that's the way it's supposed to be. But if only she weren't so damn curious, with her also surprised that he had any time to work on it, seeing how busy he was.

Lucas laid his prints out before him where he studied them each and every time. Wanting to have full sight of what it will look like when it's done, he stuck to the same steps, obsessively.

A box containing five restraints came in last week, rested on one of the shelves of the locked closet behind him. The cuffs, designer ones, he ordered exclusively because of their features. Luke chose them overall since the cuffs could be released either wirelessly or by phone or tablet.

They also featured a timer built into the app, should he want Taylor to remain for a set duration. The restraints, which resembled black robotic hands, could grasp an appendage, with the fifth much-larger one for her neck. His penis pressed against his pants aroused by the lingering thought of Taylor during a future bondage session involving the piece.

Mostly submerged, Taylor relaxed in the large white porcelain tub while the smell of lavender rose up from the heated sudsy water. Pondering, she tried to imagine what was going to happen tonight, at the same time as the onslaught of ideas of a new job and what she left in Fairbanks clouded her already flighty train of thought.

Lucas carefully aligned the pipes on the drill press before carefully boring holes through each one. These will be used as adjusters for the length of the supports. Once finished, the poles would be bolted to the base, to provide the pivot.

The tops where Taylor's body will have the most contact will be finished off with a thick black foam padding, providing a comfortable area to help hold her upper torso as well as Taylor's lower half too. An adjustable slide lock on all four steel legs will incorporate the new restraints, which should safely and securely hold each of her limbs.

He loved when it was time to construct his projects, starting with an idea and having it come out exactly as he had envisioned it. It was like a trophy or an attaboy tap on the back, for him. Of course, it wasn't that time yet. After sanding, the entire lot will be shipped out to a business in Portland, which will powder-coat them in a brilliant color of his own choosing, with his of course being black.

With Lucas having to get ready for tonight as well, he locked all the items, placing the keys on a nail, under the top front of the workbench. He left everything neat and tidy, so again no one would ever know what it was transpires behind those closed doors. Doing one final scan of the room, he exited.

Of the two dresses Luke had picked out for her, she knew which one she wanted to wear first. It had to be the short royal blue and black one. Not too short but long enough, with a plunging neckline that allowed for what she felt was the right amount of visibility to her cleavage. The outfit even contained a hint of lace, making it even that much more feminine.

Standing in nothing but a black thong, Taylor attempted to try on the leather bodice, to see if it could be concealed beneath an outer garment like the attached tags said that it would. She eventually got it tied to where she was pleased with its fit, with her only other concern, which was if tonight's dress would hide it without noticeable protrusions.

Still skeptical, she carefully brought the dress down over her, and to her surprise it covered the bodice perfectly. The dress, which is a medium-thickness material, seemed to hide the grommets and eyelets of the undergarment, making it virtually unnoticeable.

After pulling on her nylons, she spun around to see the nearly finished product multiple times. The mirrors didn't lie, as she grinned that it all pieced together so nicely. Feeling sexy, she sat on the bed.

Taylor tucked the first of her hosed feet into the black stiletto and clear spiked heels. These are by far the more stable of the two she tried on earlier. Probably not that comfortable since they aren't broken in yet, and well, they are heels. But you can't wear flip-flops with an outfit like this either. Feeling pretty and a little naughty, she took one last look and then cautiously stepped out of the bedroom.

Taylor had to remain clearheaded tonight and not jump the man's bones, even though right now that is precisely what she wanted to do. And she wasn't sure what kind of evening this was to be yet, whether it was sex or D/s activity, so she had to let him lead, with her finding out later.

Only her guy knew the answer to that question. Plus, she had to remember that being a submissive, even though it wasn't 24/7, meant she could be called on at any time, and she had to be ready and able. And she, of course, had no problem with that.

With one cheek planted on the stool, Lucas sipped from his drink when his vision of loveliness sashayed the beige carpeted hall toward him. His face portrayed that the time she took and the purchases he made were well worth the investment. She strolled only to stop about six feet from him as if she was on display.

With a broadened smile, he spun his index finger inaudibly telling her what to do. She took the hint as she rotated clockwise in front of the man, making sure that her shoes were not to be her downfall. "Can I ask what our plans are for this evening?" she inquired, knowing he mentioned a reservation for tonight.

"Well, I thought it would be nice to take you out for dinner and dancing," Luke replied. The man himself cleaned up rather nicely, as he was clean-shaven, wearing stylish dress attire and an unbuttoned tweed sport coat. He was nearly perfect except for a dilapidated belt that didn't fit the rest of his sexy image.

"That will be fantastic!" said an excited Taylor.

"By the way, you look beautiful this evening. So are you ready to paint the town red?" he asked.

"Absolutely!" she replied. With that he suavely took her by the hand and guided her out to the driveway. Lucas opened her door and made sure Taylor was seated correctly before closing her in.

Entering the foyer of the French restaurant, Taylor observed the customers who calmly awaited a table. She couldn't believe how romantically lit and gorgeous this area was, as the woman grew anxious to see the restaurant itself.

She took in the view of the entrance noticing the beautiful white marble, centered in the middle of an oval gray slate and brick floor. On the edge of the bricked border were a half dozen cast iron benches, which perfectly capped off the lilac topped stone partitions. Lucas and Taylor followed the bricked pathway to get to the host.

"Monsieur Calderone! How are you this evening?" the host asked.

"We are fine, François."

"That I see! Mademoiselle looks quite exquisite, indeed!" Lucas smiled at that remark. "We will have your table ready in just a minute!" the host exclaimed as he turned into the dining room to check on what tables were available.

"Thank you," Luke answered moving aside with his toy astride. As they talked, his eyes never left her. For that matter, neither did the other three men that were seated around the central water cascade. But neither Luke or Taylor noticed as they were just enjoying each other's company.

"Monsieur Calderone, please follow me, your table is ready." The couple grouped in behind Francois as the couples without a reservation watched the woman in the little blue-and-black dress disappear into the entryway. The two strolled the center aisle, following the tall, dark-haired French host that carried two rather large gold embossed menus.

Taylor's eyes wandered as she explored the large dining room that incorporated multiple archways that subsequently divided even more private rooms. Slowly strolling behind the host and in front of Lucas, she gazed like a young girl on Christmas Day. Taylor viewed the customers, which appeared to be quite happy and content.

She saw them sitting around different size tables that were covered in fancy white linens that she could make out even from a distance. The centerpiece for each of those was a small bouquet of delicate purple and white flowers. The overall sounds she made out, was that of pure joy and contentment.

She reached back for Luke's hand as an instantaneous feeling of love enveloped her. He held on tight as if he owned her as if he possessed her. Without her fully realizing it yet, he already did.

The three traveled down the hall to a double-wide doorway with a scrolling placard above that read "Bein-être," which she later found out meant "Comfort."

The twosome was brought into the small room that was inhabited by only two other couples. François promptly seated Taylor placing a white linen napkin across her lap and oversized dinner menu diagonally across her plate. Pulling the chair out for Lucas, he received the same treatment of napkin and menu before saying, "Your waiter Liam will be with you shortly. Please enjoy your evening!"

"Thank you, François!" Luke stated before the man offered a short bow with him retiring from the table.

Luke locked onto Taylor once more. However, she was having trouble as she'd never viewed a more beautiful restaurant. There was the room itself, the tables that are done up impeccably with the sets of elegant flatware and the crystal goblets along with the flower vases that Taylor noticed each and every table. And lastly, she noticed the fireplace. It wasn't an overly large hearth for the room but an incredible sight just the same.

Their candle flickered and danced, as a young man approached and proceeded to fill their glasses, with the owner not more than a few steps behind. "Monsieur Lucas, it is so very nice to have you here this evening," announced the tall thin, slightly balding gray-haired man.

"Good evening, Henri!" Luke replied.

Henri pulled up a chair between the couple and struck up a conversation. She thought it was a little peculiar, until she found out that Lucas was more than just a regular. As a matter of fact, he wasn't one. Luke took this moment for the introduction. "Taylor, this is the owner and my good friend, Henri, and, Henri, this is my girlfriend, Taylor!" There he did it. He called me his girlfriend.

"Well, I must say it is a great honor and pleasure to make your acquaintance, Mademoiselle Taylor," he said following it up with a kiss on the back of her hand. "Did your boyfriend happen to mention this restaurant to you?"

She lightly shook her head and quietly stated, "No."

"I should think not!" Henri said of his modest friend. "Do you like what you see here?" Henri asked inquisitively.

"I have to say that I have never been to France, but if I had, I would say that this is what I would want to see. It is gorgeous!"

"Well then, I must tell you that your Lucas is the main reason why this business thrives. He brought to this place, a wonderful ambiance to every nook. He designed it and built it, including much of France's feel. And because of that, I will be eternally grateful. He even brought some ideas that even this seasoned Frenchman would not have thought of."

She looked at a very humble Luke. He glanced over at her with a head tilt and a ever so fractional hint of a grin. The words as honest as they were said coming out of Henri's mouth, modestly embarrassed the man. Luke appeared speechless. "Well, I must let you two enjoy your evening!" He kissed her hand once more before rising and departing from the table.

"You've gotten quite the write up there," Taylor said about the eloquent words that just befell them.

"Well, it's a long story. My dad was stationed in Paris when he was young and met Henri, who was a cook at the time. They struck up quite the friendship and later my parents, and I went as my graduation present to visit."

Lucas added, "We ate at the French restaurants and café including the place where Henri had worked every day. I mean we had to, we were in France! Back when my dad was in the Italian army, he talked to Henri, driving home how people would pay well for his authentic cuisine."

"Since my parents lived in Seattle at the time, he urged him into thinking about the city. My father was right. No French restaurant around could compare. Henri started the business here over thirty years ago, and then once I moved to town, he hired me, to rebuild everything you can see and even the places you don't."

Taylor was shocked. "You did all this?"

"Well, technically, my dad helped a lot with the design of course, but he insisted that the project was mine. He said something about it being the feather in my cap. And the truth of the matter is that people came for the food, but they told others, all because of the look that it enveloped."

"So this was one of your first ventures?"

"No, it was my first. And when I used this as a reference, other jobs fell right into my lap. Many of the ones that wanted work done had dined in the restored restaurant, although they still remembered the look of the old place, citing the changes and how it now made them feel. But I never would have gotten this job without my dad knowing Henri."

"I'm thinking the man would give you his kidney if you asked," she said, partially meaning it as the waiter approached the table.

"My name is Liam, and I will be your waiter for this evening. Would you care to see the wine list?"

Luke, not needing the menu, ordered the wine, but in French, once he knew the waiter spoke the language. "Oui, Liam. Je voudrais une bouteille de votre 1988 beaufortain valley Bordeaux." After the waiter left, he went to continue with their conversation.

"What? You speak French too?" Taylor asked beyond surprised.

"I ordered us wine, and yes, I took four years of it in high school. I know that you must have taken a language!"

"I did! I took Spanish, but I wasn't that good at rolling my tongue for the r's."

"Well, maybe that's something we should work on." He grinned.

The waiter returned with the wine, placing the glasses before showing Lucas the bottle. He nodded, signaling Liam to uncork the provincial red wine. After handing Luke the cork, and after it was given the proper inspection, Luke drew in a long even whiff. He gave a second nod as Taylor watched the show on wine presentation.

Liam poured an ample tasteful into his goblet where Lucas swirled and sipped before nodding in approval. Once the waiter got the okay, he poured half a glass for Taylor before pouring an equal amount for the man of the table. "Are monsieur and mademoiselle ready to order?" Taylor forgot to look at the menu because at first glance, it all seemed like Greek to her.

"I will order for the lady!" he said as he began to rattle off their order in what sounded like perfect French, to her anyway.

After the waiter left, Taylor commented, "Now you're just showing off!" She followed it with a smile that couldn't be contained.

"Yes, I can do all that and roll my *r*'s!" Lucas stated in jest. Taylor let out a subdued laugh as she was overwhelmed with the feeling that this place, and Lucas was stirring within her.

Dinner had them both sharing Luke's choices of coq au vin and gigot d'agneau pleureur, which was basically slowly grilled goat that was a treat for the eyes, as well as the stomach. She especially enjoyed sharing the bowl of piperade as the appetizer. Since dancing's the next thing on the agenda, they both decided against the dessert.

With their napkins down for the last time, Lucas called for the check, but the waiter said there wouldn't be one. After a few attempts, Liam stated, word for word, what Henri had told him to say. "Monsieur Henri said to enjoy the rest of your evening, and he hoped you enjoyed your meal."

"We did, and please thank Henri. And thank you, Liam." Realizing he wasn't going to be able to pay, he promptly left a fifty-dollar bill for the man's impeccable service. Taylor never saw the exchange from his pocket to cradled under the basket of mini croissants.

So far, this didn't seem like it was going to be a night of dominance and submission. It appeared to be more like a, like a date. As he pulled into the parking lot of Club Royale, Taylor suddenly felt woozy possibly from the wine and she hoped that the dance part, was not going to land her flat on her ass. He went to help her out of the vehicle.

Taylor whispered, "Luke, can we skip the dancing and just go home?"

"Sure! Is everything okay?"

"I'm fine. I'm just a little loopy from the alcohol and tired from walking in these heels. I mean, I love them! They are new, that's all."

"So, you are all right?" he said in concern.

"I'm okay. But I don't want anything to ruin this evening."

"Why don't you sit back and rest then," Lucas said as they were both back in the car.

He pulled into the driveway and sat quietly in the darkness of his sedan. Giving her a few moments, he lightly shook Taylor on the shoulder. She looked so peaceful and yet stunning too. "Taylor, time to go in the house," he whispered.

She answered with an incoherent, "Hmm." He exited the car and then somehow managed to get her to her feet. Lucas, with her heels dangling from one hand, assisted Taylor, who was waking more with each passing second. Not wanting to stifle the flow of the evening any more than she already did, she asked if he felt like dancing now.

Lucas took the hint as they convened to the backside of the living room. Calling up a song on his phone, he excused himself, "I'll be right back!" Taylor waited as she leaned against the back of the couch while she tried to do a little bit better with any incoherence because of her brief nap.

Propping herself there for a couple of minutes, she spied a reflection off of what revealed itself to be a set of stainless-steel handcuffs, dangling from Luke's right index finger. It made her think that maybe that is what he picked up at the toy store, when he had sent her off to look at something during check out time.

Taylor glowed as the simple idea of being locked in them, instantaneously made her feel better, awake, and in the game. And with nothing but her body language, she gladly submitted. Seeing she was a hundred precent in for this, he brought the steel set up behind his now standing sub. He stared into her brown eyes and encircled one wrist, clamping it down, as the metallic clicks made her body quiver. A second set of clicks and Taylor was melting.

With her in full meltdown mode, the guy had her lean against the couch so that Lucas could help with her heels since she couldn't. Standing her up he followed it with a well-intentioned kiss, that the woman savored as part of the role play that she had no control over. Luke reached back for his phone, so to start the song that he had picked out for an occasion like this.

Holding her close, his captive waited for the music. The slow song he had carefully chosen was "Possession" by Sara McLachlan.

The deep lyrics reached to a phonetic breakdown of depths as one-line kept resonating within Taylor: "And I would be the one to hold you down, kiss you so hard, I'll take your breath away."

Taylor relished the casual but empowering dominance as it exuded from the man, bringing him to sway her gracefully to and fro like the rag doll that she was. And for her, she loved this. On top of that frequently the chain clanged, sending a signal straight to that specific place. Taylor closed her eyes so to take in all the beautiful lyrics as the song finished with one embracing and the other being embraced.

"Hey, since we did the dancing thing, why don't we go to bed," Lucas whispered in her ear.

"Absolutely, sir! You know you sure do know how to make a woman happy," she answered.

"Well, you deserve to be!"

They both broke away with Taylor still shackled. Lucas, who was now apprehensive about Taylor's light headedness from earlier, backed off and unlocked the first cuff. However, Taylor was too wired as she had thought up a way to thank her master properly for all of today.

Taylor suspended her release as he reached out for her other wrist. "Master, can I please you?"

Luke was entirely thrown by this request as he combatted those eyes that called for the man to just go with it. "Sure, Tay, please me!" he exclaimed. She stood and stripped Lucas before moving him to the bed. Then exposing her hidden corset, and slowly for his pleasure alone, he lay there as Taylor turned off the mood-killing overhead light.

Lucas leaned back motionless, ready to see what her gratuitous imagination would bring out. However, the submissive was in no rush as she took her sweet time, since she wasn't sure what she was going to do next. Waiting for some inspiration to come her way, her grin told him that she figured it out.

Taylor, seeing the one loose end of the manacles, reached across his chest dangling it high above him. "May I, sir?" she questioned.

He thought about it and then replied, "Sure, why not. Yes, my toy, please do." Still not sure what she was up to, Taylor leaned in and gave him a kiss. But it wasn't just a kiss but a impassioned one that reached deep within him, curling the man's toes.

She had never kissed him with such desire, with him reevaluating what they had up to this point. Thoroughly enjoying the role reversal, he leaned back. She studied and when he least expected it, she clamped the shiny steel closure around his wrist. It bit hard, but he wasn't about to stop this for anything. Luke felt this was more than he would get from a submissive, but he was enjoying her impassioned form of gratitude.

Taylor sucked his neck and chest for a few minutes, purposely to drive him crazy. She incessantly kissed him until she pulled back hurriedly and dropped her mouth over his engorged cock, while his eyes remained sealed.

When she thought he was about to explode, she climbed on top and straddled him. Taylor was horny as hell, sliding herself back and forth across the entire length of his shaft. Knowing he could unload at any second, she took the initiative and pushed herself down upon him. With everything in place where she wanted it and her locked firmly to her dominate, she awaited his explosion.

Taylor watched intently to behold the sight of Luke during his climax. With his eyes closed tight, he came while she remained still, to feel each spasm as it was shot deep inside her.

Luke bucked as he tested the hold between them. He was somewhere else, heavy but floating at the same time, with him feeling like a spectator for part of it, as he imagined watching his body going through all its various stages. When the ripples finally succumbed and his body didn't have the urge to jump any further, his eyes opened to see her donning an illuminated smile. He remained speechless as he tried to catch his breath.

"Did I do good, sir?" asked the sarcastically smug woman.

He took a few seconds and then responded. "Wow. That's all I can say!" Lucas bellowed, reaching for another labored breath.

"Really, you don't think it was too pushy?"

"No, I think you pushed just right," he stated.

The next morning from the kitchen, Taylor heard his footsteps, and she called out, "So how did you sleep?"

He answered, "You're unbelievable, you know that?"

"Me? What did I do?" she said, trying not to laugh.

"You? You, borderline went dominant on me."

"What are you talking about? I was just thanking you for our evening out, that's all!"

"Okay!" he said as he checked out her left wrist looking for any lingering marks.

"Mine are gone, but it looks like yours are still there. It's because you were thrashing so," Taylor stated.

"Yeah, that and you had me clamped tight!"

"Well, it was dark. I was horny. What can I say?" she answered with a chuckle.

# CHAPTER 8

Monday morning, Luke ran through the intricacies of what her job would entail, reiterating once again what they discussed the past evening. "What I need is for you to run the business from the office standpoint, which will operate, at least for now, out of the house."

"You will also be doing things like fielding calls, making appointments, addressing problems, and picking up something and running it out to a site. And you can handle it by phone or over the internet." Lucas paused. "I have a business phone for you, but I'd like it to remain with you during normal business hours."

Luke restated that since he was explaining it, this time on the fly, that she most likely would have questions. She was thrilled about this idea from the moment she heard it. Based out of the house! It sounded perfect. Plus, it would be helping him.

Already in work mode and with one foot out the door, Lucas puckered up and left it upon her lips. She looked out until he was gone, with the new employee gradually drifting to her new office of a chair, desk, and file cabinet. She studied the monitor, with its multiple apps emblazed across the lower part of the screen.

She clicked on the first, which featured all his client and business listings. The second one was for the business GPS that appeared to give both traffic tie-ups and the best ways for construction vehicles to make their way from point A to point B.

Taylor knew other aspects or tasks will come up that she was sure she would have to undertake, but she was looking forward to dealing with clientele from a phone instead of from the backside of a bar or tray.

She opened the metal cabinet next to browse many of his past clients, so to hopefully become familiarized with his previous work, which he had maintained alphabetically.

On the back corner of his desk behind the table lamp, she adjusted the five-by-seven picture of them at the sports bar, the same night they screwed out at the overlook. Taylor looked down upon it as she held it and gleamed.

While settling back in the chair, she received her first business call. Being new and moderately nervous, she pressed the green button and answered, "Calderone Enterprises, how can I help you?"

"This is Underwood Electrical Supply, and I just wanted to let you know that your wire and boxes are in," said a man with a very husky voice.

"Great! And what time are you open until today?"

"Six o'clock!"

"I will make sure someone picks up the order and thank you for calling." She hung up and then proceeded to make her first outgoing, with that being to her boss. The phone rang a few times before he answered.

"What's up, Taylor?" She wanted to make it quick since she was sure he was busy.

"Underwood Supply just called and said your wire and boxes order is in and could be picked up."

"Fantastic. The order was due in Wednesday." Lucas paused. "Is there any way you can run down and pick them up and bring them to the site? The GPS has the address built in and the address of the site also. They bill us directly, so you won't even need to use the credit card."

"I can do that. But what if I get a call while I'm on the road?"

"Well, pull over safely and take the call. If you miss it, then just return the call when you can!"

"I will do that and then text you when the car is loaded! I'm hoping that this will all fit!" Taylor said.

"Yes, it will. Well, I have to go, but I will see you later!"

"Talk to you soon," she said just before hanging up the phone and reaching for the keys.

She liked the GPS business system that he had installed on the company cell. It also appeared as though he set up an entry for every plumbing and electrical supply dealer as well as the many Lowes and

Home Depot's. When he needed one, it seemed all they had to do was call up the address and phone number for the closest one to him at the time. That could be a real time saver, and it was all without having to figure out which one they needed.

Lucas was outside talking to one of his guys when Taylor pulled into the site of the partially restored fire department. She was so glad that she could do this for him, with her sole intention of wanting to make the man's life a little easier.

Taylor climbed out as Lucas and the lead man approached the vehicle. Luke made the introduction. "Steve, this is my girlfriend, Taylor!" Wow, there it was again!

"It is nice to meet you, Steve!" she said with sincere conviction as she stuck out her hand.

"Yes, it's so nice to meet you too, Taylor," Steve replied as he had trouble holding up his jaw.

He looked at Luke with that smirk that guys give when they haven't gotten the whole story. Noticing that their delivery was in the yard, Lucas turned around. "Hey, Kenny, can you get over here with the cart and take this?" Kenny the assigned lugger, knew what he had to do. As Taylor watched, Kenny opened the trunk, surveyed the items, before matching them up with the ones that they ordered. Once the order matched, he took the boxes and bales of wire and dropped them onto the flatbed cart and turned back to the rear of the station.

"Taylor, thank you for delivering this today," Steve said, omitting his initial facial greeting.

"You're welcome!" she replied as he departed behind Kenny. With the two standing there, Luke asked if she wanted to check out the revamp.

"Sure, is it close to being done?" she asked.

"Hardly! Nothing is finished yet. We are only up to the heating, cooling, and electrical stage. What they had before was archaic. I don't mean like from thirty years ago, I mean from more like the turn of the last century. We just had a team out here to take care of the asbestos. That took four days before we could move back in and start tearing things up."

She followed Lucas two steps behind into the side door. At first look, she saw the light brown paneling of the 1960s as it covered the halls from floor to ceiling. How anyone thought that this would make it look better was beyond her. And then the flooring, a heavy linoleum, was either scuffed beyond repair or had tears that someone attempted to fix.

It was then that Luke explained. "The city just doesn't have the funds to completely tear down a building and start anew. They are at least getting new guts and a cosmetic makeover this time."

But Lucas knew if the job was done right, and the money comes through someday, then he is favored to do the job. He compared that to another project where they renovated a grocery store that got a full makeover, and then years later, he had his team build a new store on the other side of their parking lot, purely because they needed something bigger. Taylor was impressed with her hearing of more of the man's past work.

"I know this isn't much to look at, but for this especially we have the building inspector in here to check each step because of the cities ordinances. There are so many in place that it makes it very hard for any commercial and residential renovations. The problem is that no matter who they go with, those ordinances are in place. You break the rules, and they can shut down the project and the building too." He pushed through the door open at the end of the hall.

"We are setting up the central air and boiler in here. The contract called for all new vents, making sure that they address the circulation issues. Many of the returns are fine." Taylor listened as she tried to comprehend what it was that he was saying. However, she followed him around the room to the large boiler, with the piping that came through the back wall of the building. "Any questions?" Lucas asked, bringing her to look back in his direction.

"I don't understand it, but you do, so I guess that's all that matters."

"By the end of the week, I will have you on the business account, so you will be able to pay the bills when they come in. Don't worry, you are going to be great at this," Lucas said as he lightly pinched her chin.

"I'm not worried. I know this is going to work out, but thank you for giving me this job and for installing the GPS on the phone. Otherwise, there is no way I would ever be able to find my way home!"

"You'll figure it out after a while. Hey, I will walk you to the car, because I need to get back to work."

"No problem!" Taylor said. The two retraced their steps to the driver side of the car when she questioned, "Hey, I was wondering what Steve was doing when he gave you that strange look?"

"Oh, that! He just thought you would be prettier!" he said as he received a hefty smack on his arm from Taylor and a smile to go with it.

She gave him a fast peck on the cheek before departing, but not before saying, "See you tonight?"

"See you, Taylor!" Luke watched as her tail lights headed west onto Main Street.

As the time surpassed five, Taylor punched out on her first day as the receptionist and delivery person. With only one real hiccup to speak of, she truly got the picture when he emphasized how some customers were never pleased. At two o'clock she thought she met the example, maybe even the king of them.

By the third call, Taylor had it. Somehow completing the last extensive conversation, she was confident that she had soothed all of his frustrations. And that led her to wonder how Luke got any work done, while dealing with these people.

It was just after six o'clock when Luke texted that he would be home soon. Taylor decided to cook up a nice meal of pasta and steamed vegetables. With everything set and two tapered candles lit, she turned down the lights. The woman wasn't necessarily looking for sex, but basically wanted it to be a relaxing meal for him. However, after dinner if it ended that way, she wasn't going to say no.

Luke put his key in the door. It was unlocked, but she could see that this was not the same man that she saw just seven hours ago. "Lucas, what's the matter?" she called out in concern.

"I'm home," Lucas answered.

"What happened? What's wrong?" Taylor called out to him.

"I have a migraine."

Luke never smelled the pasta, sauce, or even the aroma of fresh buttered vegetables and rolls. He totally missed the open bottle of Malbec and the candles that illuminated the table. He did, however, manage to raise his hand to his forehead, and that's when Taylor could see that he might be in the room, but he wasn't home yet. She leaned in to hug him. He was not very responsive as he was as quiet as a mouse.

"Do you feel like dinner?"

"I'm sorry. I need to go to bed!" Luke countered, already making the pivot to their room. She followed him into the bedroom where she tucked him in before quietly closing the door and getting back to the food. Taylor was hungry but decided to stay that way. After putting it in the fridge, she sat in the living room with her wineglass and peered out at the moon as it peeked out from behind the fast-moving clouds.

In the morning, Lucas struggled with the alarm clock answering it with a smack, rising like a man with a hangover. He felt like crap, having all the aftereffects that he usually got from a migraine. Lucas tried to cheer himself up by thinking he could call in sick. That didn't work.

The hot steamy shower pounded down over his head and neck, hollowly resonating within his ears. Hopefully, his jolt of java would break him free of this. The silence boomed as he turned the shower off with the remainder of the hot liquid, dripping out from the pan showerhead. He stepped onto the dry bath mat, where Luke left impressions on his way to the hanging towel. The bath cloth masked him from the outside world, dulling the sound and the light in the room as well, if there was any to speak of.

He snuck across the carpet and opened the dresser to get his clothes, and he almost made it out the door when a faint voice called over to him. "How are you feeling?"

He turned so he wouldn't have to repeat himself. "I had a problem with the building inspector, who showed up yesterday unannounced and stopped our work to address his questions. It wasn't him, but that is when I started with a migraine. I know it wasn't him, but it is difficult working with one," Lucas explained.

"So are you better now?" Taylor inquired.

"I'll be fine, oh, I get migraines, like a couple of them a year," he said, trying to add levity to the sullen situation. "Do you get them?"

"No, but I heard they can be intense. My other grandmother used to get them. She would go to a dark room and just lay there motionless."

"Well, mine isn't that bad, but I do understand."

"I was worried about you. I didn't know what to do," Taylor spoke, concerned.

"I'm sorry. I get like two of these a year and not as bad as this one."

"Look, you don't have to be sorry. I'm just glad that you are snapping out of it."

"I am fine!" he stated, trying to hold some semblance of a smile. "So how did everything go for you yesterday?" he asked, wanting to see if she had any rough spots on her first day.

"Well, I got to talk to your client Morris Dunleavy, is it? And we had quite a talk, actually a few of them," Taylor said as Luke nodded.

"I meant to tell you about him. He is the kind of person that once you've done a project for him, you find out you are never really done."

"He did seem like a fascinating man, though!" Taylor said.

"Oh, he is, but after a while, I just stopped calling him back. He could spend an hour on the phone with me no problem."

"I believe it!" Taylor agreed.

"The meal would have been better when it was fresh," she said as she covered the bottom of his lunch box. "I am not able to pack the beverage that went along with it. I drank it," Taylor stated, referring to the wine that she polished off.

"Well, tonight I will pick up something. I owe you that after spoiling last night's meal."

"You didn't, but that will be nice!" she stated.

"I hope I didn't spoil any other plans you might have had."

Taylor lightly shook her head. "No, it was just that I was so impressed by your company's process that I figured I would do something nice for you. If I wanted anything else, you would have been dining on one of my grandma's recipes," Taylor said.

Luke got the correlation in an instant as he remembered Tilly's food and the way that she fed the people of the inn year after year. Then that same woman turned around and taught her granddaughter how to cook them too. Lucas gathered his stuff as he wanted to be to work early after the fiasco of yesterday.

The man drove off not thinking about work or Tilly's cooking and not even Taylor, not directly anyway. He did, however, consider taking them on a boat ride up to Puget Sound for some incredible fish at Wake's Seafood. With it being his last, slow weekend before his busy summer kicked in, he thought it would be perfect. Plus, the forecast was going to make it that much better, as he looked forward to showing his girl around.

With Luke returning home basically early, the two of them sat bundled up under the overhang of the second floor, sipping wine. Using the features he designed mainly for those long bouts of wet weather, a pair of six-foot cantilevered panels and a heater from above kept them encased, keeping the couple from retreating back to the dry, warm house.

The wind and cold did keep them at bay tight against the door, as the view of the Pacific Ocean kept them anchored to their seats. She lifted her glass and placed it in front of the sunset that would disappear in a few minutes. "There is nothing I like more than a good glass of red wine!"

"Not even a little Casa Noble?" he asked.

She realigned the glass up to the crimson sun. "You know how I feel about my Casa," she said as she never shifted from the panoramic view.

"Taylor, I don't want to spoil this moment, but I need to let you know this is going to get crazy soon, with me working late almost every night. And I don't want you to get bored around here waiting for me to come home." He was reluctant to say much more about this because she just moved in and he didn't want her packing up and heading home.

"Okay, but you were home by four today!"

"That won't happen again. I did that today, but I have to be at work, especially in the near future. However, I am kind of worried that there won't be enough for you to do here work-wise," he commented. "I mean, if there are any hobbies that you want to pursue, then this is a great city for that."

"You know I'm enjoying the silence right now. I was working in a busy, crowded bar, and I lived above a semi-noisy restaurant. It is the getting away from everything that I truly need right now."

"You're sure?" he asked and then saw her nod. "Well, since things are going to get busy soon, I wanted to take you out for seafood right on the Puget. It serves the most incredible delicacies. And the fact is, if I lived closer, I know I would be a hundred pounds heavier."

As Lucas no sooner finished his sentence, Taylor's phone rang. Not wanting to lose sight of the conversation, she answered it without checking the number first.

"Hello!"

Taylor listened as he first thought she was trapped on the line with a telemarketer. For her, it was far worse.

"Look, I don't have anything to say to you. I'm not even sure how you got this number," Taylor answered, trying to keep calm in front of Lucas but losing the battle. "Seriously, Marty, we have nothing to talk about. Why aren't you getting it? It's over! Don't call me again. Goodbye."

Taylor hung up, knowing that there was no way to explain her way out of this one, as Luke's jaw hung slightly ajar. He didn't know what to do as he was afraid to get her talking about something that she clearly wasn't ready to divulge.

After resisting the urge to toss her phone far out onto the lawn and with still enough temper to hurl it far out into the ocean, she sedately let it go atop her lap. She tried to lighten the mood even though deep down, Taylor was still fuming. She stared out at the sun that was nothing more than a crimson highlight cresting the horizon. Then to her amazement and maybe because of the wine, her mouth just opened, and she began to spew words that she swore no one was ever going to hear.

"Luke, I have to talk to you about this!" Taylor declared as she threw out her hands almost as if to show that she carried no baggage.

"No, you don't!" he answered keeping it light.

"But I have to." Taylor looked back at the horizon once more. "I'm sorry, but I wasn't honest with you about Marty. I haven't been honest with anyone." An unviewed tear dropped and rolled down her face as Lucas sat quietly. "I told you that Marty and I split up because the marriage just wasn't working anymore. That wasn't entirely true. The rest I haven't been able to tell Lauren, my parents, or my grandmother."

Luke reached over and clenched Taylor's hand that he noticed was trembling. "Taylor, then why tell me? I don't need to know."

She stewed as the tears, and the words began to seep through the locked lips of hers. "Marty came home one night, and we had been arguing, with us both seething toward each other."

"You broke up because you were fighting?" Luke stated.

"No, that's not it. Well, during that one fight, Marty carried it one step too far and backhanded me across the face. He paused, seeing what he had done, but for me, I was devastated. It was the only time Marty did it, and I made sure it was to be his last time too," Taylor said as more tears dropped. Luke fell silent, with him still not sure as to what he should do or say.

"It's an endless turmoil whenever someone asks me about him, as all I want to do is forget. Hey, I'm sorry about ruining the mood tonight. I changed my number, and he must have gotten it from one of our friends," Taylor said, as she brushed away her tears with her thumb. After five minutes of quiet, where she used the time to compose herself, she asked, "Tell me more about the Puget, please?"

After tiptoeing back into the conversation, he eventually said, "I was thinking early Saturday into Sunday." Her brows rose. "We will stay at the Grand Allusea Hotel and stop at any bar that suits our fancy and then have some seafood later. How does that sound?"

"Wonderful! But what about clothes?" she queried, still trying to put the phone call out of her mind.

"We will load a backpack! Are you game?"

"Of course, I'm game," she quickly answered. "Drinking and not having to go home after. That sounds perfect."

"Great, then I will make plans Monday!"

"Are you sure you don't want your assistant doing it for you?" she questioned, wiping the remainder of the dampened display.

"No, I've got this," Luke said wryly. They followed it by clinking glasses with joy conquering sadness this time. When he thought that she was back to hearing, Lucas told her about his only visit to the pub crawl while the two occasionally stared out at the ever-darkening sky.

Saturday morning, Lucas hopped out of bed before the alarm sounded, eager to get this weekend on its feet. But knowing he still had a few things to do, he checked the updated weather on his phone, which was forecasting it to be as good as you could ask for the end of March, with only partial clouds and a very light wind.

On a later pass through the bedroom, and as Taylor was packing her clothes, he snuck up and brought his arms around her. She dropped the blouse she was folding, onto the comforter. "I wish I had known. I would have stayed in bed."

"No, it's not that. It's that I am getting very comfortable with having a girlfriend."

"Me too. A boyfriend, I mean!"

Taylor lagged behind as they carried their luggage and cooler out to the boathouse. With his hands full, she came around and opened the door where his twenty-one-foot Chris-Craft was garaged. He placed the items upon the table, just a couple of feet from where the boat was docked against the mooring. Playing the gentleman card, he helped his damsel safely aboard. Then with one foot on its side and the other on solid concrete, he transferred the items to the boat.

He meticulously stowed everything in the cabinets, before he found himself afront of the wheel, with the vehicle awaiting ignition. Lucas remotely opened the overhead door and started the engine, revving the inboard. Taylor helped by reaching over and throwing off the bowlines before she took her place by his side.

"Are you ready, Tay?" he asked with her pointing straight ahead. He slowly pushed the throttle away from him as the boat inched out. Was the use of Tay a prediction of what was going to happen this weekend? Taylor wondered. She wasn't sure, but she wanted to keep her head straight so that either way, she could enjoy every second of their time together.

The craft crept into the depths of the sea so he could give her a new vantage point of the house and the shoreline. As the boathouse door closed completely, and with Taylor seated, he flipped up the throttle and adjusted the trim as the boat lunged like a playful dolphin wanting to take the lead.

When he was far enough out, he turned the boat, making it parallel to the shoreline while it rocked slightly from the swells that pushed against its port side. The air was frigid as even the sun wasn't cutting through the early morning spring cold.

In their travels, he made sure she got to see the homes that were part of the ritzy waterfront district. The ones with the perfect lawns that looked like you could putt on them, and these were the people that never had to do any of the work, besides maybe writing the check. And he was sure there was someone to do that too.

None of the homes had any sign of being inhabited, most likely because most were living in their winter places somewhere south of here. Lucas never thought about having the more than one home thing. He loved where he was at, especially now that Taylor was here to be part of it.

Once they passed millionaire acres as he called it, Lucas let her take the helm. He had no worries as Taylor was no stranger to being on a boat. Her grandfather had her out on the water once a week just so her grandmother would have fresh fish for the inn's guests. She had always been an experienced fisherman, and maybe someday if he finds the time, she could teach him.

Lucas kept an eye on the GPS as she continued north at about a half mile from land. When there was about fifteen minutes left to their desired destination, he took over and had Taylor sit back down, while she attempted to brush out the windblown look. With their location within view, she scoped over the bow to the distant island.

He slowed the engines and crawled toward the tiny island. She wasn't sure where they were heading, but she was quite confident this wasn't Puget. The boat glided in slowly up to the slip. When it was alongside, she exited and tied off the boat with the expertise of a person that had done it many times before. Lucas, making a mental checklist, grabbed the cooler, a big canvas bag, and a couple of other bags before following a confounded Taylor onto the aluminum dock.

She walked ahead slowly to the shore since she didn't know where or what they were doing. A show of confusion blanketed her face. As he passed, she asked, "Where are we?"

"Well, I wanted to make a whole day of it, so we are going to hang out and picnic here for part of the day. It is so quiet and tranquil. It's one of the smallest islands in the area."

"Okay, but you still didn't tell me where we are."

"Oh, this is Eliza Island," he said as he placed the items down along the shoreline, just north of the docks.

With a quick visual check, Lucas unzipped the lengthy canvas bag to reveal two fishing rods. Taylor smiled immediately. She knew that when it comes to fishing, you can't get much more serene than that. She held the pole, checking out the reel. "Are these yours, Luke?"

"No, Steve, let me borrow them for the weekend," he answered.

"So you did this because you know I like to fish? Do you fish?"

"Not really. And besides this is just for fun. This here is our lunch!" She looked down after he opened the lid on the cooler.

*Crabs? Wow, a day of fishing and crab too. This is going to be great,* she thought while Lucas proceeded to fire up the propane stove. Taylor prepped the poles and baited their lines, making sure to send out their first cast of the morning, as Lucas continued his couple of kitchen duties. She checked the lines while their bait swam freely about forty feet out. The few clouds that hung overhead were not looking to be any real threat, so Lucas kept an eye on the pot, waiting for the water to boil.

"I would say about ten minutes till lunch!" he stated as the bubbles in the pot climbed to the surface. Luke hooked the butter cup to the inside top of the vessel, allowing for the steam to melt it, while two motionless crabs sat in the boiling water. Since they were waiting, he placed out the hammer, cracker, and a tray.

"Fresh crab for lunch and seafood later? Are we going to be all fished out before we even get there?" she said right before she dipped a chunk of the crab meat into the buttered liquid.

"This, no! It is just an appetizer leading into tonight, and well, I just wanted to make this a special day seeing that I can't recreate the fall pub crawl. And I also can't guarantee that we will be able to attend either. It is something to see, though. I know I told you a little about it, but the first time I was down here, I was with Steve and my co-owner at the time, Trent Collier. They made it a birthday present for me, when actually it was the breaking up of ownership of our business," he added after a short pause of where he chomped into another bite of crab.

"You split up? Why would you do that? You couldn't work together?" Taylor questioned.

"No, it was quite the opposite. Trent moved to Salem to start his own company because his girlfriend at the time lived there."

"So how is he doing with it?"

"Not too good. Trent got married, and his wife quickly turned around and divorced him. He said she was cheating on him. I hear from him occasionally because he wants to move back here and he has worked hard to try to buy back in," he answered.

"Are you going to let him?"

"I don't know. We were great together, and Trent had an even better business head than me, but I think we both have run ours, as each of us has been the bosses. I think something would not go right this time. He really doesn't like Salem at all. He was born and raised right here in Seattle, and he misses it." Luke took another bite of the hot buttered seafood. "I do believe though, if he doesn't get the answer soon that he wants to hear, he will start up one and will be a solid competitor."

"So do you feel like you are being pressured into making a decision that might not be beneficial to you?"

"Yes, soon I will have to bid against him or have him join me. I don't like thinking about it because I would have to underbid to get some of the jobs. I don't think he will be back for maybe a couple of years. It costs money to start this, and Trent has to have enough for the banks even to consider him."

"I see!" Taylor said sensing how the atmosphere and conversation had changed.

Looking at her, he took a breather and said, "You know if it's all right, I would rather talk about us this weekend?" He disclosed before waiting for her answer.

"I think that's a great idea." They finished their meal and gathered everything before they repeated their steps back to the boat.

"Next stop, Puget Sound," he said right before he started the engine.

# CHAPTER 9

The royal-blue-and-white boat advanced slowly into the mouth of the Puget, following the guidelines of its no wake zone. Scared that Taylor was going to miss something, she stood to make sure that as she was experiencing the famous Seattle seaway.

She squinted far-off at the fishing docks and the non-stop ship-yard where hundreds of containers and bulk lumber, laid dormant, as many as five high, in wait of being hauled away. Taylor spied the crane operator as they connected and cautiously placed the large con-tainer onto a temporary spot, piling them like monolithic building blocks. She also eyed the neighboring marina where small boats up to massive yachts docked.

The brunette found it fascinating how the gulls hovered over and swarmed the fishing boats, waiting for any rejected fish. The birds never let a single piece of rejected fish make it back to the water, since they wanted to be the first to have gotten their fill.

Their chatter filled the air, along with the occasional horn from a passing ship. Even the wind was in on it, accounting for that unknown clanging. With the hotels, bars, and restaurants now in view, their trek was nearly over.

Luke made a call and hung up. Moments later, he cut the engines to half as they slid into the dock for the hotel, where two young male employees dressed in nautical-themed uniforms awaited their arrival. The first man secured the boat and assisted the couple, while the second employee took the bags and the two of them safely across the pier to the hotel.

Lucas and Taylor followed the young bellman with the few bags up to the docking elevator. Once inside, Lucas saw his boat being cautiously driven away and under the vastness of the Grand Allusea Hotel.

During the short one floor climb, Taylor studied the airbrushed picture of the hotel that covered one of its side walls. She even joined the other two as they faced the back. When the doors parted, Taylor looked out into the massive lobby of the oldest hotel on the Sound. The man with all that they had brought moved afront of the second opened elevator, ready for them once they completed their check-in.

A short bald manager expressed abundant courtesy as the two stood at the desk. Luke casually mentioned the pub crawl specifically to Taylor, which brought the supervisor to sheer elation. The man drove home that Pier Point, their hotel bar that beautifully overlooked the Pacific, was at one of its ends. Then he raved about the many mini decadent desserts and pastries, saying it was their contribution to the crawl.

The man even walked them to the elevator, saying their part of the crawl was the best. Lucas didn't have the heart to tell the man that he never finished its entire length. Once they were ready, the two entered the elevator followed by the bellman, enroute to the third floor.

The employee placed their bags on the luggage racks, where the teenager was tipped for his services on his way out. Not taking even a breather, Luke quickly suggested that they should freshen up before heading to their first stop.

After cleansing themselves of the day, the two looked briefly out the large paned window of their room, to scan the seaside. Seeing that same body of water each and every day, their need for libations quickly deterred them in the direction of the boardwalk.

Taylor was famished, most likely from the hours of sea air today. Passing many restaurants, including Wake's, the two walked for what was equivalent of about three city blocks before eyeing their first stop, with Taylor jubilantly choosing it.

And the place she opted for was purely because of its befitting name, the Salt Lick. They entered and looked around before finally finding a couple of hidden seats at the backside of the oval bar. For their first drink, they were educated but not surprised that this place specialized in her mind-numbing medicine, tequila.

When ordering from the mostly tequila menu, Luke asked, "We would like a couple Casa Noble's on the rocks please?"

"I'm sorry, we are out. The next shipment should be in soon though." The female bartender expediently apologized. She then remedied it by pointing out an alternate choice. "We do have Herradura! It is quite popular here at Salt's."

"That'll work, but make them doubles please," Lucas called over since neither of them were looking to be sober this evening. After the occasional chit chat about the crawl itself, and with their drinks depleted, they were about to stand and head to the next bar, That is when Taylor said something quite unexpected. "Hey, did you notice our bartender?"

"Yes, I guess. She's female, right?"

She smirked before turning solemn and whispering. "You know she is! But you know what else? I could kind of see myself being with her!"

"You could what?" Lucas said since the loud music might have been a distraction to what he thought she said.

"I said I could see myself being with her! Did you hear me that time?" Taylor said, turning up the volume two notches.

He leaned in close and said, "Yes, even my penis heard you." Smiling, she reached down under the bar and lightly groped his manhood, letting her hand linger before finally withdrawing it.

"So are we done here?" Lucas asked.

"I don't know. I think one more wouldn't hurt, would it? Oh, but you were looking to hop!" Taylor answered.

"No, we are on no schedule here, and I just want for you to enjoy yourself," Lucas stated suavely.

"Well, I am, and the Herradura is quite good, especially when Lydia is bringing it to us. Can you get me another, but make it a single so that I can walk out of here later?" Taylor asked before adding, "I'll be right back!" The woman beelined it to the ladies' room as Luke watched her back-end sway away from the barstool.

Luke turned towards the bar and called over the blond-with-black-streaks bartender. "Can we have a replay on the drinks, but at half strength this time." Within seconds, she placed the beverages down in front of him, leaving the man to look back before he opened his mouth.

"Lydia, I was wondering if you could help me play a little prank on my girlfriend. She is pretending to have the hots for you and is trying to get a rise out of me. Would you mind going along with this, so we can catch her reaction?"

"So what do you want me to do?" Lydia broke her grin in time to nonchalantly signal the man, that his woman and the intended mark was exiting the restroom. Taylor slid onto her stool as the woman dubiously wiped the counter near them. Lucas within seconds excused himself, thus giving Lydia her moment to set up the charade.

He donned a crooked smile as he imagined the scenario. "Pardon me, but would you like some water?" asked the thirty-something-year-old bartender.

"Sure, that would be great, thank you."

Lydia placed the glass down next to the freshly poured tequilas but spilled some across Taylor's right hand. Taylor went to reach for a napkin that wasn't there, but to her surprise, Lydia had already wiped it and was pawing at the back on her hand and fingers. "I'm so sorry. I am a bit nervous. I have been wanting to talk to you from the time you and your brother walked in."

Taylor was thoroughly shocked when she mistook him for a sibling. "No, no, he is my boyfriend."

"Well, I am sorry. I know this can't go anywhere now, but I wanted you to know that I find you extremely attractive."

"Wow, well, I don't know what to say," she said as she was starting to smell something. Taylor scanned behind her briefly. "Lydia, did my boyfriend put you up to this?" The beautiful curvy server didn't know how she should answer that so she finally came clean. Taylor thought for a second.

"Can I borrow a pen and a clean bar napkin? I know how to get back at him. Just do me a favor and let me know when he is almost here, please." Lydia nodded. Taylor jotted down something on the napkin and whispered to her. The bartender's eyes told her quietly when he was just fifteen feet from them.

He couldn't make out the conversation until he distinctly heard as clear as a bell. "Look, we are staying at the Allusea, and I wrote down the room number for you. Get there when you can," Taylor said as she handed the woman the folded napkin. Lucas moved in slowly flummoxed at what he knew he just heard. However, the bartender stood, with her mindfully wondering what her next move was since Lydia was now unaware as to what part she was to be playing.

"Tay, what are you doing? Or should I say, what are we doing?"

Taylor shot a quick. "Got you." It brought her fellow actress to clap at its unexpected outcome. The ladies laughed at the handsome hunk who instantly was speechless.

Taylor leaned in and gave him a big kiss after dropping the creased napkin onto the bar. "And you thought you were going to get me?"

"Wow, you turned that around pretty fast," Luke said shocked as to how she orchestrated it all in just a few minutes. That sparked another round of female laughter, with Lucas finally joining in. Lydia went back to the other end of the bar to tell a fellow coworker about the hijinks that just transpired as the two sipped on their drinks.

Lucas paid the bill and left an ample tip for Lydia's acting services. With their jackets on, they thanked the woman as they strolled past. Taylor grasped Luke's forearm and said she would be right back as he stood near the exit. She approached the blonde and semi-surprised her with a hug. "We had a great time thanks to you, Lydia. You know I'm not gay, but I am a little curious after meeting you. I think the three of us could have had some real fun."

"I think so, too, but I am not sure what my husband would think." The two shared a smile as she offered up another hug.

After a quick wave over her shoulder to her fellow actors, Lydia scooped up the empty glasses, tip, and the napkins. She was about to release the thin folded paper into the trash when the bleeding pen mark caught her attention. Curious, Lydia opened it and viewed Taylor's name and cell phone number. With nothing but a brief grin in their direction and a hesitant thought, she crumpled it and tossed it into the trash.

"So are you going to tell me what you two just talked about?" Lucas questioned.

"You know, I don't think so. Not even if you whip it out of me!" she answered as she shook her moneymaker a few feet in front of him.

He called up to her loud enough for her to hear. "If I weren't so hungry right now, I would bring you back to the hotel and take you over my knee."

"Promises, promises," she said as he scurried up to her. With the many tequilas assisting her outward brazenness, they headed the one block straight to the best seafood place around. Closing in on the busy restaurant, a pink-and-blue neon sign proudly displayed its name with a smell that welcomed them in, even as the brisk sea air made them realize just how much the tequila had won.

They neared the rear courtyard which was entirely enclosed with the white fencing that they use to protect the dunes from erosion, giving it that beachy feel. Pushing through the gate, they inched into the backside of the restaurant as the aroma again toyed and taunted with their ever-growing appetite. The couple parked themselves at a recently vacated table where they got their firsthand fill of dazzling scents that tantalized their nasal cavities.

An older male employee approached to clean the not ready for the next customer's table. "Welcome to Wake's seafood. Have you dined here with us before?"

"Yes, we have," Luke said, knowing how this goes.

"Then you know when you are ready, you can order at the counter. The specials are still on the board on the right. Enjoy your meal!" the man said as he claimed the semi loaded tray and exited.

Taylor eyed the menu, scanning for a sampler with everything. Even though they both were starving enough to order right then and there, they didn't know what. She was too hung-up on the fact that all the fried food items on the menu are battered or marinated using a different kind of beer. It looked interesting as the picture of the food was right alongside the bottle of beer that they used to make it.

The two settled, opting for the Pabst Blue Ribbon-marinated grilled seafood platter, and the Widmer Brothers' zucchini bites, the

Newcastle brown ale eggplant fries, and Asahi calamari. If it smelled half as good as the aroma that surrounded it, then she knew she was going to be quite satisfied. Then her eyes went wide. "Are we going to be able to eat all this?" she questioned.

Luke quickly answered, "No, not a chance, but we will have more to snack on from the fridge either later tonight or tomorrow morning."

Fifteen minutes later, with it being standing room only, Lucas brought over the trays and with Taylor's help they managed to cover the tablecloth with their seafood selections as steam rose from the food. Taylor's eyes were bigger than her stomach, but she was insistent that she was somehow going to try everything in front of her.

For most people, there is that moment when you know that you had had enough. Well, they had eaten so fast that it went far beyond that point. At least this time, it wasn't just the alcohol that pushed them back and made them stop to take a breath. It was going to be a chore for them to walk the rest of the way, back to their hotel. *What were they thinking?* She wondered as Lucas carried the remains in a medium-sized doggy bag.

Sauntering a little heavier and much slower, Taylor pondered if this is what it feels like when you get older? The taste of the seafood reminded her that in this case, it didn't matter.

The last fifty feet from the elevator to the room was the hardest since she was exhausted. The combination of fresh air, food, and alcohol was acting like tryptophan. Next to the bed, Luke moved in for an embrace. He looked as though he was ready to start something, although she addressed it swiftly knowing that this was going to be awkward.

"Luke, I don't think I can give you what you want tonight?" she said, whispering it into his right ear.

"Oh, good! I'm tired too. I just thought that if I didn't try something now, I might be asleep before you!"

"Can I take a rain check?"

"Sure, how about in the morning?" he asked.

"That will be great. Did you put the leftovers in the fridge?"

"Yes, don't worry! So why don't we get ready for bed then," he said. The two of them performed their nightly ritual. She however did it much faster since that four-poster bed was calling out to her. As she climbed in, he added, "Why don't we go to bed naked!" She agreed since at this point she would have agreed to anything.

Taylor gained consciousness to the smell and thought of lobster with its accompanying essence of butter. Was she dreaming it? Becoming aware of her surroundings, she knew that she had done that to coffee more than once but never once to seafood. Still partly in dreamland, she eyed Lucas while he sat on the side of the bed with his back turned to her, chewing away at some of their aromatic leftovers.

Reaching a hand out to him, she found it strange that she couldn't perform this minor task. She followed it up with her next option and quickly realized that she couldn't budge any of her limbs. Noticing her activity and that Taylor was finally awake, Lucas took a balled-up handkerchief that he had next to him the entire time he ate. He turned only to tuck it neatly in her mouth.

The plot unfolded as Lucas pulled away the blankets and pillows to reveal that she was tied spread eagle to the cherry bed. Her surprise vanished after the initial jolt of where this was going.

"Hey, baby, I hope it is okay, but I have missed you badly," he commented as the quarter-inch cotton rope firmly held her wrists and ankles, far from any of her other limbs. Finishing his last bite of Lobster tail, he took his sweet time, knowing she would be there waiting for him. Luke slowly returned after thoroughly washing his hands of his morning snack.

As he strutted to the other side of the bed, he eyeballed his snared prey, checking the bindings. Taylor's eyes followed him as he eventually came back to where he began. Her anticipation increased as he reached over and picked up a jar of white stuff, which she recognized as coconut oil. He rolled it in his hands, softening it until it finished as a clear emollient.

Using the warmed liquid, he took the opportunity to massage her hogtied body, stroking her neck lightly down to her shoulders, but that was where he stopped. Reaching out to the tip of her left hand and caressed her fingers as they stretched out to him. With that, he moved on down, making sure to cover her palms up to her wrist.

Luke moved at a snail's pace down to her armpits, to which she mutedly moaned in disappointment as he went over and did the same thing to her other arm. Each time he neared any of her erogenous zones, she would moan in disappointment as he purposely avoided her pussy and breasts.

The massage brought on more saliva, more straining from the ropes, and more excitement that he would eventually go much further. He took what must have been almost a half an hour covering all her limbs, making sure that she relaxed. Lucas then slackened the lines for her legs, placing them right where he wanted them, pulling her calves tight to her thighs, before tying them and spreading them so he had room to play.

His fully grown member reached out toward her like it was trying to say "It's my turn." He slithered up from the foot of the bed, dropping his head casually into her sweet spot, while tugging at the ties that bound her.

She would have been perfectly happy with him just being able to keep his head there, even though hers thrashed about. With the handkerchief locked in place, and Taylor's legs separated, Luke wedged his shoulders between them, as he persistantly exerted his control.

With the lower half of her body immobile, Taylor remained still until her eyes opened wide with a scream from the muffler that all but silenced her. She shook violently. When he stopped, she basked in the afterglow as Lucas kissed her with her doing her best to return her side through the gag. The restraints were a bit troublesome as she couldn't hold him. Then as she was being enamored with a barrage of kisses, he pushed himself into her. She jumped as her body hadn't finished convulsing yet.

He rocked back and forth, trying to urge her body to get in perfect time with his. A minute later, she was there. With no arms to hold him and no legs to wrap around, she was getting fucked and could have cared less, with her anticipating his climax. Lucas kept the timing the same as the rest of the morning's calculated attack, slow.

She brought her knees in desperately trying to grasp at his sides and hold him. As he neared, she could feel him growing. He shook hard, leaving his entire contents within the well of her pussy. Lying there on top of her for a few minutes, he eventually climbed off, but she barely noticed.

He undid her ties as she lay partially awake and partially asleep. Taking one of her wrists in his hand, Luke rubbed it lovingly with some of the oil. The indentations, or marks as they were, were there as a reminder of what seductive captivity can do to you. So he made sure to cover all of the bondage scarred areas with the oil. The pink that surfaced was already starting to fade. The others that were left, well, not so much. Lucas then climbed in and spooned his delighted Taylor.

The two slept for another hour plus, before she woke to the thought of lobster. After a brief trip to the bathroom, she broke into the fridge. Good, he didn't take all of it! Taylor picked it up and attacked it like she hadn't eaten in days. Lucas pulled himself up to spy the carnivore in action. "Hungry?"

"Shouldn't I be?" Taylor stated.

"I suppose. You probably burned off a few calories this morning!" he said.

"I should say so, thanks to you. And by the way, you did a number on my wrists!"

Lucas just grinned ear to ear and stated, "Technically you did that. I just kept you there in place. You, my dear, kept trying to move."

She returned the look and nodded. Finishing the lobster, she asked, "What are we doing for lunch?"

"Don't you mean breakfast?" he said.

"No, we have breakfast right here. Did you think this was going to make it all the way home?"

"All right, that sounds good Tay, leftover seafood for breakfast. For lunch, maybe we can go back and say hi to your girlfriend at the Salt Lick."

"Get over it, Luke! We are never going to have that threesome! Although she would have looked fantastic, all bound up here in front of us!" she said while he chuckled.

"Is there something I should know about?"

"Not really. It's just the first woman that ever turned me on. I'm not even sure why," she answered.

"Yes, she wasn't bad looking. But maybe with her tied up right alongside you?"

"I think we should stop talking about this before we are back in bed again," she commented.

"You know, I'm thinking I created a monster," he stated.

"Yeah, but a monster that only you can handle!"

Because of a very wet and chilly boat ride home, the two admired tonight's beautiful sunset but this time from the confines of their living room window. Taylor warmed herself as she rehashed their incredible weekend, of the food, drink and the kinky sex. Sure, it might not have gone the way she thought with the bar hopping, but Lucas made it fantastic, just the same.

"So are you going to tell me about what was going on with the bartender?"

"I'm not sure. I've never had that feeling before. I know I wouldn't ever act on it, but it was strange," Taylor said, still amazed. "I know it's off topic, but did you drug me last night, because I was sleeping and then I was tied up. How did you do all that, without waking me?"

"That was funny. It took a half an hour to coerce your limbs to reach out fully. I had you tied up loose, and you were already naked, so when the time was right, I just took in the slack and spread you out."

"Oh, you make it sound like it was just that simple."

"It wasn't, but you should have seen your face," Luke stated proudly of his imaginative bondage accomplishment. She shook her head in disbelief.

"Hey, how long do you think I am going to have these marks?"

"Oh, that? You were marked the second night at the inn when you allowed me to tie you up on the bar," he answered haughtily.

Looking back, she knew it really began when she gave Luke permission to spank her.

Monday morning, Lucas gathered everything he'd require for this upcoming week. Like at least the past years told him, was that the slowdown was over this week. And seeing the schedule for the next twelve weeks, he knew there wasn't any room to fit anything else in. Today, they would be back to full force, that is if everyone makes it in as expected.

The only problem was from the office end, with him having Taylor there primarily to make his job easier. However, he now found it harder to think beyond his girlfriend, hence the problem. And having more staff wasn't going to cut it, as it was only cutting into his bottom line, that same line that he wanted to rely on in the near future, for him and Taylor. Lucas thought he might want to revisit Trent to see what they could do, as far as the two taking the business to the next level.

Lucas glanced at his watch and headed out the door after giving Taylor a quick peck. His mind was racing, and it looked as though he was in a hurry to try to catch it. Nevertheless, the memories of this past weekend were locked away in the archives under favorite memories, that he might not access again for months.

That evening Taylor had a meatloaf cooked for the time she figured Luke would walk in the door. Usually, she got a call about five thirty saying he is on his way. Well, here it was almost six and nothing yet. She felt a bit antsy. *Was this what he said might be considered as late?* She checked the app, finding he was still at one of the sites, calming her some.

With the meal cold and back in the fridge. In bed an e-book caught her attention with the pages practically turning themselves. Getting caught up, she spied the alarm clock to see it was eight forty. Luke's location was still there at the fire department, so this time, Taylor went to call him as she felt that she had to. She jumped as the phone rang right there in her hand.

"Lucas?"

"Yeah, baby, it's me! I'm on my way home!"

"Are you okay?" Taylor asked.

"Yes, just one of those days. I'll tell you when I get home."

"Are you hungry?" Taylor inquired.

"Starving!"

"I made a meatloaf, but I will have it reheated for when you get here."

"Thanks, girl," he said as his voice dropped off at the end. The phone disconnected on his end, with him sounding like he was ready to fall asleep.

Taylor warmed a plate of meat, mashed potatoes, and broccoli in the toaster oven. Thinking about how most nights they would be turning in soon, she was hoping it wasn't going to be like this, because this girl needs to eat.

Lucas rested for a minute before he forced himself to get off his butt and into the house, with him pushing the door open to a curious Taylor. He planted a struggled kiss on her cheek as he beelined slowly to the kitchen sink to clean his hands, to wash away the day.

Instead of heading to the fridge for a beer, he plopped himself down in his usual chair at the end of the table. Luke leaned back and ran his hands through his gnarly hair, though he probably just got them dirty again from the look of things.

Lucas, who wished the day had never happened, tried to put the events of today to bed. Taking a breath, he picked up a fork and made a feeble attempt at spearing a piece that frankly a two-year-old child could have done better with. The first bite of meatloaf seemed to give him an ounce of energy, as she noticed his sideways smirk. But it wasn't until the second bite that he dipped in the potatoes that he outwardly showed signs of savoring it.

"Taylor, you are one fantastic cook!" he said quietly but profoundly.

"Thank you." She paused. "I was starting to worry when I hadn't heard from you!"

"I'm sorry, but I told you that the summer is going to be like this. I hope you don't have a problem with that?" he asked, concerned about whether she was going to be able to handle this day in and day out.

"No, I am fine. You told me. I just can't believe you do this every day."

"I don't, but it certainly seems like it sometimes," he reassured. With that last sentence, he grew quiet again.

After the pause, Taylor spoke, "I think I will consider a hobby." He sat there eating and nodded late after noticing that she had spoken.

Luke was not able to mask his exhaustion, as opposed to Taylor who was wired to the max, with her wanting to dive right into all the internet had to offer. From their bathroom she was reluctant to ask him if he minded if she stayed up. But his heavy breathing and light snore made it possible for her to creep out before her first word was even spoken.

She picked up her phone and keyed out a few words to Lauren to see if she was free. While she cleaned up the rest of the kitchen, she grabbed a notepad and sat on the leather couch. She wrote the word "Hobbies" on the top of the sheet. She even underlined it, so to get those creative juices working. She paused wondering what it was that she wanted to do.

Through her monotony and with no real train of thought, she only put down a question mark for the first line. *Writer's block already? Okay, being a writer was out,* she said to herself. Taylor's phone beeped. She read the text. "What's up, girlfriend?"

She typed out a quick two sentence reply. "All is okay. Can you give me a call when you are free?"

The phone went silent. Finally, the phone rang a couple of minutes later. "Hello," Taylor answered.

"Hey, stranger, how's it going?" Lauren asked.

"Good. Very good."

"Tell me, does master Luke have you chained up in the dungeon and I was the first person you thought to call?"

Taylor giggled. "I've missed you! No, everything is all right. Things are super crazy with the business, so I had a minute and I thought of you!"

"I'm glad. It's strange not seeing you all the time. I have no one to drink with. I mean without you it's just Carl and myself!" Lauren said with a subdued chuckle. "So why did you call Taylor?"

"Well, Luke has been telling me how crazy it is this time of year for him. Well, today I got to see it. He hinted it is pretty much like this, although today he got home four hours late."

"Well, he is in that type of business," Lauren stated.

"Yes, I know, but he did mention to me I might want to look into some hobby, and I am drawing a blank," Taylor stammered.

"You're drawing a blank?" she said somewhat in surprise.

Taylor looked down at the near-empty pad and commented, "No, actually I'm drawing a question mark. I just drew that on a pad, right before you called."

"Okay, then we can do this. You like gardening!"

"I already have that underway."

"How about you read. You could do more of that," Lauren piped in, trying to help her friend.

"That's a possibility, but I was looking for something that interests me, maybe socially," Taylor said.

"Humm. Well, you seem to like this new lifestyle. So how about a social gathering in town or maybe even the city?"

Taylor thought, "Maybe, you hit on something there. Luke was saying a while back that he had attended a few meetings for bondage and discipline," she commented as she walked to the refrigerator for a glass of wine, "But speaking of that, Lucas took me to the sound, and we had a wonderful weekend. It was romantic, it was fun, and it was also kinky."

"Well then, you better spill the one you know I want to hear first," Lauren urged.

"Do you have time?"

"Of course, Carl's watching his basketball."

"Then I am going to give you the whole story!"

# CHAPTER 10

Taylor woke to Lucas as he soft stepped across the cocoa brown carpet partially dressed. "Good morning," she said as an icebreaker.

"Good morning," he answered.

"Why didn't you wake me up? I wanted to make you breakfast?" she said as she checked her phone, knowing that it should have gone off.

"You looked so peaceful. Besides, I don't want you getting up this early every morning just because I have to," he said as he grabbed his cell and then diverted to the kitchen. She followed behind.

"I have a few things for you for lunch. Do you know what you want?"

He thought and then stated, "Can you make me a meatloaf sandwich? I enjoyed that last night."

"Sure!" she said even though she frankly was surprised that he even remembered it. Once built, she placed the sandwich and an apple to help cover the bottom of the lunchbox. Taylor poured his coffee and set them both on the kitchen island. With his morning grab and run, she made sure to stop him on the porch on his way out.

"Well, I want you to know that I haven't forgotten our weekend! You treated me like a queen. And I know that you have got to go, but I also wanted you to know that… I think I love you," she said out loud, surprising herself just as much as it did him.

"And you know how I feel about you too, but you felt like a queen for the whole weekend? I find that very surprising!"

"You know what I mean, but yes, even then." She leaned in again to give him a lighter smooch.

"Hey, I'll bring home dinner tonight and hopefully at a reasonable time," Lucas stated.

"Great! Then I hope you get out on time."

With Luke on the road, she transported herself and her nearly full mug of java back to the kitchen island. In Luke's absence and with nothing to do until 8:00, she started to think more about Alaska, with her missing her parents, her grandmother, Lauren, and yes even her brother.

Taylor thought at some point she was going to ask Lucas about going back for a visit, but it was way too early. With being here less than two months, the woman knew that she had to find something to fill some of her free time. And wanting to come up with a solution, she stared at the nearly empty pad in front of her.

She brainstormed anything she could come up with and wrote it out legibly, hoping that would bring up something that she hadn't thought of yet. The brunette began with gardening. Next, there was reading and volunteering. Then she jotted down attending a social meeting. There is also painting, drawing, fishing, yoga, the gym, or taking the boat down the coast.

Before long, she had managed to comprise nearly twenty possibilities. With her mind still searching for more, she went to the fridge for a small piece of meatloaf that she centered on a napkin that she palmed, before moving back to the table where the pad sat dormant.

Looking at the list, she began to cross off the ones that were not going to make the cut. She wasn't an artist by any means, so painting and drawing were crossed off with a single line of blue ink. Gardening, she was already doing that, and she could take care of it every morning before work.

Boating and fishing could be saved for Saturday and Sunday since she was thinking that he would be working some hours then too. Taylor labeled those as weekends. Join a gym, she quickly crossed that one off. She wasn't ready to commit to something that might take up that much of her time, not to mention the financial commitment. And reading she reserved for some of her free evenings.

After everything else had been either knocked off the list or assigned to possible free time, she had only two viable options left. Taylor liked yoga when she was younger. And even though she might not be nearly as limber now, she still thought she could do it. Then the sheer thought of a social meeting got her excited.

Of course, if anyone were to look at her notes, they would never gather what type of forum she was contemplating. But it was not like many people make their way through the house here, for her to be the least bit worried about. Taylor finished hand feeding herself the meatloaf, balling up the napkin when she was through.

With the workday far behind her, she felt uneasy and surmised it to be simply another dash of being stir crazy. From the desk drawer, she tucked the tablet and hobby choices under her left arm and marched off to the bedroom. There she messed up the throw pillows and all the others to create a makeshift nest. Turning on the handheld, Taylor waited, as the screen with its bright orange sunset wallpaper came to life.

*Where to start? Use the right search words, and hopefully I will find exactly what I'm looking for,* Taylor thought. *But what was it that she wanted to do?* She had all day to think about what kind of social gathering she wanted to be part of, so she started with the obvious. BDSM meeting. She tapped enter and waited as the choices loaded right in front of her.

Most of the options turned out to be porn, contained both pictures and videos. And not that Taylor had anything against it, but it wasn't what she was looking for. So not to get sidetracked, she scrolled through the first page. Taylor put the brakes on her pursuit as she couldn't believe that she had forgotten to enter the location for which she was looking. She knew that adding Seattle would help, although she was sure that porn would still consume a significant amount of the results.

When she entered the next time, there was not much more there. The porn, which pretty much flooded the typed page before her, wanted her to choose one and come on in and look around. She opted for a completely different approach.

She slowly typed in, "Becoming a better submissive." The first few entries narrowed it down to a few blogs of mostly lifelong people who succumbed to the hand of another. Most of the choices were women, it looked like, with there being a few men also.

She picked one that was written by a female. Double-clicking the link made a blog materialize, which featured a young woman in leather cuffs on all fours. A thick black collar encircled her neck, with its lead extending toward the foreground. She appeared very confident in who she was, and Taylor thought the woman even epitomized empowerment.

The write up had many comparisons as to both the dominant and the submissive. It also said that a submissive's prime responsibility was to choose the one that led him or her carefully. Because being in this position, they had to be in charge of their own safety, with a sub needed to find the right fit before finding out that there was no point of return.

It also mentioned sadomasochism. Taylor didn't have to fully understand what the far reaches of this term led to, but it only reminded her that this was the road she didn't want to take. She didn't need to get beat up or abused to get turned on, and that she knew already.

Reading more, it appeared it was covering not just bondage and discipline but the stronger stuff too. They did make comparisons between both, and it kept stressing safety.

Taylor wondered if opening this can of worms was going to make things more defined, if she continued or would it just muddy the water. Backing out of this blog, she moved on to the next on the list. Again, it was a female, which she felt was the right viewpoint that she was seeking.

The second site was better in the fact that the woman did whatever her female dominatrix wished. But it was the things she did that made Taylor look out of the corner of her eyes. To her, the stuff wasn't kinky; it was downright weird.

Going back to the drawing board, she exited again. It appeared that the twenty-five or thirty words she was reading, wasn't giving an accurate depiction of the text it contained. Taylor scrolled until she decided to open one that highlighted the words, The Bottom Line. There she was hoping to find something substantial as the search up til now had her becoming disinterested.

The picture located just below the main headline was that of a woman on all fours, with her head resting down to the floor. The sub's hands were also extended out in front of her, presenting a riding crop that laid across both of her open palms.

And even though she was unable to see the woman's expression, the picture was that of sheer devotion, with her not seeing one restraint, or any marks of redness anywhere upon her body. This to her epitomized what it was that Taylor was looking for.

She could see that this woman, the submissive, was there because she knew her place and was not forced into it. Her blonde hair was even flawlessly kept. Taylor wanted to be there in that very role that the woman alone chose, as it appeared that there was trust and a bond that made her and her master simpatico. It was true; a picture was worth a thousand words. Then maybe the text contained therein would hopefully reflect the image it featured.

She found that she had to break the stare, from this woman that bowed down to dominance. Taylor wanted to read, but for the second time in less than a week, she found herself ogling a person of the same gender. *What was happening to her?*

It had to be the fact that she had dropped her wall of so-called sexual independence. But she didn't feel like a mouse under normal everyday life situations. So what was it then? She opted to put that on the back burner for now. But it would be a great continuation on a previous talk with Luke when there is time.

Evicting it from her mind, she started to read, after of course checking the time. Lucas could be home in about an hour. She had no dinner to make, and the house was spotless. She nuzzled into the nest that she had surrounded herself in, as Taylor was absorbed within the article, with her reading faster and forgetting about the time.

The sound of a door closing outside brought her to look down at the time, making her place the tablet softly onto the nightstand. When the door swung open, Taylor was there to greet him. She waited, unsure as to which Luke she was going to get tonight.

He appeared in good spirits at first glance. "Hello, baby," he said as he lightly stroked the side of her face, with a touch that made her melt.

"Hello, yourself! How was your day?" Taylor asked.

"Very good! Just busy, that's all."

"Should I make us something?" Taylor lightly asked, knowing that his hands were empty after saying he would bring home dinner.

"I know that I forgot, so why don't we just have delivery tonight. How about pizza?" he said somehow managing to read her mind. Taylor was amazed that her man had thought of the Italian flat crusted delight, when she was thinking that it would hit the spot.

"That sounds wonderful! I'll order it," she replied.

He parked himself on the deacon's bench just to the left of the door. He unlaced his boots and grunted at each tug, as he yanked them clear of his aching feet. Standing, he lifted the hinged cover and carefully placed the pair of well-worked construction boots to bed inside the storage compartment, totally hiding them when he was at home. The cover let out a light rapping sound as the top closed.

"Do you want a beer?" Taylor said, standing there with the bottle in hand.

"You know I'm not sure what I want. I do know that I have a long night ahead of me, and I have a lot of parts to order for the new job."

Taylor was besides herself after another possible evening with loads of free time. But she didn't whine or complain. He told her from the get-go that this was the way it was for him. Although she was slightly disappointed, she managed to keep it to herself. Grappling with her emotions she picked up her phone, dialing the Italian place down the road. "Are we getting a combo?" she asked.

"That will be fine!" Lucas said as he took the beer from her hand.

Luke sipped the cold Heineken before handing it to Taylor, when her phone made its way to the counter. She accepted it by bringing the bottle up to her lips and wetting her whistle. The taste was refreshing as it washed over her palate.

She wasn't one for drinking beer for the most part. It was an acquired taste, and for now it wasn't hers. Taylor passed the bottle back to Lucas as they both sat at the table. He wanted to spend the next few minutes with it being just the two of them, before he surrounded himself with a pile of papers and of course his overused calculator.

While holding Taylor's hand, he asked, "So how was your day?

"It was all right. I started doing a bit of light reading!" she answered, meaning that she was just getting into it.

"Anything good?"

"Yes, I'm not that far into it, but I am definitely liking it." Taylor paused before asking him. "Are you going to tell me about your day?"

"Not really. It was uneventful, and I wanted to hear about yours. Is that okay?"

"I guess," she said a little sad.

Lucas looked at her once more before speaking. "Taylor, are you missing home?"

"A little. I have been missing everyone that I haven't saw in a while," Taylor stated before wishing she had kept her trap shut. "I didn't mean that you know. I have just missed my family from time to time, that's all," she said, trying to make light of what he had just heard.

"I know you have. You can go up to visit your parents, or you can even move back if that is what you want." Now he wished he hadn't mentioned the last part, even though it had to be mentioned.

"No, I'm just babbling. As you said, I just need to find something to do with my free time, that's all. And I have absolutely no intention of leaving unless you are growing tired of me."

"Taylor, that could never happen. Never." He ran his hand up and down her forearm soothing her. A long pause followed before he broke the silence. "So what have you been thinking about for hobbies?"

"Well, like I just mentioned, I want to get back to reading. I have also been dabbling with the thought of taking up yoga or go to the gym. And I have also been thinking about maybe joining a group!"

"Oh, what kind of group are you talking about?" he asked.

She looked him in the eye and then shied away, looking for the right words. "Well, I want to be better for you, you know, when it comes to being the subservient that I know you want me to be."

Lucas braked her right there by exposing his right palm to her and lightly exclaimed. "You know you have learned very quickly and the last thing I want is for you to be a cookie cutter sub. Plus, what we do is just for fun," Luke stated only to continue.

"I'm not going to tell you that you can't go, but I just want you to understand that there are some over-the-top relationships that I don't think you will want to hear about, never mind be a part of. There are also some guys that will try to own you, if you know what I mean, not to mention the couples that are always recruiting for a third. I'm just saying you have to be careful."

She stewed over his precautionary words. Keywords seemed to reverberate in her head as if trying to break through her thin-walled defenses. Her eyes locked with Luke's again. "You know I will think about it!" she said. Changing the subject, she peered outside and suggested that they have their meal out on the deck. She knew that it wouldn't be for the sunset, but it would get them some fresh air on such a beautiful day.

"Sure, that sounds fantastic," he answered. As Taylor collected the plates and forks, Luke reached around like a magnet grasping the items he was going to need shortly, stacking them in a pile on the edge of his desk. But that didn't keep him from enjoying bites of the six-item treat, while it was still hot.

The sauce which Luke had had many times before, reminded him of the sauce that his mom makes. And it resembled in and the same way with it being so thick that you could stand a spoon in the center of it. Lucas thought back to his childhood, with his mother standing over the pot of sauce, thickening it until it was a meal in itself. And she was such a good cook that he didn't have any real favorites, because there was no meal that she didn't excel at.

Her lasagna, her carbonara, the bolognese, and chicken piccata, were just a few that made him run to the table as a kid. She also made a risotto that went with any other dish, and it was to die for. Just thinking of it now was making the man hungry, even while he was sitting there eating his Seattle-style slice.

Lucas piled up his crumpled napkins in the center of the marinara spotted plates before weighing it down with the empty green

Dutch lager bottle, with him using it as a paperweight. Discarding the pile, Lucas found himself at his old padded desk chair.

This chair had been with him for a long time. It was his first piece of furniture that he had ever owned, along with the desk which was a housewarming gift from his parents. And for the last seven years, he and the two items had been inseparable.

He hated taking another evening away from Taylor as he knew she deserved more than this. But for now, he didn't have a choice. She sat six feet away, cross legged at the island as she periodically sipped her wine.

The sight of her there made Lucas call out to her. "Honey, I'm sorry, but I am probably going to be here all night. This is a huge bid, and I want this one. Is that okay?"

"Sure," she said while walking across the floor to steal a kiss. "I'll be in the bedroom, reading." Taylor left the man with a painted smile before turning out of sight. There she eyeballed the grouping of pillows that was still in the same place she had left them. Batting her eyes, she wished she had thought to refill her wineglass before she left the kitchen.

Taylor opened a drawer and pulled out her favorite T-shirt of his before sliding out of her own clothes. As she brought it down over her head, she bunched the material in front of her face, hoping to catch some of his smell. She wondered if he liked it as much as she did. She knew she wasn't going to be up late tonight as reading in the evening often put her to sleep, even though this one is a very entertaining blog up till now.

An hour later, Luke must still have been working, or she was sure he would have been there with her. Taylor looked back at the tablet as she was overtaken by the comfort around her. She closed her eyes for what she thought was just a second, and it was lights out. The tablet went black, with it joining her in her sweet, sweet slumber.

Lucas powered down the calculator and computer before gathering the eight-page estimate from the printer. Placing them in a gray folder, he slid them into the side pocket, laying it like a book on the corner of his desk, with only the bold logo of his business located in its center, to show that it was from his company.

Turning off the desk lamp last, the man pathed his way down the dimly lit hallway and slid through the partially closed door, where he spotted Taylor sound asleep. With him being wide awake, he decided to make a detour to the garage, to work on his project.

# CHAPTER 11

A box from Portland Precision Paint sat atop one of the corners of his workbench. The work might have taken a couple of extra weeks more than he had figured, but he knew by just looking at them that it was well worth it. This was the third time Lucas had used this company. but it was only the first time for personal use.

He opened the box to dig his hands into the cardboard separators, bubble wrap, and tiny foam pieces. Reaching in like a parent taking their child out of a crib, he extracted the first item. The piece, a leg that Lucas referred to as the staple, was entirely covered in a thin outer skin foam. Holding it carefully, he placed it upon a padded blanket that covered the top of his workbench.

Peeling away the semi-transparent layer revealed a beautiful glossy black enamel finish. Lucas eyed it meticulously before setting it down and reaching for one of the next four. The second leg, what he called the tee, opened up to expose it to be as perfect as the first.

The final three were the shins, as he called them, which connected directly to the base. Painted just above the adjuster knuckle, the trio was designed as the medians to join the legs to the base, using changeable settings for the ideal fit. He placed them neatly side by side on the work area while the shop light shown a glaring stripe of light across the lengths of each item.

Lucas grabbed for the keys that hung beneath the front face of the workbench's top. Unlocking the padlock that hung from the cabinet, he removed it to allow the fixed hasp and door to swing freely on its hinges. Within the unfinished and unstained locker, Luke removed the base, which was delivered a little over a week ago.

With the base riding two furniture dollies, he positioned it to the center of the floor. Lifting it, he swiveled the dolly away to place the thirty-by-forty-two-inch foundation down firmly upon its thick rubber feet. He then reached into the toolbox and grabbed the wrenches he needed, laying them down. Then he carried over the box of heavy-duty stainless-steel bolts.

The man really should have gone to bed since it was late already, but here it was the almost June and he had to get this project finished. He set himself a time limit of forty-five minutes, knowing he should be able to get it done before then.

Connecting the first of the shins to one of the ends of the staple he tightened it with a bolt, before affixing the other. Then he cautiously lifted the unified piece that resembled a wicket in croquet, to the base, making sure not to scratch any of it. After aligning one side, using both eyes as a guide, he bolted it hand tight. Lucas connected the other side and was pleased, fastening the two as the washers cushioned it into one immovable unit.

With the front-upper-torso part done, he attached the shin before torquing the T-shaped piece as well. It was looking like what he had envisioned nearly a year ago. Now all he needed is the padded sections which are supposed to be in, in a next week or so.

Since the legs were designed to adjust for the right fit, Lucas retracted the pin for the placement he wanted, allowing the locking pins on both sides to fall into place, with only a faint click.

Getting excited about the next part he went to the shelf for the last box, the restraints. He decided on these because they were high tech, with them being Bluetooth ready. The claws, as they were called on the website, were designed for wall attachment and could be unlocked in many ways including a cellphone.

It also had an instant release, which could be used by the captive one, since these were designed for self-bondage unit. There was also a timer, that allowed the captive or captor a release time of their choosing. *So many options, so little time*, he thought.

Luke was getting horny as the thought crossed his mind of his girl spread out over it. Seeing the time, he swiftly connected all five to their prospective places. The four smaller ones for Taylor's wrists and ankles and the larger one that would be for her neck. They supposedly were designed not to apply much pressure but to hold you tightly once they were closed, and that is what he intended on testing first.

With the bondage horse, as he had named it previously, plugged into the extension cord, he tried the wrist cuff. He pushed down on the small button within the manacles palm, and it retracted. Since he depressed it with only his finger, it closed entirely and then opened again on its own.

Curious, Luke aligned his arm to depress the rubber plunger. The closure moved slowly and stopped at just the right pressure, much like the movement of a Venus flytrap. He then tested it by attempting to pull his arm free of the three-finger manacle.

He actually lifted up the front half of the base as his arm never budged, with his limb going nowhere. He pressed down on the remotes unlock button, and then it instantly and noiselessly became free. He did it again testing the app on the smartphone to perform the release. It all worked as stated. With it getting late, he wheeled the base back to its locker and placed back into hiding, although this time nearly complete.

Taylor, who must have awoke in the past hour slid herself under the covers. With Luke ready to join her, he plucked the remaining pillows aside that hadn't already found their way to the floor. She nestled close, even though she was in dreamland.

He loved watching her. She was so beautiful that he wished he could do this more often. He buried his nose into her long flowing hair as he didn't have the nerve to wake her for a kiss, or to help him with the erection and the thoughts he still had floating around in that brain of his.

Another May weekend day alone had Taylor feeling very antsy, with an anxiety that refused to yield. And this had her thinking about grandma again, as if she was summoning her. Taylor did the same yesterday, as she thought that the woman might be suffering, but after a call to Willow Creek and speaking with her directly it put her fears to rest. However, today her intuition was much stronger, so much so that she had to tell herself to calm down, otherwise she would be talking to the nursing home every day from here on out.

Today Taylor was lonely, pacing the kitchen, searching for something different to do. She eventually pulled her workout bag down that was perched on one of the wooden pegs, just to the left of the front door. Packing a couple of waters in her small pack, she walked out the door to begin an early-morning jog up the coast.

From the fire station, Luke stepped back from the blueprints, searching for it before it went to voice mail. He pushed the green button. "Hello!" he said as he didn't recognize the number.

"Lucas, this is Susan Naughton."

"Hello, Mrs. Naughton is everything all right?" he asked of Taylor's mom.

"Well, I have been trying to call our daughter for the last hour, and she hasn't answered. I just wanted to tell her that we think her grandmother is dying and I know that she would want to know."

"I'm sorry. Taylor must have shut her volume off. Listen, I am leaving work right now, and I will get in touch with her and have her call you back as soon as she can. Is there any other information that you want me to give her?"

"No. That's it for now!" Susan answered.

"Okay, then you will hear from Taylor soon!"

"Thank you, Lucas. Bye," the woman concluded. Luke yelled to Steve before driving west to their residence. With it being over a half hour away, he had so much to do, first of which was locating his girlfriend.

He tried her phone, expecting that she wouldn't pick up, so he left a short message anyway. Not having the proper resources at his fingertips that he needed, he made another call and waited. A man's voice answered, "Hello!"

"Hey Dad, can you do me a favor if you're not busy?"

"Sure, what is it, son?"

"I hope you have time for this, because I need you to book a flight for me and Taylor today from Seattle to Fairbanks."

"Is everything okay?"

"Taylor's grandmother is dying!" Lucas phrased. Even Luke's father knew how detrimental that was to Taylor.

"I will call you right before I purchase them," his dad said.

"Thank you, dad. I hear mom in the background. Please tell her everything is all right."

"I will, and I'll call you soon!"

As Lucas pulled into the yard he spotted the car, so he knew she was here somewhere. He heard from his dad but couldn't commit since there still was no sign of Taylor. He called one more time finding that her phone was ringing on the counter behind him. In the bedroom he located two small suitcases from the closet, and with lightning speed, he proceeded to pack them both. Not knowing what to take in the few minutes, he winged it.

"Luke?" he heard from down the hall.

"Taylor, I'm in here." Lucas picked up the phone and had his father book the flights, hoping that they could still make it there today.

"What's going on? Why are you home so early?" she said calmly, at least until she saw the suitcases.

"Taylor, your mom has been trying to call you. Your grandmother is not doing well." To that Taylor had a look of shock. "My dad just booked our flights, and we need to go now. Can you think of anything else you need before we go?"

Dazed, Taylor looked over the contents within. "I... I guess that's good."

On the road Lucas sat belted in as Taylor sobbed, leaning in for emotional support. "We are going to make it," he said. She didn't hear it as she was staring out the window with her only thought being that her grandmother might be leaving this earth soon.

At the Willow Creek nursing center, Lucas and Taylor swiftly exited the vehicle, as Kyle brought them expediently into the building. He had informed them that she was alive, but Taylor feared that she still might not make it in time. She slid under Luke's right arm. Following Kyle into the large oddly shaped building, they made their way down the hallway.

Once Tilly was in view, Taylor broke free of Luke and passed Kyle into the room, before carefully laying herself across her motionless grandmother. She could feel that the woman was still here. Seeing that Kyle walked away to make a call.

Luke huddled in close since he knew that Taylor was not going to take this well if her grandmother doesn't pull through. His thoughts wandered to the woman lying motionless on the bed.

He had always found Grandma Tilly and her husband to be the nicest of people. It was because they always treated people with respect. Her grandmother had this unique way of making their home feel like your own. It was the little things.

Beautiful seasonal flowers, albeit plastic, were placed carefully on tables, walls, bookshelves, and even walkways outside, making all feel comfortable and welcome. The meals she put together every day made your mouth water. And when you left to continue your life somewhere else, you felt like you were leaving friends behind.

Taylor leaned back slowly onto the folding chair that Luke had pulled up behind her. There she rested quietly as tears clouded her eyes. Her gaze never strayed from the eighty-seven-year-old matriarch. Kyle however, remained outside in respect for his sister while he waited for the rest of the family. Then with the room as quiet as it could be, Tilly's right hand twitched, followed by some finger movement.

Taylor's eyes grew as her grandmother began to whisper. Luke couldn't make it out, and it didn't look as though Taylor was getting it either. Tilly was muttering words, but they were gibberish and unrecognizable. Moments later she noticed it wasn't that; it was her native language.

The woman picked up on this and was looking for anything that she might know. From the mashing of words, she finally understood just the one, as it was now as clear as day. "Tehya." Taylor stood there and began to sob. The word was like an endearing embrace. Tilly was calling out her nickname, and it grew louder and more evident with each passing second. Tehya stood for precious, which her grandmother had called her from as far back as she could remember, and probably because it sounded very much like Taylor.

Finally, she couldn't take it anymore. "Grandma, it is your Taylor!" Tilly lay face up on the bed and flashed her award-winning smile, although her eyes remained clenched.

"Taylor, you are here, baby?" she whispered with much less energy than her expression. Tilly strained to draw her eyes open. The light worked against her, sealing them tight again.

"Grandma, Tehya is here, and I miss your hug." With that, Tilly's eyes opened for only Taylor and Lucas to see. She took a few deep breaths and then struggled to talk.

"Then what are you waiting for, baby?" she stated as a tear welled up in the corner of Tilly's eye. Taylor hugged her and then crouched over and looked at the aged woman looking back. Lucas grouped in alongside, making sure not to miss this special moment. Tilly, seeing a blur in the corner of her eye, questioned, "Is that Kyle with you?" Taylor spied the room, making sure it wasn't.

"No, this is Lucas, Lucas Calderone. Do you remember him?"

"Of course, I do! Nice to see you, Lucas!"

"And you too, Grandma Tilly!" he stated, trying not to distract them.

"Are you here with Kyle?" Tilly said, rephrasing her last comment.

Taylor didn't know how to answer. Even Luke felt unsettled about what should be said. "No, Luke is with me!" she commented, pausing. "Luke is my boyfriend!"

"I know. Your mom told me, and I'm so happy for you," she answered, barely exhaling a chuckle, with her next words trailing off. "Taylor, your grandpa has been here today. He's calling for me to go with him," Tilly whispered. "I must go. I must see my Michael."

"Then you should go," the granddaughter replied as tears involuntarily welled up. Right then Taylor quietly cried as her grandmother close her eyes for the last time. Unbeknownst to them, a silent gathering of Kyle and her parents filed in quietly behind Lucas.

Tilly gasped a few times, and then the grip on Taylor's hand became fainter until there was no movement at all. Her grandmother was gone. Taylor leaned in close and embraced the woman. Tears poured from her face as her equally teary-eyed mother, and Luke stood behind, each with a hand on her shoulder.

Her grandmother had always been the one she could tell her secrets to. She did the same with her mom, but with her grandmother it was different. It was like she was passing it on to a friend, as she never got judged for it.

Lucas dropped to one knee. He wanted to hold her as he noticed that she was quite withdrawn. Luke felt as though he had to do something for her but didn't know what. With one of Luke's arms around her, she leaned back in the chair.

She had all but forgotten that there were others in the room. Taylor stood and turned for the most significant shoulder around. Lucas reached out and held her close shielding her from the pain she was experiencing. Luke swore he could feel her pain, with him seeing that Taylor had lost something of ultimate importance. When the two separated, it was only so the two Naughton woman could cry in each other's arms.

It was impossible to tell what time it was by looking outside, as time crept about as fast as the sun that spanned the Alaskan summer sky. The family, along with Luke's help, eventually got Taylor to leave the nursing home, her grandmother's final resting place.

The following day at the restaurant, Lucas was properly introduced to Isla. His initial impression of the woman was that she was a tad shy but very down-to-earth. Seeing them together for the first time, Luke also thought they made a great looking couple.

He took another swig of the dark draft beer in front of him. Here amongst her loving family, Taylor was more with it, with her only a few times falling into a funk, as others were talking at the table. But Lucas somehow got her back, by just touching her hand and sending her a look that he was here for her.

Luke knew that the next few days were not going to be easy. Their relationship was already strained as of late since Taylor had moved to Washington. However, he didn't have to look at the phone bill, to see that she spent lots of time talking to her family back home.

Taylor, who was sitting right there at the table with her parents, and brother was mostly disconnected, with her showing up late emotionally to the gathering. If a joke had been told, she laughed but later than everyone else, and then for the life of her Taylor didn't know why. She did know that they were all talking about the lives of her grandparents though.

The woman kept thinking about her grandfather and how he died about seven years ago. After that Tilly went into a descent, with her missing her husband, with her not wanting to forget one minute, of their fifty-plus years of marriage.

Because of his absence and how painful it was for her grandmother; she needed the pictures that were plastered around the entire room. It kept her mind from stealing the recollections that her mind was supposed to protect. So Taylor made it a mission to bring her a new picture in every week, and then she would pull one down and would explain it to her, or maybe on a good day, Tilly was the one that told her granddaughter.

Taylor's dad, Ken, stood to walk away from the table. He caught Luke's eye and gave him an unspoken head tilt. "Taylor, I will be right back!" Luke said. She looked on offering him a rented smile.

The two made a stop in the back room where the pool table waited for someone to pick up a cue. Kenneth who had a look of concern chose a stool that bordered the wall. The room was quiet dark except for the lone pool light that hung down over the center of the green-felted playing surface. Luke sat on an angle, just a couple of feet away.

"Lucas, I needed to talk to you, and I wasn't sure how I was going to do it." Luke looked on, unsure as to what the man was about to say. "I have been worried about my little girl. Is she okay there in Seattle?"

"Yes! Of course, she is!" He said, wondering where that came from.

"I'm sorry, but she seems very lonely lately, and I just hate to see my little girl sad in any way."

"Mr. Naughton—"

"Please, Ken!"

"Ah, Ken, she is missing Alaska in general. She had never been that far away, and she misses her friends and especially you guys."

"Okay. I am sorry for asking, but ever since Taylor's breakup with Marty, I have been so worried about her."

"I understand, but I care very much for your daughter, and I already couldn't imagine my life without Taylor. I love her, and I realize it more and more every day. I will do anything to make sure she is safe and happy. And if it turns out that her moving back here will do that, then that is the way it will have to be! Do you understand?"

Kenneth leaned back a few inches, with him happy to hear words Luke had just delivered. "Yes, I do. So I guess we are both on the same page then?"

"Yes, sir!" Luke answered.

The two exited the game room as Kenneth took from their conversation a nearly hidden smirk. His daughter was going to be all right. He never once had a question about Luke's character. Both families had been in each other's company enough times for him to know that. He knew the Calderone's and had known the family to be honorable. He just never thought in a million years that his little girl from Fairbanks and Luke from Seattle would ever see each other again, not to mention end up living together.

The two men replanted themselves in their prospective seats. Ken looked across one last time to check on Luke, who offered up a light peck on Taylor's cheek instead of an explanation.

Taylor's mother, Susan, whispered in her husband's direction. She looked as though she knew what he had done by taking Luke away for those few minutes. Their conversation was quiet, and it was meant to be that way.

Lucas turned to Kyle and Isla. "So who is watching the inn?"

"We have friends that volunteered to watch it when they heard about grandma!" Kyle replied.

Taylor took a sip of her wine. She was becoming more okay with the fact that it was her grandma's time. She did make it to eighty-seven, with not too much in the way of health complications. Her weight slowed her down, which played havoc with her breathing for the past ten plus years. But then she somehow managed to see her Tehya one last time before passing, which was a true testament to how strong the woman really was.

A series of memories flashed before Taylor's eyes. She was eating her chicken sandwich, but in her mind, she was having a private "This is your life" picture show for only her to see. There she saw glimpses of them decorating the inn for the holidays when she was probably around five. She also recalled at around twelve when she began to learn all her grandmother's renowned recipes and times when she and her grandmother sat down to checkers and eventually scrabble when Taylor got older.

After a bite of her sandwich, Luke wiped a dab of guacamole from the side of her mouth. He could see that his girl was coming around, as she was now noticing the food she was eating.

Lucas was warming up to being in Alaska again, despite the circumstances and the fact that he knew he would be leaving soon. If only he could slow down to where he could thoroughly relax and enjoy the time he had here, instead of what he had to do when he got back home.

For days, the best he was going to be able to stay away from work was maybe a week, or less, depending on what the family comes up with for the funeral arrangements.

That made Luke feel a little more in the way that Taylor did as of late. He didn't have the family that he got to see regularly. He hadn't visited his parents in parents in almost a year, and yet he went and called his dad to book flights for them.

He slowly scanned the table as the other five were now active in conversation and laughter, with it pulling Taylor out of her dreary disposition. And that was mainly because of Isla, who was lightly picking on the defenseless Kyle, with it drawing in Taylor because it was her way of joining in on the hilarity.

Laughter engulfed the table. And because of that very interaction Luke missed his parents, as he wished for the first time that he had a sibling. It wasn't often that Lucas wanted more than he was already lucky enough to have, but today he did.

Luke picked up his phone and texted into his to-do files, to invite his parents to the house for a visit. He didn't think that this was something he was about to forget, but being as busy as Lucas was sometimes, he appreciated the reminder.

Lucas closed the app and joined in because who knew Kyle better than his best friend. The man never stood a chance. Kyle leaned back enough to see all his attackers, as he laughed right alongside them. No retaliation was possible, as the best that he could do was roll over and take the verbal beating, of course, with a smile.

Ken and Susan sat there, noticing that their girl was happy again, with her acting the part of the archer, with her setting her sight on her favorite target. Her eyes glistened as her, and hopefully her someday sister-in-law took harmless pot shots at someone they both loved.

Lucas was envious indeed as it was a luxury he didn't have, with having a brother or sister that he could mess around with verbally. His parents just didn't have another child for whatever the reason was. But for him, it still was a good life.

Luke had plenty of friends, good friends that helped to fill the void, which made living in Point Hope bearable. And when he was young there were sleepovers and kid parties, in which kids had attended and that he had also been invited to. All in all, it's been a very good life.

# CHAPTER 12

Four days later the family stood within the quaint foyer amongst much of the revered woman's recorded past. There Luke studied the many boards that contained almost a hundred pictures of Grandma Tilly's life. Because of her lifespan and what she had accomplished in that time frame, she was considered the town's matriarch.

The earliest depiction in the photos was when she was just a young girl of maybe nine or ten, with her mother who was preparing vegetables for dinner a few feet behind. Her father was also caught in the frame as he dropped a basket of fish onto the clothed sling that they must have used for the days catch.

Another was when she attended the first school in Point Hope, and to this day, the building still stands. However, it was now a memorial library to a man who had developed the town and made it into a small but booming fishing industry, which soared from 1943 to 1988.

The town's primary industry was still that, but it diminished slightly when many more ports popped up along the coast, sometimes creating fierce competition. Tilly was not part of this movement, even though her father had been.

Then the pictures of a young Irishman and a teenaged Cheesh-Na plastered the right side of the brown corkboard. Lastly, there was the rest that encompassed their lives as a married couple. From the time when the groom had to borrow a suit for his own wedding, and the mother of the bride hand-stitched a gown for her daughter, Tilly.

There were others like when the inn was shown during the stages of being built. It exhibited humungous piles of wood, then a partially constructed frame and lastly the siding and roofing in various stages. The inn had been completed and in operation in 1958, and it has been the Point's beacon to the Pacific ever since.

But here today, the family and all who had known Tilly knew that she had reunited with her husband, with only the pictures and memories to show for it. That same loving, caring woman then turned over who she was to her grandkids, in the hope that her grandchildren would benefit and walk humbly on her same footpath. All in all, Tilly was pleased with what she had done in her eight plus decades of life.

The service was beautiful and uplifting with not many tears, but stories of those who had been close and had just happened to cross her path. The townspeople who attended all crammed into the small funeral home. Luke watched the pride in Taylor's eyes until he was distracted by the sight of his parents as they entered through the arched entryway. Swiftly excusing himself from Taylor, he walked to meet them.

"Mom, Dad, I can't believe you came," an astonished Lucas said.

"Don't be too surprised, son. We wanted to pay our respects to an extraordinary woman!"

"Well, I'm glad you could make it." Luke gave them a quick hug as he could see that they were there for another reason right now. His father gave his son his trademark light smack on the back on their way through.

Anthony and Gia after making their way to the front stopped in front of the casket to kneel before Tilly. Then they rejoined Lucas a few feet before the receiving line.

As they stood before Susan, the deceased woman's daughter, Anthony displayed his condolences eloquently, making sure that both her and her husband knew just how much Tilly meant to them. When they got to Taylor though, Luke's dad and his very quiet mom came alive as they treated her like one of their own, as it was from the talks they shared on the phone, mostly when their son was still at work. However, talking to the woman directly about her grandmother, who she idolized, seemed more heartfelt with in being in person.

When they got to the end of the line they met with Kyle, whom they often referred to as their second son. Not only was he at the house a lot of the time as a youth, but they even had one of the spare bedrooms made up just for him. Kyle hugged them tightly. After meeting Kyle's girl, the older Calderone's eventually dispersed and found a couple of seats in the back of the room.

As it was quiet at that point, Lucas took Taylor by the hand and went to the back to join them. With nothing but standing room Lucas inquired, "So why didn't you two tell me you were heading up?"

"Well, we knew how important this is to you, Taylor, and because of that, we needed to be here. And we thought it would be nice to see your whole family again," Tony said as Gia sat by his side.

Luke nodded. He felt good having someone from his family here. "Hey, we're almost done here. You guys must be hungry?" he asked.

"Are you kidding me? We each had two bags of those airline peanuts on the plane. We are stuffed," Luke's dad quipped. Luke and his mom just sat there looking on at the jester that couldn't stop from smiling.

"Well, if for some reason you find yourself even a little hungry, you can join us at the tavern later."

"That sounds good. Taylor, is that where you use to work?" his mom said, recalling the place from one of their past talks.

"Yes, I worked there when I was still in town," Taylor replied.

Almost three hundred people attended the service, with many just stating their words of kindness before exiting. The place might have been the only funeral home in Point Hope, but it wasn't equipped for such a great showing. It truly was an incredible turn out since the population was slightly more than seven hundred.

When the week was through for Luke anyway, he looked out over the ocean during the second half of his four-hour flight. Many hours ago, he said goodbye to his parents, his best friend, and most importantly, his girl that he missed already. Lucas was able to stay an extra two days, but he had to get back to work. He was appreciative that he has two guys like Steve and John to help him out, but it was time.

Emails and texts kept him in the loop on all the progress, which wasn't always good, but it would have been the same even if he had been there. It was just the nature of it. After tucking away his trash, he recalled the conversation he had, when he got those same two bags of peanuts. He chuckled briefly as he thought back to his dad's reply.

Luke's parents flew back to Saint Pete after spending some time with them all at the inn. Before he left, he had made tentative plans with his parents to visit Seattle. From that talk, they were swaying more toward late fall or Christmastime, with only a slim chance of it being this summer. If that was the case, then Taylor could visit with them until he got home.

Taylor spent most of her week with her family at the inn but still got to hang out with Lauren for a day, while her husband took a day off from work. As things were getting quiet again, all Taylor could think about was home, now calling the state of Washington home.

She missed Seattle and not being there with her boyfriend. Yes, she had the daily calls with Luke, but it wasn't enough. With Lucas being busy most times until the end of the day, she sometimes wanted to hear from him sooner. However, she reminded him each time that she would be home soon.

On Friday night, Taylor's flight landed about twenty minutes early, leading her to anticipate being home in about an hour. She snaked her way through the cluster of people leaving the Alaskan Airlines plane she just disembarked from. She was exhausted from being wedged in the center seat between two enormous men. They might have paid for their seats, but their bodies went far beyond the armrests.

Walking for what felt like twenty minutes through the winding terminal, she finally got to baggage claim at the bottom of the escalator, where she saw Luke. She ran over and hugged him as she didn't want to ever let him go. But when she finally did, it was a mainly quiet trip home.

As soon as they got in the house and put the suitcases down, Luke had a glass of red wine out for her. They sat at the kitchen island as they often did. Taking a sip, relaxation quickly took over. "I've wanted to talk to you about something all week, but I left it until now when we are alone. I never thanked you properly for what you did."

"You know that I didn't do it all, but I just had to try to get you there in time to see your grandmother."

"No, I know your dad booked the flights, and by the way, I had an almost hour phone call with him and your mom. I wanted to thank him and you for pulling off the impossible. My grandmother was so much a part of my life, and I know she always will be." She paused as the emotion in her words got to her.

"To think I almost didn't have that chance to see her one last time, and it was all because I didn't have my phone with me." Taylor started to tear up as they quickly made a path down the side of her face.

"Don't worry about it. Your grandmother was the strongest woman I have ever met, and she would have stayed alive for another month if it meant seeing you one last time. But you know that!"

Taylor shook her head in agreement, pulling him in for an embrace, and this time held on even longer. "Look, why don't we go get ready for bed. It's nice to have you home, but now I think you need to get some sleep." She pulled back nodding one last time.

The wine and beer went untouched as the lights got turned off, with them both sauntering slowly to their room. In bed, Taylor climbed into the waiting arms of Lucas. She knew without a doubt that this was the one place in the world that she genuinely wanted to be. They embraced, with Taylor resting her head on his shoulder.

It was followed up by kissing, caressing, and gazing deeply into each other's eyes. No conversation happened at this point, even though each knew that this was their point of destiny.

Taylor and Luke spent a good part of the day in bed on Saturday. She found that with all the playtime, she was tired halfway through, and because of it, she had to nap just to continue until nightfall.

By Monday she felt different. Taylor was no longer missing her family but instead yearned for something much different, as it had been some time since her last session. With her mind already venturing in that direction, it called up thoughts of the bondage and those such meetings, which often controlled her mind.

Lucas was off for work, and at best guess, she figured he would be gone for up to fourteen hours. And her job was only tiring in the fact that there wasn't enough to do, which left her with way too much time on her hands.

Pining again about the meetings that lingered in the corner of her brain, Taylor knew that this was only going to work if she didn't attend too many. She also wasn't about to make this a weekly thing, where it would rob each other of their rare time together. But even with that as a barrier, she knew she had to do something because she never figured she would miss this newly introduced lifestyle so much.

The woman had no friends here yet, and it appeared that Lucas didn't have many, if any, so far as she could tell. But working most of the year with long days and sometimes as many as seven in a week, when did the man have time?

Then out of her jumbled thoughts, a crazy thing crossed her mind. Lucas was turning thirty-five this September. Seeing the light from the bulb that figuratively turned on over her head she thought, now that is something that she could do, to keep her busy, at least for the upcoming weeks. Her eyes gleamed, as she compiled and considered the steps she would need to do to make this manifest.

It began with "What if I have a party for him?" Hopefully, things would be a little slower by then. And she could ask his parents. This was worth getting excited over. And if she made it sound like she wanted to do something with him on the weekend of his birthday, or better yet go away, then Taylor was sure she could entice him. She was getting giddy as she ran off for some paper.

She first thought about a party at the house and having a meal catered in. Maybe a gathering out on the deck? Taylor wasn't sure about the weather, seeing that you couldn't count on it, being that far-off in the future. And having it inside the house could only work if there weren't too many people.

For a venue, which was probably the best option, she circled one place quite a few times with it being a strong possibility for the where part. *He will love this*, she thought as she went online to do some research. This was going to get her some serious girlfriend points.

With the help of the internet, she was able to lay much of the groundwork right from home. The websites, along with the phone numbers, were right there to get the party ball rolling. The hardest part for her would be the guest list. To go and venture outside of the immediate family, was to extend beyond her very limited resources.

Taylor decided to talk to Kyle, Luke's right-hand man Steve, and his parents, and maybe anyone else he has mentioned in the past months. In as much as she still didn't know a lot about the new and vastly improved person that she was now living with, she thought that was the best place to start. Changing it direction her list filled up quickly with ideas, with them not being neat by any means, but they were there for her to filter through at a later date.

Her first call was going to be to his parents, which even though it was a fantastic hour-plus, all she got was a definite maybe. But they did give her a lot of names and even some numbers if she was looking for past friends.

His parents didn't have much going on with Alaska anymore, but they kept in touch with many of their generation that did. Their kids hung out with Luke, and therefore, they still had a link to his past.

She hung up thinking she really enjoys talking to Tony. He was just like Luke, but he didn't have the everyday restrictions to slow him down. He was free of his job, so he had a retired carefree attitude. Or maybe it was just when he talked with her.

Next, she decided to leave a text for Kyle. She knew he might be busy, and he probably wouldn't be able to call her until later because of his duties as the innkeeper. This for them was the busy season, as Isla was likely doing the cooking with Kyle's help and room changes which her brother didn't really care for, with him not having the woman's touch.

Taylor probably shouldn't say that since that was years ago, and she knew that her brother would do whatever he had to, to keep the inn in business. The Kyle of late has much of the same swagger that her grandfather did since they both have had the satisfaction of ownership of such a fine establishment. Kyle didn't call, and that led to a brief pause in her search for partygoers.

Unaware of the time, she put down the notepad as a text came in from the second site that had her running supplies from the first. This was going to play out in her favor as Luke was at one of the sites, while she knew that Steve or John would be at the other. That would give her time to speak with one of them, without Luke catching on. She took hold of her keys and phone and headed straight to the site.

In the most straightforward delivery yet, Taylor drove to point A, where she saw Luke who put the boxes in the trunk for her. A minute later, she was driving thirty-five minutes to point B. There, a second guy took the boxes out, and she was done. Instead of leaving though, she followed the young man to the rear of the building, searching for Luke's second in command.

Steve looked up and thanked Taylor promptly for running the items. It saved them almost an hour and a half of downtime for one of his guys. "Thank you very much for doing this for us."

"No problem, but I did want to talk to you about something if you have a minute," she said, flashing her eyes that any man would have trouble saying no to.

"Sure," Steve said as he brought her into the makeshift office. He pulled up a seat for her and cleared off some small boxes from the center of his so-called desk. "So what did you want to talk about?"

"Well, it's about Luke. He is turning thirty-five this year, and I was thinking about having something for him, in September. I am not sure where yet, but I only started coming up with this today, and I was wondering if you knew some people that we should invite?"

"All right, I will get back to you, but just off the top of my head, I would have to say some of his work crew. That would be as many as five. And I will get back to you on the rest. You know for the place, one comes to mind. You could go with the music on the Sound. You know for the pier pub crawl? We have been down there in September, and it's fantastic, but I am not trying to change what you came up with."

"No, that does sound good. I'm sure Luke told you that he took me there back in April. He went to Wake's for their seafood."

"Oh man, that place is incredible. Oh, and is this going to be a surprise?"

"I think we could do that. Hey, I don't want to take up any more of your time. I know, time is money!" As they both stood, Steve said he would come up with a list and send it to her by email. Then he moved in and surprised her with a very awkward hug.

"I am sorry to hear about your grandmother, Taylor!" She quickly thanked him and then walked back to her car as she pulled the yellow legal pad in front of her. She scribbled down his suggestions. For the venue, which was already down on the paper, she repeatedly circled the Sound.

Taylor drove off, knowing she was combatting the boredom of having too much free time, for now anyway. After all this she knew she had to come up with more to do if this arrangement of theirs was going to work. But she also understood that this shindig was only a quick fix, and she shouldn't misconstrue this as a cure.

She instinctively reached to make sure she had her phone. That small piece of plastic was almost always out of arms reach, and someday it was going to get her into trouble. A prime example of when the call came in about her grandmother. She tucked her phone deep into the abyss of her small but overstuffed pocketbook.

Lucas was to be expected shortly, and dinner was cooking on the stove. Her phone rang. It took her a few seconds to get to it. "Hello, Taylor, I'm just calling you back. What's up?" Kyle asked always using these same two words at the start of all of his phone conversations, whether he was making the call or getting one.

"I'm having a surprise birthday for Luke, and I am of course inviting you, but for now, I was looking for some names of friends from home."

"Okay, yeah, I can probably come up with a few. Some of the guys still live here. I have run into them at the bar quite a few times in the past year, so I will mention it."

"It was so nice to see Isla again. She is a great girl!" Taylor said, changing the subject.

"Yes, she is, and I would say that even if she wasn't just a few feet away from me."

"Oh, make sure you say hi from us and when are you making her my sister-in-law?"

"Hey, I think we have a bad connection. But when you find out more about the party, get me the information and I will ask around!"

"Thanks, Kyle. I'll talk to you soon!"

"Bye, sis." She no sooner put down the phone, and it rang again. It boldly displayed the call as being from her parents. She knew they didn't travel much, so this might not be an easy sell.

"Hi, Mom," she said once the connection was through.

"Hi, Taylor, sorry we weren't home for your call. Your dad and I were doing volunteer work at the nursing home."

"That's nice. Have you been doing that long?" she said, not hearing of this before.

"No, they have been so sweet to your grandmother since she has got there, and we just wantedto pay it back somehow."

"That is very nice! Oh, the reason I called is that Luke is turning thirty-five in September, and I wanted to have something special for him."

"You mean there in Seattle?" her mom stammered.

"Yes!" Taylor said, picking up on the first hurdle.

"I can talk to your father, and then I can get back to you soon. So when will we know all the arrangements?"

"Soon. I just started this today." Pausing, Taylor added, "So how are you doing, Mom?" Taylor said since she had lost her mom two weeks ago.

"I'm fine, honey!" Mom exclaimed making sure to add, "Your grandmother had a full wonderful life, and I am happy that she is now with your grandfather."

"Yes, that is the way I'm looking at it too. They were a special couple, and she had missed him so," Taylor said, adding after a very long pause. "Oh, about the party, it's a surprise!"

"I understand."

"Well, Mom, I hate to let you go, but Luke should be in at any second, and I'm cooking."

"That's fine. I'll call you soon," her mom stated.

"And say hi to Dad from us," Taylor asked.

"You got it, angel."

The phone went blank before returning to its wallpaper, exhibiting a selfie of the two of them standing on the edge of the pier, with the marina behind them. It was almost comical that she had been trying to come up with a place today, and it was right in front of her the whole time.

She stirred the vegetable medley as the oven released a pleasant aroma that seeped up from the juicy pot roast. With her wired ear buds in, she called up her music app and was bebopping to some seventy's tunes. She pushed the curtains back looking for Luke. No sign of him yet.

Taylor was swaying to the music when Luke entered. If he had made any noise, it was negated by John Lennon singing "Imagine." Luke moved in silently behind her. Lightly startled, Taylor drove her derriere up against him. She unplugged the headset, so he knew what it was that she had been dancing to.

He wrapped his arms around her and held her tight. Luke forgot all about the other part of his day. It wasn't that bad, but this here made him feel wonderful. He was thrilled that she came back to Seattle, and with that, Luke promised that he would do whatever it took to keep her here.

When the song concluded, she moved away from him to shut everything off. He took the hint by heading to the alcohol cabinet, where he pulled out an unopened bottle of Casa Noble. The woman grinned in thanks.

Taylor turned up the volume as the next song "Take a Walk on the Wild Side" began. She played the song loud, hoping that the dinner and this song might get them not only in the mood but the right one.

He dropped a few ice cubes in the bottom of the glasses, making them clink. Cracking the seal, he poured the light-brown liquid down over the one-inch square cubes. The ice bounced in a sign of jubilation as the liquid immediately made it less of what it was a few seconds ago.

He handed her a glass as she studied its liquified contents. She tapped up against Luke's as they both sipped the tequila. Taylor closed her eyes briefly relishing the taste as it flowed down and across her taste buds. With the hot stuff out, she ushered him to the table.

"What are you looking at?" Taylor said, mimicking his expression.

"You! I'm looking at you."

"Okay, but make sure you get some of this while it's hot," Taylor said.

"That was my intention," he said as he tipped his glass up to his mouth.

"You are such a sweet talker." He went silent as he lifted a small fist-size chunk of the brown meat to his plate.

"So how was your day?"

"It was perfect. Oh, and I went to lunch with Trent Collier."

"Wait that was your old partner, right?" she asked.

"Yes, it was nice to see him."

"Did he talk to you again about sharing the business?" Taylor questioned.

"Yes, I hope you're not mad, but I still don't want to do that. I worked very hard, and I am not willing to hand over half of all of this, no matter how much Trent is offering."

"I understand! So how is the pot roast?" she said with her trying to get him to take his first bite. Lucas let the forkful of the out-of-this-world beef do its trick. He savored the blend of roast along with its lightly spiced gravy.

"This is incredible, Tay." Well, you might have thought she resembled a deer that just got hit with a pair of headlights because she went motionless. *Did he say it by accident, or is he in the mood?* she wondered.

"Are you all right?" Lucas asked.

"Well, it's just that you said," Taylor quickly answered.

"I know what I said!" He exclaimed displaying a devilish grin. She didn't expect this kind of talk during the week. Now, the weekend, that she could understand.

"So am I going to meet Trent?" she said, slowly moving back to her last subject.

"No, not this time. He was just passing through."

"That's too bad. I would have liked to meet him," Taylor said as she realized he would be as a good candidate for the upcoming party. The two fell silent for a few minutes while they ate the food on their plates.

It was probably the combination of them both wanting to get dinner done and maybe a lack of appetite that was pulling them away from the table. However, the bottle tipped a couple more times, with the ice accompanying the tequila until within time the alcohol won the battle of liquid and solid.

That familiar warmth was creeping in. By the beginning of the third, Taylor heard it again as clear as a bell. He called her Tay once more. Something was going to happen tonight she was sure of it. She sat there opposite him as she was intoxicated in the alcohol and the presence of Luke's eyes and the way that he was looking at her.

The talk was mostly innocent, but she could sense his thought process but not the effect of what it was doing to her as she studied him. From deep inside she had this feeling that she was being over-shadowed by his presence, while she sat buried in her chair. It didn't strike up fear but a desire to be ravished by the one that she loved. It was then that Luke took her by the hand, making her eyes glisten.

The next day a beaming Taylor dropped off Lucas, since his work truck was out of commission. She would rather have slept later, but then she would have been without a vehicle for the day, and she needed it to check out a few party locations in person.

By the afternoon, she drove into the city, on a mission of completing the where with Chez Henri's being her first stop.

Taylor waited for a party planner to walk out with the oversized function book and sit with her to let her know what they could do. What she got was the owner himself. "Mademoiselle Taylor?" he said from behind her as she was kind of shocked that he even remembered her name.

"Henri, I didn't think you would be here this early."

"Early? I live upstairs, my dear. I am always here," Henri said, sitting across from her. He clicked his fingers, and the reservation book mysteriously made its way to the table in the arms of the young ebony-haired hostess. He placed the book down and then looked up at Taylor, who was sitting patiently across the table from him. "So what exactly are you looking for?" he asked slathering his thick French accent.

"Well, Lucas is celebrating his thirty-fifth birthday, and I am out today looking for the place."

"Okay! So what is the date that you are interested in?" he asked.

"I am thinking Saturday, September 17."

"That should not be a problem. The summer weddings are done, and it is a wonderful time of year for a gathering." He thumbed through the large oversized book when he finished talking. Trying to avoid the squint, he extracted a pair of black-framed glasses, resting them upon the bridge of his nose. Henri flipped the pages until he got to that very week in September. "Okay, we have one of the rooms opened for that night. How many do you think there will be in your party?"

"It is too early to tell, but I would say between fifteen and thirty," she said since she didn't have a clue.

"Well, you are in luck then. The very room you sat in last time is not booked yet. It is small and quaint, but it would be a little tight for more than twenty-four people."

"That sounds good, but I am very interested in what you have for menu choices."

"That is the best part, mademoiselle. You can pick what you want from the menu or pick as few as one item, and we can serve it all family style."

She nodded in approval. "Is there any way I could get a copy of the menu to go because I have to get back to work?"

"But of course."

"I can let you know for sure by Monday, if that is okay? The number of people might take a little longer."

"That will be fine," Henri exclaimed as he penciled it in for that date.

The owner excused himself and returned shortly with a copy of the menu before escorting her to the door like the gentleman he was. She exited the restaurant, knowing that she was going to have at least one viable choice. Still leaning toward Puget though, she thought she had more than enough time to find one or maybe two more places right on the pier.

While multitasking Taylor quickly ruled out Wake's since they were a restaurant and it was a Saturday night, with that being something that she couldn't picture happening. Then there were the bars that had an outside seating area. They were covered for the weather, but they didn't look like they served food.

She wanted this to be good, but she was beginning to worry about the finances part of it. Taylor couldn't have everyone from out of state chipping in, and that was going to be at least 80 percent of them. They were going to be opening their wallets for lodging, not to mention travel. And that quickly got her frustrated, as she considered how extensive this little party was getting.

Taylor was about to turn around to reconsider her options, forcing her to pull onto the shoulder of the highway. She sat there and closed her eyes as the brunette began to second-guess herself. Seeing it was just planning a party, Taylor opened her eyes and continued to Puget. Taking a breath, she looked out at her side mirror and cautiously pulled back onto the highway.

# CHAPTER 13

Exiting her car, Taylor fancied the warm ocean breeze as it toyed with her hair, while the darkening clouds high above visually contradicted the weather report that she read on her phone earlier that morning. However, a little rain wasn't going to prevent her from completing this task she was giddy about.

She kept thinking about that the pub walk, and how Lucas recently couldn't stop talking about it, with live music that played every weekend through the end of September. And that made her jubilant as she strutted across the parking lot towards her first destination.

Taylor was feeling more confident that the Sound would be the locale, with her imagining that any of these neighboring places could be the one. Since the seafood restaurant was not an option, she thought the obvious choice was where they had spent the night, at the Grand Allusea, the same place she was walking into.

The woman placed a foot into the lavish almost all-white lobby. She was quite sure that she couldn't afford this place, but Taylor wanted to see just how far her budget for the party could go. So she sat down with a short bald middle-aged man who introduced himself as the manager. He was very professional in having everything ready, so as not to take up too much of her time and probably his also.

After inquiring about the number of people to attend, he led her to the pier-side room, a room that was large enough for what she wanted. The walls were white, except for the windows that lined the entire outside wall and a couple of large skylights above.

Oh, this is going to be out of her price range for sure, but she figured she would stick it out. "As you can see, this room is very nice in the fact that you have your privacy. The servers enter from the side of this wall." She did like the feel of the room. Hardwood floors, beautifully designed accent pieces, and gold hardware, just to name a few. "So what is the budget that you have for your…it is a surprise birthday party, right?"

"My budget is two thousand dollars," she said, keeping a straight face, although deep down she knew she wasn't going to close out her bank account for one party.

"We can work for a lot less than that," the man proclaimed. She grinned, thinking that maybe she had a chance for something already.

"Of course, you know, we don't serve food, here, right?" the man explained.

"You don't?" Crap, she knew it was too good to be true.

"No, we don't have a kitchen, but we do work with an outside catering company down the street that has a very nice menu from which to choose from. As you can see here, whether it is beef, chicken, or fish, we can make your party experience here, one you will talk about for years."

She thought the last part was a little corny as she looked over the menu. There were no prices on it, so a red flag went off over her head. "So do you have live music here during the crawl?"

"The music is down in the bar below, and we do not have a speaker system from there to here." After that comment, the manager was beginning to sense her reluctance to look on any further.

"I think I have a lot to think about," she said, starting the turn that was going to get her closer to the exit.

"You know, Miss Naughton, we can still do all this with the catering for under the amount that you were looking to spend."

"I will keep that in mind," she said with her already taking her first step.

"Please, take the packet. It has the prices for the hall, catering, and even room choices, should you decide to stay here."

"Okay, thank you. I will give it some thought." As she walked down the stairs and out the door, she did think about it. She thought about the man who had called her Miss Naughton. Taylor had made it official last week with her changing back to her maiden name, and

Taylor just heard it out loud for the first time. It was good to have it back.

Taylor wanted to dump the folder in the nearest trash can. After all she didn't have the funds for it, and it barely met any of her criteria. But she was also sure that she wouldn't find anything on this stretch that could measure up to this. Reading a sign on one particular place on the way here, she thought that should be her next and last place for today.

She wished she hadn't been in so much of a rush to leave since she went out the rear exit, the same exit that she and Luke had used when they had stayed in this hotel. Questioning the clouds that loomed, she thought a brisk walk might be in order. As she saw the bar off in the distance, she hoped that the weather would cooperate as her car was hundreds of feet away in the parking lot of the hotel. With only the bar up ahead, as a focal point in the foreground, she recalled that this was the one that the two would have visited, had they tried another place besides the Salt Lick.

Taylor tried to stay locked on the many clusters of flowers instead of the darkness that was rolling in, and fast. She loved the combination of Shasta daisies, her favorite, and primrose and cardinal flowers. The colors of white, pink, and red added such appeal up against its preserved cedar shakes. And she surmised that as she ducked into the place, before the rain fell hard.

Inside the entrance, she shook off her somewhat waterproof jacket, before stepping more than a few feet in. The room was pretty much empty, except for the regulars who spun around just long enough to see the woman ridding herself of Seattle's waterworks.

With less eyes on her she dawdled up to the bar and asked for a glass of Chablis. Turning, the young man reached into the divided stainless-steel pond that held the white wine. Pouring the glass, he set it down in front of her.

"Thank you. And one more thing please, do you rent out your side room for parties?" Taylor asked as she dropped a ten on the counter.

"Yes, we do. Just one moment. I will get Sheila, our manager, to speak with you." After giving her the change, he walked to the employees only signed door as she looked around and brought the wine to her lips.

The young man returned with a woman that had to be in her late sixties. "Hello, my name is Sheila, and I understand you are interested in booking a party?" Taylor was taken aback from the raspy voice of a woman that must have spent many, many years with a cigarette in her mouth. And it wasn't just an assumption, as she reeked of it.

"Yes, I want to book a surprise birthday party for my boyfriend."

"I see. And how many people are we talking about?"

"Twenty to thirty!" Taylor answered.

"And what is the date you wanted this for?"

"Saturday, September the seventeenth." Sheila was listening, but then went over and reached blindly behind the bar for the small black book.

Before she escorted Taylor to the sunroom, she checked to see if the room was open. She thumbed to the right week. "Saturday, the seventeenth? We have a wedding reception booked for that night. But it looks like the night before just opened up!" Taylor could see that there once was something penciled in and then erased. "Are you locked into having it on Saturday?"

"Well, no, but I would like it for that weekend."

"Honey, let's look at the room, and I will tell you about the rest." They walked over to one of the two open doors. Taylor stopped in the center of the room, so she could check it out from every angle. Immediately she noticed that is was very nice, but it couldn't compare with the last place. And that is when she prayed that it was something she could afford.

"As you can see, it is a very large room that is well lit during the day and has very nice outdoor lighting that overlooks the courtyard at night." Taylor decided not to laugh at the comparison of the area she was looking at, to what this woman was calling a courtyard.

"So do you have a menu I can look at?"

"No, I'm sorry, we don't serve food, besides the occasional sandwiches and chips," she said. Wheezing a bit, she added, "But if you want to bring in food or have something catered, then that's okay.

We don't have a kitchen. And we do charge a small fee for this service, for cleanup."

"So how much is it for the room?"

"It is two hundred and fifty dollars, and that includes a bartender for the room, or if you want, two hundred dollars and your guests will have to get their own drinks. I suggest having your own bartender since we are always busy on the weekends."

"So I can hire my own caterer then?" Taylor questioned.

"Yes, chafing dishes are the norm. We don't want any open flame here, for obvious reasons."

She thought for a few seconds. "How much do you want for a deposit?"

"Fifty dollars. And if you cancel up until two weeks before, you get your money back. You can even use decorations so long as you don't pin or nail anything to the walls. We also have speakers to get the live music from out front, straight into the room. The bands are out there every Friday and Saturday night this year from mid-July to the end of September. They are starting that this year, because of the great turnouts we get. You can also run the volume to whatever level you want from right here," Sheila said, pointing to the volume control.

"Well, it all sounds good. Can I give you a check?"

"That will be fine. The rest I will need by the second of September. Are you going to want the bartender in your room?" Sheila said as she jotted down the info into the book.

"Yes."

"Then that will be two hundred and fifty dollars, with two hundred as the remainder."

Taylor finished writing out the check and handed it to the woman. "So it is for Friday the sixteenth and what time can we be in here?"

"You can come in as early as we open to set up that day, but you must be out by two in the morning when we lock up!" The woman handed her a business card with the time and date on the back. Taylor shook her hand and then left. The pitter-patter on the glass told her that the rain had not subsided. Why didn't she grab her umbrella when she saw that the sky was clouding over? Well, it was too late now.

Taylor finished the rest of her wine before pulling up her hood and zipping as high as it would go. She hoped that the few extra minutes here would be enough for there to be a change in the heavy precipitation. It didn't change. Deciding not to wait any longer, she made her way back to her car.

Friday, she paid the bills, just like she customarily did every other week, for the business. For her it was fun playing with thousands of dollars, which were not hers. She was growing to like the online banking feature, as it was much faster than writing out checks.

Her phone chirped that she missed a call. It was Henri, and he probably wanting to know if she made up her mind yet. She was going to call him back later anyway and tell the man that she had found another place for Luke's thirty-fifth.

Not knowing if her decision was going to hurt the man's feelings, Taylor called the number he provided in the voice mail. "Henri?" Taylor said after she heard his voice.

"Mademoiselle Taylor, it is very nice of you to call back. I was wondering if you made a decision for Monsieur Luke's party."

"Actually, Henri, I have been leaning more toward a different place. Luke loves attending the crawl on the Puget." Henri didn't have to pretend he hadn't heard of it.

"I see. Where is the place, might I ask?"

"It is at Flynt's Bar on the pier."

"Ah, yes, but do they serve food?" he said, working the accent.

"No, they don't. I will be looking for a caterer next," Taylor stated.

"Please let us do that for you," Henri pleaded.

"I couldn't. I can't have you drive a half hour to the place and—"

"Please, I insist. There will be no charge for the food either, but I would like to attend, if it is all right with you?"

"Of course that's okay, but I wouldn't think that you would leave your establishment on the weekends. And it is on Friday the sixteenth now."

"It will be good for me to get out. So that is a yes?"

"Yes!" she said emphatically.

"If anything changes, you will get in touch with me, yes? And don't worry, we will be ready, and it will be magnifique. Lucas Calderone deserves it," Henri exclaimed.

"Yes, he does. Thank you for this, and we will talk soon!"

"Bye for now, Mademoiselle Taylor."

Taylor danced to no music, ecstatic about the no-cost catering results. Her movement got away from her with her accidentally hip-checking the file cabinet. It was then that a folder dropped forward from between the metal storage unit and the wall.

Picking up the lightly textured, thick-papered medium-brown folder she held it on the palms of her hands. It only contained two words in the center on a white square label, with that being "The Project."

Taylor felt like she should just put it back where it belonged and forget about it. Maybe it was intuition, but she had a feeling it was about the secret project that Luke had locked away in the garage and not a project that he had done within the business.

She went over to the desk and sat, spying the outside of the file that was quickly getting the best of her. Taylor was only supposed to know what he let her know. That's how it worked.

Breaking away temporarily, she went to the kitchen and heated up some soup. And all the while it was saying, *"Taylor, how will he know."* She kept her back to it while she stirred the liquid and got a cup of coffee.

She cut up one of their ripe tomatoes from the garden and took a bite. With her willpower dwindling fast, she sat snacking on her food while her back was turned to the binder that she could not get out of her mind.

When she was done cleaning up, she twisted around, and there it was, right where she placed it. This was crazy! Why was she even considering it? Maybe because if it was what she thought it was, then it was going to get her sexually turned on, even more than she was right now.

Taylor picked it up like it was a magazine she was about to place back on a rack. The only problem was that even though she was going through the motions and heading the few feet to the file cabinet, she somehow knew that she needed to find out if this was what Luke was making out in the garage. To that she did an about face and sat at the desk.

She fingered the cover and ever so leisurely opened it, letting it drop off to her left. Her eyes went wild. She was in awe. She turned the pages and tried to absorb what she could, from a layman's perspective that is. She looked voraciously at the computer-designed images, but could really picture it, when she got to the 3-D rendering.

Lucas had come up with this, and he was constructing it out in the garage, for her to use. Taylor didn't have to be a rocket scientist to realize that this contraption was going to restrain her. And from the look of the restraints, hold her tight. She was dripping, and there was no stopping it. Well, that was it; she had to see more, even if it wasn't complete yet.

She closed the folder and headed straight to the garage, venturing past the laundry room like it wasn't even there, closing the doors as she went along. Taylor instinctively yanked at all the sealed enclosures, to no avail. There had to be a key in either the garage or laundry room that could grant her entry.

The woman checked out the walled storage and said he wouldn't put it here. She slowly spun to her left, and there was the garage door. After a few seconds of looking, she turned around to the rear of the garage. She felt around the window and door casing and still felt nothing. Frustrated she turned to the workbench.

Putting her phones down on the smooth aluminum top, she moved items aside to see if they concealed a key. She could sense that it was near. The ordeal was like playing hot potato when she was a kid, when the word hot told you that you were very, very close. She looked at the rear panel to see if there might be a key there to open those, now very annoying locks.

Taylor checked out the tool panel and still nothing. The bottom shelf was clear. Finally, she reached under the wooden supports of the bench's top. Feeling a light pinch on her finger as she came to the head of a finish nail—that was holding a key, and that was right before she was about to end the search.

The metal piece dangled back and forth as her hand tried to pass it, when she finally realized what it was that she just came across. Holding the key tight, the woman daintily slid it off the nail. Taylor then made her way to the big cabinet. Placing the key in the hole, she turned it. The door slid open a fraction somewhat welcoming her. She grasped both of the wood panels and pulled them ajar.

Now, she knew that she had to remember to put everything away like it was, so Luke wouldn't know that she had ever been there. She also had to replace the key and, lastly, put the folder back where it was initially.

Taylor leaned the entire piece up on its side casters to steer it to the open floor so she could see it better in the light. She looked it over thoroughly, mindfully comparing the drawing she had just looked at to the three-dimensional finished item. Taylor toyed with the claws but quickly figured out they weren't working.

Looking down, she unwound the cord and plugged the extension into the outlet, powering up the apparatus. Bubbly, she activated one of the restraints by depressing the stylish half-inch-thick button, setting it to close, and then watching it open again.

Finding the remote that hung on a hook she clenched it tight, ready to see what this bondage piece could actually do. Getting beyond aroused, she bent over the apparatus, just to feel how comfortable it is. Taylor knew it was early and there was absolutely no chance of Lucas coming home before five o'clock, so what's wrong with giving it a little test run?

Taylor gently ran her hands over the molded cushions that she longed to lean herself against. She thought for a second and looked back to make sure she had both phones there. Beyond excited, she just had to see how the cuffs fit, for real this time.

She decided to lock one leg and then pushed the remote button. Just as quickly, her left leg was free once more. Fascinated she locked in both legs and bent over, to have it comfortably close around her first wrist. She tried desperately to move.

It was the wildest thing. It was not at all painful, but it was kind of like being held by someone's hands. Taylor could not budge her wrist or ankles, beyond the point in which they were being held. Taylor could feel the wetness of her panties now, and she yearned to have her last limb stuck tight too.

While reaching down to make this a complete bondage experience, her cell phone on the workbench blared, vibrating across its butcher block surface, totally scaring the living shit out of her. With the same feeling, as if Luke had just stepped in behind her, she brought her free hand up, smacking it against the adjuster, making the remote drop and bounce across the black-painted base.

"Oh fuck," Taylor screamed in sheer panic. She tugged at the bonds like a trapped animal. Frustrated, she reached for the remote, which was just beyond her grasp. "Oh my God," she screamed as she accidentally depressed the collar restraint locking her neck tight after not knowing it was there.

Freaking out momentarily, she was at a loss for what options she had. She had to come up with something. Otherwise, Lucas was going to find her right there. Within the next fifteen or thirty minutes, she had two more missed calls.

Taylor was unsure as to how much time had gone by since her cells and the clock over his workbench were directly behind her. She only knew that Luke was not going to be happy over this one, not to mention how he constantly had said that she misplaces her phone.

Well, technically in this case she didn't misplace it, it's behind her. She just couldn't get to it, that's all. Taylor knew there was no way that she was going to avoid punishment from this. Her eyes grew large as she did a quick calculation of how long she could be stuck on the piece.

Seeing it was a Friday night and redoing the math in her head, Taylor figured it could be six or more hours. Adding to her woes, the woman came up with *What if I have to pee?* she thought. Great, now she felt like she had to. With nothing to do and a steel piece and padding that was in the way, she couldn't even use her free hand to play with herself.

After who knows how many hours later and a nap she took out of boredom, Taylor was getting sore. It had been very comfortable, but that was a long time ago. She kept thinking back to the three unanswered calls that she couldn't get to, as she was sure that the ring tones were not from the business phone.

Debating it in her mind, she was convinced that it was on her personal phone, which she prayed would make her punishment possibly a little less severe. Going back and forth with who it could have been, Taylor heard a truck as it came to a stop, maybe fifteen feet away from where she was being held. She braced herself as it was now time to pay the piper.

Lucas turned the key in the door and entered looking for the nonexistent Taylor. He put down the two suitcases he carried into the house. "Mom and Dad come on in. I'll be with you as soon as I check on Taylor." Luke was befuddled. He ran the locator on the phone earlier, first at the airport and twice since, so he knew she was home.

When the three Calderone's walked into the living room, he urged his mom and dad to sit and get comfortable. Luke was panicking a little and said I'm just going to check to see where Taylor was when he saw "The Project" folder, in a place that he knew he hadn't put it. "Can I get you wine or a beer?"

They both replied, "Wine, please!"

"I will bring it out to you. I want to show you the boat. Maybe we can take it for a ride tomorrow if you like?"

"That sounds fantastic son," his father said as the two parents exited through the rear door to the deck.

After putting the binder back in place, he gave them a few seconds before he darted to where his project and maybe Taylor was probably located. He grasped the handle of the laundry room door. The light was on, which was a sure sign that she could have been through here. He took a breather and slowly opened the other door.

"So is this why you haven't been answering your phone?" he phrased as he entered to see a bent over and mostly bound Taylor. "So how long have you been here?" he said as he picked up the loose remote.

"Since around twelve thirty!" she said coyly.

"You know you can't unlock yourself without the remote?"

She wanted to say something sarcastic; however, she bit her tongue and only managed to say, "I know."

"Are you comfortable?"

"I was hours ago."

"Well, I thought I would tell you that my parents are here for the weekend." She had the biggest look of horror. "Oh, and they tried to call you twice to keep this a surprise from me. So when I release you, I want you to come out after you fix yourself and tell them you had a migraine and was sleeping."

As she viewed the remote in his left hand that slipped from her grasp, he reached down and locked her last limb, checking it for tightness. He then reached over for a clean work cloth and balled it up and tucked it in her mouth.

"So are you clear on what you are to do after you are released?" She nodded. "Yes, sir!" He went to leave but wedged the remote in her butt cleavage between her shirt and form-fitting pants. Total confusion set in, as she realized the conflict in what he said and what he did with the remote. But she wasn't about to ask because she knew she was in trouble.

Lucas pushed himself through the opening of the sliding door carrying three glasses of wine. He met them at Taylor's Garden, which was starting to show a bumper crop. "Here you go," Lucas said as she passed out the drinks. "Well, I just found out why Taylor hasn't been taking your calls. She was in bed, sleeping. She said something about a migraine and this one was a doozy. She will get up when she can."

"I know how bad those can be. Very painful sometimes," Luke's mother Gia said.

"So do you want to take a look at the boat?" Lucas asked.

"Yes," they said as they patiently waited for their son to show off his pride and joy. Well, at least it was until he started dating Taylor.

They were entirely in awe of the boat since the best and only boat Tony ever had was a fixer-upper that never saw much time in the frigid arctic setting. And a worrisome Gia made sure of that. "Tomorrow morning, we will check out the coast!" Luke insisted.

"As long as Taylor is all right," his mom interjected.

The three of them went out to the chairs on the deck, where Lucas sat opposite his mom and dad as they struck up a conversation. Lucas casually viewed the camera for the garage that he had linked to the security system. The camera that pointed down faced the garage door, showing a wonderful side view of his captive cutie. He was so pleased that he made sure to snap a few screenshots, so he could show it to her to remind her on why she shouldn't do this again.

There wasn't much movement, except the occasional turn of the head that had Luke very excited, even as this was a trial run which he didn't plan on. It was an unfortunate chain of events, but once he found out that she was safe, Lucas knew that he had something on her that he would be able to use for her first, earned punishment. The conversation and eye contact dwindled to where they noticed that Luke was preoccupied. "Everything okay over there, son?" his father asked.

"Yes, I'm sorry., I was just checking in on my latest project," he said, noticing the rag still lodged neatly in her oral cavity.

"We are so proud of you, Luke! You have done well for yourself here!" his mom boasted.

"Oh, I meant to tell you I got a call from my buddy, Henri," the father and son both said, mentioning his name at the same time.

"Speaking of which. I want to go to the French restaurant this weekend with you two if that's all right?"

His dad stated, "Of course it is, but only if you let us pay?"

"You know your money is no good here, old man," he said with a smile. Because his father and mother had made his start here in Seattle possible, with their financial backing, there was no way that they were going to pay one red cent.

Lucas peeked at the app timer that he had set, as this was the best time to use it for her eventual release. Then he looked in on Taylor, who still filled the center of the screen.

During his conversation with his folks, he wondered what Taylor was thinking. Lucas would give a thousand dollars to find out. She was most likely sore both physically and emotionally from the ordeal. The fact is that Taylor was getting mad but kept herself in check.

After all, she was the reason why she was in this predicament in the first place. If she didn't let her curiosity get the best of her, she would have been able to pick up Tony and Gia at the airport and keep their secret intact until Lucas got home.

*But, why did he put the remote down the crack of her ass, resting it where there was no way she was going to reach it? He must be making a second trip in to release her?* She thought to herself. What she was sure of was that he was punishing her, but there had to be more to it than this.

Somewhere down the road she surmissed that this would resurface with her having to face the music. Taylor was so sore that she figured she might need a massage or a good long bath to remedy the situation. She most likely had a better chance at it later, and hopefully, he would feel a little compassionate and do the first for her.

Just then, there was a quick low-level beep that came out from somewhere beneath her. All five of the restraints retracted, giving her access to leave. The work rag was the first to go as the cotton fuzz that was in her mouth seemed to stay with her. She stood slowly and straightened up. Wow, even though he had this padded for her, too many hours on it made it feel like there was no cushion at all.

She stepped back, and that was all Luke saw right before he let out a hint of a smile and shut down the app. Taylor slinked through the doorway of the laundry room after grabbing her phone and putting the remote back in its place.

Her fury returned with her not quite sure why she was so mad. Taylor had to burn off these pent-up frustrations soon, and she knew exactly how to do it. She rapidly stripped and leaned back on the frame of the tub. While maintaining her balance, she reached down noting she was still wet.

With her finger tips full of pussy, she let her fingers do the walking, by slowly massaging her clit in a constant steady circular motion. Not intending it to be a quickie she relaxed entirely, acclimated to the bends and hardened curves of the bath she conformed herself to.

The motion sent her to another place, hypnotically inducing her skin and her bones, right down to her very core. As a palette of vibrant colors smeared her retinas like fireworks illuminating the sky,

Taylor's body went taut, starting a frenzy of neural firings that pulsed and convulsed. When her orgasm subsided, all negative energy was gone.

Still achy and moving erratically because of it, she cleaned herself up, just as she had been instructed before making her way out to her viewing public of Luke's parents. Having to act as though she had been under the weather was going to be easy since she looked as though she had suffered from a migraine recently. She hobbled gingerly from the soreness that hadn't left yet to find a new change of clothes.

"Taylor, are you okay?" Gia asked like she was talking to a crash victim.

"Yes, I'm sorry I wasn't able to get your calls earlier. I couldn't make it to the phone, you know, because of my migraine," a stone-faced Taylor declared, declaring it specifically toward Lucas.

He totally loved the way this had played out. It's too bad though, he was going to use the newly finished device on her soon. With it not being a surprise anymore, he thought he will now make her wait.

Taylor scampered past to sit to the right of Luke, where he lifted a glass of ice water to her left. "Here, you need to hydrate after the day you had!"

"Thank you," she said, drinking a few ounces of the refreshing liquid.

"Can you excuse me, Mom and Dad, I'll be right back," Lucas said, heading in the open door. His parents and the still very humble but ill-acting Taylor sat and talked. Right away Luke's dad, Tony, after making sure she was okay, quietly inquired how the arrangements were going.

Taylor led them to the garden with a simple hand gesture. As she got far from the open door, she gave them an updated rundown. "The party has changed to Friday the sixteenth. I have a block of rooms that are right on the pier, not far from the gathering. And that's about all I have for now," she said while reaching for a tomato.

The three were back in the sitting area before Lucas rejoined them. He came out wearing a different outfit along with some of his cologne, which she pleasantly caught as he passed by her. Thinking about it now, Taylor wondered if she was supposed to put the bondage horse away, but she knew he wouldn't want her touching it again.

The conversation that he walked into was about her garden. Luke's parents mentioned what they were growing, in their tiny community parcel in Florida. "So what kind of tomatoes do you have?" Anthony asked of Taylor.

"Well, the ones you saw that were hanging as normal tomatoes do are called Stupice tomatoes, and the ones that hung straight down in the long bloom lengths of endless tomatoes are the sweet millions."

"It looks like you are going to get a lot just from the sweet millions plant," Tony stated.

"Yes, I'm sure glad I didn't put in any more, or we would never be able to eat them all."

"Well, if you ever come up with too many, Gia could show you or tell you over the phone how to can them. Luke loves his mother's sauce, and this might be something fun for you to learn."

"Maybe, I'll do that. I don't want us getting sick of eating them." The verbal exchange lulled, although he had heard some of the talks Taylor had with his parents over the phone, and he wondered why they were less social now. He figured it must have been because of the flight, and Taylor's situation with her getting caught.

Lucas broke away, stepping across the deck and down the stairs, and pulled his phone from his front pocket to make a call. He wanted to make a reservation for tomorrow evening at his dad's favorite French restaurant. Luke, recognizing the voice, spoke, "François, my friend." The rest listened in.

"Yes, Monsieur Lucas, what can we do for you?"

"Well, I would like a table for tomorrow night."

"Let me see. Okay, and what time would you like?" Francois asked.

"Seven o'clock," he said and then waited.

"Well, we have eight fifteen or six thirty open. But if you wanted, let me see. We do have an opening for seven thirty tonight on the terrace!"

"One moment please," Luke said as he put the call on hold.

"Are you guys up for Henri's tonight?" They all agreed, even Taylor, who was having trouble keeping up the migraine charade.

"Seven thirty will be fine, Francois. Oh, and could you tell Henri that my parents will be dining with us tonight."

"Excellent, sir, we will see you at seven?"

The four were ecstatic that they scored a reservation, a couple of hours from when they called at the prestigious Henri's. With the parents off to their bedroom to freshen up. Taylor walked off in the other direction, just a few feet ahead of Lucas. Once the door closed, she wanted to be the first to say something.

She cringed knowing that she was about to poke the bear. But it wasn't like she worried for her safety, however there was that not knowing punishment that she knew would be forthcoming. "So my toy got a bit curious today?" Lucas blurted out.

"Yes, sir," Taylor said instinctively dropping her head.

"And you know that I told you to stay away from that, right?"

Again, "Yes, sir!"

"And then you know that you will be punished for this, Tay!" She nodded her lowered head in front of him.

"Let's get ready, but I would like to know how you felt."

"When I was restrained, you mean?" asked Taylor.

"Yes!"

She traipsed into the bathroom and pulled off her top dropping it into the opened hamper. "Well, I do want you to know I was upset."

"Upset at me?" Luke asked.

"No, the person I was most upset with was myself."

"Taylor, all kidding aside here! If something were to have happened while I wasn't here, you never would have been able to get free."

"Yes, I am aware of that. I had a long time to think about it when that was all I could do." Luke stood in the mirror and ran his hands through his scruff of a beard.

"So did it make you feel anything else?"

"Yes, I was horny, very horny."

"And did you play?" he asked.

"I couldn't reach because of the centerpiece."

"So you wanted to see how it felt to be restrained, fully confident that you could release yourself when you finished?"

"That is it exactly," she said, putting on her little black dress. "So how does this look on me, Luke?" she said, trying to get him all worked up and distracted.

"You, baby, are hot. But then again you always are."

"You always manage to say the right thing."

"Oh, one more question. Why didn't you have the remote in your hand so you could let yourself out?" Luke said inquisitively.

"Well, when the phone rang the first time it surprised me so much that I smacked my hand up against something on the whatever it was you made. I almost attached my last arm by accident. Instead, I managed to lock my neck while trying to reach for it on the floor. I didn't even realize it was there." Luke cackled as he kissed his blushing sub. The girl oozed embarrassment as she needed to be through talking about this.

Luke changed his pants again. His comfortable jeans weren't what he felt was the dress code for Chez Henri's. Going to his side of the closet, Luke pulled down a pair of medium-brown dress pants. He slid into them and then went back and spied Taylor who was looking in the mirror.

She tugged and pushed at the skin on her face and neck. Now that she was beginning a new chapter in her life, she noticed her youthful look wasn't quite there anymore. It's not that she looked much older, but it had changed.

# CHAPTER 14

The four followed the host past the room that Luke and Taylor had dined, with it bringing up recollections of Taylor's first full day in Seattle. She looked over to see that it was hosting a party of ten, with their table they had, used as part of it. Francois continued through the rear door and around to the restored outdoor café, to a rectangular cast-iron table out on the bricked patio.

The group were seated with the women being helped first by the host, pushing in their chairs for them. The men followed and sat opposite of each other, where he placed the menus in front of them, and stated, "Matteo, your waiter, will be right with you."

A young busboy stepped in mutely to fill glasses, allowing for the group to start up a conversation, that is until the very lively Matteo centered himself to where they all could see.

"Good evening, messieurs and mesdames. I am your waiter, Matteo, and I am here to ensure that you will all have the most special evening here at Chez Henri's. I understand you are good friends with the owner, and he will be here soon to greet you," he said and then paused. "Is there anything I can get you to drink this evening?"

Anthony, who was already familiar with the wine list, ordered a bottle of wine, in French of course. "That is an exquisite choice, monsieur!" The waiter said, before giving a bit of a head bow and leaving the table.

Taylor, who was in shock, just had to say it. "Do all you Calderone's speak French?"

"Well, these two here do," Gia said, getting them all to chuckle.

"I'm guessing that Luke told you some of this, but back before we were married, I was stationed in Paris. I visited the café's trying to experience some of France's best." Anthony continued talking directly to Taylor. "And I got lucky trying some of the best dishes I have ever had. I met Henri, a cook at the time, and before long, we were pen pals, and I told him he should come to America to open his own restaurant."

Henri stepped in, finishing the story for him. "But what my good friend Anthony forgot to tell me was that they were moving to Alaska just as I decided to start up Henri's here in Seattle."

"Yes, I didn't know he was moving here, and that is when we had moved to Point Hope," Luke's dad said as he stood and spun to give a hardy two-handed handshake.

"Sorry, we couldn't get you into Bein-etre. But it is such a wonderful night, I thought you would want to see the finished café that your son designed and built for us here," Henri said and then added, "Might I interest you in a little tour?"

The four complied, rising altogether to lag behind the proud proprietor Henri, by trekking back toward the other end. Tracts of manicured trees lined the outside terrace, as strings of white lights dangled high above the diners from the rear of the bricked building, to the wrought iron that stood beyond those same spruces.

Henri led them between the tables and down to the right, where a swooping pathway adjoined the large oval terrace with its centrally located white fountain. The terrace alone was lavish and had enough room to house a rather intimate dinner party. It was also lined with many iron benches that faced the impressive fountain.

"My mother had this fountain shipped in from her home in Limoges. She believed in me, the same way that my friend Anthony did. So that is why, with all the incredible work of Monsieur Lucas, the restaurant, the outside café, and the courtyard look as good as they do."

Tony interjected, "But there is no way you would still have been in business if you didn't have the best French cuisine that you do."

"Well, I thank you for saying that, and I assure you, tonight will be no different."

A minute later, they were escorted back to their table, where the waiter timed it so he could pour their wine, with them seated. Instead of leaving, Henri spoke directly to Lucas in his native tongue. The only part Taylor understood was when she heard her name.

"But of course," Lucas answered the man. He turned to Taylor, who was still trying to figure out what he had just muttered, and said, "Henri would like to take you for a quick tour of the kitchen and the wine cellar. Is that okay?" She turned to Henri and put out her cupped hand for him to take. Henri helped her gracefully to her feet.

"I will have her back momentarily!" he said as the two sauntered into the building, past the Bein-être room, which Lucas had finally taught her to pronounce. Just after the small private dining room was a somewhat-hidden hallway into the kitchen. And the sound of clinking dishes and the occasional open door told her she was about to be in the thick of it.

The kitchen was spotless. Apparently, that was Henri's way, and the staff seemed to follow it to the letter. Here the Frenchman introduced the kitchen help to her by title even though they didn't hear or have the time to turn to greet her.

He began with the executive chef, Enzo. He was preparing duck along with multiple parts of other entrees all at the same time. Next was his right-hand man, the sous-chef. He was prepping meals, but he was also the divine force behind the ever-changing menu selection. Then she was directed to the chef de partie, which oversaw multiple stations.

The underlings beneath him were the sauce chef, also known as the saucier; the boulanger, who was responsible for the bread; the concise, who took care of the candy; the poissonier, who was responsible for all the fish and shellfish items. And then it got blurry from there, as she never realized how much there was to running just the kitchen.

There were people in white everywhere in the large meticulous galley, and yet no one was in anyone's way, and for the most part, the ones in charge got their points across without screaming what they wanted. When this part of the tour was done, he led her down the back stairs to the much quieter wine cellar, where she came face to face with wine racks that filled the stone walkthrough.

"As you can see, these here on both sides are all the wines and champagnes that are on the menu." The racks stood a full six feet high by about twelve feet across. He let her gaze across all the corked white and red wines. When she was through, she followed him to a separate section on the back wall where he stood solemnly.

Here he appeared to be a bit emotional as he gazed at the few wines that inhabited the rack. It had black painted steel locking bars that were meant to keep these apparently invaluable wines safe.

"You know I am a romantic at heart. And I do not necessarily mean between a man and a woman. I am romantic in life. I have always understood that life is precious and that we should remember these to keep us on the path to where we are going," Henri said before adding.

"These wines, the ones that are left, were left to me by my parents. They gave us a dozen bottles when we were wed in a small town outside of Limoges," he said these were to be for all the special moments in our lives.

"The very first bottle we used to celebrate our life together during our honeymoon in Barcelona. Not knowing yet what other special moments there might be, two of the bottles did vanish for the births of our two sons." He unlocked the bars and continued.

"Another two were added to fill our sons' dozen when they were both wed. One was for our first twenty-five years together, as man and wife. Then two were for the opening of our two boys' own restaurants, one in San Francisco and the other in Los Angeles." Here he began to get a little choked up.

"Four of these were not designated for anything. But this one was…" He fought back the tears, trying to finish what he was saying without becoming too emotional. He carefully lifted the bottle, and his hands shook as he handed it to her. She looked down at the label. It was a Bordeaux from 1950.

"You see this one bottle was to be for our fifty years together. But six years ago, we were no more, as my wife, Sabine, passed." He struggled to keep it together. Taylor even teared up as she was now emotionally drawn in.

Not wanting to drop the wine, she handed him the bottle and took a hold of his forearm until it looked as though he had regained his composure. He placed it back in its dusty cradle and locked it safely away again.

"I am sorry, Mademoiselle Taylor. These wines represent so much to me, and no one knows of this story. I must get you back to your party, but I just want you to know that most people look at wine as a party, to feel good or even mask their pains. I look at it differently. These wines epitomize the best moments, we have throughout life and would otherwise overlook, by moving past them too fast. Like I can see that you and Monsieur Lucas are very much in love, yes?"

She nodded as tears still inhabited the corners of her eyes. "Then we must get you back up to dinner then!" He grabbed a bottle of Bordeaux off the rack and had her follow him through the rear of the cellar up the stairs and was about to unlock the door.

Henri turned to her and added one last comment. "May your wine rack never be full and never be empty." She retook his arm as he went to exit before explaining.

"Henri, that was beautiful! Please tell me what it means."

He simply stated, "If your wine rack is full, it means you have never caught the special moments you have had in your life. If it is empty, then you have nothing to look forward to." He then opened the door, which was just a few feet from the entrance to the terrace.

She thought about the words he had just offered as he walked her back to the table. The impact of that grouping of words made her emote what it is she thought the Frenchman was saying. *It had nothing to do with wine!* Taylor reminded herself. Rejoining the party she sat, while Henri placed the bottle down and kissed Taylor's hand before leaving. Lucas peered over at her. "Are you all right?"

"Yes, I'm fine. I just didn't realize how much of a romantic Henri is."

Luke ordered for Taylor in her extended absence. As they conversed over wine and mini croissants, Taylor drifted again. The second part of Henri's phrase was calling her back. And never be empty, wow. Those words resonated like a beacon of light. Luke hadn't even noticed Taylor's odd behavior since she appeared to be there at the table with them drinking and nibbling.

The quartet of diners rose from the table, with the taste of the cuisine still massaging their taste buds. Luke went to pay, but of course, Henri never let the bill make its way to their table. And the bubbly Matteo was happy since he had a C-note tucked into his hand as they left.

They made a scheduled detour to the lower terrace again before they called it a night. Two other couples, who most likely had finished their dinner, partook of the grandeur of the marble fountain that stood there before them. Lucas, seeing it for the first time at night, checked it out in complete darkness.

He noticed Taylor being much more affectionate since the tour; however, he didn't question it. Taylor and Lucas, along with his parents, sat on separate wrought iron benches and looked at the spectacle that transformed, using the darkness as its backdrop.

It indeed was a sight to behold. They watched as the water shot up and trickled down across the bowl down to the other below. The mood lighting did primarily what it was meant to do.

Even his parents were drawn into the romance of the evening, forgetting that they had stepped off a plane four hours ago. Henri's had this strange way of making people feel like they were always celebrating. True, it wasn't France itself, but when you walked out of there with your belly full, and yes, your wallet empty, you knew you were in France even if it was just for a little while.

Lucas led Taylor a few feet from the base of the fountain when Taylor stopped him abruptly. The woman totally surprised him with a kiss that was not meant for show but as a sign of how she truly felt about him right at that very moment.

Anthony and Gia relished the affection that Taylor was showing toward their son. It was a romantic atmosphere here, as even the two of them could feel it. Lucas looked deeply into Taylor's eyes as they withdrew from the kiss, without a spoken word. Then eventually the four strolled out of the restaurant knowing that Henri had performed his magic once again.

During the hours when everyone slept, Taylor gazed up at the star speckled sky above, where she yielded a heavy blanket out on the deck. She hadn't looked at the stars like this since the night she was out with Luke at the overlook. With mixed sentiments for him and those of missing home too, she reflected.

Taylor pondered over her building on her new life here in Washington. Why was it that she had the most to think about in her life at a time when she didn't need to? Why was this such an quandary?

At times she felt as if her grandmother was trying to call her back to where she belonged. But with Lucas doing so well here, he wasn't about to call it quits and return with her, and she didn't want that either. So why can't she just be happy being here with him?

For the first time in her life outside of living with her parents, Taylor had found some real direction and not one that she wanted to divert from either. Maybe it's because she was going to be thirty-three soon, which only enabled her clock to tick louder.

Tears of joy and those of sorrow trickled down her face, as one quickly washed away the other. If she had to guess it would have been about her age that needed to stop so her new life could stand a chance. But Taylor knew that the world didn't work that way as she ran the fleece blanket across her dampened eyelashes.

She could never tell Lucas exactly how she felt because to be honest she wasn't sure herself. What she did know undoubtedly was that she loved him and that this was where she wanted to be, by his side.

The recent endearing wine comment from Henri was new for her. It subliminally made her think about life itself, like a dissection extruding each element to the surface and acknowledging them for what they truly were. Tonight, was a night to remember for many reasons. And it opened her eyes to where she stood in their relationship, to where she wanted to hold on tight and not let herself forget how meaningful this all is.

Lucas lifted his head off the pillow and reached across for his morning squeeze. With his hand feeling nothing but the sheets, he turned around seeing that her side of the bed was vacant.

Curious, he peeked down the hall at her standing in the kitchen with his mom. They were whispering, so as not to wake the men, while they cooked breakfast. He could make out the strong smell of bacon and coffee. The ladies halted their talk once they realized they had an audience.

"Did we wake you?" Luke's mom asked.

"No, I think it was the coffee," Luke said moving in close with a mug in hand, to pour himself some caffeinated joe. "You know we could eat breakfast later?" Lucas called out between sips.

"We couldn't sleep," his mother speedily replied. He looked at the clock. Six thirty and it was his day off? Why was he even up?

Taylor checked the bacon in the oven, while Gia sat still facing her. "Good morning, Mother!" he said as he placed a kiss on the side of her face.

"Good morning, Luke." He walked around the island and gave Taylor her morning peck too.

"How did you sleep?" he said to his girl.

"Fine," came the comment. Looking around, Luke asked, "So Dad's not up yet? That's a first."

"He's stirring. His arthritis is acting up. Sometimes he loses a lot of sleep over it. Actually, we both do!" Gia declared.

"So do you still want to take a cruise down the coast today?"

"We wouldn't miss that for the world, son," his mom said as his dad poked his head out the door and slowly hobbled his way out to join them. He sat on the stool nearest him.

"I swear it is getting harder and harder to get going in the morning," his dad intervened. Luke let out a smile. "Are you getting any pains from getting older yet, son?" his dad added.

"Well, I'm not sure if it's from getting older as much as the work that is doing it."

Taylor brought a cup of coffee over to Tony. "Do you want anything in it?"

"No, just hot and black."

Luke called his dad out to the deck. He followed right behind still with a bit of a limp, out to the barely lit day. The brisk air had his dad close the door behind them, so the cooling air didn't flood the warmth of the house. When they were both standing along the railing with sea in the forefront, Lucas opened his wallet and extracted a check. His father was about to comment on it when he realized it was for the flights, he had booked for the two of them. "Thanks, son!"

While looking out over the ocean, Tony asked, "So when are you going to propose?"

"Soon. I am just looking for a special time when it feels right."

"I understand that, but you don't want to wait too long, you know," he said as he looked back, making sure the door was closed so that their secret was still their secret.

"It will be soon. I know Taylor is still in conflict over staying here in Seattle. Even though she doesn't have her whole family living close together, she has ties to there that she continues to fight with. I just need to know she is ready before I ask," Lucas stated.

"Son, every man that has ever asked their woman to marry them has this momentary fear that they might say no. I had it, but when you get that yes, nothing else in the world can take away from it. Besides, I know that she is very much into you. And she gets along great with her future in-laws. How good is that?"

"Yes, it's going to happen soon, old man!" Luke quipped. The two made their way back into the house. He happened to open the door, just as he said, "I am going to check the weather. I know there is a chance of a storm for today, just north of here."

The men got hit square in the face from the cacophony of smells that played with their nostrils. Tony smelled food too but didn't see them on the stove. "Everything smells great. Are we having eggs?"

"No, your wife turned it into a quiche. I hope that is all right?" Taylor questioned.

"Are you kidding me, I would eat mud if she prepared it. Only she could make it delectable."

"But what if I cooked the rest?" Taylor said playfully. "Look, little lady, I remember where you came from. You learned from your grandmother, and that makes you a very good—no, great cook."

Taylor knew she was all right when it came to cooking, but it was nice to hear. Lucas never complained. Seeing it was time to eat, she went to the fridge as Gia began to parade the food out to the table.

In the silence Luke's mother recalled early this morning when she woke and went to the kitchen for a little something to drink, which was a nightly complication of the medicine she took. During her return to bed, the woman felt a cold breeze that coursed through the slit of the open slider.

As she reached out to close and lock it, she barely made out Taylor, who was wrapped in a blanket, sitting on one of the chairs. Looking around, the woman grabbed an afghan from the couch before accompanying her in the darkness.

It wasn't apparent to Gia that she had been crying since Taylor began with her whispering about the man that meant so very much to both of them. Before long, any sign of tears were gone, with the inspiring talk about Alaska, Florida, and everywhere in between. Gia remained neutral even as she was glad to see that Luke had someone in his life that she now knew loved him.

Right before breakfast, Taylor was checking on the quiche when she got a text from her gal pal Lauren. Sometime soon, they were going to continue the conversation that they hadn't finished last time. And she knew that if anyone could make her walk in the right direction again, it was her.

Lauren always had her back, even when her last relationship with Marty started out. But Taylor was in love. At least she thought so. But because of that Taylor never saw the man for who he really was, even though Lauren had.

She was love stuck, and after years of not realizing it, it finally reared itself and hit her both barrels, right between the eyes. She did everything she could to prove to herself that the self-awareness she now acquired was as sharp as a tack.

The four chowed on the few item buffet before them. It was hard to believe that this same group could eat anything, after the meals they consumed last night, including the two new appetizers that Matteo said were from Henri, wanting their opinion. And at the end, a crème brûlée and even a lemon soufflé made its way out to them.

The morning ocean tour had to be postponed until the evening as the storm did move through from late morning to later in the afternoon. They would have done it tomorrow, but the visiting

Calderone's were set to drive into northern California for the week before heading back here and flying home the following Sunday.

Shortly before bedtime, the boat teetered against the swells that surrounded it. Luke's parents were up front, feasting on the panoramic view of the coast from the sea, as the lights illuminated not just Luke's backyard but the one's abutting it. The brighter lights even created a reflective glow that sat atop of the water producing a visual masterpiece.

The cruise was pretty much silent as their senses were tested, like the lights and the sights, the waves, the salt from the ocean, and even the light breeze as it tried to go through them, unobstructed.

Tony lightly manned the wheel with Gia seated off to his left. Luke and Taylor, in the meantime sat cuddled up on the white-and-blue leather bench at the rear of the cockpit. A blanket that was loosely wrapped around them helped the two fight the chill of the night ocean air as Taylor's hair whipped around like a flag on a mast.

"I want my parents to stay longer!" Lucas exclaimed loud enough for her alone. Taylor thought it was strange that she was hearing this with her wanting to talk it out, but this conversation was not for now. She just nodded in agreement appeasing the man, who should be happy he has his family here with him now instead of missing them before they're gone.

Luke's dad piloted the craft cautiously, knowing this was a casual evening cruise. The boat clearly looked as though it was designed for the warmth of summer, with it able to control the open waters with abundant speed and manageability. As for Anthony, it had been some time since he had driven a boat in the ocean with Point Hope being the last place.

The saltwater had Tony thinking back to the summers at the Point, which were magnificent, with the grass being its bright green up against the many other hues that the town possessed. It's too bad it was so cold, with the real summer beauty being a couple of months out of the year. Yet after returning from the funeral, he could see them visiting again.

Anthony started the engine, before heading back to the boathouse. Maybe in September, when they return to Seattle, Luke could play hooky for a day or two. At the restaurant, they even heard Luke saying that the two of them would like to fly down this winter to darken their doorway. He hoped so, as he looked over at Gia who was buried in a gray wool blanket, with her face barely poking through.

Luke talked his parents into borrowing their car, with him using the company truck to resolve their single vehicle dilemma. The visit might have been short, but it was evident that it left both the parents and their son wanting more. His parents set a tentative Friday the earliest or Saturday the latest as the date of their return, so at least they could have another day or so together.

The next morning, they handed out hugs and kisses as they sent his parents on their way with a small cooler of drinks and a bag of snacks. With the truck down out of view, the two turned and walked at a snail's pace back to the house hand in hand. Lucas was very quiet as he sat silently on the couch. Taylor squeezed in next to him slowly, seeing he looked as though he needed his space.

She didn't know what to do and what not to do, as there appeared to be an impenetrable wall around him. Her hand covered his as he sat like a mannequin. She nuzzled, bringing her lips up toward his. Taylor made a move, and Lucas didn't even acknowledge it. She got up and kissed him on the lips and said, "I'll be in the bedroom if you want to talk."

Of course, she was taking his actions or inactions personally with all kinds of things popping into her head. *It is because of me. I touched his project. I am driving him crazy with the way I need to be doing more to keep busy,* just to name a couple. She climbed into bed and turned out all but one light. She lay there for an hour before, her eyelids closed for the last time, while she waited for him to come and talk.

Lucas snapped out of his depression long enough to see that Taylor was not there. He headed to a lockbox that he had buried in the rear of the bottom drawer of the filing cabinet. Luke took out a small notepad that had all the changes he wanted to make, and they all included Taylor being there with him. As he sat at the desk, he also extracted a ring box, which contained a one carat stone and a beautiful setting that held it tight.

The guy had to remain focused and pay attention to details to help keep his thoughts straight. He entertained the idea of bringing Trent in as his partner again. He still wasn't crazy about the guy moving back into town and putting his name alongside his on the business card. But the changes he needed to set in motion were taking too long.

Lucas took the ring box in hand, studying its golden band and stones. He paced and even walked down to the bedroom to make a proposal that couldn't be rationalized as a great idea by either of them tonight. He was about to enter through the nearly closed door when he saw her fast asleep.

It was a fool's notion, and as special as he wanted this to be for her, this wasn't going to be it. He knew that he had become withdrawn, and even more so he was attuned to her seeing it too. It was just that he had so much on his mind. After placing the ring and the notebook under lock and key again, he gave into his depression, one that had him quietly climbing in bed beside her.

The morning was a reticent one, with Lucas having no real answers for an equally quiet Taylor. She drove him to work and dropped him off at the site, leaving the man with a tender kiss before she did. Each of them wanted to be the first to get the ball rolling, but it never happened.

There he watched as her taillights disappeared around the security fencing. It was going to be a long day with his personal life that he knew would be hindering his work. Luke also knew by the end of the day that Taylor was going to want to talk, and he didn't have any answers yet.

Getting home this late, he wondered if Taylor was still awake. Turning onto his road, he squirmed as his back was throbbing. Earlier with his mind somewhere else, he hadn't paid attention to what he was doing, and to no surprise, he tweaked his back. It wasn't anything serious, and he wasn't going to use this as an excuse to put off their inevitable talk. He still was quite unsure as to what he was about to say to Taylor. But she deserved an answer.

Lucas came around the last corner as he saw not only the front light on but the one on the porch too. As he climbed out of the truck, trying not to wince in pain, he noticed Taylor sitting on the swing. He pulled at the door handle and dropped his head before the screen door closure emotionally and physically locked him in the bullring. He reluctantly opened his mouth and said, "I think we need to talk."

"I think so too," she answered wanting to know what was wrong and equally as scared to find out.

"I have done a lot of thinking about life lately."

Taylor sat motionless as he paused before continuing. "First of all, I am very sorry I didn't let you in last night. I have had so many things on my mind lately that they have been clouding over what's good and what's real with us."

She sat as a wave of uncertainty swept over her. Maybe she didn't want to know. Maybe her perception of them was different from Luke's the entire time. "I don't know exactly why, but my life has changed because of you. And I'm not saying it as a bad thing, but I know the things that have been troubling you are getting me too," he said, pausing long enough for a breather.

"Taylor, I know you miss your family, and it reminds me of how families should be, you know, close. I am working out some things, but I think we both need to see our family more." She nodded, slowly agreeing.

"I do want you to stay with me here, but it is important that my work doesn't interfere with our life too." She stopped him right there by pulling him to sit on the swing.

She looked at him with a stray tear moving down her face and said, "I am not going anywhere. I think it is wonderful of you to realize how important being with your family is. And I couldn't be happier that you continue to look out for my welfare, even though you are pushing your own needs aside, sometimes in the process. I will be fine. You make sure of that," she paused, letting him absorb what she had said. "So are we okay then?" she asked wanting to know the answer.

"We are," Luke exclaimed. "But I really want to see my parents in the fall or winter if that is all right?"

"I insist that we do. Just let me know when and I will be there with you!" Taylor exclaimed.

"Thanks, baby," he stated. Taylor rubbed his leg, wedging herself closer to Lucas. They swung for almost an hour, not saying a word. She wanted so much to tell Lucas about his soon-to-be celebration, even though she still felt that it needed to be kept a surprise.

Taylor slept in, as Luke insisted, feeling guilty about the pressures he invoked, even though that evening they didn't fight. He also made sure that she wasn't doing anything business related today by seizing the business cell from her too. She awoke aware that the two might have hit a speed bump but were back on their way down the same path.

With a whole day to herself, Taylor arose eventually not adhering to the schedule that she ordinarily had set for herself. This vacation day was the ideal day to notify all the potential guests, of the party or the change of date for those that already had been asked.

It was probably a good time to call her best friend before she switched roles becoming the teacher to her two oldest. Lauren had said she was going to do it until the kids were fighting it too much or when she felt teaching the soon-to-be three was too hard to handle. After waiting for Lauren to pick up, Taylor left a message.

# CHAPTER 15

Forty-five minutes later, her phone rang. "What's up, girlfriend?" she asked even though Lauren already knew by the few-word text.

"Well, I'm having the party I was talking about for Luke."

"And it is still on his birthday on that Saturday?" Lauren interrupted.

"No, I had to change it to that Friday. But wait, do you have a few minutes?"

"Sure honey, I've got the kids stuck to the walls with Velcro." Taylor cackled but pictured it anyway.

"You know how I was talking about opening the vault up for this?"

"Yes, the piggy bank," Lauren corrected.

"Well, there is a client of his that is going to cater the whole thing for us, for free."

"Are you kidding, why?"

"It's a long story, but he keeps saying that he owes his popularity of the restaurant to Luke. Basically, it would not have thrived without all the visual changes Luke had made to his place."

"For real? Luke did a job and got paid for it, and he is still reaping the benefits?" Lauren said in amazement.

"Yes, and a couple of times we went out to dinner there, he never let us pay the bill."

"Wow, I want to see this place. It must be a Taj Mahal."

Taylor snorted. "It's French Lauren!"

"All right, it must be an Eiffel Tower then!"

"There you go. Hey, I know you are busy, but I am free to talk later because I wanted to know if you and Carl could make it?"

"We're in, but you know he has only met us once. Is that okay?"

"I want you there!" Taylor pleaded.

"Then it's done! Maybe I can even come in a few days early to help you with stuff."

"But there won't be any stuff to do," Taylor phrased.

"Great, more time for us to drink!"

"All right, I'm not saying we won't enjoy ourselves, but you have to remember that I am on the clock with Lucas and he can't know you are in town either. It could spoil the surprise."

"I understand! I will be in on Tuesday night, and Carl will probably get there a couple of days later."

Taylor was ecstatic that her best friend was heading to town. "Girl, I've got to go, but we will talk soon, okay?" Lauren said.

"And maybe I will tell you about the idiotic thing I did."

"No, you have to tell me now, please," Lauren begged.

"No, get back to your kids, Lauren. Call me soon!"

"Okay. Talk to you, Taylor," Lauren said, surrendering.

"Bye."

This had the making of a very long call. Taylor, of course, was going to let it slip on the story of her untimely stupidity. But all her friend was going to hear is kinky, kinky, kinky.

Taylor, for some odd reason in the noiseless house, imagined Lauren with an alter ego. A stay-at-home mom by day and dominatrix by night. In each case, she would rule. She visualized her friend as she snapped the whip to get the attention of her submissive, while wearing a tight leather corset that showed off her still great bod, even though it previously had been used as a launchpad, as Lauren often referred to it, to birth her three kids.

Taylor braked, knowing she wasn't going to get anything done if she didn't start soon. In the process, she thought briefly about Luke, prevising that family does matter, with it being every bit as important as his work.

The fact that it's just surfacing now was no real barn burner either. But Taylor was astonished that there hadn't been some form of verbal disagreement or squabble yet between her and Luke. With Marty... Taylor cut off that thought before she could finish it.

After a full day, Taylor popped the cork on a bottle of Moscato. All the calls and texts were done, and most gave a yes, with a couple that had to get back to her. And for her, it was time to celebrate. It really looked like her man was in line to have that party. She reached over and poured her standard six ounces and a second light pour as a pat on the back for her excellent job, following it by raising the glass to her lips.

Instead of consuming it the way she had been accustomed, she savored the sweet wine. Closing her eyes, she thought, what should this bottle represent? She didn't pretend to compare it to the sentimental quote of Henri, but the realization of one of its extrusions, that for her being, to notice an accomplishment, both in work and her own life. This one was for so many things, but it foremost had to be about a second chance with Lucas, although many would say it was their first.

If she had chosen a different path, she definitely would have looked at Lucas differently. Standing there, the woman viewed the wine again as it sloshed around the bowl of the stemware. Lucas would not have been just Kyle's best friend, but something that she would have focused on, with there being maybe another fifteen years of bondage. Drip!

Taylor prayed Luke would be home early, with something good for dinner. She didn't feel like slaving over a hot stove tonight. Wow! Slaving and bondage basically in the same breath. She smirked, rehashing the images of a few days ago. That project of Luke's had gotten her so turned on, until the fear of being trapped set in, and then not so much.

The brunette yearned to be locked to the bondage horse again. She wanted to be shackled tight and maybe spanked for her punishment. But there was no way that Taylor was openly going to come right out with it, asking to be punished, for the second time, with the first being at the inn. More than ever, she hoped that he would read her mind.

A truck pulled into the drive. Taylor didn't recognize it. Lucas walked into the house a minute later carrying a wet brown bag with the contents of an Italian meal, with him being every bit as soaked as the food. "I forgot you had the work truck this week."

"Yeah, it was strange for me also. I'm having problems with the clutch, so remind me that we have to get this one into the shop when my parents get back." Taylor was good for that. She didn't have to set alarms or write herself notes to remember things she had to do, even though she did just forget about the truck switcheroo.

"So how did your day go?" she asked.

"The beginning was rough, but I would have to say it finished on a good note."

"I figured so, with you being home so early," Taylor said.

"Yes, but don't expect that tomorrow. Inspection day again. It's almost done, and then we will all be out in Monroe. Oh, did you call on the conduit mix-up?" Luke asked.

"Yes, they said they would drop off the order first thing tomorrow and pick up the other items. They said you are getting an extra 20 percent discount for their screwup."

"Good that should more than cover this morning's mistake that we made."

"What happened?"

"You know, I only want to talk about sitting down to a plate of osso buco and a bowl of zuppa Toscana."

"Hey, isn't that what your mom makes?"

"Not, the same, my mom's is better, but this isn't half bad," he claimed.

"So you wish she was still here?"

"No, I wish she was in this kitchen doing what she does best in those pots and pans over there," Luke phrased. Taylor went over and grabbed a couple of plates and a glass and poured some of her world observances into its belly, while Luke took out the foam containers and placed it gently in the center of the table. He fondled her ass as he passed by her to retrieve the utensils they would need.

Luke leaned back in his chair and undid his pants as the containers sat empty between them, leaving only a little bit of the pork juices that he couldn't scoop out. Taylor didn't indulge nearly as much, knowing that Lucas needed his fix.

"Wow, you really do miss your mom, huh?" Taylor stated making him aware that that meal could have fed them twice.

"Yes, you know I do," Lucas answered, somewhat embarrassed as to the damage he had done.

Taylor, with the horse and punishment still taking up residence in her mind, contemplated how she would break the ice, without it making her look like she wanted it. She relished the last sip in her glass. She was tipsy, considering she only had a half bottle of wine in the last couple of hours.

"You know, Luke, I do want you to know that I am very sorry about the way you found me Friday night!" she said on a genius whim.

"What are you talking about, the way that I found you?"

She looked at him oddly since she knew that he couldn't have possibly forgotten. "I mean, I shouldn't have looked at your file and—"

"Yes, you shouldn't have looked at it and unlocked the project I was working on for you. And you shouldn't have gotten ensnared in it. Is that what you were going to say?" Lucas said now sitting up straight.

"Well, yes, I apologize immensely. I was just so curious that I guess I did those things. Will you ever forgive me?"

Lucas sat quiet reaching for the words. "Taylor, you will not be getting your punishment tonight. I am not hurt, but I am surprised that not the girlfriend part of you, but the submissive part didn't listen to me. But I assure you that when you do get the punishment that you so rightly deserve, there won't be any warning, and all you will be able to say is 'Yes, sir!'"

She was enraptured by the talk that he wielded to her. Taylor thought and then replied, "I understand. It was wrong that you had to come home with your parents and see me helplessly strapped across the horse that you had built. I mean, if they weren't there, you could have done anything to me, anything. And heaven forbid, what if I had been naked?"

"Touché, Taylor, I would have to declare this one a draw," he said as his package wanted out from his pants and from under the table. "With that being said, there will not be any punishment tonight. Besides, I'm too full." She cackled at that, and he joined in.

But rest assured both knew that one of them was going to be handing out the punishment and the other would be receiving it. And there was no doubt that both were going to be overjoyed when it finally does.

Wednesday, her phone rang just after 9:00 a.m. while in the middle of cleaning the house for his parents' return. She was surprised as it was them calling her. "Hello," she said, catching it before it went to voice mail.

"Hello, Taylor. This is Gia."

She already knew but continued. "So how is your week going?"

"Oh, fine, just fine. Hey, the reason I'm calling is to see if it would be all right if we got back today?" Taylor looked at the house, sizing up what she had to finish.

"Um, that would be great. What time do you think you will be here?"

"Tony, what time would you say?" Gia delayed just long enough to get the answer. "We will be back at around eleven twenty, I mean if that's all right?"

"No, I'm looking forward to seeing you guys. Lucas will be so surprised."

She hung up and went straight to work. The clock on the wall over the desk didn't lie, she had to get this place back in shape soon. An hour later, she put the last items in place after the floors dried that is.

Not wanting to appear disheveled, her shower was the last thing she did. Coming out with a sensible outfit on, she twisted and formed a quick braid for her hair. The mirror was kind enough to agree with her that she did at least look presentable. With whatever remaining time she had, she decided to open the task manager again. It wasn't to work on but to be used as a refresher to get some insight from them hopefully.

Like clockwork, Tony and Gia drove into the driveway with Luke's truck within a few minutes of what they had said. Gia waited outside her door as Tony grabbed their suitcase from the rear seat. "Wow, what a lovely day," Gia said as she saw Taylor coming through the screen door.

Taylor threw up her arms and wrapped her limbs around the woman who had made sure her husband was all set before coming in. "Oh, honey, we barely pulled out of here, and Tony was complaining that he hadn't spent enough time with Lucas."

Her husband spoke up right away. "Mother, please. She doesn't need to hear what it was that you thought I said," Tony stated with a grin as they all headed in. The two entered the porch as Taylor held the door. Gia went right in and sat at the dining table, watching the hot water bounce off the tea bag that the lady of the house was pouring. She sat with Tony, pulling up a chair once his hands were bag free.

"So what did you two do this week?" Taylor inquired.

"Well, we stopped in to see our friends in Portland and then we saw some of the sights."

"I thought you were mentioning heading into California."

"Well, Gia missed her baby so much, I was lucky that I got her that far."

"Tony!"

"You know I'm only kidding dear. We or I thought about it and decided we should spend some time with you. I mean we are on the phone together all the time, and I think this is much better, don't you?" Taylor nodded in agreement, flashing her signature smile. "And that's why our boy is so crazy about you. Your smile lights up the room!" Tony added.

"You Calderone boys, I don't know about you."

With the lull in the conversation, Gia piped in, "So how are the birthday plans coming?"

"I think everything is in place. I haven't had any definite yesses yet, but I just set the date and contacted everyone yesterday. What I am having the most trouble with though is a present for Luke. I mean, we have only started dating so I don't think it should be anything too expensive. However, I do want it to be something he will use, you know, something special."

"Wow, that is a tough one. Maybe something for Luke's boat," Tony commented.

"I bought him a very nice dress shirt because he looks so nice when he's dressed up. The other thing is I think he needs a belt. He has this old stretched used-to-be-black, holes are too-big, dress belt."

Tony cut her off. "I know it well, it used to be mine." Noticing Taylor standing there with her foot in her mouth, he promptly added, "I used to be thin like Luke, but fine Italian cooking for all those years, and that is how that belt got to be that way."

"Okay. Don't I feel awkward," Taylor said, somewhat embarrassed.

"Don't. Tony had that belt for a lot of years, but Lucas didn't let him toss it out when it became an eyesore. Lucas thought it was the coolest thing," Gia said, trying to appease her comment.

"Then how about a belt made from fine Italian leather? I know I always wanted one of those," Tony stated. Taylor's eyes lit up the fraction of a second when a beam of light from a lighthouse crosses your path.

"Oh, that's it. I'm not sure how much time I have on this, but what if I order one online from Italy? That would be more symbolic. Do you think he would like that?"

"I think he would like that a lot," Gia proclaimed.

"Look, I know you two just got here, but is there any way I can check this out? I will need to order it now and hope I can get it in time."

"No, go, dear. We will need a nap after that long drive today anyway. We can help you later, and I will still have time to throw a lasagna together for all of us tonight."

"Lucas will love that! Thank you!" Taylor exclaimed as they left the table with Gia, waving to her to get to it. Using the tablet, she typed "leather belts made in Italy" into the search bar as soon as it was ready.

She was surprised that there were more than a few that do this. Taylor clicked on the link to one of the southern villages just outside of Florence, where Tony had said both of their families were from. She was pretty sure that this was the one. Since the belt was coming from Italy, it was only right that she made it even more personal for him.

She tapped on a link. It loaded up very slow as she awaited its completion. It was like watching grass grow until the site finally came on. The main header with some of the home screen text loaded up, blurry at first, before eventually focusing.

The other text, followed by thumbnail pics, took their sweet time loading. She finally clicked on Italian-crafted belts. And in what felt like ten minutes later came pictures and descriptions of nearly thirty styles of belts. The first page had only ones that she didn't mind skimming past.

After going on to the next page, she saw something that she fell in love with. The dress belt she had chosen, was a braided solid black dress belt, Italian leather, of course. Because of the texture, it was very eye-catching. The braid she thought resembled many thin strands of rope. It was available in two colors or a two-toned brown with black.

Taylor added two more things to the cart before finishing the order. She did pay extra to have it shipped, where it should be here about two weeks earlier. It was also linked to a tracking number that would go into effect once it made it to the United States.

The woman got to the last page after filling out all her information and pushed submit, making her want to run into the other bedroom and wake up Tony and Gia. She decided against that with her wanting to wait until they made their way out on their own. Besides, Taylor still wanted to get an opinion on the shirt.

She took a screenshot of the confirmation number before she exited the site. Taylor wondered what good that would do, with the company being fifteen thousand miles away.

Later, she had to make a point of parking the truck in the garage so that Lucas would get the full surprise. She never saw a vehicle in there yet, but Taylor figured out first hand why that was, with there not being room for that and his bondage equipment.

She reheated the water for the tea again, with her thinking it barely having time to get cold. Taylor sat on the love seat, looking at the sun-drenched lawn, when Gia exited from the spare bedroom.

After setting her up with a fresh cup of Earl Grey, she had to show Gia what she found and subsequently ordered.

"You don't know it, but Tony's parents were from there. He and I lived a little more than ten miles from that same village." She was happy for Taylor because Lucas was going to be happy. Taylor sat back a little proud of herself. She knew the rough vicinity, and now just hearing it made the purchase that much sweeter.

"Tony is going to be excited about it also. You may not be able to get him to stop talking about home, though. But it's your choice on whether you want to tell him or not," Gia said joking, but not really. Taylor thought it was amazing that after forty years that they still referred to Italy as home.

"Hey, we need to get food for tonight's dinner. Anthony will be sleeping for a while. Should we go to the store now?"

Taylor knew that Gia didn't drive, so she suggested, "If you make me out a list, I will run for what you want."

"Don't be silly, we can both go. Anthony will be fine here until we get back."

"Okay, then let's go." They left a note and grabbed their pocketbooks and went out and climbed into the cab of the truck. Taylor adjusted all the mirrors and then put it into reverse. Gia didn't speak again until the Ford F-150 was moving in a forward direction.

Tony limped his way to the door. It was very quiet, and he wondered what kind of trouble the two women could be getting into, in his absence. He was incredibly sore after the morning's drive, and it was one of those pains that had to be temporarily healed by his prescription that only his wife would be able to find.

Gia would always tell her husband where it was, but after so many times and so many years, he thought that she had to put it some place different because he could never locate it himself. He tried looking for them most of the time with Gia's directions, and he still couldn't come up with it.

He did, however, see the note on the table and then his question was answered. He then turned around to spy his favorite cushy chair, which happened to be Taylor's favorite too. He ended up parking himself in the love seat by the window admiring the afternoon sea side view.

Tony who was absorbed in a magazine, when he heard the garage door open and then close thirty seconds later. As two voices became louder, Taylor eventually passed through the door, carrying four paper bags. "Did you pay for the food?" Tony asked his wife as it sounded like this was well thought out in advance.

"No, she wouldn't let me!" Gia said, sounding slightly flustered.

"No, you are our guest this week, and do you think Luke would let you pay?" Taylor asked.

"Probably not," said his mother.

"Okay, then we would like to take you out for lunch tomorrow," Tony declared and then added, "You and Gia can sample the grape, and I can be your designated driver."

"Now, that sounds wonderful, but I still have to check with Lucas first though. I am working right now, even though it doesn't look like it," she said quietly of a job that for the most part didn't have much to it.

"Then we will ask him tonight, if he says you can't go, then I will insist that we take you two out to dinner."

"Hey, you two can fight about it, but I really like the grape thing," Taylor said pausing just long enough to change the subject. "Hey, I did want to talk more about your son's party?"

"Okay, go ahead, honey?" Gia said, not knowing what they didn't talk about during the whole time they were gone.

"Well, I was wondering if you two will be able to make it to the party?"

"Well, we did talk about it, and we will be there!" Tony confirmed.

"Fantastic. I am going to block off some rooms for all the out-of-town guests for two nights at the Grand Allusea. I would like to pay for your room. Your friend Henri is paying for the catering, and I want to take some of the savings and do this. You will be springing for more flights, which I wish I could help you with."

"Taylor, don't worry about it. I will dip into our bonus miles, and if you want to pay for the room, then we appreciate it. We are not going to fight you every time!" Tony exclaimed.

Gia feverishly worked to prepare the sauce, so it would have hours to simmer. She tried to join in on the conversation as her backup accompaniment buzzed from the nonstop electric can opener.

To save on time, she opened and added the sauce, paste, and the cans of crushed tomatoes into the large stockpot. Gia even used a dozen fresh ones from Taylor's Garden. The stockpot sat upon the gas range, standing tall above the gas flames below. On the second pass, Tony and Taylor retrieved more of the veggies for tonight's salad.

She didn't much mind not being out there. She was in her element, cooking for her men. It was what she always did, since that is what she was taught. She stirred the recipe after adding the fresh garlic, salt, sugar, oregano, and basil.

Gia smelled after each step, so she knew how much of each ingredient to add into the mixture. The tomatoes of the Pacific Northwest added a succulent flavor that she welcomed as one of her items of making a perfect sauce by first smelling a wedge and then tasting it. Since she took the easy route of not making her own pasta, she at least was going to have fresh bread for this evening.

Tony held the tray as Taylor stripped the plants leaving only the unripe or underdeveloped. He caught his heel as he backed out of the garden box, forgetting the wood frame was right behind him. Taylor picked up the tomatoes that managed to roll from the tray and, with the help of gravity, made their way successfully to the ground. "Let me help you with those," Taylor said as she plucked up the rest of the produce from the ground.

With the tray steadied, he commented, "I just thought I would let you know that Gia wants to teach you some of her recipes."

"I would love that. And I didn't know if you knew, but Luke and I have been talking seriously about visiting you this fall or winter. I think he wants to make it at least a week."

"Both of you? Coming to see us?" Tony said following it with, "But what about going to see your folks too?"

"He said we should be going to see them around the beginning of March."

"That will be good. After seeing your mom again, I realized how much she looks like your grandmother."

"Well, thank you," she said, not knowing what to say to that. There were some facial similarities, but she found it hard to compare anyone to her grandmother when she was alive. And now with her being gone, Grandma is even more saintly to her.

When back in the kitchen, the tray came to rest on the island. "Getting back on topic, what day do you want us in Seattle?"

"The party is on Friday, September the sixteenth. But I think if you fly that day, you might not be able to make it on time. Plus, you will be exhausted from the flight."

"Well, we will look at it, but maybe we can come in a day or two earlier. We will pay for the extra nights, and then we can help you with whatever you need."

"That would work. Oh, and I am planning on picking up Luke at work that day. He could be working nearby or many miles away, so I will figure it out when it gets closer," Taylor stated before pausing. "So I'm putting you both down as yesses?"

"Yes," they both said in unison.

Gia went over to the stove and stirred the batch. Its fantastic aroma was now filling the room. "My good friend Lauren and her husband, Carl, will be in early too. She will be in on Tuesday, so you would have someone to visit with if I'm busy with work. She is a real hoot. I am getting very excited now, so I hope this all remains a secret."

"Don't worry about us, Taylor, we are the king and queen of keeping secrets," Tony proclaimed.

# CHAPTER 16

Lucas pushed through the door as he was greeted kindly by his past, in the form of a heavenly and distinct aroma. He recognized it immediately to be that of the scent of Italian. Turning, he looked over at Taylor, stirring slowly at a red sauce as he inched in behind her.

He was confounded. And now he was even getting a whiff of a freshly baked bread. "Taylor, what's going on?" he questioned as he took hold of the wooden spoon that he stood up in the center of the pot.

"What are you talking about?"

He spied the room one more time. "Well, I smell my mother's cooking and…" He paused long enough to pull her back so he could turn on the oven light, catching the sight of lasagna and a nearly finished loaf of bread. "I am pretty sure that you have never baked bread before."

After a very brief silence, a round of laughter came up from behind him. The two moved in to join the party. "So you're saying I don't cook as good as your mother?" Taylor questioned. He didn't want to have to go there but decided to just the same.

"No, what I am saying is that you can't cook this meal as good as my mother," carefully emphasizing his words.

Gia gave her son a quick kiss and hug. "Thanks, Mom." She thought it was for the meal when he actually meant thanks for being here. His dad made his way still chuckling. "So why did you guys get back so early?"

"Well, we ended up going to Portland, and we just missed you!"

"Well then, I'm glad you are back because tonight I am eating the best lasagna in Seattle."

"Don't get too excited. I bought the noodles," his mom, Gia, confessed.

"Mom, I would eat anything if it had your sauce on it!" Luke stated.

"I'm hoping the meal is much better than that," mom joked back.

Luke joyously thought back to when he was young and when the winters never seemed to let up. He would come home chilled to the bone to that same glorious smell that had a warming effect from the second he stepped in the door. If it hadn't been for his metabolism, he surely would have had a serious weight problem.

His parents were drinking wine for the prelude and during the meal while Taylor switched over to tequila. Luke did the same as he partook but at a sip for taste pace, not the drink for drunk and get horny one that they had followed before.

When his last bite consumed, Lucas let out a series of grunts of enjoyment. Lucas undoubtedly felt like he must have gained five pounds. It was so worth it, though. He pushed back from the table, seeing a gauntlet laying there on the table before him.

He stared at a four by four-inch square of layered pasta sat in the corner of the baking dish, taunting him as it cooled with each passing second. His better judgment took hold and said leave it for another day. "You know, Mom, I still don't know how you do it!"

"Yes, it was incredible, Mrs. Calderone," Taylor added.

"Please call me Gia."

"Yes, Gia!" Taylor dittoed.

"So do you two have anything planned for tomorrow?" asked Lucas.

"Well, we were thinking about taking your best girl out to lunch, but she says she is working," Tony stated.

"No, she's not. She phoned in with a personal day," Luke answered as Taylor smiled through her own pain. She too indulged more than she should have and thought it was supposed to be a little lasagna and a little bread, not seconds to boot. "So do you know where it is you want to go?"

"No, I personally only want there to be an assortment of menu choices," his dad asked.

"Okay…there is Campbell's diner, which is just down the street from where I'm at tomorrow. I would like to join you guys if I can get away," Luke answered.

"Oh, you're welcome to come, but I already told Taylor that we are paying."

"That's fine," Lucas blurted out as he saw Taylor nodding for him to agree to it.

The following day Taylor and Luke's parents were about to pull into to the diner after they had driven past the site. "Really?" Taylor answered into her phone in disappointment. The passengers figured by her demeanor that it wasn't four for lunch today, and also noticed that she wasn't all right with it either. "Okay, bye!" she said disappointedly. She gently placed the phone down on the console next to her.

"Lucas won't be joining us today?" Gia asked.

"No, something came up, and I don't know."

"This diner does it serve alcohol?" Tony hoped.

"I am not sure, maybe not," answered Taylor.

"Well, I did volunteer to be your designated driver today, so take us to a place so that I can get you some."

Taylor stopped at the parking lot of the Holey Donut and searched for restaurants in the area while trying to cover up her last outward display. They immediately all decided on barbeque, which happened to be a couple of miles up the road. Taylor was happy earlier that she was without work today but got equally excited when she thought there was a chance that Luke would be joining them.

She kept her feeling to herself knowing that it will always be like this. Oh, he might have a day when he could probably slide out for an hour here and there, but she would never be able to pinpoint the exact one. Just another thing that was continuing to claw at her. And that prompted a fear of having a lavish party with no birthday boy in attendance.

In a booth, the three studied the menu. The waitress came over as Tony rapidly called for a pitcher of sangria, seeing today a couple for each wasn't going to do it. He ordered an iced tea for himself anticipating that he will have to be the designated driver. After the waitress turned toward the kitchen, Tony asked, "Taylor is everything all right?"

She was pissed that she hadn't kept her face from showing how she was feeling. Taylor liked them a lot but didn't want to have to explain that their son's barely being around in the spring, summer, and fall was already causing a rift. And because of that she didn't want to say that she might be beginning to question their relationship

"Taylor, are you okay?" Gia said thinking that maybe she didn't hear her husband.

"I'm sorry. I just wanted to have a nice meal out, with just the four of us, that's all."

"And that's all that is bothering you?" the woman asked.

"Well, I am apprehensive that I am having a party for him next month, and he might not be able to make it. And then there is no guarantee that some of his employees that I invited will be able to attend either." Taylor felt as though she was going to start crying. The waitress returned, placing the pitcher and glasses in front of them.

"Are you ready to order?" the waitress asked. Tony could see that the young lady was in distress on the other side of the bench, so he did it.

"Can we have the special for three please?"

The waitress read back the order, making sure it was what they wanted. "Okay, you want the pulled pork, beef brisket, and beef short ribs, along with cornbread, beans, and slaw, for three? Is that right?"

"That sounds good, but can you make it for four, please? We love leftovers," Tony stated, upping it before she left the table.

"That will be for four," the waitress said while collecting the menus. With the waitress gone, they had to get back to the problem at hand.

"I'm sure he will be there and on time, and you will have the guests there also," Gia said even though she couldn't even convince herself. "Is this what this is all about?" Gia quickly added.

"Yes and no. You both know how I feel about your son, and I think he feels the same about me too."

Tony stopped her to say something. "Taylor, you have got to know that he is crazy about you. Luke and I talk all the time, and he is head over heels for you!"

Taylor interrupted, "I mean I shouldn't be saying this, but I wake up now, knowing I'm over thirty and I keep thinking that I should be at a certain point in my life, but I'm not anywhere near it. Do you understand what I mean?"

Gia could only say, "You just have to give it a little more time, that's all!"

Tony, which had already had many conversations about the couple's future, was in a predicament. He wasn't going to spill the beans to Taylor and Gia, no matter how bad this got, but he definitely had to address this with Luke if this couldn't be sugarcoated.

"I see your point, but did you feel this with Marty?" Tony asked.

"No, that's just it, I didn't."

"Then that should tell you something! He is worth waiting for. He will do whatever he has to, to make you happy," Tony chided.

"And how do you know this?" Taylor asked Tony while looking at both of them in a pleading way.

"I know this because my boy is just like me. Good or bad, he is just like me!" Anthony said, driving his point home.

Taylor sat there feeling a little better, even though she still couldn't see at this exact moment the part of Lucas doing whatever he had to do, to make her happy. Unknowingly, she had already downed an entire glass of the fruited wine, but she never recalled lifting her drink more than once.

She wanted to reach for the pitcher to refill it, hoping they didn't notice, as she didn't want to look like a lush. But a sympathetic Gia filled the glass for her. Taylor sipped this time. "Can we talk about something else? How about Florida in the winter? What is there to do?" Taylor said, wiping the tears away with her napkin.

"Well, St. Petersburg is around seventy in December, but there is still a lot to do, although it is a little chilly if you wanted to sit out on the beach. So an Alaskan woman like yourself would fit in wonderfully," he commented jokingly, trying to put this subject to bed.

They laughed halfheartedly with her, even though they could see that she still wasn't okay. Tony might have put a bandage on this problem, but it was not going to fix itself and definitely not soon.

The three pecked at the tasty portions that the waitress had brought over, making the food as nothing more than a mere deterrent to the issues. Tony knew that sometimes addressing an issue was best not addressing it, or at least not right this second. Taylor was going to be all right, and Tony knew that; however, he thought it was time that he had a talk with his son.

Tony got Lucas up to speed about today's dealings, while the ladies ran out for pie and ice cream after dinner. Tony hoped that Gia was careful about how she was speaking with Taylor. But with her not knowing about her son's intentions, she couldn't use a proposal to cloud the issue.

The two men sat out on the deck, watching the sun go down before he decided to talk about it. "I know you probably don't know this, but Taylor is a little scared right now?"

"Scared? Scared of what?" Lucas asked, surprised after not seeing those words coming.

"That's where I'm not sure. How long is it going to be before the women get back? I don't want them walking in."

"At least fifteen minutes. Is this why Taylor has been so quiet tonight?" Lucas asked.

"Yes. I think Taylor was on the edge of a near breakdown. She's torn because all of a sudden she's getting older and I think Taylor doesn't know where she stands."

"Pop, I have never done anything that would make her think there isn't a future for both of us."

"I know, but this is where I think she is scared. Taylor knows how your work is, but I think she is finding problems with it."

"Is that what she said?" a riled Lucas questioned.

"No, it bothered her, well, a lot today that you weren't able to join us. I don't think she wants you to put her above your work, but she needs to know that she will be at least be a close second."

"Well, what do you think I should do? Should I propose to her sooner?"

"No, I don't think you should get married, not yet anyway until you have, I mean you both have a plan." Lucas stewed after hearing this.

"Well, I was looking to make some changes, and getting married was just the first one. Now, I won't know when the moment is right to do this," Lucas said.

"I'm sorry, son. I can see you both making it through this, but you should advance with kid gloves."

"I had no idea. I know if we could move back to Alaska, she would be the happiest person around. This is my first real chance at a long-standing relationship, and now I am afraid I will blow it," Lucas stated.

"All I can say is eggshells for a while. Walk on eggshells!" Tony said with him starting to take it personal since Taylor didn't have this problem until they arrived. Maybe they shouldn't have come. And his fears continued, with the two women out talking about God knows what.

The ladies poked their heads out the open door. "Miss me?" Gia said to her husband with a little smile. The men sat there waiting for the ladies to join them on the Adirondack chairs.

"So where is the ice cream?" Tony questioned.

"It's in the freezer. Did you want some already?" Gia asked.

"No, actually all I have done is eat since we got here. I'm good."

"Yeah, he says that until the first person reaches for a bowl!" Gia said sarcastically.

Later, in the bedroom, Lucas looked on as Taylor went silent, with both knowing this had to be a topic for when the two were alone. Lucas had always said that she could leave if she weren't happy, but he just couldn't lose her to something they couldn't work around. It almost felt like she was mad at him but in a speechless sort of way.

He wasn't going to be able to come up with answers until his parents left, so that they could figure this out. It wasn't going to be covered over instantly, but Lucas needed to smooth things at least. She snuggled in close to him, reminding him of when his dad had said that she was scared. "I love you," he said in a moment of panic.

"I love you too, Luke," she said, not even turning to make eye contact.

Friday, after Luke left for work, her head went into a nosedive, with a form of gloom that was sinking in fast. She didn't want to talk to her best friend about this one, but Lauren's call was either going to be coming in tomorrow or Sunday, for sure.

She had to snap out of this. His parents were finishing up their visit, and they were starting to look at her different. No more alcohol for a while. This was the instigator that was fueling the fire. She decided to go back to bed and try to get a little sleep.

Taylor tossed and turned, rustling the covers. Picking up the tablet, she figured that she would continue the blog, but her mind just wasn't into it. As soon as she read a line, it disappeared from her brain. Becoming frustrated at not being able to clear her head, she stood and went into the bathroom.

She reached down and proceeded to pour a warm bath to soothe her nerves. If this didn't work, she was going to find a sleeping pill, and maybe it would at least slow down these thoughts, so she could rationally deal with them one at a time. The bath water brought her in and made her drowsy. The hour or maybe two that she had last night was now calling out to her for more sleep.

When she was done with the bath, some of her problems spiraled down the drain with it, or at least she hoped they did. She gathered herself and went back to bed, thinking of nothing but closing her eyes and taking in some uninterrupted slumber.

The idea of Lucas with his job was beginning to create a wedge, as she needed more time with him. Another two months and he would start the slowdown as he called it. It was when he had more time to think about his personal life and more time to breath. She drifted off, remembering happy thoughts they shared in Alaska.

Taylor awoke to the faint clink of dishes from out in the kitchen. She fixed her hair and then forced her way to the kitchen to a concerned Gia, who promptly asked after seeing her, "Are you okay?"

With her brain still blurred, she replied, "I'm fine. Why do you ask?"

"Because it is after eleven o'clock and I was a little worried, that's all," Taylor replied. *How could it be that late already, when she felt as though she had just closed her eyes?*

"So where is your husband?" Taylor asked, still trying to catch up.

"He went for a walk. We just finished lunch. Do you want me to make you something?"

"No, thank you. I'm not hungry, but thank you."

Then a silence befell them, and Taylor was the first to open her mouth. "I know that I have not exactly been myself lately. I don't have any real reasons, but to say that I am dealing with some things, but I assure you that Luke and I are good." Gia was cautious when she delivered the next line.

"Taylor, it's all right if you don't want to tell me, but are you dealing with depression?"

Taylor sat at the table. "I do not have depression, but there was something that haunted me yesterday about my direction."

"What do you mean?" Gia asked.

"Well, I am not sure I have this all figured out. It is like, even though I am happy with us as a couple, I still feel like roommates most times. His job is keeping us from totally being us. But it's not his fault. I am just having trouble dealing with it. Do you understand?" Taylor assured, finalizing to his mother that Lucas was not the reason.

"Actually, I do. You want there to be more of the romance thing day in and day out."

"Exactly! You know maybe I shouldn't be talking to you about this," Taylor said, noticing the weirdness.

"Look, we are just talking as friends. If I were hurting, I would want someone like you, listening to my woes. And besides, who knows more about romance than us Italians?"

Taylor instinctively arose and hugged the woman for being there for her. Lauren was a great phone friend, but right now, this was what she needed, real table talk. She broke the bond before setting herself back in the chair next to her. Gia mentioned how romantic her husband has been since the time that they had met.

Taylor was shocked to find out that they almost never came to be since Gia was to be part of an arranged marriage. Gia lightly cried right there at the table. "Anthony had to beg my parents, who finally gave in, due to the love they saw in us both."

Gia wiped her eyes and then continued, "It was shortly after that that Tony was called up to serve. He had not been part of any front-line wartime, but he was stationed in Paris for a year. The separation was unbearable as I was still not married, and my parents began to push again to get me wed. I was in a terrible place. I mean I had parents who loved me, and they were just looking to make me happy. I also missed Anthony so. It was the most when I needed him to protect me from all this."

"So how did you get back together?" Taylor asked, finding she was drawn into their life story that Lucas had never told her.

"Well, Tony eventually came home, and then we married a month later not far from the town I was from. We then moved to Seattle. Immigration allowed us to stay in the States after our visas ran out. But almost two years later, we moved to Point Hope. Tony and I went there because there he heard about the mill yard. That is where we met your grandparents, and it is where he retired. We settled down, and I want you to know that even with all the hardships we endured, it was more than worth it."

"So Tony is romantic?" Taylor asked.

"Oh God, yes. Anthony excited me as he was always a take charge kind of man. He stood up to my father, who wanted livestock for my hand. If I made any part of our life sound simple, it wasn't. He always surprised me, but he's always made me feel like a queen. Tony was tough when he needed to be and sympathetic when I was vulnerable," Gia said.

And then she added, "I don't regret one thing about our life. And you know what? You won't either. I understand that you feel confused about where you are going, but you will make it as long as you are together. You just need to give Lucas time to prove it! And he will, I promise you."

Taylor took the information that Gia handed her to heart. She wasn't going anywhere, but now she had to make more of a point to tell those that have become vested in their future together. "Gia, we will be fine. And because of what you just told me, now even I know it's true," Taylor said as some of the worries washed away from Gia's face.

Tony opened the door. "Do I need to come back later, because I don't think I can walk anymore?" The two ladies giggled at his approach to lighten the mood.

"Get in here, will you?" Taylor said as the laughter continued.

The moment had passed, and she wasn't going to rehash it with him, not when she was sure that Gia was going to fill him in, most likely with an abridged version. Taylor knew enough by her parents that, that was the way it worked. A close couple was as one. Taylor jumped into the subject that Tony had brought up. It was not head-lined material, but it at least pulled her out of the limelight.

At around five thirty, Luke slogged in thinking he was getting the same Taylor as yesterday. However, it was quite the opposite. With Gia dragging out her photo album from their Point Hope days, Taylor was in hysterics. She laughed so hard when he poked his head in that she thought she was going to pee herself.

The album had all the best of Luke's past. It had those—oh, isn't he so handsome moments, and there were many. It had the ones of him naked, which was of course, the most embarrassing to the one who was in the picture. And it had the pictures with friends and those he dated, dressed for different occasions.

"Mom, I can't believe you are showing her those pictures."

"Well, I never had an opportunity to sit down and show them to Tara or the older woman you were dating. What was her name, Celine?"

"No, it was Celeste!" he said mildly in disdain.

"We never got to meet her because it never worked out for the two of them."

"Mom, can we talk about something else please?"

"Sure, Lucas! I didn't think it still bothered you."

Not knowing what to say, he whispered, "Well, it does." Taylor understood with him showing outrage over the woman in the past, with her apparently knowing much more than either of his parents.

Gia then pointed out a picture of their young son in the tub. She was trying to get his goat, and it was working. "Dad?"

"Sorry, boy," he said, staying far and away from this conversa-tion. Lucas finally just gave in and went and grabbed a beer. He sat down quietly with his hands raised in the air, surrendering.

Taylor enjoyed the stories that went along with almost every picture. Luke might have heard it one way, but Taylor saw it as how proud she was of her son because if it weren't for them, then he wouldn't be here.

The parents went to bed their usual time around nine thirty, spurring Luke to ask Taylor to come with him. "Let's go for a ride!" Lucas exclaimed. She climbed in next to him, where they rode a mile up the drive and pulled off onto a cul-de-sac.

At the end, he parked against the curb and dropped the shifter into park and shut off the engine. Lucas, without wasting any time, turned and point blank asked her. "Are you happy?" he questioned inquisitively. She was hoping that this wasn't going to show its face so soon but knew he was going to befall her soon.

"What do you want me to say?"

"I just want the truth. I hoped this could wait until Sunday after they left, but I think we need to get this out of the way if we are all going to salvage this weekend. I know you are hurting about something, and I just want to help you through it, even if the problem is me."

"You are not the problem. I just got excited that all four of us might have been going out to lunch together. And then you had to cancel."

"You know that I couldn't get away. I would if I could have! Something came up that I had to take care of myself."

"I realize that, but it's going to be like this a year from now and in another twenty-five. Sure, you might have times when you can break away for lunch, but we might never be able to pinpoint when that'll be."

"But this is the way that I told you it was. I never sold you lies that it was any better than this. Am I right?"

"Yes, you told me. I just thought there would still be more us time."

Luke peered over and held her hand. "Are you regretting what you did?"

"No! I just thought when I fell in love with you that there would be more romance to go along with it."

"But—"

"Hey, I know you are tired at the end of the day. I would be shocked if you weren't. But don't you want more?"

"I know what you're saying. I do want more for us. Let's just get through this season, and I will be open to any reasonable decision that we come up with," Lucas stated, combating his own set of fears and tears.

"Now, do you feel the same way about me that you did months ago when I first moved in?" Taylor inquired.

"No, I don't. I fell in love with you without even noticing exactly when it happened. I'm starting to think that I always did. And now I don't ever want to let you go, and I would fight to keep you if that is what it takes. But more than that, I just want you to be happy!" Taking a breath, he added, "So are you staying with me?"

"I am staying."

"Then I want you to find a hobby. I will even help you in my spare time if you want the help that is," Luke said, pushing away a tear.

"Even if it is the meetings?" Taylor questioned.

"Yes, the meetings too!"

"I'm sorry that I have put you through this," Luke said sincerely.

"There is nothing to be sorry for. I knew what I was in for and I know it will all be worth it someday!" Taylor concluded.

Lucas drove up the road that led to the parking area that overlooked the ocean. Here they didn't venture out to proclaim their love for each other, by having sex in the darkness that was everywhere. They didn't even walk down to the beach below. They just sat there looking for answers that might help them stay together while being happy doing it. Tonight, the partially hidden summer moon was offering no freebies, so the couple eventually drove home no surer about what they should do.

Sunday morning the Florida visitors came out freshly showered with packed suitcases in hand. Yesterday turned out to be a much better day with the wounds that Taylor had healed over from talking to the right people.

Luke, however, knew that this problem was going to be like the tide out there. It might ebb for now, but it for sure was going to show itself again. He needed this work season to be over soon, even more than she did as Luke had the ring to give her. And he truly thought that it was the right thing to do, and even more, he believed now that she would accept it.

They feasted on scrambled eggs, chorizo, home fries, and toast that Luke's mom was told not to help with. There was a little sadness in the air, which was normal seeing their visit was coming to an end. It was easier though for three of them, knowing they would all be back together in eight weeks.

Lucas lifted the bags out of the car, just the same way he walked them in, a little over a week ago. The Floridians rattled on about how the two of them should try to come down soon. Lucas said, "We will." And Taylor knew he meant it.

With the four exchanging goodbyes inside the terminal for the last time. The two women hugged, allowing Gia to whisper a few words that were directed just to her. The cordial compilation toted a promise if there could be such a thing that Taylor and Lucas were going to make it. It was something that Taylor wanted to work on with all her heart even though she thought it might not happen today or anytime soon.

Luke pulled back from his dad as like usual, his father had him in stitches over a joke he just told. The two looked each other in the eye, and then they hugged before finally saying their goodbyes.

# CHAPTER 17

They peered out the windshield, with both not uttering a word for the better part of their travels home. Off the highway, Taylor stewed getting the nerve to spit out what had been bothering her for the last few days. "Lucas, I am so sorry. I had no intention of ruining your visit with your mom and dad."

"You know you didn't. It is not your fault that I haven't been spending enough time with you. That will change soon though. I just have to do this at my own pace. I just want this to be real and not forced, okay?"

Taylor blindly answered, "Okay."

"But I think you should take some time later and look into your hobby choice, a little more in depth. And I meant it when I said I would help you. Whatever it is, I want to help!" Lucas exclaimed. She looked out at the highway as they took the exit off the rotary that would lead them up to their drive.

"So what is it that you think you want to do?" he asked innocently enough. She thought but knew the answer to that one.

"I want to pursue more of who I am as a sub. I know this is one of those facets you talk about, but I want to be better."

"Then that is what you should do. When we get home, I will clue you into a secret website that covers that and much more. I mean if I can still get on it that is."

"Secret, what is so secretive about it?" Taylor asked.

"You'll see."

Taylor held the tablet, awaiting instruction. Lucas found the paperwork that he had hidden in the bottom drawer of his desk. Taking the tablet from her momentarily, he signed on to a website called DD247. She watched as he filled in his username and a password, which sent him a text that he had to enter in the next minute.

To her, it was looking more like stuff a spy would do. But he said it was merely a hidden site that covered the Seattle area, and it would have what she was looking for. When he logged onto the main page of DD247, he had an option of sponsoring a visitor. After clicking on that box, he carefully handed her the tablet.

"So what you will have to do here is fill out all the information, and don't worry, it does not contain your actual name, address, or credit or banking information. I will let you start this. If you need any help, I will be right here." He left her long enough to get them both a glass of ice water. She began by looking at the username box.

"What should I use for a name?"

"You can put in anything you want but do not include your real name."

"Any suggestions?" she questioned.

"How about kneed2please?"

"Oh, I get it." She entered Need 2 Please.

"No, I was thinking more like this, and it has to be one word also." He typed in the word "kneed2please." She looked at it, seeing the simplicity and genius of it.

"Oh, that's good. All lowercase and an act of submission, which shows through the double entendre. I like it." When she was ready, she punched the enter button. Almost instantaneously, the username came up as already taken but showed follow-up options. The obvious answer was to add at least a double-digit number after it. She thought for a second. Taylor slowly entered "kneed2please49."

"Why did you add the number 49 after it?" Lucas said in wonder.

"Well, Alaska was the forty ninth state." She paused and then tapped when she was ready. Next, she was instructed to set up a password. After a few minutes, Taylor sat gazing at the main screen. Once she was officially on the main page, she was asked to set up one more name, which was optional. It was for a nickname. "Do I have to do this?" she asked knowing that he had gone through this process before.

"It is your choice. You can stick with your username or part of it, but a lot of other people use one to make it more personal. Also, you can use that name throughout the whole site, including chatrooms."

"So I could just put in something like Hope?"

Lucas rocked his head up and down. "That's a perfect choice. Using part of our hometown as your nickname, I like it."

She entered her newly chosen alias in the box. This time she got right through as the DD247 expanded, visually morphing into Dark Desires 24/7. Seconds transpired as the words evaporated into the background exposing a dark alleyway.

There a scene showing nothing but a darkened city street focused where sources of light peeked out from places like a phone booth and assorted other storefronts. It reminded Taylor of a Thomas Kinkade painting except without the brush marks.

"What do I do here?" she inquired, not finding any menu across the top or bottom.

"Um, the site has updated since the last time I was on a couple of years ago, but I think you need to touch the light sources."

An eager Taylor studied the screen, even though she didn't know why yet. If it was anything like the title of the site, then she was getting excited for the right reason. She tapped on the phone booth. It left behind a word that read Chatroom.

Still curious, she touched on the newsstand. It showed the words Items for Sale. Taylor feverishly knocked on each storefront window to see what it had hidden within. A few of them she found interesting. She acted like all the others that must have graced this updated site for the first time.

"So what do I do from here?" she asked of Luke, that had been quietly looking over her shoulder. He hadn't been on the site in some time, so he went off some of what he remembered.

"Well, you need to decide which of these you want to check out."

"I don't think fetishes is what I want. S & M is a definite no. B & D is a yes, but D & S is where I want to go first. I do kind of want to check out meetings in the city. But I'm not sure if I would go into a chatroom."

"You can go into them but do it from a very overly cautious viewpoint. Be very careful of everyone and anyone."

"I'm still not sure if I want to do this, but I will not give out my name, address, or anything else that will leave me vulnerable. I promise."

"Okay, that is all I ask. But I am going to leave you to this so I can get some sleep if that's all right. It has been a long week." Taylor got up and presented him with a hug and kiss that a young couple might give.

"What was that for?" he asked.

"I just wanted you to know that I love you and appreciate you for helping me with this."

"Anytime," Lucas said, turning away and then back to her. "By the way, I didn't forget about your punishment!" he stated. She was elated. "No, not tonight, you have things to do. Enjoy, Taylor!"

"Good night, Luke!"

Lucas turned and disappeared around the corner for the last time. "Don't stay up too late," was the last thing she heard as she reabsorbed herself back into the screen.

She double clicked on, the Tall & Short clothing store, and that led her straight to the next page, which was Domination & Submission. The page was a silhouette in the foreground of a man towering over a woman who was kneeling before him. Again, there were no menus. The much smaller beacons of lights were not as evident as those on the main screen, since she was focused on the artistic way it was being portrayed.

A single candle sat on the small table beside them. Another glimmer refracted from the woman's steel collar. Then there was the moon in the window. But as before, through a click, that would reveal another option. One had meetings, like the last page, but it was refined to the specific category of the section that she was in at this time.

The chatrooms must do the same, as there were even lessons, which Taylor figured she would view some other time. No need to get turned on while her man is sound asleep in the other room. Plus, the last time she got her panties in a bunch, she found herself totally restrained and she was the culprit who had done it.

She went to the fridge for some vino. Taylor poured the remains of the white wine that was uncorked last night. The sweet aroma swept up from the glass she held as she drifted back to the tablet which had just turned off to conserve its energy.

Tapping at its glass, it awoke. Taylor continued by clicking on one, which defined in great detail the two variances in the sexual scale of controller and controlee. Slowly reading the definition, she dissected it to where she thought she had it figured out.

Taylor had learned much about it already, with most not being the same exact wording but carrying the same context of how it worked. Once the words were read probably as much as twice, she went on to meetings. She looked at the calendar for the next three months, which had meeting dates and times for the next few days.

There was even the bold negation that stated "Please keep these meetings confidential" at the top and the bottom of the calendar. Taylor found it interesting that beyond a couple of days, the time and place was not posted. Even though it wasn't explained, she thought it had to be because of the discretion of the site.

She opted not to attend meetings, not yet anyway, with Lucas strongly fearing for her safety. Exiting back two screens was a chore as it took her a minute to do. She fell in love with the artsy way that they had the shops displayed.

There was a podiatrist office, complete with a white lined foot drawing stuck to the window, which covered fetishes. Law offices of Payne & Plezure, for S & M. A hardware store with rope and chain hanging on the left and right edges of the windows, for B & D. And a coffeehouse for meetings. And the clothing store she had just visited. The site builders must have had a lot of fun constructing this website.

After getting caught up in the moment of what the art was hiding in its picture, she decided to return to the Tall & Short clothing store. She touched the other light orbs and went on to video training. And even thought she said she wasn't going to tonight, she sat and studied videos that pertained to making her a better sub.

The woman eyed the title for the exercise, but figured that she might look at Lucas differently, perhaps if he wasn't following the guidelines the two of them practiced. Some of the videos were quite elaborate as they stopped and broke down and played out scenes to show up close the right and wrong way of being submissive.

Taylor lost track of time until she was texted a very familiar word, "Idiot." She already knew who it was because she had another one just like it from the other day. It was yesterday when Lauren called, wanting to find out why her best friend referred to herself as an idiot. Well, after hearing the whole story, she definitely agreed.

In fact, by one of the other texts yesterday, she thought the story was so good that she wanted to tell her husband. But after a quick reply, Lauren of course, declined. Taylor wondered if this was going to be the last reminder of her stupidity. She wouldn't bank on it. After all, it was damn funny, now that some time had passed.

She backed out of the site and shut down the tablet, with it reminding her that it was time to be charged. After plugging it in, she went to bed. Taylor strutted softly across the bedroom carpet, making sure not to wake the man that had to get up early for work tomorrow.

She closed the bathroom door but not before the sight of Lucas sleeping spurred the last thing he had said to her. "I did not forget your punishment," came back to her as if she heard it straight from his mouth again. After brushing her teeth, she got changed. The thought resurfaced once more of her wanting to get stuck on the horse, but this time with a minor tweak of her master looking down at her, deciding her fate.

The weeks flew by with Taylor totally engrossed into getting everything ready for the party. The days were now down to three. Her guest count had grown beyond what she had expected, with it coming close to maxing out the room. She found herself even more grateful now that she wasn't having to foot the bill on all of this.

Kyle had done more than his share, as her brother had managed to get in touch with a few of their classmates that Luke knew from school, some from the mills, and even the bar in Point Hope.

Taylor, a couple of weeks ago, received a yes, with no urging from her, saying that her parents were coming down. It turned out that they were hung up on it being a loud party, when Taylor thought it would be all about the flight. But for whatever the reason, her mom and dad were going to be here.

As the days disappeared, she became a little apprehensive about Lucas being able to get out on time. It was no problem selling him on them getting away, once he heard the when and where they were going. Luke didn't even ask any questions about it. And when he heard that she wanted to book a room at the same hotel, he was in a hundred percent.

Taylor managed to push through the week, with their bank or its website screwing up on their online transactions yet again. Luke only told her that it was time to move to the other goliath bank to keep this from happening again. So the next day, she spent what felt like hours with the account manager of the new institution, making sure that all was right.

After a quick ten-minute stop to sign papers for the new accounts, Lucas joined Taylor for lunch at the diner. Then with Luke gone again, she headed home, to initialize Calderone Enterprises, to the online banking part. Taylor felt as though she genuinely earned her money today.

This week she was praying would be much easier as Lauren was getting in late tonight. Tony, Gia, and Carl will be in on Thursday, so the four could finally meet.

It was all aligning, with the pinnacle being that Luke had to... never mind. She didn't want to get all worked up about it. Flynt's Bar even called after receiving the payoff balance a couple of days ago to say that they could set up the night before.

Taylor decided against it, even though the manager assured her that the room would be locked. She instead opted to get there early, giving herself time to decorate the room before picking up the birthday boy for his surprise drive in.

Lucas announced last night that he had another day that went pretty well, by his standards and this was scaring her, as he was due for a not so good one. Today she met for a very relaxed hour of just her, his parents and Lauren. The seconds were ticking loudly now.

Taylor's job, as if by design, was thankfully running in the background without her. With it starting to get late, she said goodbye since she didn't want to have to lie to Lucas about why she wasn't home.

Lucas stepped in portraying a fantastic mood. Work was once again, somewhat tolerable. A surprise inspection this time caught them with only one minor infraction to correct, which he considered an overall win.

With less than twenty-four hours until the two of them get to the pier for the party, Taylor sure hoped she didn't slip up now. "So how was your day?" Lucas asked.

"Good. The deposit showed up in the account the first thing this morning. I also have all the paperwork for you to read?" Taylor questioned.

"Read. I don't feel like reading tonight. How about you?" he said, portraying a crooked smile.

"No, I guess I'm good," Taylor said in a malleable tone.

"Let's eat quick. Do we have leftovers?" Lucas questioned.

"Yes, I think we have enough for a meal."

"Good," he said, flashing the same look once more.

Placing the dirty plates in the sink, Taylor was instructed to wash up and return to the kitchen. She didn't respond with any excitement, but answered with a "Yes, sir" just in case. She promptly did as she was told and returned. "I'm back, sir!"

Waiting as she thought she should, Lucas sidestepped through the recently opened door of the laundry area. Taylor had good reason to be thrilled about what she thought and hoped must be happening tonight. "Tay, I want you to follow me out to the garage!"

Whoosh was the feeling she had deep within her. "Yes, sir." In what seemed like a long walk to the garage, she realized that this was likely to be her first session since she moved to Seattle.

With her being so busy these last two weeks, she had forgotten about her chastisement. But here was the night, with Lucas opting for tonight as the night for her punishment, even as she was ready weeks ago to accept it. Lucas stopped a few feet into the garage and stepped aside to show the piece that aided in her punishment in the first place.

Taylor looked it over not with hatred but with sheer anticipation. She had been learning how to be a sub and tonight she might refer to those notes, to make her performance genuinely spectacular. Taylor moved in next to him and stopped by his side, so as not to lose eye contact with her puppet master.

"I would like you to stand still here while I undress you!" His sub became a mannequin as her master came around the front of her and pulled her top off, showing some of her bare brown skin. Next, he undid and dropped her pants and pulled them out from under her, leaving her barely covered. Next, he guided her up to an oh-so-familiar location and had her wait.

Without hesitation, he took one of her legs and moved it close, depressing the switch, which brought the closures securely around her left ankle. Taylor lightly chirped with her closing her eyes relishing the rush. He did the same thing to her other leg, locking in her lower half.

As Taylor stood straight, she leaned in tight against the firm foam piece that will be one of the two supports for her tonight. Lucas walked up behind her and unhooked and did away with her bra as her breasts roamed freely.

He brought her top half down slowly against the upper support. The neck closure grabbed softly at her neck, keeping her from moving anything but her still two loose limbs. Lucas suddenly remedied that by bringing them to a locked position at the same time. She let out a louder groan, that this time came both from her and her eager pussy.

Restrained, she anxiously awaiting the words she hoped to hear. Lucas slid her panties away from the support and down to her ankles. "It looks like someone has been waiting for this?"

"I'm sorry, sir!"

"Sorry for what, Tay?"

"Sorry for finding and using the surprise you made for me before you were ready to use it."

"Okay, well, it is time for your punishment, my toy," he stated to her and her nearly cloaked elation.

"Yes, sir." Then without warning, he disappeared. She couldn't turn to see where he had gone since that was not what a submissive would do.

Soon she heard footsteps, and a noise like from a piece of furniture that sounded behind her. With nothing going on for a few seconds, her body shuddered as she felt something sloshing up against her very wet lips. Then there was a push as it slid between and parted her captive vagina, entering her.

What she couldn't see was that Lucas was making a meal of her inviting lips before him. As he went through the motions, she began to moan. He drove his tongue as deep as he could inside her while she was paralyzed to fight back in any way. His actions were like a safecracker working a safe, with him searching for the right combination and then boom.

Taylor shook so hard, she thought the house was going to feel it, but in reality, it only quaked her insides. The apparatus did its job and never let her move a muscle. When he was done, he delighted in every last drop of her expelled orgasm before he backed off.

He swigged from his newly opened brew and then moved alongside her. She could barely see his feet as she kept her eyes steadfast. He ran his fingers across her ass that still quivered. Taylor let out a barely audible cry as he cracked his right hand across both of her cheeks at the same time. The contact made her motionlessly dance with both pain and satisfaction from the punishment she had been expecting for so very long.

The intensity escalated as the spanking sustained. Taylor tried not to show how much it hurt, but she had no gag to mask it. So she took it until it ceased, bringing Luke to run his palm and fingers into and around her still convulsing pussy.

He played with her juices, using it to soothe her red battered cheeks. To her, it felt like butter on a burn. His hand dove back in for more drippings. This time he used it to force her to come for the second time.

She did fight it since she was still sensitive from her first climax. But Lucas didn't let up as her shaking changed to wanting that second climax. This time her head lifted out straight as she felt all the parts of her body trying to escape.

Luke let her be as waves of the orgasm attacked her like warranted convulsions. She wished to be released, even though she wasn't strong enough in her role to ask. The punishment must be over, Taylor thought as she lost track of everything around her.

Lucas, who was still toying with his submissive, ran his penis across her still quivering clitoris, with a feeling that surely would have brought her to the ceiling if it could have.

He sawed across her lips like a musician would play a stringed instrument, moving at a level, before inserting himself at just the right time. With that, her head shot up again.

Within her cavity, he plunged deep into her pussy before deciding to take this stationary horse for a ride. He moved back and forth with no give to the pieces that held her tight, and Lucas received moans of enjoyment in return.

The pace rose until he came within her. Luke might have crumbled if Taylor and the piece hadn't been there for him to hold on to. When he regained enough control to stand, he pushed the button on the remote and Taylor was released, with him finding her exhaustingly spent.

She stayed huddled over, while her mental faculties tapped her on the shoulder, and said, "Your punishment is over. You are free." Well, it might have been from inside her, or maybe it was Luke that had said it, but either way, she was hoping it was bedtime, and very soon.

Lucas helped her up. "Are you all right?" he quipped. With her starting to get a little bit of the feeling she had when she was stuck there the last time, he made up for in the activity he asserted.

"Wow, am I?" she eventually answered.

"So you probably don't want to be punished again, right?"

"No, that definitely makes me want to do the right thing from now on," Taylor said, trying to force enough energy to not show a grin.

"Why don't we call it a night, then."

"I was kind of thinking the same thing," she said, pleased that they were both on the same page with about eight hours of sleep.

Primarily because of their busy day tomorrow, that he still doesn't know about.

On Friday night, Taylor left the bar after putting up the last of the decorations. With help from about ten people, they had it all set up and they were able to do it and still have time to socialize. Henri's crew tended to getting their table ready while all in the background.

Now, all she had was a short drive, and thanks to a call from Lucas, it looked like they should have enough time to check in at the hotel if traffic wasn't too heavy. She replayed the incredible idea that her brother had come up with, and she couldn't wait to spring it on him.

Jubilantly she sang to the radio as she drove toward a still-unsuspecting Lucas. She looked at the time on the dashboard. She could make it to the hotel by five thirty, and that's with traffic.

She had the weekend luggage in the trunk and everything in place. If the timing was right, this would be an excellent surprise. If not, well, they were all going to have a great time anyway. She got off the highway and headed toward the town hall restoration in the small town of Binghamton.

She drove up to the front of the site, where it looked like most of the employees were still working. Taylor picked up the phone and waited for him to answer. "Hi, baby!"

"Hey, I'm outside," Taylor commented.

"Okay, I will be right there." She put down the phone and looked around. Across the street, there was a two-tiered gazebo that reached down the hillside toward the town hall. She checked it out as the late day sun shone through the trees and down over the structure.

That would make a pretty picture. Lucas interrupted her as she looked over the beautifully landscaped area with people that were bundled up a little but were still out enjoying it. He put his lunch box in the back seat and then tapped on the driver side window.

"Let me drive," Luke stated as she unbuckled her seat belt and climbed out. Luke grabbed a handful of ass cheek, not allowing her to walk by without a grope.

"So how did it go today?" Taylor questioned, trying to mask her excitement.

"It went well. I've had so many lately, but I don't get tired of days like these," Luke said, then asked a more personal question. "So how tired are you today? Quite the workout, huh?" Lucas joked. She ran her hand over his leg and beamed her trademark smile.

"Yes, you worked me very hard," Taylor said, emphasizing the word hard.

After a pause, Luke exclaimed, "I can't wait to take a shower! You wouldn't believe the dust from an old building like that." She looked across to him since he mentioned it. "Steve and three of the guys went back to the office to grab some supplies. They are going to work until nine tonight."

Taylor thought about it, thinking that sounded like a reasonable way to get out of work early today, even though she got a text that said they were on their way a while ago.

"Is it okay that I am taking you away since they decided to work?"

"No, I am right where I need to be tonight, with you!"

After a brief smirk and a set of admiring eyes, Taylor questioned, "You know we should go out to dinner with Steve and his wife…"

"Vanessa. And yes, we should," Lucas interrupted.

"They live on the Southside, right?" Taylor asked.

"Yes, they have been there for about ten years now," Lucas said before adding, "So what do you feel like eating tonight?"

"Well, if we want seafood, we can go to Wake's, but I can't eat as much as we did last time!"

"Yes, we did overdo it! Maybe we can find a buffet or restaurant down further and leave the seafood for tomorrow." He offered.

"That sounds good to me," Taylor said, wondering if he was on to her. She quickly dismissed it, figuring even if he did know some of it, he didn't know everything. Otherwise, Steve's arm was going to be black and blue when they meet later. In a couple of hours, the sun would set, making her waver with time passing so slowly. She just had to keep calm for a little longer.

Luke told Taylor to head into the hotel as he went to the trunk to get the luggage. While in the grand foyer, the door closed behind her. She clacked as her soles sounded until she stopped at the counter of the front desk. She desperately hoped that Lucas didn't hear those words that she now feared most, with those words being "Are you part of the Calderone party?"

It wasn't asked, which was good because Lucas came out of nowhere and was right there behind her. "Okay, here is your room key, and Brian will take you to your room on the fourth floor, suite B." Lucas had heard about the suites. It was a huge and incredible room that was atop the hotel. They were told that their room has a balcony that looked at both the Sound and the ocean too.

"Wow, you went all-out," Lucas stated in anticipation while they moved toward the elevator.

"I just wanted this weekend to be perfect not just for you but for me too. I can't wait to see the pier all done up in lights and the music playing. You made it sound like Disneyland."

"Yes, you are going to love it," Lucas agreed as the elevator doors opened up. He signaled with his free hand, doing the gentlemanly thing and letting her go first, with the bellhop a few feet behind. An acoustic song played softly from the speakers overhead. Moments later, the door reopened to a hall of only four suites.

After tipping the man who closed the door on his exit, Lucas opened the suitcase and asked if she needed a shower. She passed. When the shower water eventually hit the tiled floor, Taylor slinked out to the hall to call her brother. "What's up?" he said.

"We are in the room now. How are things going there?" Taylor asked.

"Great. The food smells incredible, and there is plenty of it. The guests are all here except for one of the guys from back home, who let me know last minute that something came up and he couldn't make it. We are a go, and I will have everybody ready when we get your text."

"Okay, I'm thinking about thirty minutes. I'll text when we are a couple of minutes away."

"We will be waiting!" Kyle replied. Taylor hung up and typed in a text so it would be ready to send off later.

Luke and Taylor did one last check of their appearance. They were semi-dressed, with Taylor opting for a green dress and white flats for walking. Lucas had on his old ratty dress belt, which she vowed he would not be wearing after tonight. It was time for that thing to go.

They sauntered from the elevator to the pier level. It was a beautiful night with the sun, which will disappear into the ocean in less than an hour. Everything was perfect in the world. Taylor sent the pre-typed text and then dropped it in her purse. On their right guiding their way were white lights that hung from the poles that secured the edge of the boardwalk.

The couple, walking at their own pace, made their way hand in hand while gazing into each other's eyes. They strolled up to the first band that was positioned between the Allusea and their seafood restaurant. The band played a melody that they didn't recognize, but it was rock, and it was nice just the same. They stood for a minute and then continued their speechless gaze. The smell of Wake's reached out and tried desperately to pull them in. Still, they strode on.

The resonances of the next band far-off grew louder as they approached. It played an inspiring version of "We Are the Champions," even though it wasn't enough to break Luke's view of his captivating girlfriend. The band, which was known as the Z-tones played on with the lead singer belting it out.

Then mysteriously without notice, the song ended, with the female stepping forward to begin another number. Lucas and Taylor were still a hundred feet away, but Luke wondered why they would stop a song before it was through. She swung at his arm. It was then that this beautiful tall, thin redheaded woman started a very sexy version of "Happy, Happy Birthday, Baby."

Luke's trance was broken now. The tall, slender woman crooned as nearly thirty people stood in of all things, New Year's hats. He was confused, but he was drawn in by the beautiful music that the young woman was belting out.

They stood at the rear of the crowd getting as close as they could. As the song ended, an a capella rendition of "Happy Birthday" was sung by the hatted group, with the rest joining in. Lucas tried to look past all the hats looking for who this was being directed toward, and Taylor looked on from the corner of her eye recording it in her mind as a memory she never wished to forget.

When the song got to the part, where you would insert the name, he was caught off guard. The majority of them sang Lucas. He looked over at Taylor, who just managed to barely spit out, "I love you!"

Then like a swarm of piranha, the cardboard capped ones all turned to wish him a happy birthday. It felt like everyone he knew from his whole life. There were classmates, coworkers, friends, and family, both from his side and Taylor's. He was dumbfounded and shocked.

With all the greetings and handshakes exchanged, the group filed inside where they were directed to the party. The room proudly adorned yellow tablecloths, streamers, and decorations that hung from the many window panes. There was also a bar, a table for chafing dishes, and even a small table with gifts. Lucas even heard the music on the pier piping into the room.

Kyle approached Lucas and handed him a rock glass with a drink in it. Taylor, who had been standing by his side, said, "Don't get too excited, it's not Casa." He took a sip of the liquid but not before he kissed his lady. He was surprised as she was outwardly proud that she got him. Lauren and Carl walked over to be introduced by Taylor. Lucas had spoken to her a few times on the phone but was glad to see them here.

At the end of one of the long tables, the four parents grouped together with Henri, a face that Luke was shocked to see outside of his restaurant. The parents talked the way that they had, the last time they all were in Alaska.

All of his classmates came up to talk to him as a group. It was a bit awkward since the conversation was mainly about who they had been instead of who they were now. They also talked about classmates that had moved, and Lucas was glad to hear that two of them, Sloane and Phil, were still in Point Hope and doing well. They mentioned changes to the port town. Luke saw some of them and agreed with the two, telling him that he had just been there months ago.

Having this surprise sprung on him, Luke wondered if it was going to change his own plans for the weekend. The female bartender who kept busy for the first twenty minutes, stood with her arms behind her back, awaiting refills a few feet behind Lucas, who still couldn't contain his awe. Henri approached the birthday boy. "You are surprised, yes?"

"Yes, very surprised. And is it my imagination, or am I smelling some items from the kitchen of Henri?"

"You are, my friend. Enjoy your evening," Henri said, shaking his hand and walking off toward the table of food.

Taylor pulled herself in close, noticing the break of people walking up to him. "Well, do you like?"

"I love it, baby. I still don't know how you got all this done and without me even knowing about it but thank you!" he said, finding another reason to reach in for a hug and a kiss. Henri, after getting the groups attention, announced that the food was ready.

A line gathered afront of the selections that were a mix of both French and American cuisines. The first four chafing dishes opened to coq au vin, beef bourguignon, a stew named blanquette de veau, and sole meuniere, which covered the French side. The second set of plates held pot roast with mashed potatoes, pasta with meatballs, grilled mixed vegetables, and a pork pot pie covered the American side.

The smells were utterly heavenly as everyone tried the European fare. Henri, along with his assistant, kept an eye to make sure this part of the festivities is nothing short of grandiose. The food was a hit as, before long, many even made their way back for seconds.

The four-member band made an appearance during their break for some food and drink as previously arranged by Taylor. The foursome congratulated Lucas, with the beautiful redhead planting a kiss on his cheek before they headed to the buffet. Taylor graciously handed the woman money for their outside contribution earlier.

Lucas, when he was finished, excused himself from the parents and Taylor and joined Kyle at the bar. "So tell me you weren't surprised?"

"No, she totally got me, but I wouldn't be shocked if you didn't have something to do with this!"

"Yes, I helped. Like the birthday song, when you two walked up. That was me. That was fun! And didn't you recognize the party hats from New Year's Eve?" Kyle asked as Luke, who clearly didn't recall them.

"So have you figured out when you are going to propose?"

"I was going to do it in our room tomorrow."

"Well, tomorrow is your birthday."

"Yes, but this moment seems right. And by the way, when are you doing yours?"

"Soon. I was thinking the last week before Isla heads home."

"That will be nice. Isla must be expecting it after all this time?"

"I'm sure she is," Kyle said while he looked over at his girl who was gabbing with his sister.

Coming up with something, Luke asked, "Hey, would you mind doing me a favor?" After Kyle's nod, he looked around and whispered. Kyle disappeared into the main bar area as Lucas took two drinks back to the table and placed one in front of Taylor.

"Thank you," she said while still listening to the Calderone's.

They talked about the way things were back in the old country. Henri agreed with his longtime friend that things were so much different, even though his home in France was over eight hundred miles, or fourteen hundred kilometers, away as the Europeans knew it.

# CHAPTER 18

People assembled for the white frosted cake, while Henri offered scalloped crepe shells, with a homemade apple filling, and a spiced ice crème to be served as a second choice. While standing in line Lucas found out that most of the attendees were also staying there at the Allusea, which made him again recognize Taylor for her ability to plan all this out while working.

Visiting the bartender often had Lucas and Taylor feeling no pain, as the music from out front played into the speakers overhead. With dessert done, Taylor urged the birthday boy to sit and open his presents. Lucas fought it for a few seconds while some of the partygoers turned their chairs to watch. He shook his head as he was still in disbelief.

Taylor handed him the first gift. It was very light, and it was from the sports bar back home. They weren't even here, and yet they were here. Lucas opened it to find two coupons, among the light-yellow tissue paper.

One was for a pitcher of beer, and the other was for twenty-piece wings. He didn't have anyone to thank, so he just told everyone what it was and who it was from. The next present was from his parents. It was an outdoor solar lighting system to light the way to the boathouse. "Thank you, Mom and Dad!" he called out.

The next was from Taylor's parents. He opened it to reveal pictures of when he was a kid, mostly at the inn with Kyle and a very young Taylor. There were even pictures of Grandma Tilly and her husband and the most special one was when they were part way through constructing the bar. When he finally got to the bottom of the box, he pulled out a photo album for all of them to go in. It was entitled Beginnings.

Lucas thanked them both as he realized these were some of the first moments that he had with the woman he now loves. Then lastly, he received Taylor's second gift, with the first being a satiny royal-blue dress shirt, just seconds before. Luke opened the box slowly to reveal a belt that she was clearly excited about. Once Lucas was okay with it, she did the honors and reached for the old tired one around his waist.

"May I?" she asked as she was about to drop it on the tray with the remains of the dirty dishes. Then using her other hand, she handed him the new one. He smiled as she dropped it off as trash. With her urging to search further, he found a wallet under white tissue paper.

He opened the leather billfold and instantly recognized the name of the village from one that his dad had talked about before. A happy tear snuck out over the thoughtful idea. He hugged and kissed her, making it known that he was going to talk about this with his dad. When he was through, he called out to everyone and thanked them again.

As the two of them walked toward their seats, Kyle called out, "Wait, there is one more here!" Lucas and Taylor turned back and stepped toward a tiny box in the center of the white tablecloth.

Taylor didn't remember seeing it and was shocked when she noticed her name written on it. All a dither, she wondered what this was and why was it for her. Luke, during this, picked it up and opened it to reveal a smaller box.

He opened the velvet outer container like an oyster and held it out for her to see. Her jaw dropped. "Taylor, I want to thank you so very much for today. You totally surprised me and now I would like to do the same for you." Her eyes remained steadfast on him now. "I need to have more wonderful moments like the ones we have already shared."

The crowd was a wonder as they couldn't make out a word of what was being said. Lucas moved in close beside her and knelt down on one knee and asked the four magic words. She stepped back a few inches, startled from his action. "Taylor, will you marry me and make me the happiest man in the world?" She looked down at the ring, which was a beautiful cluster of three white diamonds, and then peered back at him.

Even though she was still in a daze, her tears found their way down the contours of her cheeks. She looked briefly over to her parents, although she couldn't see them clearly at this point. He patiently awaited her answer. There was only one word that came to her mind. She didn't think this was going to happen so soon and certainly not tonight. "Yes," she said, crying harder now.

Kyle was the first to applaud, with the crowd following suit. Luke and Taylor kissed, and for an ever so brief amount of time, they were the only ones in the room. She was all aflutter over what was said to her and even more so over her answer. Only Lucas could take a party for himself and upstage it by turning it back to her. He was undoubtedly a man of surprises, just like his dad. There truly was a lot more to her boyfriend like she originally thought.

Lucas slid the ring upon her left hand of the newly engaged Taylor, and she couldn't believe it. Lauren ran to check out the ring. "Let me see, let me see!" she said before she pulled her hand up to view it. "Girl, I am so envious. I wish I had a man who loved me," Lauren joked, knowing that her husband was right there with her.

Still dabbing at the corners of her eyes, Taylor whispered over to Luke, "I'll explain later." She referred to her friend's unseemly comment.

Lucas shook many hands and even got a hug from his mother while she talked with her best friend. His dad came in for a hug to congratulate them. With Lauren and Carl breaking away, Tony and Gia stepped in and checked out the ring. "Well, I guess we don't have any more secrets!" Tony said as Taylor gave an excited hug to her future in-laws.

"So you two knew about this the whole time?" she said.

Gia popped off, "No, he did. It was just as much a surprise to me." Her parents came over and the two of them couldn't have been happier.

"To think we almost didn't come," Ken said as his significant other gave him a light glare. The rest of the party followed suit and congratulated the newly engaged couple.

The oldest generation called it quits hours ago, leaving the rest to party. They even danced out by the pier to a six-person cover band that played Alabama music that went by the name Old Flame. Taylor and Lucas slow danced, happy that they were away from the booze for a little bit.

Lauren, Carl, Kyle, and Isla even kicked up their heels too, as Kyle smiled at the sight of his sister and best friend. The alcohol might have been their fuel, but the moment made them think of the friends and family who flew in to be part of this.

Eyeing the last twenty, who hadn't given up yet, Taylor held Luke tight to the slow song "Forever's as Far as I Will Go." Lucas reminisced all that happened, with not wanting this night to be over.

After the song, Taylor told him that Trent was invited but couldn't make it. Luke thought maybe it was time to rethink the partnership, about bringing the man in. Trent was a great business-man and a good friend, who happened to run into a little trouble when he got divorced. Had it not gone that way they still would be partners today.

For Lucas, he knew any changes must happen soon. He couldn't lose what it was that was standing right there in front of him. He dropped his head down and kissed her. As that was the last song for them, he took her by the hand and led her to their private bar. Many of the others followed as their fuel wasn't cutting the latest drop in temperature.

Even as Taylor was still a glow from the proposal, he opted not to tell her about any other impending upcoming decisions; however, he did want them all to be done in less than a year. She loved today's surprise, and he knew in his heart that she will like the others too.

Taylor and Lucas left as they were closing down the place. Henri paid the bill for the bar tab way before Taylor got to it, at the end of the evening. She was mildly irked since he had done so much for this party already, and she had planned for this expense.

A hand full of people put on their jackets and made their way out the doors. Taylor and Lucas were tired and yet so full of life at the same time. They didn't want to miss one second of this incredible day, and they didn't. The series of lights strung along the pier's edge guided their way as the alcohol had them slaloming.

Lucas met Taylor out on the large balcony of their room, illuminated by the full moon that worked as their nightlight, lighting all they saw with its soft bluish light. Standing wrapped up in a blanket, they gazed the ocean as carabiners and spring clips played a winded song, clanging against the aluminum masts far below. Lucas held her tight, with her feeling the gift of sheer contentment.

Once visually satisfied, they lay upon the window bed, thinking back to the evening they shared. With not enough energy to move, the two watched intently the movie that was now to be a lifelong memory.

Lucas awoke to notice what they had done. He went over and turned down the bed and scooped up the still out cold Taylor, placing her gently like a feather upon the mattress. Luke climbed in next to her, allowing them both to sleep the rest of the evening in comfort. He closed his eyes, and rejoined her in sweet, sweet slumber.

The moon outside their windows through time became enlightened by the rising sun. The alarm wasn't set because that wasn't a priority for them, even though they planned to breakfast with everyone else for nine o'clock. They didn't wake up until after that.

Taylor awoke in a fabulous mood despite having a hangover. Lucas however felt the need for another hour of sleep. "Happy birthday, sweetheart! Hey, why don't you stay in bed a little longer?" Taylor urged.

"Hmm," was his only reply as he placed his head back down on the pillow.

She climbed into the shower and tried to disperse her aching head. She just got a good lather going when she heard the shower door open up to Lucas, saying, "I'll do that."

"You know we said we would be down there for nine o'clock," Taylor stated since she wasn't sure if he was there for more than a shower.

"And did you or anyone else really believe that? We will still be there by ten," Luke stated.

Mr. and the someday Mrs. Calderone entered the room that the hotel used for its breakfasts. A scattering of guests, some they knew and many they didn't, was in all stages of dining. But a few of their clan ate already and were awaiting the arrival of the pair. The elders were the only ones who managed to get down here on time and finished eating since they all appeared to be hangover free.

The older generation sat with dirty plates before them at one of the tables as they customarily ate much earlier than this. Luke figured that even though his dad had eaten already, he could coax the old man into going up for seconds.

Lauren felt like crap as the tequila, which she never did, was doing a tap dance on her head. Wanting it to go away and fast, she went straight for a Bloody Mary, using it as the hair of the dog that bit her cure. She mentioned to Taylor in passing that Carl tried to convince her that he had three mixed drinks during the night, but she thought that one or two of those were ginger and ginger. They both knew the man as a teetotaler.

The engaged couple scoped the buffet, finding that they were starving, as Anthony and Gia followed closely behind. Anthony obliged, plating himself up a half a plate of the piping hot food, while Gia followed along until they made it to the pastries. Lucas wasn't about to be shy, leading the group, as he looked for a cure to his hunger.

Taylor piled some fruit and cheese, to go along with her one pancake, since she overdid it eating from the French side of last night's menu. Henri and his team had a way of making their food sing. Last night she found herself making noises like the food seemed to thrill her. If she had ever done that before, she didn't remember it.

When they all stood to disband, it was happy trails for many of the guests as they wanted to venture out and see the city and its sights. They said their goodbyes as many of them vacated to discover the Pacific Coasts, Emerald City.

The following afternoon Taylor brought out more beer and wine and placed it in the cooler to get it cold. It was a hot day in September, with Seattle clouds that were rolling in fast, to a resolute forecast of rain later. Her mother opened the photo album and was placing the pictures within the cellophane sleeve, making it so that

Luke didn't have to perform this task that she waited so long to complete herself.

Lucas stood proudly, wearing the dress belt Taylor had given him, while he flipped ground beef patties, keeping one eye on the food and the other to the clouds. The lot of them knew the weather was going to get bad soon, as it appeared that the sky was about to unload.

The group sat back but were ready to jump when it was time. Taylor's family and Lauren and Carl filled all the chairs that Luke could come up with. Kyle sat with Isla on his lap, as Taylor sat next to her dad, who was nursing his first beer.

Taylor reached for one photo in general of Lucas and his father working on the bar. Her ring shimmered as she pointed the picture out to her mom. Lucas was just finishing up with the hamburgers and buns as the sky decided to interfere. A big gust brought in the rain, making them all bolt into the house except for Luke, who was still manning the grill.

Kyle came to the rescue, to help Luke pull the grill under cover to keep the food from getting ruined. Lucas was already pretty wet, as his curly locks were hanging low. His T-shirt contained remnants of the pitter-patter splatter mother nature dropped down over him. He trayed up the picnic meat and bread before they scurried into the house.

After lunch, Taylor's mom sat on the couch with her daughter on one side and her husband on the other as Kyle, Isla, and Lucas stood behind. She laid out three albums on the coffee table in front of them. She opened the first and recanted stories about Lucas, for those times when he had either visited their house or the inn.

They even received knowledge of things they had forgotten about themselves as youths. And a few laughs broke out when they finally did remember. But the picture that got the biggest laugh was when the three of them had gotten dressed up for Halloween. The pic was inside Kyle's album.

Lucas, who was maybe eight, dressed as a cowboy, with the toy gun and holster, and a looped rope at his side. Kyle dressed as an Indian, with the full, but very scaled headdress and fake leather buckskin top and tomahawk.

Taylor, who was probably about five, wore her dark hair in a braid with a single feather. The young girl adorned a knee-length buckskin dress. It was then that they found out that the Native American garb was made by their grandmother.

Taylor stood so cute among the taller boys in the picture. Luke knew that she must be seeing the rope hanging off his right side. His hair was shorter back then, but the curls were even more pronounced then.

After finishing the walk down memory lane, Lucas asked if he could borrow the Halloween photo, as he wanted to have a copy of it made up for their album. She slid it out and handed it to him. Taylor looked back with that glimmer of why he wanted it.

When it came to bedtime, her parents headed to the spare bedroom, with Kyle and Isla were upstairs in the newly redone bedroom. Taylor and Lucas settled in and quietly talked about the day. She, of course, had to bring up the picture and how manly he looked with his rope, even back then. Lucas smiled, knowing that the photo didn't escape her.

On Monday, with the family together and Lucas at work, Taylor concocted some of her grandmother's stew. They gabbed, something this family was good at. Then when there was a momentary break, Isla spoke. "It is wonderful that you all get along as well as you do. I wasn't that lucky, with me being an orphan at an early age," she said silencing the room. "There weren't any family members to speak of, so I got taken in by foster parents that were okay at best." Isla took a breather.

"They never treated me special, but they never mistreated me either. We just barely got along, with me thinking that is how I thought a family was supposed to be. Many years went by with them not even remembering my birthday or Christmas, which was nothing but a token day off for them."

Isla sat there regaling the Naughtons, while Taylor's eyes went to Kyle, who she thought must have heard some of the story before. "I do want to tell you something, Kyle. My life changed for the better the day that I met you." She looked him straight in the eye, directing the statement to only her boyfriend. "I look forward to every summer when I can help you at the inn. And knowing you and your family has only made me stronger, so thank you!" Isla exclaimed, not caring if they all heard.

Kyle looked as though he had not heard this part before. He held her hand as it was clear that she had relinquished the floor.

"I love you, Isla!" Kyle proclaimed. The other three didn't know what to say. Her life, which wasn't terrible, was still not much of a life at all. And because of that, Taylor was now pulling for the two of them more than ever before.

Later, Taylor was quiet as she whispered the story of Isla. Lucas was quite surprised and would have never guessed it. He thought that maybe she was just an introvert. It was no bad thing; he just figured that she wasn't outgoing.

"Wow! Did she say what happened to her parents?" Lucas asked, continuing the whisper.

"No, with her finally opening up to us, no one was going to ask."

"I'm still shocked your dad didn't."

"Well, he wouldn't. I know that he likes Isla a lot and he would never screw this up for his son."

"That makes sense."

Wednesday night, Lucas finally arrived home. "So did your family get to the airport okay?"

"Yes. My brother forgot his phone cord. I texted him later, and he said just keep it. They should all be home soon."

"That's good," Lucas said as he went to the fridge and grabbed a bottle of water.

"So what can I get you to eat?"

"If you have any more of that stew, I would love that." She turned to the fridge and dumped out the remainder of the meal into a pan and turned it on to heat. "I see you are drinking water!" Taylor said, noticing the water bottle in his hand.

"After this weekend with all the alcohol and food, my body needs a detox."

"I know what you mean, but it was so good. That beef bourguignon was incredible. I could have eaten that all night long," Taylor stated. After the quick dinner and cleanup, they retired calling it a night.

"So are you going to be looking more into the website?"

"Yes, I am, and if it is all right, I would like to check out one of the meetings."

"I don't mind. Just be very leery and don't get sucked into anything. There are some shady characters out there," Lucas said in a muffled voice.

"I will be careful, and I will let you know the date, time, and place before I go."

"And always keep your phone on you too."

"Yes, sir," she said this time in a condescending tone.

"Have you found the site informative?" he said, changing the subject.

"Very much, but I'm still not sure why it has to be so secretive."

Luke turned his head. "It is because dark desires are about following up on your deepest wants while doing it in complete anonymity. You know like Superman but if he had hobbies." She laughed as he compared a fictional animated superhero to someone that was maybe just a little bored and horny. She wanted to look more into the meetings now but under the criteria that Lucas had just given her.

Today, Taylor had to catch up on all the business stuff she had put aside for the past week. No Taylor time until she's caught up. She remembered that the garden needed to be stripped soon, as the cold weather was going to move in destroying whatever was left. But first, it was paying the bills for the company.

She spied the balance, making sure it was always where it needed to be. Any issues and it meant a long phone call to straighten it out or the twenty-minute ride to the branch itself. The balance looked accurate. Next week she balances it, but that is not for today.

Then, she paid all the bills and filed the receipts. After exiting the site, she caught up with the unanswered emails that had gone unopened, adding a little something about getting back to them so late.

She checked the inbox, thinking she was going to have to run something to Lucas, but by text, he replied that he already had an e-copy. She then tried to figure out what else she needed to do as she didn't want to bother Luke a second time to find out. Confident she was done, she closed the book on her work for the day, barring any unforeseen phone calls.

Passing her tablet, Taylor thought I am going to need that later. Earlier she took a morning shower that was late enough to be called an afternoon one. Returning, she made another pass to the desk where she had put the work phone down.

# CHAPTER 19

Wednesday, Taylor eyed the calendar of the dominant/submissive section of Dark Desires, logging the pertinent information into her phone. Finding a topic she was sure she'd like, she decided that next week was the week to check it out. She hoped it was what she wanted, but the few words didn't say much to her. If it wasn't, she figured she would give it a second chance before she stopped this pursuit or tried something different.

Taylor was pleased that she was going to learn and be more open to this way of life that she now finds she craves. The info she entered was her meeting on this coming Tuesday, at six thirty, at the underground café. Taylor tried to picture the setting where dominants and submissives alike, gather to learn.

The woman brought the tablet to the chair in the living room, looking for a comfortable place to sit, to view the video. She also carried in a bottle of water, placing it right on the sill of the ocean view window, before parking herself.

Clicking on this week's lesson, she found the video was long with it being about thirty minutes. She studied it, finding a few similarities in the way that the dom and sub performed their actions. She also found this dominant to be more loving than the last one. It appeared he was more defined. Taylor liked this version, as she could identify with this guy who she thought was much like Lucas.

Later she went for a jog. Taylor wasn't up for a full workout, so she figured she would burn a few calories and all she had to battle was a little bit of wind. She turned and trotted up the street, wondering if she could make it to the scenic parking area before she had to turn around.

It was so quiet and peaceful as she felt like she was the only one on the street. Taylor spoke too soon as there he was. A man that must have been in his early eighties was out mowing his lawn with the smallest lawnmower she had ever saw. She wondered where he could have gotten it. Taylor waved to the man who was watching her as she passed.

Making sure her sneakers were clean and that she didn't pick up any dog droppings, she put them away and changed all the rest of the bedding that they had used the past few days. She carried the sheets and blankets out to the laundry area. At the end of the workday, she was pleased to know that her business phone never left her side, not once. Maybe she was starting to figure it out.

After dinner, she sat on the couch with Lucas there next to her, she just came out with it. "I found a meeting that I want to attend next week."

"And what day is it?" Lucas said, trying to be happy about her choice.

"It is on Tuesday at six thirty."

"And where is it?"

"It's at the Underground Café."

"That's a nice place, or so I've heard," he said.

"It is along the commercial district on the north end, isn't it?"

"Yes, it's a good section. And you are sure you want to do this?"

"Of course, I do. Why? do you not want me to go?" Taylor asked.

"I didn't say that. I just want you to do this for you and not me. You know that I have not found anything that you need to train for."

Taylor was unsure as to what she should do. She had been saying that she wanted to do this for herself, but did she? "I am going to think about it some more, now that I have a date and a place to go to," she disclosed while looking him in the eye.

Lucas wasn't looking to confuse her, and he wasn't about to stop her, but he wanted to make sure that her choice was not based on him. That made Taylor a little standoffish, with the sudden realization of if she went, it would be her choice. She sat there with him, but her mind was stewing over her next step. Lucas turned on the television, something that they never did and flipped through some channels.

Sunday night, she turned to Lucas, who was almost asleep and told him what she was doing. "Luke, I am going Tuesday!"

"That's fine."

"I am not sure what time I will be home, but I will call you when I'm on my way."

Lucas just leaned over and kissed her on the lips and said, "I love you, baby, but I will not be asleep until you get back!"

"Then I'll try not to be too late." She closed her eyes, briefly wondering if she had made the right choice. And would this affect her decision to continue going, if she did think it was right for her? If she didn't at least try this out, then she would always wonder. Taylor didn't want it to keep Lucas up late while she's gone, but she would have been very surprised if he was asleep when she did.

Two days later and after several outfit changes, Taylor finally was going to check out the café, before the meeting. Having her mind ready, she somehow felt as though she was stuck in quick drying cement.

A quick turn of the key and a deep breath had her backing out of the driveway. It also had her letting out a sigh of relief before she even made it to the highway. She relaxed as she got further from home.

Taylor thought a little less about Lucas and more about the things that she found so intriguing about their hidden life. Planning on being there at least thirty minutes early, she thought she might sit in the car at first, to see what kind of people were going in.

It was a very long drive with her running scenarios in her head, about the way the meetings might run. Taylor took a sip of water and proceeded slowly as she got onto the highway heading south.

Idling across the street from the hip year-old coffeehouse, she sat as the exhaust from her tailpipe billowed into the Seattle chilly night air. She chose street parking, not wanting to do what turned out to be a much longer walk to the garage than she initially thought. She was there a half hour early like she wished to and had a half a mind to put it in drive and head home.

Taylor carefully watched as people went in and others left. Some of the patrons exited, carrying the trademark underground café cups, demonstrating to her how harmless it was. Maybe, if she didn't want to use the emailed barcode they sent her, she might at least walk away from this with a great cup of coffee. Taylor shut off her car and locked it.

Crossing the busy street, she stepped in as a man graciously held the door for her during his departure. She lingered by the doorway as she wasn't sure how this worked. A young waitress dressed in almost all black said, "If you are ordering your coffee to go, there is the standing bar, over there, but if you are drinking it here, have a seat at any of the tables."

Taylor wanted to stay on her feet until she figured out whether she was making an evening of this. She walked over and stood in front of the long tall tables, as she was still not sure what to do. With her leaning on the tabletop, a section lit up that shown a monitor. It had no audio, but it greeted her through an integrated video that led her to the menus.

From that digital layout, she was able to select all different types of coffees and even snack items. Taylor was shocked by the prices, but she knew that this was a trendy place and it must be paying for all these monitors that she first thought were tables. Pivoting, she looked around to see if any of the group for tonight had been walking by her as she got caught up in this new way that they were using to sell java.

She couldn't tell, but she thought there had to be a backroom or a downstairs for events like these. Taylor was ready to order, so she looked down to the touchscreen menu that had blacked out already. The same woman walked by. "Do you need any help?" the waitress asked.

"I do. I just want to order a cup of coffee," Taylor said, a little frustrated.

"Easy enough. Let me help you!" the woman said as she steered her to the right screen in seconds.

"Okay, if you are ordering it to go, you can choose the size here. Any additives? We do serve a few blends with alcohol, but you can't get those to go. You can even purchase a reusable cup." Taylor tapped the screen and got her completed order and just had to pay. Her no-frills large coffee came to a whopping seven dollars.

"Do I pay you?" Taylor asked curiously. The waitress tapped place order, and a credit card slider lit up. "Or you can just hit cash here, and you will pay for it when we bring it to you."

"I'd like to pay cash."

"Then I will be right back with your coffee!" the waitress said, departing before she could ask her a question.

She turned to check out the place more thoroughly. The café was dimly lit to give it the feel they were going for. But it still was cozy, clean, and warm, at least what she could see of it. Again, no people stood out, with no neon sign that boldly exhibited Kink Fest.

The waitress, who was busy serving others across the room, was fast at clearing tables, delivering coffee, and assisting those that needed help. Her next stop to the kitchen brought her back with her drink order in hand. She marched up to Taylor and placed it down in front of her. "That will be seven dollars and fifteen cents!" Taylor pulled two fives from her pocketbook but didn't release the money until she asked her question.

"Excuse me, but is there a meeting here this evening?"

"Yes, it is downstairs. If you are staying for it, I can put this in a mug?"

"No, this is fine," she said as she told the woman to keep the change. As the waitress started to pick up momentum once more, Taylor said, "And where are the stairs?"

She pointed off to the other side of the building. "The stairs are back between the restrooms," she exclaimed as she vanished again. Nervous at least on the inside, she made her way around with coffee in hand and sauntered past the small grove of tables. The flight of stairs was between the bathrooms, just as the woman had said.

As she slowly moved closer to the door, a tall beautiful black woman passed her. Taylor was trying to figure if she was just looking to relieve herself, but no, she descended. Taylor was not timid in the least, as she followed distantly at a slow pace. She was glad for a second reason that she wasn't carrying a mug. By the time she got downstairs, there wouldn't be any left from the jitters that were coming on.

She was very close and was about to place her foot down the first step when she opted for the bathroom. After a quick piddle, she washed her hands and checked herself in the mirror. She toyed with her bangs using her hand for a brush.

Taylor opened the restroom door. From here, it was left to go home or right to see what this is all about. A small sign stood at the top of the railing boldly stating PRIVATE PARTY. As she read it she heard voices, that drew her in, as she put her free hand on the railing. The noises became increasingly louder as she came around to where she could see people waiting to enter.

She took a sip of her beverage, wondering what a seven-dollar coffee tastes like. Not bad, a mixed bean blend for sure, and it said its organic. Watching what the man in front of her was doing, she stepped up when she was next in line. Calling up the barcode, she faced it down to the scanner.

A green light and a sound told her it was okay to pass. The young man running the station just gave her a friendly "Enjoy" as she instinctively reached into her pocketbook and fed the donation jar that sat on the table.

With a room that was at least three-quarters full, she quickly noticed that they were dressed no different from any of the patrons upstairs. It almost saddened her, not that she would ever wear in public the outfit that she wears for Lucas. Wow, she just thought about him for the first time since she left the house. Taking a seat in the last row, against the wall, she sent a concise text: "I am at the meeting. Call you later!"

She felt at ease seeing what kind of people were in the room here tonight. Average was the word she would use to describe the crowd. Almost as a game, she tried to come up with who were tops and who were bottoms. It wasn't as easy as she thought. There were old and young males and females that, for the most part, sat as if it were waiting for a comedian or show to begin.

Taylor kept her knees wedged tight, after a well-groomed forty-something-year-old man sat a few inches from the padded wooden seat she was on. After a brief look at her, the man parked himself and held his head straight forward.

Her stance relaxed just a touch, as the show was about to begin. Also, her head straightened as the guessing game that she wasn't winning came to a close. Her main focus now was the man and woman, placing props upon the backside of the area that was to be their stage for the evening. Taylor turned as the door beside her closed, ensuring the privacy of who was there and the lesson that they were being taught.

The brunette peeked at her cell before turning off the ringer. Lucas left a reply: "Stay safe." She knew he was worried, but she felt like she was at an opening for improv. And later all she had to do was walk across the street to her car. It was a task that she wished to do safely so that Lucas would be okay with this, in case she decides to do this again.

The lights in the room dimmed, allowing for the couple up front to get total attention while eliminating any visual distractions. The man and woman sat upon the barstools and scoped the mostly silhouetted figured that kept their eyes straight forward. The man was a fit, attractive blond-haired guy of about five feet seven, and the curvaceous woman was maybe a five-foot-nine brunette.

Not a word was uttered, and yet she already couldn't turn away. The man was the first to stand from his seated perch. He arose and brought his two hands together in a single clap, pausing for a few seconds as he readied himself to speak.

"I would like to welcome you all to this week's edition of Dominance and Submission. Before we get started, I will have you know that as employees, so to speak, we must inform you of the ground rules in which Dark Desires operate. Oh, and by the way, if being an employee means that we get paid, then I guess we don't fit that criterion. That is why we have the tip jar out there on the table. Under Dark Desires' rigid guidelines, we here will not be plying for names or any other information. We also will not be asking for role play participation from you, the audience either." He paused to briefly look back at his co-teacher.

"So for the exhibitionists out there, we are sorry. Our end game this evening is to teach you or lend some insight into the role that you have put yourself in but by doing it in the safest way possible.

Also, if you are here to see lewd and lascivious acts, then you have wasted your time. It's not going to happen."

The woman alongside him stood. He backed up to the stool and out of the limelight so to give her the floor. "We have given ourselves a fake name so that you might feel more open to this. Tonight, we will go by the names." She paused just long enough to look at him in his eyes. "He will be Adam, and I will be Eve. I was this close to picking Sonny and Cher." A light round of laughter erupted.

"I will be speaking first from the dominant end. It is not because I am the sexual take-charge kind of person. It is because I get to talk first tonight. By the way, we are both switches, but I assure you everything we are bringing to you, we have experienced from both sides."

Taylor took a sip as she might have possibly blinked too. The woman got serious and said, "These are the ground rules of a master or dominant. A dominant is one who cares about the well-being or safety of the submissive. It is not about the control that they hold over the other. It is about how they bring it across. Now there are sometimes mixed reviews on who's pleasure it is. The scale is hard to read as some would lean towards the one with the heavy hand, when in retrospect a sub can get just as much out of it."

She stopped to drink before continuing. "And there is nothing wrong with this. Again, being on both sides, it is easy to feel the sexual energy being transferred from one to the other. And please if we talk about being a switch, it is not to talk you into it or out of what you do. Only you know what feels good and, most of all, feels right."

Taylor listened to the woman as she explained the definition of a dominant, showing how it directly related to a different but formidable relationship. The woman spoke for all of forty minutes, sometimes using Adam to demonstrate the techniques that make it work so well. When Eve was through, they called out for a ten-minute break, whether it be for the bathroom, smoke break, or even more coffee.

Taylor stood, making sure that she was still in possession of her purse and phone. She walked out with at least half the audience behind her, seeing that the other half were mostly up and about. A few stepped up to the two switches and may have been asking some questions instead of waiting to the end. Going to the ladies' room, she held the cup of coffee that was now easier to drink, now that it had cooled some.

This was informative for sure, with her noticing the similarities to some of the videos Taylor had been watching on the site. But now she was waiting for the other side of it. Taylor wasn't sure if it was going to have the same impact coming from a male sub. Trying not to think bigotedly, she pictured it as a male master, female sub.

The doorman told all that were in the hall that they needed to take their seats. He made sure to say it loud enough, so at least the ones in the restrooms could hear. The ten or so people still outside filtered back into the room with the very eager newbie student.

She excused herself as she passed the man that had been next to her. There had been very few people talking like before it began and during the intermission even. As a person that enjoys talking, she just thought that was peculiar. And for the ones that were speaking with the instructors, she thought they might possibly know each other.

The couple took their spot back on the stools. Adam took a few seconds as if he was looking to the heavens for some divine wisdom. Well, he found it because what the audience got from him was the equivalent of gold. He had started with how it was for a submissive. "From the first time that rope encased wrists, or collar encircled a neck, or subconsciously bowed to another, there has been that division of power and respect. Even though that may not have been a basis for which we all identified with or acted on, it was still there, silently lurking in the shadows."

He ran his open hand up and across his chin and then continued. "These experiences, whether they seemed bad or good, are ones that have helped to mold the person you are today. I mean, a person can't just wake up and say 'I am submissive.' It doesn't happen like that."

Adam took a breather and called out to the crowd. "Is there anyone here that is here because your master or mistress had told you to?" No hands raised. "Great, then you are all here because it is your choice. And I understand how that can change drastically when some of you get out and are not within your private world. So make sure that you take in what works for you. It might be the meeting in the upcoming weeks that switches on that lightbulb. You will learn from these, but it will be your refinement that will leave you perfectly polished." He reached for his bottle of water and slugged down a few ounces.

"I think the two most important things a sub can possess is making sure they are always safe. Have you heard about safe words? They are there for a reason. Use them. Without them, you have ventured over the line from D & S to possibly S & M. The second thing is you must trust your partner. If you don't have trust in the other, you will not be at ease, and that is where the letters could start to change. If you are a newbie to this, that is okay. Take it slow, as you don't want to be caught up with a dominant that is out of your league, new or otherwise."

As the man talked, Taylor thought of how she never questioned her master but felt assured that she already trusted him with safety not being an issue. She looked at her watch. It was eight fifteen, and Taylor was thinking it must be wrapping up soon. She wasn't losing interest, but she didn't want Lucas worrying.

The rest of the evening included Eve who stood in as the Dom, while Adam showed proper form in the unassertive role he was teaching. She gulped the rest of her coffee, holding the empty cup in one hand, waiting for the end. She had to go to the bathroom before she left since there was something about coffee that always made her have to pee.

The question and answer segment at the end had only four questions asked. The duo took turns answering, and this encouraged the crowd. It probably helped their tip can too. When Eve asked one last time if there were any more inqueries, Taylor stood to exit the room. A few remained to possibly ask questions of a more personal nature, but she didn't know that seeing she had had rounded the corner in a rush to go home.

Taylor stopped to the left of the door to bundle up and let a few of the people from the meeting pass. The place looked busy as the crowd inhabited the café for trivia night using the very screen's they placed orders on. As Taylor looked out at her car, and pulled at her zipper, a woman stared from the window that looked out towards the street. The blond never diverted following Taylor's every move as she walked down the stairs across the street to her vehicle.

The woman who was perched at the table, drinking a cappuccino set her mug down, and studied the brunette as she climbed into the seat of the red Honda Civic. She watched intently until she drove off and out of sight. She took one last sip of her drink before reaching and dropping a five-dollar tip to the table as she exited.

Taylor got to the light when a car pulled up behind her and stopped. The light turned green, with her pressing the pedal, advancing to the speed limit. In the right lane, she exited onto the Seaway drive connector. At the end, she took the rotary turning off at the first exit to their drive. The other car, which had dropped back, lagged at a distance of about three hundred feet. As Taylor pulled into the driveway, the vehicle that was following her slowed, and then drove off.

Taylor got out of the car and went into the house, only to find Luke sitting at his desk going over a bid proposal. He never led on, but he found it hard to concentrate on while she was gone. Taylor went straight to him and gave him a great big kiss. "Did you have fun?" Lucas inquired.

She beamed. "I had a ball."

"So are you going to continue?"

"Are you kidding me? I learned a lot, and you know how much that means to me?"

He nodded. It wasn't exactly the response he wanted to hear, but Taylor did seem happy, and how could he squelch that? "Well, what type of meeting was it exactly?" Lucas asked, genuinely curious.

"Tonight, was D & S," she said like she talks this way all the time. "Next week is something different. It is only listed as Bondage so far!"

"So are you going to skip that one? Since it isn't what you are looking for?"

"I am thinking about attending the first so many weeks of meetings and then I will cut back since you will be home earlier. I don't want it moving into our time together."

She sat in his lap. The night had her feeling rejuvenated. "I thought you would have been in bed by now."

"I might have been, but the school committee will be taking bids on their expansion project in November, and I wanted to get a jump on it. It is a big job, and I'm not sure I can come up with the workforce to cover it. I might just toss the proposal out."

"Well, what if you had Trent helping you?"

"I don't know, but he would have to have been in place a month or two ago, for this to work."

"So are you still thinking about it?"

"I… I have been thinking about a change, and for that to happen, he would have to be involved." Taylor smiled and got up and grabbed a soft handful of his leg.

"Well, it is time to get you to bed!"

With her first meeting behind her, she looked at the calendar to view this week's information and what they had coming. She filtered to have it include only the coffee shop as she wasn't ready to venture outside of the place she was already comfortable with.

The details were just as it had been the week before. However, Taylor didn't realize she could get a brief synopsis of what it was going to cover. It seemed that tonight was going to be less about bondage than she originally thought. They were selling it as the artistic side, as bondage shown by a renowned Japanese expert.

The title for the upcoming event was "The Knotted Sculpture." She didn't think this was what most were going to ask a lot of questions about, but it could be incredibly hot watching it, as the artist tied what she only assumed was a woman up. Thinking of it in that context, she was looking forward to this one, and just as much as the last.

Taylor made it through the next days, getting turned on, by this form of art that had absolutely nothing to do with sex. She realized immediately that the turn out for this one was much busier as she hadn't even made her way part way down the staircase. On the calendar, there was a ten-dollar cover charge to be in attendance.

But it was kind of like going to a movie, except there were a lot fewer seats and it was cheaper, but the coffee in her right hand helped to tip the scale the other way, she thought. Taylor plodded down three more steps. She recognized the same doorman that sat by the door the previous week. Everyone took out their smartphones and shown their barcodes, and shelled out their cash to be part of this secret meeting in the basement of the coffeehouse.

Taylor was ready as she paid the man her money and held her phone over the scanner, like a seasoned pro. The beep sounded as she walked into the room and took her same seat. She sipped from her coffee and then carefully put it under her chair.

They planned for a packed house as they filled as many chairs as the place could hold, just beyond the area that they were using as their stage. She looked around as she did the week before. It was much harder to see with most people already seated. This time she mainly was checking out the back of their heads.

Up in front, a steel six-plus-foot-high stand, a series of different-sized ropes hung there, catching her attention. So much so that she hardly noticed as a tall lanky blonde woman crossed in front of Taylor, taking a seat alongside her. After making sure the woman was clear, Taylor pulled out her phone to put it in silent mode, following the text that she sent minutes earlier.

She dropped it into her pocketbook as the woman sat with eyes forward. When the place was full, and they had to turn others away. The door was closed, leaving them there for the private show.

Taylor felt lucky to be one of the roughly sixty people in attendance for something that was so rare to see. She sat up tall as she was now rethinking her seat choice. Taylor was not short by any means but felt like it, sitting behind rows of equally tall people. If only she were a little taller like the Amazon sized woman sitting to her left.

The brunette stood and plucked her jacket from the back of her seat, folding it to prop herself up. Sitting on the thicker pad of the chair, she was somewhat pleased with the new vantage point. From the back of the room, she saw the artist, the model, and some other woman as they stood against the back wall of the stage, speaking

Japanese, she assumed. She figured the artist was probably explaining how she wanted the presentation to go tonight.

Taylor so wanted to take a picture of the model all tied up on display, even though there was a bold statement that included no flash or video photography on the door. She thought that Luke would enjoy seeing the way that this form of bondage was displayed.

The assistant turned to face the crowd, where she explained the style the artist practices and how she learned this art and even how many hours she practiced to date. Taylor cringed at the thought of the thousands of hours and the model or models that had to endure this day in and day out.

Next, the woman who would be displaying her skills walked to the side of the frame grasping a specific rope of choice in her hand. She untied the simple knot that held the bulk in place during its storage. The third woman must be just that, the interpreter for tonight, since it would lose some of its appeal if the artist herself talked throughout the entire presentation. The model was introduced simply as Karuko. She stood behind the metal frame and bowed her head as the artist readied herself.

The artist was introduced last, with her muttering something to the model, again not in English. The woman took her place directly in front of the stainless-steel frame. The model stood tall in a white leotard, with her long jet-black hair free and flawlessly maintained. The artist clenched the violet shade of rope in one hand, surveying the model before even letting it touch her skin, up until the time that Natsumi, the rope yielder, was ready.

Karuko stretched her limbs, preparing for what she was about to do. The artist touched her shoulder, making the model stop and stand erect. She held her head high as Natsumi reached around with the center point of the purple cord to form a knot leaving a loop.

She lifted the ringlet placing it over her head, leaving the bulk of the braided line hanging straight down her back. The artist lifted her long black hair, bringing in over her right shoulder clear of the bindings. Taylor sat on the edge of her chair and wished again that she had chosen something closer to the front.

Natsumi brought the model's arms behind her so that her wrists were together with her arms laid in a V down her back and over her derriere. Taylor could see that this woman was very pliable, and that must have been the reason why she was chosen for this.

Quickly crafting an artsy restraint that held Karuko's arms, a new bond for every few inches was added, as the young ladies' arms looked as if they had been artfully cemented to her backside.

Natsumi moved from one side to the other, making sure that the rope was not crossed, and it laid just so before starting the next. The dark ties had a beautiful contrast against the white of her material. The woman was diligent in her work, as she made her way down to the wrists of her assistant.

Next, with a word again that no one in the crowd understood, she had the model separate her legs a couple of inches. Natsumi spun the model around so that the spectators could see. She brought the rope down the center of her bottom and drew the two leads past her crotch and pulled them taut. She fashioned another simple knot in the way that she did when she began and strategically positioned it between her modest breasts, tying it off behind her neck.

Natsumi turned to Karuko before she continued. With no more rope to work with, she brought out a bright yellow piece and uncoiled it. She tied off the center bringing it through the ropes that were currently holding her arms behind her. She ran each of the ends through and around her upper arms. Weaving it from the front piece and back to the rear ones that she designed, to create a stylish cross-weave pattern.

Taylor was getting wet, even as she watched it from the artistic side. She pictured herself bound tight, with the rope between her wet pussy lips. The model, when she was done, stood turning slowly for the full visuals of everyone seated.

Natsumi never took her eyes off the woman, who was probably critiquing her own work. She looked as though she strived to be the best at what she did, and that must take lots of effort and practice. The next part had the model tied with black ties this time, having her arms bound differently.

She was then seated, as the rope master crossed and tied her ankles, leaving her legs lying flat on the round wood platform she was placed on. Running a new short tie, she had the young model's upper half of her body pulled down and tied about a foot from her well-restrained ankles. When Natsumi was through, she spun the model on the platform slowly to show her handiwork.

The crowd applauded as Taylor, being in the very last row, just felt she had to stand to view it. And she wasn't the only one. The translator at that point said there would be a brief intermission and that if anyone wanted to take pictures, they could do so now. Taylor did have to go to the bathroom, if for nothing else to wipe up, but there was no way that she was going to miss this photo op.

Taylor walked the aisle following others who were before her in line. She waited her turn but still managed to get a couple of good pics to show Lucas later. She cringed at the sight of the young lady with her hands tethered behind her back and high up by her shoulder blades. If she ever thought that she was remotely flexible, she didn't think so now.

# CHAPTER 20

After Taylor had taken the pictures she wanted, she darted to the bathroom. It wasn't to relieve herself this time, as much as to tend to her own dripping faucet.

On her return through the threshold, an employee was mopping up the floor in the exact area where she was sitting. Taylor looked down at the woman that she vaguely knew as the one beside her. With a look of guilt on her face she apologized. "I'm sorry, I did it. I knocked your coffee over!"

"That's okay," Taylor said, shrugging it off. With the floor modestly damp and their seats back where they were in the first place, the two sat.

"I feel bad. It's my big feet. Can I buy you another one?" she whispered, trying to make amends.

"No, seriously, it's all right!"

"Then at least let me give you money for it. Those things aren't cheap," the woman continued.

"I'm all right, but thanks anyway."

As the two eyed the set for the second half and not more than a minute in, the woman leaned in to whisper to her. "The bondage is very hot, don't you think?" Taylor nodded to her. "I am the model at home. My master has been doing this for years," the woman stated in soft tense. The show hadn't officially restarted yet, but the blonde uttered something that invariably caught her ear.

"He ties you up like this?" Taylor replied in question.

"Yes, not nearly as elaborate because it is a part-time thing for us, but about half the time it is foreplay, you know?" Taylor smiled. She did know, and she didn't have to picture it. The lights dimmed with the thoughts playing havoc in her brain.

She wanted to pick the woman's brain, but there was no time. Taylor sat, trying to concentrate on the show up front, as the model for the last piece came out from behind a silk partition wearing nothing but a G-string. Taylor was in shock as she knew that she wasn't going to be able to take pictures of this one.

*Holy crap*, was her first thought, while the crowd acted like she was fully dressed. That was something Taylor couldn't do, go completely nude in front of about sixty people. Her seatmate watched Taylor as she stared down the model up front.

The tall blonde studied and compiled as much information as she could about the woman seated to her left. She was driving the car of someone she knew and knew well. From that, she needed to find out who this brown-haired submissive was.

Crushing her coffee cup was just the start. Feeding her the bogus story about being a submissive also fed on the woman's obedient heart. It wasn't at all hard to figure that one out. Doing this for this long, she eyed her next trophy, bringing her face to steadily morph into a broad commandeering sneer.

Taylor sat for the next twenty-five minutes while Karuko was tied up with one leg high in the air and her two arms above that, to the stand that sat all night in the background. She was suspended using the cross pole so that all could view her. Her limbs were then webbed to each other, exhibiting the vibrant red rope that held her snuggly underneath the stage lights that highlighted the bound beauty.

The woman kept her head motionless as if she was a still-life sculpture. Her black ebony hair glistened over the rope pattern as she looked to the sky, with one of her breasts that peeked out through the woven material. Karuko stood only using the front half of her right foot. She was suspended enough by Natsumi, to where she did it with ease. When the evening was over, the artist gave a head bow to all that watched.

The crowd stood and applauded the works of a woman that had given much of her life, for something that she loved. Taylor clapped and then looked down at her watch. Unbeknownst, the woman next to her slid her arm into the sleeve of her jacket. "I still owe you a coffee?" she said beginning a conversation but keeping it short.

Taylor, who wanted to get home, replied, "Sure, you can buy me a coffee sometime!" The woman slid her other arm in, then pulled her jacket onto her shoulders and reached for the zipper.

"I hope I didn't make you feel weird about the bondage stuff. It is not something a person should say after spilling their drink," she quipped.

"It didn't make me feel weird. That is why we are here in the first place. Actually, I wish I had time to hear some of your stories if you didn't think that's weird."

"Not at all," the woman said as they headed to the door. Taylor, among others, cleared the room, with most leaving for their cars.

Taylor stopped for a minute so not to be rude, as her curiosity made her want to talk with the lady, to at least be sociable and get her name. "Excuse me, I'm Hope!" she said, calling on her newly named site persona.

"Hi, Hope, I'm Ellie, well, Elinor."

"Nice to meet you, Ellie!"

"I have to get going since I have to work in the morning," Taylor stated.

"Hope, here is my DD chat name if you want to talk sometime," the woman phrased. Writing down her site name, she handed it to Taylor. She looked at it to make sure she could read it before she left.

"You know what, we can chat, and I might see you here next week."

"That sounds good, Hope. And it was nice meeting you," Ellie said.

"And you as well." Both women exited to the public garage. Ellie gave a brief wave as she passed Taylor, who just unlocked her car. As the blonde left, a sinister grin engulfed the lower part of her face. She was confident that the wheels were in motion, with her sensing that it was nearly time.

Taylor couldn't wait to show Luke the pictures. She wished it was possible to have developed the ones that were still fresh in her mind though. The Japanese model all strung up in bright red. It was something she would not soon forget. During the drive home, she thought about trying out the chatroom feature.

What could it hurt? Maybe she could grow to like this woman, with her someday being a friend. Elinor, if that was her name, was a long-legged beauty that looked like she might be as old as fifty, she thought. And that had Taylor wondering how long she had been in this lifestyle. That and so many more questions randomly popped into her head.

Luke just finished putting the chairs and hoses from the yard away. Winter could come early by the predictions for Washington, so he wanted to clean up the boat and put it on the lift. Getting home so late made it hard for him even to consider doing it tonight. He just wanted to keep busy while Taylor was out having fun.

He felt a little more okay with it after the first one. Lucas figured she should be in the door again, any minute now. He closed the rear door to the garage, only to get back in the house a few seconds after Taylor had walked in. She was in the fridge, getting some water and quenching her thirst.

"So how did it go?"

"Fantastic. Have you ever been to any rope exhibits?"

"No, I haven't."

"Well, I had a good time. I struck up a conversation with a woman there. It all started because she knocked over my coffee."

Luke's instinctual defenses went up. "You didn't give her your name or anything, did you?"

"No, she doesn't know who I am. I told her my name is Hope!"

"That's good," he said, relieved. "You just have to be careful."

"I know. We might chat this week on DD. That should be okay, right?"

"Just as long as you don't give her any more than the site will give them."

Changing the subject she asked, "So what did you do while I was gone?"

"Not much, just puttering."

"Then you weren't worried about me," Taylor stated.

"No…well not as much. But I'm thrilled that you had a good time."

"I did…oh, I have a few pictures to show you," Taylor said going to her phone gallery.

"Look at this," she said, pointing her phone at him.

"Interesting!" he said with one brow slightly raised.

"I know, and the model was on a turntable for the viewing when she was done. It was very hot. And there is one that was even better than that. The model was nude in the last one."

Getting Luke's full attention, he said, "Let me see!"

"They wouldn't let us take pictures of that, sorry." Taylor paused. "And she was all knotted up in this rope web that you would have had to be there to understand."

"I get it, I wasn't there!" he said jokingly.

The next day she went to the website to see just how hard it was to find this woman. Locating the chat box, she took out the paper and typed in "sub4u112," then hit Enter, which instantly opened a message field. Taylor left a note. "I will be on at nine if you want to chat."

She closed down the site and went back to check on the business emails. The first one was from a man who said that he came home to find the stone and mortar retaining wall they did for him wasn't right. She was pretty sure it wasn't done yet, but she gave Lucas a quick call anyway. "Hello, Taylor, what's up?"

"I'm sorry to bother you, but the Anderson back wall project, the guy is saying it isn't right!"

"Well, Steve is there now, and I think it was because he didn't get the mortar done yesterday."

"That could be it. The man did mention the mortar! I thought you might want to get Steve to give him a quick call."

"I will have him do that. Anything else?"

"No, I was just going through the emails, because I don't like to fall behind on them."

"Good. Thank you. I'll see you later."

"Bye, Luke." She hung up, finding it hard to leave her normal personal touch at the end. Saying I love you felt so natural these days.

But she understood that he could be there with a client or even the mayor for all she knew.

And most times he was on speakerphone so that he was hands-free. She put down the phone because her next task was to replace the plumbing stock that was depleted. She started up the computer on the desk and logged into the contractor supply website.

Once she was signed in, she went in and found the length, thickness, and diameter of each material she needed. Lucas had left a detailed note since he hadn't got to it. She typed in the amount on the lines she wanted and then went on to the next item. When she was done, Taylor entered and paid for the product with their company credit card. *Check*, she thought as another thing was knocked off her mental work list.

Taylor kept thinking about the chatroom, with her wanting to go back and see if there had been any activity. She needed to hear the woman's real-life stories firsthand, from someone that has lived a good part of her life in servitude to a master. Nothing, she guessed she would have to wait until later. Taylor who had a lapse in work, grabbed a tray and went to strip what ripe vegetables were left in the garden.

At bedtime Lucas said goodnight to Taylor with a gentle kiss. She told him she intended on chatting tonight and didn't want to go to bed yet. After he was asleep, she went to the fridge for some wine. Well, the bottle made its way to the window sill, with her parking her glass on the small end table to the left of her. From there the only other thing she needed was the tablet, that she left on the dining room table.

She hoped that Ellie had noticed her post and was free to talk. After getting on the site, this time a red dot and a single beep sounded in the lower-right-hand corner of the screen. She tapped on the dot. The message read, "kneed2please49, I will be on later. I was informed this morning of a session for this evening. Should be on by nine thirty the latest."

After reading it, she figured that it's not proper to use a person's name on the site. She made a note to play by the rules, although Ellie might be an alias for her too. Either way, she opted to keep it from the digital media.

Taylor took a sip and pushed back in the overstuffed chair, reaching for the folded throw behind her, with her searching for comfort as she sat there. She wondered what she was going to say to the blonde woman she had just met.

She thought she would be very careful and read before she sent anything. Although, Taylor was okay with telling Ellie that she too is submissive. This is going to be much harder than she thought, as she wished she could have taken a class on chatrooms.

It was almost nine thirty when she saw the first entry from sub4u112. The line read, "Sorry about that. I wasn't free to chat earlier."

She replied, "No prob. I was just sitting here, sipping my wine."

"That's nice. I'm hydrating. I always need lots of water after an hour and a half." Taylor's jaw dropped open.

She knew what she meant, but that was a long session. "I hope you had fun?" Taylor asked.

"Always. My master insists on it. But I am the submissive, so I must endure."

"I do know that, but it is a lot of fun, though."

"Yes, I agree. So how did you like the artistic bondage the other night?"

"It was incredible. And you two do that?" Taylor inquired.

"Sometimes. If you could see my wrists right now. My master keeps me limber, or should I say, he tells me he wants me that way."

"Wow, and you don't ever fight any of those requests?"

"I am what I am, and if you are one, you wouldn't either, would you?"

Taylor thought for a second and then typed, "I don't fight it either!"

"Oh, so do we have a fellow sub?" Ellie asked.

"Yes, guilty as charged," Taylor confessed.

"I don't feel bad about it, I think I had known from the time I was a young girl. Just didn't know the term and it didn't make any sense until I came across my first Dom," Ellie explained.

"That is how it happened to me too," Taylor agreed.

"So is your counterpart a man?" she asked already sure she knew the answer.

Taylor hesitated and then answered, "Yes, he is!"

"So what are you two into? For us, it is dominant/submissive stuff with rope for our B, but he has dabbled with the S & M stuff too."

"Oh really, no we are mostly B, with the D being that he takes the lead."

"I understand that. It is complete chaos if no one leads the other. But the imagination this man has always surprised me."

"Mine too," Taylor said after putting the wineglass back down. She was having fun, and this was innocent enough.

"My master has built different things for me in the basement. It is nothing I can show anybody, and I would be strung up somewhere right now if he knew I was telling you!"

"Well, mine has built me something too," she said but erased it and just put, "Yes, they can be so imaginative and crafty." She just couldn't send the other statement.

"Hey, kneed, I have to shut down. It's not because of my situation. It is that I have to get up real early in the morning for work."

"That's all right, it is nice talking to you!" Taylor said.

"And you also. I can be on as early as eight thirty tomorrow night. He always gives me a free night to recuperate. LOL."

"LOL, I would like to hear some of your stories, if that isn't too personal to ask."

"Hell no, but I would feel safer if I am not typing my personal stuff over the internet for the hacking world to see."

"Yeah, I didn't think of that. I'm sorry I asked!"

"Don't be sorry. Maybe we can do lunch next week at the coffeehouse on Tuesday. From two to three thirty, they have free eats for the customers. It is not a meal, but they send out some pretty amazing stuff."

"I don't know. I will have to get back to you," Taylor said apprehensively on her end anyway.

"Oh, you are probably working. I sometimes forget since I get to work from home. It is just something to think about."

"I will let you know. I might be able to work something out," Taylor said.

"Okay, maybe tomorrow night then?"

"That should work for me. I really want to do lunch," Taylor answered.

"And I owe you a coffee, remember?"

"Yes, and there is that too," Taylor said.

"Good night, H, I have to go."

"Good night, E, I will talk to you soon." And then in seconds, sub4u112 was gone. Her green light had turned to white.

Taylor finished the rest of the bottle of chardonnay and sat there in the low light of the living room, stewing over what she was going to do. The woman was a submissive, and no kind of red flags went up when Taylor met her for the first time, or chatted with her now. She thought the lady must have some incredible stories, with some of them revolving around S & M. She still didn't want to try it, but she was intrigued.

Thursday, Taylor made it through the entire day, getting only a few things accomplished. It took her longer than it should have because her mind had wandered so many times. She was also worried on how Lucas was going to take it tonight, with her possibly going to the chatroom earlier.

Eight thirty? He might be okay with it, if she said it was the last time this week that she would do it. Taylor thought it was worth a try. She even figured she would make a special dinner for him tomorrow night and then offer herself up to him. That he might be all right with. She smiled as she let her imagination roam.

At dinner, the two were talking, as the topic had the two chatting about everything but mostly about their future. With Taylor being excitedly nervous, Lucas picked then to bring up their wedding, looking for a date.

"Well, when do you think it might be good for you? And are we talking next year or the year after?" Taylor asked.

"As late as May or as early as September? And I am okay with whatever year we decide on, but I don't want it to end up a few years down the road."

"I agree, but what about kids? I know that you are okay with that, but how many would you like?" Taylor asked, wanting to hear the answer to this one.

"I am thinking two," he said, cringing like he just pulled the trigger during a game of Russian roulette.

"What is that face for? I was thinking two," Taylor agreed.

"So where do you want to get married?" Lucas asked.

"My first choice would be at the little church in Point Hope?" Taylor answered.

"I frankly don't care where I get married to you, as long as we do!" he exclaimed. Seeing her look at her watch for the second time in the last few minutes he asked. "Am I keeping you from something?"

"Um, I have a chance to chat with Ellie again. You know the woman I met at the café?"

"It is okay with me, but are you going to do this all the time?"

"No, she couldn't talk long last night, and she wanted to tell me some stories. She knows that I can't do this anymore this week."

"That's fine. I have to stay up to check on a few things anyway, but I won't be in your way."

"I know that, but I thought I would make one of my grandmother's recipes for us tomorrow night, and then I could make it up to you."

"Ooh, I hope I am home early then."

"Me too!" Taylor said as she was happy that she was getting to do this, and all while happy that she was making him feel good about it.

"I talked to Trent again about buying in. and I don't think that it's going to work the way he wants it."

"And why not?" she said a little sad.

"I can't get him on board for certain things, and it is about his end of the capital."

"So he can't afford it?"

"No, I think he could buy out the entire company outright. He is very good with his money, and even with the split from his wife, he landed flat on his feet. But don't worry, we are not done yet." She was happy to hear that as it could mean a life for him as a husband and father.

283

She went off to her chair when the time rounded eight thirty. Luke was drawing up plans for the new mall food court, with him looking forward to rebuilding the customer base there. As of late, he saw the mall, as one that will run into financial trouble someday, if they don't hit on one or a few ideas that could save it. It still might, but people were looking for something new, and they might revisit it if they find it eye appealing.

Taylor talked lightly with Lucas, who was sitting just a few feet behind her. While multitasking he asked for the white fish that Grandma Tilly would make, as the thought of it got him bubbly. To that Taylor said that she was going to go out and buy some Pacific Halibut tomorrow.

She even decided to throw in some spaghetti squash and mixed veggies for the rest of the plate. She would go back to the garden, before blending them with a little butter and spices.

The light turned green as Ellie was on to chat. Taylor only looked forward at this point. "Hello again," was the first type that appeared.

"Hello," Taylor said.

"So what are you doing tonight?"

Taylor thought and then entered. "I am just sitting here, with my master behind me."

"Oh, is he on with us?"

"No, he is doing his own thing. It is just us," Taylor said knowing that the woman would probably feel weird about the chat if someone was looking at her every word.

"I am on a break tonight. My master is out for drinks with his buddy. So I don't think he will be in until around eleven o'clock," Ellie stated.

"On a break?"

"Yeah, once a week he goes out, usually Thursday nights, and he lets me go out on Tuesday nights so that I can attend the meetings."

"Were you there a couple of weeks ago?" Taylor asked.

"I was, but something came up, and I got there late, so I just enjoyed a coffee!"

"I like them, the meetings I mean. I just started going, with me only being at the last two." She hit enter and then quickly added, "So have you ever been to any of the other meeting places?"

"No, not really. I like the atmosphere at the underground. Yes, I did go to one in an old classroom at a middle school. Didn't like it much. It felt wrong having it in that setting."

"I'm anxious to see what next weeks are going to be," Taylor stated.

"Well, it was just posted. It is actually a play. Not sure what it is about. It's a comedy, I think. Ten-dollar charge to get in."

"That sounds like fun," Taylor answered.

"It does. So have you given any more thought to lunch, Tuesday?"

"I think I can make it. I won't know until Monday for sure. I do work, but I have flex hours."

"That sounds fantastic. You will like the tidbits they serve," Ellie said.

Taylor got distracted by something Lucas was doing behind her. He had gone to the fridge for another beer, kissing her on the side of her face upon his return. She instinctually turned the tablet away from his view when he did.

She didn't want to have to explain that she was going to lunch, with what he would have said was a complete stranger. It's innocent enough, with it being in the middle of the day and she still wasn't a hundred percent positive, she was going to go yet. He sat back down. "I love you," she called back over her shoulder.

"I love you too, baby." Taylor got back to the last thing Ellie had asked. "Have you been doing this long?"

"I was introduced to this less than a year ago," she stated candidly.

"Wow, very rare to come across a novice. It has been almost thirty years for me."

"It can't be. You don't look old enough for that."

"Well, thank you, but I am old enough, and I try to keep myself in shape."

"I can see that. So are you flexible because of your training?"

"Very much so, although I have to confess, I have been into yoga for most of my life. And what about you?"

"Not really, but I wish I were more in shape."

"You know I can show you a few things some time and with some practice, you will limber up fast." Then Ellie quickly commented, "I can see the beauty which your master must see in you."

"Well, thank you," she replied modestly.

"So are you and your man married?" the woman asked.

"No!"

"Yeah, me either, we are more about the B than anything else. No real sex involved."

"And that is your choice?" Taylor asked wondering why this would be acceptable for her.

"It's complicated. We are both into what we do but don't have those feelings for each other. I don't date, just because I don't."

"So do you get lonely?"

"Not really. I do have other hobbies, and they keep me excited if you know what I mean. I am fine." Taylor almost felt bad for the woman. She's a beautiful lady, and her relationship is no real relationship. After a brief pause, Ellie added, "I suppose I should get going, lots to do around here. I have got to clean the cage."

"The cage?"

"I meant my bedroom, and that is a story for another day."

"Okay then, I will get back in touch with you on Monday to let you know about lunch."

"Sounds good, H. I'll talk to you soon."

"Bye, E." Taylor clicked off the chat and put the tablet down to her side. Feeling a little guilty she went over to hang out with her fiancé. She studied his computer diagram of the food court. It was in the early stages, but she could already make out the walls, individual restaurants, kitchens, and the restrooms.

She wrapped her arms around his neck. Looking closer at his CAD design, she said, "It doesn't look like you missed me much while I was chatting."

"I did. You know I did. This is a project for next spring. There is so much to it, with phone calls having to be made to the building inspectors, making sure it all falls within the code, which allows for the food franchises and a lot of other state guidelines. It is like what I have done with other commercial projects, only there is much more to it."

"So is this a bid one?"

"Yes, but there is much to do with getting them a mock-up of what it is going to look like without putting in a lot of work. We make a hefty amount in the win though."

"So what happens to the ones that don't?" Taylor asked.

"We don't win them all, and it's a big city, so we go on to the next opportunity."

Taylor remained quiet by Luke's side as he continued with the drawing as occasionally, he would stop and go on to the Seattle website to view their e-manuals to see if his design was under their guidelines. Many can design an incredible food court experience for the public, but that didn't mean it was safe or it was up to code.

Luke's girl was floundering, looking at all those subordinates and definitions that were pressing down hard on her eyelids. How could he even read this, not to mention figure out what it was? She got up, turned her favorite chair around, and brought it close and parked it quietly next to Lucas. She just wanted to sit next to him for once while he did his work.

The place was remarkably quiet as neither were not adding any noises to the house, except for maybe the tapping of Luke's mouse from time to time. It was a quiet evening outside too, with the wind not adding its usual early fall rumblings.

He was caught up in the printed manual he was studying; then he would cut back to the CAD program and make his changes. If he knew it was what he wanted, and it followed the guidelines he set the line color to black. The others were in sketch gray.

Taylor sat there, wanting to be the imaginative one and do something romantic tomorrow night. She vowed to come up with anything that would wow him. Unfortunately for her, it wasn't going to be tonight. Sometime later, she found herself in bed and didn't know if she walked there or Luke helped her.

The week flew by as Taylor, who finally had a few pans in the fire again, meaning since the party, had a few things that she had checked off of her calendar. After dinner Friday night, she baked the Pacific halibut in a lobster cream sauce. Not exactly her grandma's recipe but undoubtedly inspired by her. It was to die for, coming straight from Luke's mouth, that is.

Then she decided to give him some specific attention, where she showed him some stripper moves for her personal audience of one. She thought she had been somewhat complete in what she did, leaving the man with a massive smile on his face.

The weekend was fairly busy with the two of them lifting the boat from the water and cleaning it up before winterizing it. Even yesterday had gone reasonably well, with Taylor leaving Elinor a message, saying that she would be there for lunch tomorrow.

# CHAPTER 21

Taylor opened the door to the underground café. Making sure to be there a few minutes early, she looked around and noticed how empty the place was. And that is when she saw Elinor a few rows away on the backside of the coffeehouse. Taylor strutted up to the table. "Hope it is nice to see you!" Ellie said.

"Nice to see you too!"

"Can I order you that coffee?" Elinor said as Taylor pulled off her jacket and sat down.

"Sure," Taylor voiced as she dropped her coat on the back of the chair.

"What do you usually get?"

"Oh, just plain coffee with nothing in it and in a to-go cup please," Taylor answered.

Ellie tapped at the screen in front of her. "The house blend, okay? And you want the large, right?"

"Yes, and yes." Elinor placed the order for the two of them and then shut off the touchscreen.

"Ellie, do you sleep in a cage?" Taylor whispered as she had been thinking too hard for days about the topic her new friend had chatted to her.

"Wow, I didn't think that was going to be the first question. But no, I don't sleep in it per se? I get my timeouts when I have done something wrong. It's all innocent enough. I mean, haven't you ever been punished?"

"Yes, just recently as a matter of fact, after doing something I wasn't supposed to. It was my fault, for sure, and my master followed through on what he said he was going to do if I did. And mine was innocent too."

"That's the way it is for us," Elinor said referring to the plight of the submissive. "So you are not getting in trouble with work?" Ellie added.

"No, I just have to check in on business emails and texts to make sure all is well and stuff like that."

"That sounds like fun. It must be nice having flex hours. And your master is okay with you hanging out with another sub?"

"He doesn't know. He worries about me too much! I mean I am just going to lunch," Taylor stated.

After a long pause and with Ellie holding her smile, she asked. "So are you going to the play tonight?"

"I am planning on it. Are you?" Taylor answered.

"No, I don't think so. I will be busy later. I'm thinking very busy."

"I see!" Taylor said while nodding. She brought her seat closer, getting more comfortable. "So what kind of goodies do they have here?" Taylor asked, looking for a munchie.

"We can go up in a second, the waitress is coming now."

The woman came over and set the tall paper cup in front of her. "Will there be anything else I can get you two?" the waitress asked.

"No, I think we are all set. Thank you!" She disappeared from the table in the blink of an eye, but by now Taylor was use to that. "So do you want to go up?"

"Sure," Taylor retorted only to follow Elinor closely to the bar table on the business side of the split cafe. Getting to the table they looked down over a nice assortment of crackers, cookies, and mini croissants. There were also butter, jellies, and cream cheese in a large chilled bowl. Taylor didn't have to be asked as she selected and then plated a few things. Ellie returned to the table, with Taylor still tight on her heels. "So do you come here often for lunch?" Taylor asked the woman who was dressed to the nines.

"Sometimes when I'm bored and looking for new things and new people." Taylor was confused by the way Elinor answered but reached for a cracker and the cream cheese. "So do you still want to hear some of my stories?" Elinor asked as they got back to the table.

"Yes, yes I do. I mean if you don't mind," Taylor prodded.

"I don't mind at all," the woman answered. After a sip of her coffee Elinor began her story of how it all started for her. It wasn't the way that Taylor had begun, but it didn't take long to realize that Ellie was more of a slave than a sub. She felt terrible for the woman trying not to interrupt her. Ellie had been bullied by a man that said he had loved her. He had done some cruel things to her, and somehow, she made it look like it didn't faze her, almost as if to say that she felt she deserved it.

Taylor wanted to say that she was looking at it all wrong. Elinor had been abused, and if she were a better friend, she clearly would have said something. "When I was in my mid-twenties, I found out the term for the person that I was. I was past the first guy as he moved on to someone new. The next guy was the one I was supposed to marry. He treated me like a queen in public and a whore in bed. I catered to his every whim, but then he just left me. My parents said he was the nicest guy, and that I was the reason why he left. I don't know, maybe I was."

"I am just hearing it, but it wasn't you," Taylor said sympathetically and then took a drink.

"Well, whether it was or whether it wasn't, it happened. I then gave up men for a while and learned that I didn't have what it took to play the other side of the field. I was bewildered, and it never led to a good fit in the three attempts. Now here I am almost fifty, and I still don't have a soul mate or life partner anywhere in the vicinity. It was at that point when I finally met this other guy that I am still with to this day. He figured out how to satisfy my needs using nothing but restraints and the way to use them."

"Hope, I'm going up for cookies. Are you coming?"

"I shouldn't. Why don't you go ahead?"

Elinor was gone for maybe a couple of minutes when she returned with five different pastry selections. She was about to sit down when Taylor eyed the treats.

"Oh, those chocolate ones are my favorites."

"Do you want this one or I can get you some?" Elinor offered.

"No. I will be right back!" Taylor expressed with her not wanting to take a treat from the woman that had been abused for the better part of her life.

Once Taylor had rounded the corner, Ellie looked around, spying her phone under her disheveled napkin, and turned it to view the main screen. Quickly viewing the wallpaper image, gave her all the information she needed, before shutting it down and replacing it under the cloth again.

The blonde then pulled out a short paper straw-like cylinder.

Working against time and looking to make sure the coast was clear, she poured it into the opening in the top of Taylor's cup. Elinor gave it a quick swirl and then made sure her straw was discarded back in her pocketbook. Taylor strolled back smiling with her three chocolate favorites before her.

After repositioning herself the brunette subconsciously felt around for her phone. "Did you ask the man to control you when you first met?" she inquired, taking a bite of the cookie only to wash it down with a long slug of the perfect temperature java.

"Heavens, no. He read me like an open book. He said he knew me better than I did. He was right on that one."

"But you don't have sex?" she said reaching for that personal question when she probably shouldn't have.

"No, but you know what? For the first time in my life, I feel like this is right for both of us. He has his wife twenty minutes away, and I get what I want. Even if it means that I have to spend a few hours in an animal cage, now and then."

The woman rapidly changed the subject. "So how is it for you? I mean, your story and being a freshman sub."

Taylor took a few seconds as she was still absorbing her friend's story. "Well, I am from a failed marriage and ran into this guy, someone I hadn't seen since after graduation. We met and spent some time together again, and somehow I tripped and fell in love, just like that," Taylor said, sipping at her drink.

"That sounds wonderful," Ellie said, pausing. "So how did you start up in the submissive life?"

"Well, I can't go into the whole thing, but he introduced me to it, and his part was that he had done a couple of times in his past. It is something that we only do occasionally."

"So he had been with others before you! Were they men or women?" the woman said as she pressed her, searching for more fuel.

"No, it was two women. He almost married the first one, and the other one was from a couple of years ago. He deeply despises this Celeste woman for some reason. Shit, I didn't mean to use any names, even though he never did tell me why. So we reunited, and here we are fifteen years later. It was special. We both lucked out."

"I wish I could have found a man like that!" Ellie seethed, trying hard to maintain her composure.

"It is never too late. You are still a young woman!" Taylor exclaimed. Ellie nodded outwardly dropping her painted-on smile.

"So I am guessing that these were not exactly the stories you thought you were going to hear?" Elinor questioned.

"No, I wanted to hear about you. I shouldn't have asked such personal questions anyway."

"You didn't. It is mildly disappointing when I hear that my relationships were not near normal. Hey, I have to get going. You are busy later!"

"I'll walk out with you, but I have to go to the bathroom first."

"Okay, I'll wait," Ellie said as Taylor got up and grabbed her pocketbook and phone before heading to the ladies' room.

In the bathroom, Taylor brushed the back of her hand across her forehead as she felt light-headed. She reached down for some water and spread some across her face before departing. Walking to their table, she hastily reached for her jacket since Ellie already had hers on. She took another large sip of her coffee thinking maybe she was dehydrated and needed the liquids. Placing the paper cup on the table, she scurried to the woman who was quick to exit.

The two crossed the street as Taylor found it hard to keep up with the long legged woman, who was booking it to the parking complex. She knew that Ellie was noticeably agitated after talking about her life, something that Taylor had noticed more than once.

Trotting up behind her Taylor inquired, "Ellie, are you all right? I feel like I must have said something out of line, and that was not my intention." Ellie stopped at her car and turned to her. The two women stood a few feet from each other as Taylor felt no rush to go home, seeing she was going to be back here in another three and a half hours anyhow.

"I'm sorry. I don't open up to people usually. You are very nice, and I let you in. And no one else has heard this story!" Elinor exclaimed as Taylor began to waver.

"I didn't know. I… I just wan…hel…" Taylor concluded hearing the words that didn't come out of her mouth right. Then her focus became cloudy as she felt Elinor reach out for her.

# CHAPTER 22

The woman applied smelling salts up to Taylor's nostrils. The irritable sensation brusquely whipped Taylor's head away as the ammonia inhalant coarsely tore through, awakening her. "Well, look who finally joined the party!"

Taylor opened her eyes as the lingering smell and its effects dissipated. She had some disorientation, finding that she was no longer in the parking lot where she last remembered, but in a room where she stood and couldn't move.

Now fully awake, she looked over at her arms and legs that were held tight by a series of four thick metal shackles. And to make matters worse, she was restrained in only in her bra and panties. "Confused? Well, you shouldn't be, Taylor!" Taylor's eyes bugged out as she knew she hadn't told Ellie her real name.

"Let me clear up a few things before we get started. When I told you that you were the only one had ever heard this story, it is because, well, I made it up. Well, part of it anyway. And secondly my name is not Ellie, it is Celeste, Celeste Harker!" Taylor had a sudden look of horror. "So Luke did tell you about me. I am so honored. I bet it was all good." Taylor knew she was in deep shit as her head erratically spun about waiting for this nightmare to end.

Celeste paraded around in front of her in a tight form fitting black latex outfit, with tall matching heels that brought the woman to still look down upon her, seeing Taylor knew she wasn't standing on the floor.

This was not the outfit of a sub, where one of Luke's spot-on comments reappeared, with Celeste being a deceptive switch and not to be trusted. Breaking eye contact she noticed that she was held firmly to a board or wall of some type, as Taylor tried to lightly pull herself free.

Taylor tried but the restraints never budged. "So what are we doing here, Celeste?" Taylor emitted in a firm but calm voice.

"Well, I was thinking we would have some fun. I sent Luke a text saying that you were going to the meeting tonight and you will see him later. Oh, and before we go too much further, screaming will not help you, but it will get me aggravated, and I don't think you want to see me angry!" After hearing that Taylor rethought the options that she knew she didn't have.

Lucas got Taylor's text and went back to work. He was thinking if he gets out of work early tonight, he would join her, even though he understood that she had enjoyed these times away without him. He sent an "I love you" text to show that he received it, then placed the phone back in his holster.

Celeste left Taylor for a few minutes, giving Taylor time to look around and see what she could use to break free. Even if she did find something, there was no way she could reach it, to use it. She was screwed, but she refused to see it that way.

Calming herself she looked about the nearly hundred and eighty degrees that she could make out. Beyond the board that she was backed up to, with its four six-inch sides, were concrete walls that reached back a full twenty feet to each side of her, with a tall narrow mahogany cabinet against the wall to her left. In front, two chairs, an end table, and a video camera on a tripod with a red light that remained constant.

And behind the sitting area, a dozen floor to ceiling mirrors all pointed directly at her, most likely to remind her what kind of trouble she was in, displaying it twelvefold. And for what might be behind her, well, it was best to not think about it.

Celeste had plans for her, and from the talk Taylor had with Lucas, she knew it was going to be far worse than the stuff, her and Lucas had done. Taylor was scared, but she didn't want to let on that she was. Celeste returned, holding a large glass of white wine, man-ufacturing a stuttered breath, that escaped the visuals of her captor.

"I am glad you didn't scream while I was gone. If you had, then what I am going to do to you would only be quicker and not so mild. Oh, where are my manners? Can I offer you some wine or maybe a coffee?" Celeste said, laughing hard. "Oh wait, that is how you got here in the first place," she enounced, finishing her tirade. "But seriously, can I get you some wine? These sessions can be very intense and tiresome."

Taylor, as part of a stall tactic, asked for water. Maybe that would buy her a couple of minutes, even though she knew there was no way that Lucas would be able to figure out where she was. Celeste, being the gracious hostess, went around the corner. Taylor wished she could get to her phone but established an idea to sweet talk the woman into her release. And that might be her only hope.

Celeste came back with an open bottle of water and a straw sticking out of its neck. She brought it up nicely, offering her the straw to quench her thirst. Taylor looked at the woman defiantly before eventually taking a sip. She wasn't sure what she was going to do, to shut down a woman who restrained her against her will, into doing the right thing by releasing her.

She took a second sip as the woman seemed a little more compassionate at this point. Taylor released the straw and drew her head back, almost to loosely say, "Bring on the inevitable." Celeste, who had nothing but time and the privacy to conceal it, used it all to her advantage. She was going to be slow and methodical in the way she dealt with her sub, the same as she had done to others before.

Taylor tried to get out one more time while she had her back turned. When Celeste' main focus was back on the bound woman, she took out a blindfold that was hanging from the side of the box that held her and placed it over her eyes, fastening it tight. Taylor was torn up inside, understanding she might just have lost her best option to get free. Once Celeste was happy with the way things were going, she smiled at her accomplishments, but Taylor never saw it.

"Okay, maybe we should start," Celeste remarked.

Taylor frantically searched for what she should say. "Celeste, please, can we talk about this?"

"Whatever do you want to talk about?" said the huntress to her prey.

"Why…why are you doing this? And how did you know who I was?"

"Well honey, to answer the second question first, I recognized Luke's car. It was the same car he had back when we were, you know, sub and dom two years ago. And I only had to see his picture and read the texts on your phone to figure out the rest. And to answer the why, well, I want to mess with Luke, and you are far too pretty, but after tonight, he won't be saying that anymore," Celeste sneered.

Taylor swallowed at the words she wished she hadn't heard. Taking a breath, she went for it, with the good-cop mentality. "Why don't you let me go, and I won't tell anyone!" Taylor exclaimed.

"Let you go! You, my dear, are not going anywhere."

"Please don't do this," Taylor said, begging for her life.

When the imposing one finished the sentence, Taylor felt an object that was being jammed deep into her mouth. Celeste ran it behind her head and around, strapping it tight. Taylor lost her only form of negotiation now. She withdrew, emotionally bowing in momentous defeat.

Celeste left her there for another half hour, just to torment her. After that, she stood in front of her and every few minutes grazed Taylor's body with her fingernail. Taylor jumped, not knowing if it was a feather or a knife. That is when a phone rang. Taylor knew it was hers. She couldn't hear anything else, but she knew the psycho woman was still in the room and close. The ringing stopped, so Taylor lost hope again.

A follow-up sound beeped. Taylor knew that someone left a message. She hoped it was Luke, but there was no way of passing on her situation to him, even if it was. Taylor heard the keys from her phone beep as she figured Celeste was listening in on the voice mail. Seconds passed before she felt the woman breathing on her neck.

"Oh, Lucas left us a text that I didn't see until now. He said he loves you. He also said that he is going to join you at the café. Won't he be surprised when you're not there? Maybe we should call him." Taylor perked up as she hoped that the woman would make that phone call. "You know. I think not! We don't want him ruining this." With that Celeste ran her hands across the body of the barely dressed, blind, and muted Taylor.

Taylor flinched at the thought of this woman running her hands over her, and it was beginning to make her mad. Celeste got in close again as she could feel her breath along the uncovered part of her face and ear. Celeste undid the gag and let it just hang off to one side. Taylor was scared of what was going to happen next. She swallowed, that thought and the freedom from the obstruction.

Celeste dropped her mouth to the nape of her captive's neck. Taylor flinched, trying to pull away from the woman's advances. Celeste held her head tight and moved her mouth up to hers. Taylor used her head to push the woman away. The woman reminded her of her situation by digging her long nails into Taylor's side, bringing her to undeniable, and instant submission. She drew her head away, appearing paralyzed.

The blonde woman advanced again, this time unopposed. She orally violated the younger woman as she stood, with her arms extended. Taylor gasped as the woman's tongue dove deep into her mouth, barely letting her breath. Taylor endured as much as she could until the vulture was done, leaving her gagging and reaching for a breath, while saliva oozed down her face and chin.

As the phone blared again. Celeste walked over to it. "Doesn't he ever stop calling?" she said angrily, dropping the phone to the floor before stomped on it, rendering it useless. "There, he won't bother us anymore!"

She cleared those thoughts before looking over at the blood and wounds of where she dug deep into the sides of Taylor's waist. Ready to inflict some real pain and bring this up a notch, Celeste walked to the wall cabinet to see what she felt like using first as Taylor whimpered.

Taylor flailed. "Help me. Somebody, please help me!" she screamed at the top of her lungs. Celeste came over and hit a toggle on the side of the box she was in. Taylor's arms stretched out, causing her to cease her vocal outburst. When Taylor stopped, Celeste backed it off, giving her only an inch or so of play, making Taylor think she had a heart; of course, she did not.

Lucas couldn't get a hold of Taylor for the second time. He thought she would be thrilled that he was going tonight. A second call and nothing. He felt uneasy as he was getting a bad feeling about this.

The hairs on his arms stood up as a wave of panic took over. He tried one last time only to have it go straight to voice mail. Confused, he turned on the locator, thinking she should be leaving for the café soon. It came up with nothing. *That is strange,* he thought with him wondering why it wasn't working.

Shutting down the app, he restarted it as the fear pangs engulfed him. It showed no location. One last-ditch effort was to locate the business cell. Lucas froze and then gasped as he saw the area and then the address as it zoomed in. He left work. He never said a word as his tires hardly touched the ground, tearing out of there.

Taylor shifted her head, trying to get a glimmer of what was happening on the other side of the blindfold. If she had been success-ful, she would have noticed Celeste, still fighting over the inanimate phone. Grasping a knife, she stood in front of Taylor pointing it in her direction. After regaining her calmed control as she lightly ran the point of it lightly across her tanned skin.

The restrained one felt a light tug at her bra as the woman cut the material and whipped it from her hapless body. Next, Celeste got a hold of the frilly matching panties and cut them free, tossing them to the floor, like the rags they had become.

She was so pissed, having been disrobed, granting the woman total access, so to run her tongue along one of her breasts. Taylor tried to push her away. But Celeste only leaned in to secure Taylor's left nipple in her teeth, pulling it away from her body, while the bru-nette shrieked in pain.

It was a good thing that she couldn't see since her captor held the razor-edged knife a fraction of an inch from her areola, hoping that Taylor would give her a reason to do it. Not getting the response she wanted, Celeste slowly retracted it before moving on to the other breast. And the blade didn't cut this time either, as Taylor had not given her reason to.

Taylor used her plea one more time. However, because her prey didn't give her the satisfaction, moments ago, Celeste struck back. Dragging the knife just below her right breast and rib cage, Taylor grimaced in pain.

Celeste replaced the gag, not wanting to hear one more word out of Luke's play toy. Her resentment of Lucas escalated brought on by the thoughts of him deserting her. And that led to time running out for the helpless Taylor. Infuriated the woman in black ventured to the cabinet and grabbed the item she thought was fitting, for the way she felt at this very moment. The dominant reached in and pulled out a gold sixteen-inch handle with a wide wheel on its ends.

The parts that extended from it were three quarter inch pins that encircled the entire spinning wheel, a wider modification from the Wartenberg pinwheel. She walked back to her and hit another of the side toggles that slowly laid the box she was in at table height so that Celeste could look down upon the one she was torturing.

Taylor was still reeling from the gash she had just received as blood seeped from the open wound. She didn't know how deep it was, but with the pain, she now knew this was for real.

Celeste rolled the stainless-steel guide wheel softly across her breasts, abdomen, and thighs making sure to deliver her victim back to pain level zero, if possible. After the initial passes, Taylor heard a click as her attacker slid the wheel just a notch exposing a small fraction of the pointy ends. Taylor noticed the difference immediately with the pain signal getting to her brain in a microsecond.

She couldn't reason with Celeste, as she was too hell-bent on making a statement with her vowing to leave it upon her already-abused body. The woman continued her moves as Taylor had passed out from the pain. Feeling so many of the spiked needles, along with the thought of what had already been done to her, led her to black out.

But it was probably best, as it stopped Celeste from any further attacks, leaving the unconscious one to lie there with blood seeping out of each of the hundreds of punctures.

Taylor woke again only to feel Celeste pawing at her skin. The blindfold had been removed while the gag stayed firmly in place, as her jaw was sore from having the piece there for so long. Upright again, she looked down at the little one-inch circles that were being stuck to her and a few she thought might be along her backside.

What was Celeste doing? There was one on each breast, one on the top of her pubic bone and other ones on her thighs, arms, and torso. Seeing it made her more scared than mad, she found she no longer had the strength for the latter. Taylor was tiring fast. Her limbs were numb from having them stretched for so long. She also had no idea what time it was, but now she didn't care.

The cavalry wasn't coming, and she was sure that after this torture, she was going to end up dead. Taylor didn't have any fight left. She looked out blankly as the woman attached a small wire to all of the adhesive pieces that were applied to her. Celeste stood when she was done. Proud of the job she did, she undid the gag once more, not to make it more comfortable for Taylor but so she could hear each and every scream.

"Taylor, look at me. Taylor! I'm over here. That's better." Celeste beckoned when she saw the woman's eyes loosely focused in another direction. "I think you are going to love this, Taylor. You have twenty probes attached to your body. They are wired, with electricity being your way of torture. Okay, it's me that will love this. But anyhow, each of these wire's fires independently. I have it so that a jolt will be pushed through the wire and to a point or points of its choosing. It is random in intensity and to which wires it goes out to."

Celeste took a deep breath and said, "So are you ready?" Taylor just looked at her blankly. "Well, that is good enough for me." She walked over and turned on the machine beside her. Taylor didn't hear what Celeste had said. With a few seconds the first zap of electricity stabbed at her right breast and one of her ass cheeks. She screamed out as her eyes opened wide.

The pain stopped, with her body contracting from the jolt. Then ten seconds later, a lesser one grabbed the side of her neck and one of her thighs. She faired that one easier, although she still hadn't made it through the first. Celeste sat to the left of the recording camcorder, thriving on this one being added to her collection, which will fit in very nicely with the other two.

Lucas parked the truck diagonally across the walkway, fuming that the police weren't there already. He ran from the vehicle and pounded at the front door. There was no answer. After thirty seconds of knocking, he knew where he had to look. Without waiting for the cops, he backed onto the circular drive up to where he cut off and drove through the eight-foot designer fence that connected to the large home of Celeste'.

He braced himself as he didn't know about the four-foot wall that his truck jumped off, landing with ease, carving two deep paths into her lawn. He cut the wheel, so he was directly behind the basement door of the house.

Luke threw it into reverse, sending a combination of sod and smoke forward while Lucas only looked back. Luke aimed for the basement entry under her deck, crashing his pickup into the building, crushing the rear of his vehicle. Breaking the door, allowed him a direct route to where he knew that Taylor was being held.

Celeste jumped as a tremendous racket caught her off guard. Taylor never heard it as she was zapped once more. Lucas ran into the finished basement, cutting his arm on the glass, when he did. He climbed into the crash-free floor space to Celeste, who was now in his face and furious. Lucas pushed past her, sending Celeste onto and across one of the chairs. Luke rushed over to Taylor and unplugged the machine as her unconscious body spasmed one last time.

Within seconds, he found the release as her arms dropped to her side, only for her body to collapse into his. Lucas pulled her clear and rushed to get a throw from one of the chairs. As he covered and cared for Taylor, he lost sight of the demonic Celeste, until he heard her enraged scream. That allowed him time to avoid a deadly blow, with him getting stabbed in the upper arm when he veered.

If he hadn't reacted, Celeste would have stabbed him again and then killed Taylor as he watched. But without the knife, and with his adrenaline in high gear, Luke grabbed the woman and restrained one of her wrists in her own contraption, keeping the screaming banshee far away from them. With his energy depleted, he rested next to Taylor as the police charged through the same broken doorway.

Taylor awoke on the way to the hospital, to see Luke, who was crying silently. She struggled with the few words she wanted to say. "Luke, you're here!"

"Yes, baby, I'm here."

"Then why are you crying?" she said, barely loud enough for him to hear.

"Because I thought I was going to lose you," he replied. Taylor even shed a tear after hearing that.

"Luke, what happened to you?" she asked when she saw the bandage on his forearm.

Luke tried not to cry. "I cut myself, but I'm all right!"

"Are we going home?" Taylor asked quietly.

"Right after we go to the hospital," he stated.

"Yes, they should look at that!" Taylor said as she closed her eyes and then drifted off.

# CHAPTER 23

Ten long days later, Lucas fielded another call from Taylor's parents. Knowing it was unavoidable and not letting this go to voice mail, the exhausted, unkept man reached for his phone. He didn't know what to tell them, but he couldn't keep this from Taylor's parents any longer.

"Susan."

"Lucas, is everything all right there? We haven't heard from Taylor, and it's been over a week!"

Lucas drew a long pause as he felt his heart pounding. "Um, Taylor has gone through something, and I wasn't exactly sure how I should tell you," Luke finished, feeling as though his heart was going to pop out of his chest or explode before it did.

He checked in on Taylor, who was out cold from the heavy medication that was prescribed to her. "Luke, what's wrong with Taylor?" Susan inquired nervously.

He whispered into the phone, "She is sleeping, I was just checking on her."

"What's wrong, you have got to tell us, please." He could hear Ken pleading right there next to his wife.

"I do have something to tell you. Taylor... Taylor was abducted. She's fine, we got her back, but emotionally she's been having a rough time."

"Oh my God. When did this happen?" Susan asked as Ken continued to interrupt.

"About two weeks ago."

"Why didn't you tell us earlier? We have to see her!" Susan said, panicking.

"Please don't. I know you love your daughter, but I am getting her in for counseling on Thursday. She did experience some cuts and bruises, but what I am most worried about is her emotional scars. If I thought for a second that either of you could help, I would have got you down here last week. She hasn't even talked to me yet. So please trust me. I will call you every day if you wish. I will tell you of any changes, but she needs a professional for this. So can you please trust me?"

"I don't know how we can. It's our baby, you know. Parents are supposed to help."

"I know, but I don't think anyone can fix this outside of a professional, and that includes me. So can we please try this for a little while?" There was a long silence on the other end as he knew that they were talking about it.

"Okay, we will try it your way, but we need to know how she is doing, every day. And we want the truth!"

"I will call you every night."

"Then we will be here waiting for your call tomorrow. And please take care of her!" Susan sobbed.

"I will. I promise." Luke hung up the phone to the sound of the woman crying. His nerves were battered as that was the hardest thing he ever had to do. He should have told them, but his condition was as fragile as his girls with his only thread to sanity being on the other side of the door he stood behind. Lucas dropped into a ball to cry so to be there if she needed him. Hopefully no one else will call for a while.

Luke begged and pleaded for her to come back to him. He couldn't take two more days of this, with her locked within that impenetrable shell. So far she was displaying no sign of outward emotion. He checked her again, knowing she hadn't moved for hours. Lucas finally went and sat on the chair at the island and closed his eyes, hoping this would all go away.

Sometime later, Taylor skulked the length of the hall. Lucas lifted his head to glimpse Taylor with a distant look in her eyes. He broke down, meeting her, as she reached for what appeared to be a hug.

Lucas held her tight while so many things crossed his mind, like was she hungry or thirsty, which she hadn't done much in the past week. Taylor was looking so run-down because of it. She stayed motionless in his arms.

"I love you, Taylor." Taylor did nothing and then walked away from him, to the chair that she loved. She attempted to cover up, with the blanket she pulled from the arm. He helped by bringing the Afghan around her so that she was comfortable.

He was sure that this had to be some form of progress, with Taylor not having any contact with him since the incident. He felt a heavy weight on his chest as he knew that he was the sole reason why Celeste must have done all this.

Desperate to try anything, he decided to make her something to eat, hoping that she would join him. Lucas didn't want her going back to the hospital, to be fed intravenously. Luke heated a can of chicken and rice soup, which made her turn her head. Maybe it was the smell in the air, or he prayed that it was that she was famished, as she should be.

He split the soup into two bowls. Taylor, with her eyes toward the window, turned again to look over. "Taylor, are you hungry?" She sat and looked toward him and the steaming bowls. He made a gesture that he wanted to help her, as his arms were barely out. "Please!" She stood and then scuffled with his assistance to the table.

She fiddled with the spoon and then put it down. Taylor watched as Luke took a sip from his bowl. She looked in at the noodles that floated within the broth and lifted a spoonful of the now not-so-hot liquid. The woman brought it to her lips and then paused. She put it in her mouth.

Taylor continued at a plodding pace until the bowl was half gone, only to release the spoon into the bowl and slink back to her chair. He was happy. At least she fed herself and didn't just toy with the food this time. She didn't eat a lot, but at least she ate something. Taylor was showing signs of improvement, or at least he thought so. Later, he sat next to her holding her hand. She even grasped his a few times.

Thursday arrived, with Taylor being a little better still. She hadn't said one word yet, so Lucas wasn't sure how she was going to be counseled. So while Lucas was in with the psychologist, Taylor sat next to the receptionist just outside the office. Lucas felt strange, not having her right there with him.

"Lucas, has Taylor been sleeping better this week?" Dr. Conlang inquired with him prepared to add it to his notes compared to the week before, her first week.

"Only with the medication they prescribed."

"And how are you doing?"

"I haven't slept much. But I am still having trouble getting Taylor to eat or drink."

"So Taylor has been able to sleep?"

"Not all the time. Sometimes I have woken up to find her sitting in a chair in the living room, just looking outside. It scares me that she hasn't talked since maybe a half an hour after the ordeal."

"So she did talk?" the doctor asked.

"Yes, but only because she was worried about me."

"And when she knew you were fine, I'm guessing she had time to think about herself and then she completely closed up," the psychologist said.

"Yes, that might be it, but how are you going to get her to open up when she isn't talking!" Lucas exclaimed.

"Well, I am going to talk to her. Maybe something will get through enough to Taylor. But there is a strong chance that she might not speak today. So I need to bring her in here, and you can take a seat in the waiting room."

"Can't I just sit here with her?" Lucas urged.

"I would prefer that you didn't. If you are here, it might be a distraction, and Taylor won't hear what I am saying," the doctor stated as the two worked their way to the door.

The two men helped Taylor in and onto the unoccupied leatherback chair. "I will be outside if you need me," he stated as he reluctantly drifted out of sight.

Luke took his place in the waiting room, nervous as he was the last time. The whole ordeal had him feeling useless in not being able to bring her back to him. He hoped the way that she felt about him would have been the divining rod to her path out, but it wasn't.

He got up and paced the four corners of the room thinking that Taylor had to come back. Their life together depended on it. If only he had been there with her more, and maybe that would have kept Celeste out of sight and far from at least his woman. He still didn't know how she found out that they were together, when Taylor had not disclosed it.

Lucas truly wanted to choke the life out of the woman that destroyed the life they had. Why did Celeste feel she had to retaliate against him? And how did she find Taylor and do all this? That was something that he would never find out, and he was sure that she was going to be a ward of the state, and this time for a long time, with all the evidence they accumulated.

It seemed the state had been building an ongoing case, meaning they now had enough to put her away for years, life, if they found more evidence. Luke had read about how she always managed to skate out of her legal woes, and he thought it had to be because of her immense wealth. Only this time they assured him it wouldn't be that easy.

He didn't ask the particulars but was relieved to hear that, since it was personal this time. Luke had trouble staying with the whole conversation, but they would be going to court in the next six weeks.

Lucas thumbed through the subscriptions that sat neatly in the magazine rack on the wall. Not able to concentrate, he put one back and took another, just to do the same again. The silence was maddening as two other people watched him unravel, maybe thinking he was the patient.

At home he helped Taylor in the door, where she pulled away to sit at the dining room table. His girl was hungry! That he knew. He quickly made a sandwich, wanting her to eat before she changed her mind. He put a glass of water in front of her. He cut back to finish the sandwich and when he put it down he noticed the empty glass. Luke let out a tearful smile.

Even though she hadn't talked yet, the doctor said she was answering some of the questions with her eyes. Luke wasn't sure what that meant, but they have another appointment for next week, and they were going to be there for it. Taylor lifted half of the turkey sandwich and chomped into it. He thought she was showing signs that she liked it.

Sunday night, Luke heard his phone beep as he was bringing his fiancé to bed. She gave him a show of affection as she put her arms around his neck. With her safe in bed, he checked the message. Focusing, he spied the centered text notice. The man tapped it to see it was from Lauren.

Her friend had not heard from Taylor, so she wanted a call some night when she was free. Lucas thought he would do it later, after he updates her parents.

At six thirty, he hung up with the Naughton's. He had told them about her second session and how she had shown even more improvement today. They still wanted to come down, and at this rate, he figured they might be able to soon.

Calling Lauren back, he found this one not to be as hard since Luke had recently struck up a friendship with Lauren when he thought Taylor was unsure about their relationship. The call timed out as he was prepared to leave a short message, when the woman answered. "Hello, Luke."

"Lauren. Am I calling you at a bad time?"

"Is there ever a good time when you have kids?"

"You can call me back later if you want, but I need to talk to you. It's about Taylor."

"Carl, watch the kids!" she called out. There was a silence as he thought she had put him on mute.

Telling her the story, and not being interrupted the entire time, he heard as Taylor's best friend was quietly sobbing on the other end. "So she's not talking?" That was the only thing she managed to get out.

"No, she hasn't said a word in fourteen days, but with other things, she is showing improvement."

"Luke, I am so sorry. Is there anything we can do?"

"I don't know. I am at wit's end, and I don't know what to do for her. Hopefully, the second week with the psychologist will help." Lauren was still quiet. "Lauren, I needed to tell you. You have always been a great friend to Taylor, and after talking with you for the last two months, I can see why. You are the only person that knows our story, and I thought she would want you to know this."

"Well, thank you for being honest," Lauren said still crying.

After the call, Lucas felt at ease, thinking maybe tonight would be the night he could sleep, especially with Taylor who already was. Luke was shutting off the light and was about to climb into his bed upon the couch, when he heard another beep. It was from Lauren. He had instantly keyed up again because of what he read. "Lucas, I will be there later tomorrow. I need to help!"

Luke was going to call her, but he knew that she had probably booked the flight already, and he didn't have the energy to change her mind. He just texted back, "See you tomorrow, and thank you." Luke didn't have as much trouble falling asleep as he thought, with both of them sleeping the night.

Taylor looked as though she was trying to talk in the early afternoon hours. If she could just say one word, he knew that she was back. He catered to her, with her picking through the braised beef and mashed potatoes that he had made for her. She did consume lots of water, as he figured that she needed it. He even noticed that she had lost some weight from this.

A text from Lauren said that she had landed and was on her way to get the rental car and then would drive straight here. Luke felt a little better, even knowing that there was a strong chance that none of this was going to change. But maybe it would do some good.

A very long hour later, there was a triple knock at the door. Taylor was staring out the rear window again, with her mind that was emotionally far, far away. Lauren didn't say a word as she walked in, holding her hand on Luke's shoulder briefly on the way by. She stood quietly in front of her friend, and the distraught woman didn't notice her at first.

"Taylor!" Lauren called out. Taylor didn't turn right away as it didn't sink in. Turning her head lethargically, she looked up. Trying to mouth something, she completely lost it.

Tears poured down as she threw her arms out. Lauren knelt beside her and cried a combination of sad and happy, making Lucas place his hand over the lower part of his face. He did what he thought was best and went into the bedroom, where he could get a handle on his own emotions, with him not wanting to interfere. Plus, he knew that the one on one time was crucial for Taylor right now.

Taylor opened like a faucet. Sitting next to Lauren on the couch, with her so impacted that she still couldn't talk. Lauren just sat there, wanting this deplorable thing that had a hold on her best friend, to disappear forever. For the first time in however long it had been, Taylor was trying to break out, and Luke wasn't around to see it.

Lauren held her hand. "You know we love you, right?" Taylor answered with only a light bob of her head as tears flooded her eyes. "Then we need you to get out here where we can help you with this, because Lucas needs you dearly! And I do too," Lauren exclaimed.

"He doesn't know what to do. You have got to work with us girl-friend, and we are ready whenever you are," she confirmed while she held her friend's hand and still only a fraction of her attention. Taylor looked her in the eyes. She was ready to talk, but she was afraid to open the dam, for fear of everything rushing out at the same time.

Lauren hesitated to think about what she wanted to say next. "Taylor, do you remember when you and I went to the mall in Fairbanks, and my dress got caught in the elevator? I know it was a fluke, and I was probably the only one it had ever happened to. But do you remember when the elevator went down a floor, and it grabbed my dress? It ripped it off of me entirely. Do you remember that?" Taylor let out a glimmer of a smile even though she wasn't looking in her friend's direction.

"And what did you do?" Lauren said, waiting for a response. "Yes, you took your two large clothing bags out and covered my front and backside. Then a man came up and offered some assistance. You know who that was? Come on say it!"

Taylor thought and then managed to squeak out. "Carl, it was Carl!" Lauren's eyes watered as she was overwhelmed by the response.

Wiping her eyes, she asked, "And what did Carl say to me sometime later after we had dated for a while?"

Taylor just shook her head, not ready to talk in sentences yet. "Carl said he liked what he saw, and he didn't know he could get that at the mall," Lauren said as both ladies burst into a hint of laughter followed by a lot of tears. It was loud enough where Lucas came out to see. He didn't believe that it was Taylor who was part of it.

Lauren, once the laughter stopped, said, "And that is why we are married today! I guess he thought I looked good in Nordstrom bags." Taylor giggled very briefly before her friend joined in again. Lucas was drawn to the sweet sound of his girlfriend returning.

He moved in close and dropped his head down over Lauren's and said, "Thank you!" Lauren didn't say anything. "I think maybe I should leave you two alone tonight," Luke said, wanting the best for her.

Taylor let go of Lauren immediately and reached back for Luke and said, "Stay, please!"

Luke had to do something. "I'll be right back, baby. I promise!" Taylor hesitated but did release his hand. Luke gave her a grin and then headed to the laundry room, where he closed the door after looking over at both of the ladies. Once in the garage, he leaned up against his workbench wiped his tears and dialed the phone. "Luke, how is she?" Taylor's mother asked.

"We just had a big breakthrough."

"What is it?" Taylor's mother said wanting to be filled in.

"Lauren is here, and Taylor started talking as soon as she saw her," Lucas said still choked up by it.

"Oh, God bless. She's talking, that's good, right?"

"It's excellent," Lucas reiterated.

"So we can come to see her now?"

"I would rather you wait. If Taylor stays like this, I will have her come to see you, but I have to talk to the doctor to make sure we don't say anything wrong."

"Well, where is she right now?"

"She is with Lauren. And by the way, I did not ask Lauren to come."

"Aren't you afraid Lauren will say something?"

"I am, but honestly, she came in, and she has been the only one to get her moving in the right direction. Even I'm afraid to say anything because I don't want her closing up again. So can you please wait a few more weeks so the two of us can come up to visit you?"

"We will do anything, even if that means not doing anything, then that's the way it will be."

"Okay, I will talk to you tomorrow then?"

"We will be waiting and when you get a chance, please tell Lauren thank you from us."

"I will. Bye, Susan!"

"Bye."

Luke walked back in on Taylor who said, "I don't remember what happened."

"You don't need to," Lauren said, trying to keep it light.

"But how did I get free?" Taylor asked.

"Lucas saved you," she said as Lauren not sure if she was supposed to make that known. Taylor got up and instantly walked over to Luke and moved in to hug him. Cloaking her with his arms, he masked her from the ills of the world, much in the way he did when he freed her. He wanted to stay right where he was and be there to protect her for the rest of her life.

Lucas pushed Taylor away enough to ask her a question. "Taylor, do you mind if I make one more quick call? This will be the last one, I promise." Taylor nodded as she turned into the waiting arms of her friend.

From the garage, he dialed the psychologist. He waited for the receptionist to pick up. He looked at his watch, seeing what time it was. "Dr. Conlang's office, can I help you?"

"Yes, this is Lucas Calderone, calling about my fiancée, Taylor Naughton. Is there any way I can speak with the doctor, please? She had a breakthrough."

"I will give the doctor the information, and I am sure he will call you."

"Thank you." Luke went back to see the two, thinking he might not get a callback today since it was so late. The phone rang before he even made it past the laundry area.

"Dr. Conlang, this is Lucas Calderone."

"Yes, Luke, what has happened?"

"She started talking!"

"That's very good news. Do you think you can get her in here tomorrow?"

"Yes, just name a time," Lucas stated.

"Monica, do we have any times open for tomorrow?" the doctor asked of his receptionist. "Luke, how about noontime?"

"We will be there. See you tomorrow and thank you very much."

Luke hung up, elated that he didn't have to wait until Thursday. In the living room he softly kissed the top of Taylor's head. The ladies continued to talk, even though it was Lauren who controlled the mic. Taylor phased in and out throughout the next hour. Then she turned in early as her outlet of emotion had taxed her severely.

Lauren brought her in and made sure she was okay in bed before leaving the room. She walked out to the kitchen where Lucas was sitting. He was exhausted. He sat there with his eyes closed as she approached. "Maybe you should get some sleep. You look like you need it."

"I will, but what I really need is a shower. But that can wait until later. Hey, can I get you something to drink?"

"I will if you join me."

"I'd like to, but the doctor doesn't want alcohol to be an avenue out for her dilemma."

"So you can't drink anymore?"

"No, it is just while she is undergoing treatment. I figure if she's not drinking, then I'm not either."

"Then you know what, I am okay with just a tea."

"Coming right up!"

With cups in hand and steam rising up from them, they made their way to the dining table. Lauren asked a few irrelevant questions before she got to the one that he couldn't answer in just a few words.

He got up and went down the hall and closed the door, making sure she was asleep. Lauren sat quietly, awaiting his return.

"I… I don't know if I can tell you this story because you will look at me differently when you find out, or after I break down from the guilt."

"Guilt, I don't understand. I know you wouldn't do anything that would hurt Taylor."

Lucas paused before answering. "I guess I should just tell you. You will be the only person that will ever know this. Her parents don't even know since they just wouldn't understand it." Lucas stopped for a breather. "I know that Taylor has filled you in on some of our activities, and I am okay with it… Well, it is about the meetings she had attended. She told you about those, right?"

"Yes, she did."

"Well, somehow this Celeste Harker sought out Taylor, to cause her bodily harm. Taylor had gone to lunch with her after the woman had befriended her. Celeste must have drugged Taylor and dragged her into her house. That is what I am guessing anyway because I found the car outside the coffeehouse where she was going to her meetings. But this despicable woman is into all kinds of crazy shit. She used it to restrain her in the basement. That much, I do know. Then she did some things wanting to inflict pain on her." Lucas halted the words because it was getting too painful to recall.

"Luke, I changed my mind. I don't need to know anything else, really I don't!" Lauren said, seeing how hard it was getting for him.

"But I have to tell someone. I need to get this out."

"Okay, but how come?" Lauren asked.

"Because I am the reason why the woman abducted Taylor." Lucas paused. "I had something going with this woman a couple of years ago."

"You mean you went out with this psycho bitch?"

"Not exactly. I was the master of Celeste for a short while."

"You are saying that she was submissive, but what she did wasn't. I don't get it."

"I didn't either. Celeste fooled me back then too. But this is where the guilt comes in. If I hadn't been part of her life, with her being upset that we parted ways, then she wouldn't have found out that Taylor was my fiancée and been prepared to…to kill her."

"Kill?"

"Yes. This woman is in for a lot of trouble right now! She has done this to two other women, torturing them as she did with Taylor, with two others that are still missing to this day. The police even found recordings of the victims she murdered and then kept as some kind of trophy. But the only thing that worries me now is that this woman has a lot of money and might be able to buy her way out of this."

"But it sounds cut and dry."

"Yes, but if for some reason they can't use the tapes, then the prosecution doesn't have a leg to stand on. The victims from two other survivor cases were thrown out because they made it seem like they were there on their own."

"But how could they do that?" Lauren said fearing the worst.

"Because like Taylor, they were all there for those types of meetings. The recordings just have to be used as evidence or Taylor and the other women won't ever get justice. They are out looking for the bodies to close this once and for all."

"So what kind of wounds did she inflict?" she questioned.

"She has marks on the side of her torso, which are already fading. She also has hundreds of small perforation marks across her waist and breast and a shallow slice under one of her breasts. But it is the emotional wounds that I worry about. Taylor has done something good here today because of you, but we still have a long way to go."

"With you Lucas, I know she is going to beat this."

"I hope so. But it took your help to get her this far. I wasn't getting anywhere." Luke took a breath. "I have a lot of things in the works, but it all revolves around Taylor being Taylor."

"What kind of things are you talking about?" Lauren asked curiously. For the next hour, Lucas whispered his intentions. Lauren as she listened intently sat still except for her blossoming smile.

Lucas and Lauren sat in the front reception room waiting for Taylor, who had just walked in for her appointment. "I think Taylor is even better today, don't you?" Lauren asked.

"I do, but I am worried about when she will be alone. I will be going back to work in about a week if I can. And then she is going to be by herself. That's what bothers me the most."

"You don't think she would hurt herself, do you?" Lauren asked.

"No, but she could fall back into the same hole. I have to think that she can find her way out of this so she can end this turmoil."

"Taylor said you are going to visit her parents?"

"Yes, and you will know when we do, but we are there for a visit with them. With Taylor's mom and dad not being able to come down and help, it was driving them up the wall," Lucas stated.

"I understand that more than anyone. There is no way I could not be there for my child," Lauren said.

"I know, but I just couldn't tell them what happened. I mean, all of it."

Taylor sat up straight in the black tufted leather chair opposite her doctor. "Now, Taylor, could you please tell me what you can remember?"

"I can't."

"Do you mean you can't tell me or you can't remember?" Dr. Conlang asked.

"Both."

"Can you at least start by telling me the things that led up to it, the things that you do remember?"

"I don't want to go back there!"

"I know, but by burying this, you will never get over it. You have already taken the right step by seeing someone to help you deal with this." Taylor thought about it and how much she needed to be back in a happy relationship she has had with Lucas.

She rolled her diamond setting straight out where she could look at it. "We are getting married, you know?"

"I do, and you need to do this for Lucas as well as yourself, right?" She nodded.

She took a breath and then started from the beginning. "I wanted to attend meetings in the way of giving myself something socially to do. I went to the first one, and I was excited about it, and

Luke was too. The second meeting was an art show, and through the first half, everything was going great," she paused for a breather.

"The second half was where I walked in, and this woman had knocked over my coffee. I do know now that she had done this as a means of getting closer to me, one on one. After a brief conversation, she talked me into joining her there at the coffeehouse for a late lunch. During one of the two times, I left the table, I think she must have drugged me. And then I woke up in her house, I think."

The doctor was scribbling down notes as he went along, so not to hinder her recollection that she had called up to this point. "But then... I don't remember it too well. I was blindfolded for most of it, I think. I remember her having me restrained with metal cuffs, or shackles. Oh, she was dressed in black leather with the long boots that went up to her thighs."

"But this is where I forget. I think she dug into my sides with something. It could have been her fingernails. And I felt it in many places on my left and right side." Taylor slowed at this point. She couldn't remember, and her eyes moved about as she tried hard to come up with anything.

"So you said she had you restrained, was it to a wall or the floor?"

"It was more like a panel of some type. And it was boxed in so I wasn't able to see to my side, or behind me." She paused. "And she was able to tighten...and move the shackles when she wanted. They were motorized, I think. She also dragged something across my body. It felt like nails or pins being run over me. It is hard to explain, but it was unbearable. And then I know she cut me here." She pointed to the location with her fingers.

"She did it to silence me and because she was furious. I think this was only the beginning for her because I know that she wanted to hurt me. And the last thing was where she attached electrodes is it, all over my body. And I was zapped, and that is all I remember."

"I see. I heard from Lucas that this was when he came in and rescued you."

"Yes, he saved me," Taylor said.

"You remember that? That's good."

"No, my friend Lauren told me."

"Taylor, you have done very well, within the last few days. How have you been sleeping?"

"Good. I have been sleeping without the medication."

The door opened as Lucas and Lauren were talking face to face. They rose as Taylor, and the doctor made their way out into the reception room. "Lauren, this is Dr. Conlang," Luke said with him making a nervous introduction.

"Nice to meet you, Doctor," Lauren said as she reached out and shook his hand.

"Luke, do you think I can see you in my office for a minute?"

"Sure." He followed the doctor. Closing his office door behind him, he addressed Lucas.

"I want you to know that she is coming out of this. It appears that she put herself in that shell and is now ready to fight her predicament. It also appears that Taylor shut herself down as a way to heal and protect herself, much in the way a person would roll into a ball if they were being attacked. I am quite confident that she will get out of this just fine." The doctor hacked.

"Excuse me," the man said clearing his throat. "But Taylor does seem to have resentment toward this woman, but this should pass with time."

"So what do I have to do?" Luke asked.

"Just keep doing what you have been doing. Let me know if Taylor starts to have trouble sleeping or eating or regresses emotionally. If she does, that is quite normal. Sooner or later, she will be by herself, and that is when it might return."

"But what if I am going back to work in about a week?" Lucas asked.

"That is fine. Taylor has to be alone eventually, and it doesn't matter if it is next week or six months from now. You will just want to call her and check in on her a couple of times during the day. She will make it, you both will." The doctor shook his hand and walked him in the direction of the receptionist.

"I have one more question. Why is it that she came out of it when her friend was there and not with me?"

"I'm not sure on that. I bet Taylor wouldn't have the answer to that. Her thought process has already changed, and you might never now. But it shouldn't matter either," the doctor replied.

"Okay, well I don't want to take up any more of your time!"

"She is heading in the right direction, but I would like to see her a few more times just to be sure!"

"That is fine!" Lucas answered.

# CHAPTER 24

The day came when Lauren was gone, and Luke was off to his first day back to work. It was near impossible for him to turn his back and drive away. Worrying already, he planned to call Taylor for about eight to check on her. These two weeks were going to be the hardest until it was time to head up to Fairbanks. Fingers crossed he hoped that she would be fine.

Taylor looked out the bedroom window. With Lauren gone home to Carl and the kids yesterday and Luke not here today, she strangely felt more at ease once the house was quiet. Luke was jumpy, and even though he didn't mean to be, she could tell. Things were starting to get back to what Taylor called a new normal, she thought as she saw the wind carry someone's leaves across the backyard.

Then falling into her old habits, Taylor became growingly antsy, with the past of not having anything to do, coming back to her. She picked up the phone as it got to the third ring, where she heard, "Hello."

"Hi, Mom."

"Taylor, how are you?"

"Well, Lucas just went back to work today, and I didn't have much to do. I thought I should call since I haven't talked to you in a while."

"Well, we, um…we just thought you needed a little time to recuperate, that's all. We have wanted to call you. So how are you feeling?"

"The doctor thinks I am doing good. I told him I am eating, drinking, and sleeping."

"That sounds good to hear."

"So how are you and Dad?" Taylor asked.

"We are fine. My arth…never mind, I'm fine. And Dad is the same. He always is. We sit around and do our hobbies." Taylor started sobbing on the other end.

"Taylor, what is it?"

"Mom, I don't know. I thought I was doing much better, and now I can't even make a short phone call without…" she said tearing up, loud enough for her parents to make out.

"Taylor, do you need to call the doctor?"

"No, I'm fine. Dr. Conlang said there might be little setbacks and I should be ready for them," Taylor said as she pushed the tears away from her eyes.

"Taylor, we are so sorry that we couldn't be there for you," her father piped in.

"I'm not mad, I had gone through a lot, and Luke told me why I couldn't have people around. It would have made things worse," she said while she sobbed.

"You know Lucas is doing everything he can to help you. He had been calling us every day to keep us informed. But it had been so hard, not coming to see you," her mother said, then quickly added, "I'm so sorry!"

Taylor and her parents talked some more with her telling them that she and Lucas were coming to Fairbanks to see them. They knew, but they were unaware as to whether Taylor had known about it yet.

When she ended the call, she decided to take a nice long shower. As she got to the bedroom, Lucas called. "Hi, baby, I just wanted to see if there is anything you need."

"No, I'm fine. I just got off the phone with Mom and Dad."

"Oh, okay," Luke said.

"And I was just about to take a shower."

"All right, but if you need anything, give me a call."

"I will, Luke. Bye."

"Bye, baby."

She walked down to their bathroom, where she disrobed and turned to the full-length oak mirror on the back of the door. She was thinking about how awkward a conversation that must have been for Lucas and her parents. And how it was time to put this all behind her. Even the puncture marks from the attack were pretty much gone. She realized that as she peeled back the bandage to see how the incision was healing.

Grasping the edge of the sticky medical tape, Taylor pulled it away to reveal a barely visible line. It was a little discolored, but she doubted it would leave a scar. She pulled off the rest and dropped it into the trash. This was the first time that she felt like herself in weeks, and that is when she realized that she was physically missing her husband-to-be.

Taylor needed Lucas and the kind of relationship that they once had. She didn't want to think about the bondage part, but it came to mind anyway. That was going to bring back so many bad memories that this woman, Celeste had taken from her. She wanted to be angry, the kind of mad she was while Taylor was at the woman's mercy, but she just didn't have the strength for it. She wasn't that type of person, and she didn't want to give Celeste the satisfaction either.

Taylor had to fight through this. The doctor, Lucas, Lauren, and her parents were all there to help, but it was up to her to make it right. She stopped pawing at the wounds that were disappearing, climbed into the shower, and pulled the curtain across.

The water washed away more of the memories, flooding on down over her and down to the tub drain, where Taylor pictured them gone forever. She felt all of it washing away, except for one thing that she hadn't addressed yet with Luke. She had to get this out, so she wouldn't feel the sting of what she could now see.

Throughout the day he had only called one more time to check on Taylor. She sounded like she had something to talk about but said she was okay. When he walked in, Taylor was in the chair that she had come to know as hers. She was quiet, except for looking back at Luke as he neared. He knelt in front of her. "How are you, baby?" Lucas asked.

"Good. But it was a long day, so I took a nap."

"That's good," Luke stated.

Taylor leaned in and snuck a hug. Lucas welcomed it once he got past the initial surprise.

"I love you," she said as she made sure the whisper caught his ear.

"I love you too," he responded as he felt she was a little too happy. "Honey, did you have anything to drink today?"

"No, it's just that I realized for the first time in weeks how important you are in my life."

"Are you sure that there isn't more to it?" He asked.

"No, really. I just miss being with you. I need to be close to you again."

"Well, you know I want to also, but I don't want you sliding backward with this." Taylor looked him in the eyes and turned away. "What's the matter?" She turned with a tear that clung tightly to her duct.

"If you are mad at me, can't you just punish me or yell at me because I need to feel like me again?" Taylor said as she fell to tears.

"What? It's not that. I… Why are you talking about punishment?" a stumped Lucas asked while tears rolled down her cheeks. "Taylor, seriously I don't know where you are coming from on this one. What happened to you happened more because of me, not you." Luke closed his eyes momentarily once he blurted it out.

"It happened because of you?" Taylor replied with her mouth agape. Lucas was frantic as he wasn't sure what he wanted to say.

"Taylor, I was praying that this would all pass without me having to tell you that I feel guilty about the entire situation."

"You?" Taylor said in shock.

"Yes," Lucas said as he dropped his head in shame.

"I was the reason why she took you, and I was the reason why she probably was going to—"

"I can't believe you are feeling guilty. I have been because I went to the meetings."

"Tay… I'm sorry, I didn't mean to say that. You did nothing wrong. This stuff doesn't happen much and not in the middle of the day."

She brushed back a single tear. "Besides, if this is all that is keeping you from getting back to your normal life, then you have no more issues. I think maybe it is time I put the guilt to rest too, so we can both move on." Taylor didn't have a problem with that. It was time to forget this. "I think we have to stop playing the blame game, and I think we should not talk about punishment or anything else for a while. You don't need that anymore," Lucas stated.

This one was going too smart for Taylor. Because of this vile and evil woman, she was being denied something that she loved and needed. But he did say for a while, so she figured she could hold out.

After dinner, Lucas decided that they should go to bed early. Taylor knew what that meant and pleasantly agreed. He went in and poured a bath as they undressed. She looked in the mirror as if the last signs of her injuries had gone away within the previous six hours. Lucas walked up and said, "Don't do that, baby. It is going to take time."

She turned and held her naked skin up against his. Taylor felt a resurgence as she relished in the most innocent of feel. Climbing into the tub, she sat with him behind her. She thought that this would be a perfect time for a glass of wine. Taylor knew she couldn't but she still wished that she wasn't the reason why Luke couldn't drink.

She hadn't had any alcohol for weeks, not a drop, and Luke did the same for her. And that was when he would have needed it most. She reached down and lightly ran her fingers from his knees to his calves.

For some reason, something popped into her head. "Lauren called this afternoon! She wanted to see how I was doing, but I think she misses us already."

"She probably does, but you will see her in less than two weeks," Lucas said.

"Yes, I can't wait, and my parents too."

"And them too," he said as he brought his head in and held her arms and chest, with his left arm. She adjusted him by pulling hers free and placing his, with his hand cupping her right breast. In a very awkward way, she semi turned around and made the connection of her lips to his. This turned on something in him because he had her get up, and as the tub drained, they moved to the bedroom.

He laid Taylor down across the width of the king-size bed as she felt the light that had been gone for so long, coming back. He laid next to her and began to kiss and fondle her. Once he was satisfied with kissing her lips, he stopped the touch while he moved his lips down to her neck.

The comforter became damp beneath them from not toweling off before they laid upon it. Neither of them noticed though. She only laid back and closed her eyes. Lucas moved from her neck down to the top of her breast. She closed her eyes from the sensation that was sinking in. When he got to her breasts, she pushed his head away.

"Baby, did I do something wrong?"

"No," she quickly answered. "Just give me a minute, please."

When she was ready, she placed his head there again. "Go slow, okay?" Taylor said wanting him to continue.

He made love to her chest, slowly and tenderly. When she was finally over the panic attack, she closed her eyes and even smiled. Lucas moved lower, playing by the same ground rules. He could feel her tensing up, while she reached for his head. That is when Taylor stopped him for the last time.

The next morning, the first thing Taylor did was apologize. "Apologize for what?" Luke said.

"I shouldn't have started, you know?" Taylor phrased regretfully.

"What are you talking about?"

"I was having pangs."

"And that is normal. I didn't want to rush you into this, so I didn't."

"No, it was me. For some reason when I closed my eyes, I pictured her there ready to assault me."

"Baby, it was too early for us to try this," he said sensitively.

"I just wanted to be with you," she exclaimed.

"You are, and you always have been, but don't rush this. We need to move at the pace that you can handle." She nodded, thinking that it was going to be some kind of fix-all.

With the sun making its late afternoon blaze across the pacific sky, Taylor thought she would try something on her own. She went out to the garage, ready to meet her fears head-on. Taylor unlocked the cabinet that held the restraint system. She looked it over and felt that if she could get over this, she would be all right.

She had to jump this hurdle and back into their lives like she was before. Taylor ran her hands over the smooth powder coated arms that extended up from the floor base, once she dragged it out to the center of the floor. She gripped the foam padding.

Feeling set Taylor plugged in the unit. Next, she reached down and toyed with one of the restraints. There was nothing that even set off a twinge of fear.

She went back into the house and drank some water to relax with what she was about to do. When the woman was ready, she walked back up to it slowly and stood behind. Taylor leaned over, with the remote tightly in her hand in case it's needed. When Taylor was prepared, she brought one leg over and locked it in with its restraint. With no visible sign, Taylor unlocked it. She brought it away, sensing her freedom.

After about a minute, she took some breaths and locked in both of her legs. She stood back up to get ready for her top half. Another couple of minutes transpired as she held the remote, in case this test went sideways on her. When she was sure that she could do this, she leaned over and put her first arm into place. Thirty seconds later she brought the other wrist in and depressed the plunger to lock it in too.

She had her finger just above the button, thinking it should be right about now if it were going to happen. She closed her eyes to relax in the accomplishments she had done this far. But with her eyes closed, the panic did set in fast and hard, locking her neck in too. She shook, or tried to, as she had such an attack; it was hard to hold on to the only thing that could insure her release.

Taylor began to bawl and screamed for help. She was locked into what felt like a nightmare, and it wasn't letting go. None of the neighbors had heard as her screaming went unanswered. She battled for what felt like hours when it was only a few minutes.

She pictured herself at the woman's house in the hands of Celeste Harker, with the emotions being as strong as they were when they originally happened. Her mind replayed the same endless turmoil, keeping Taylor at bay, even though all she had to do was push the one red oval button, and her freedom and this horrific movie would be over. Through it all, all she wished for was for Lucas to barge in and save her again, before it was too late.

Later Lucas walked in feeling the house was a little too quiet, knowing that Taylor was home. Looking for her in the bedroom, he saw her all curled up amongst the pillows and blankets.

"Taylor, are you all right?" he asked as she lay there silently. Thinking she was sleeping he went over to cover her up. "Taylor, what's the matter?" he questioned again, seeing the woman who had apparently been crying for some time as her mascara marks were across her face. He sat down on the edge of the bed. "Taylor, please tell me what happened."

She looked up at him, still shaking over what she had done. "I... I am so sorry. I thought I was over this and I'm sorry."

"But what happened?"

"I was in the garage, and I'm so sorry," Taylor said as tears began to flow.

Lucas was already gone. He returned thirty seconds later. "Baby, please don't tell me you used it."

"I did. I thought I was over it and—"

"You shouldn't have done that," he said with him trying not to yell. He crawled into bed in front of a fetal Taylor. He caressed her as she eventually fell asleep in his arms. The thoughts of her reoccurring attack subsided, and she relaxed from being held.

He thought he should get up and call or leave a message for the doctor. Luke was going to send her for her appointment alone this week, but the doctor needed to know what had happened. He wasn't comfortable telling anyone about what they do behind closed doors, but this wasn't about their privacy anymore. It was about Taylor and getting her free from this once and for all.

The next week and a half had gone uneventful, which was music to Luke's ears, and he was sure to Taylor's also. She had been to the doctor two more times, and to Luke's amazement, she did in fact, tell him about their night of attempted sex and her harrowing self-bondage.

Onboard Alaskan Airlines, they waited with luggage in hand that Lucas had just pulled down from the overhead. Luke was looking forward to this long weekend, where he could finally relax, while being here in Fairbanks to visit her parents. The two of them moved down the aisle slowly as the plane started to clear out.

When they got down to the baggage claim, her parents were waiting somewhat patiently at the bottom of the escalator. It was a typical greeting for the four, and one that you would see at any airport. However, there were no tears or emotional outpouring over what she had gone through.

The four trudged off to the parking lot. The luggage went in, with Taylor sitting next to her father in the front seat. Her mother sat opposite in the back seat so she could see and talk with her daughter. With a tear in his eye, Taylor's dad put his hand on his daughter's knee as a sign that he was there for her. But no other talk beyond their regular life filled the vehicle.

Ken drove cautiously as he pulled out from the pick-up area and into the partially snow-covered road. Luke sat quietly as the three caught up using small talk as their outlet. All was okay, for as far as he could see. She had not experienced a setback since the last incident that Taylor had tested. And the doctor said it was quite normal for her to have nightmares, even considering how well she was doing.

The doctor didn't see any reason for her to continue appointments with him unless a problem arose. Her last visit was for next Thursday, if Taylor wanted one last get together.

The parents talked a lot about Kyle and Isla who got engaged a month ago since they didn't want to open a can of worms by saying anything else. They, meaning Luke, only responded previously to texts since Taylor was not able to speak over the phone, even though they were thrilled to hear that the newly engaged couple might stop in this weekend.

Lucas only had to come up with an excuse that would get them talking about the next subject. He hated to lie to people, but he just couldn't explain it to everyone individually. He still hadn't said anything to his parents either, although they had been curious as to why they hadn't had any phone calls from their future daughter in law.

Lucas carried the luggage into the small two-bedroom townhouse that sat at the beginning of Birch Circle. In passing, the living room was quite toasty as the fire was burning bright when they walked in. The place was tiny but sufficient. He set down the luggage in the aqua painted bedroom they had done up for whenever their kids came to see them.

It was feminine, but as far as Lucas was concerned, it was just a place to lay one's head. Lucas viewed the border with lace, prompting him only to the idea that this was not a man's bedroom.

Taylor sat out in the kitchen with her mom, as the guys stood in the doorways. That is when the edgy mom offered them something to drink out of habit, forgetting that it was one of her only restrictions. "I'm not supposed to drink yet," Taylor announced shyly as if she was ashamed.

"Taylor and I will have a little wine, please," Luke said as he thought she could handle a little, without there being any kind of incident. Susan with lightly shaking hands poured the three glasses, making sure not to overdo it. She remembered being told that and felt terrible, even bringing it up. She was trying not to appear nervous to her daughter, but was failing miserably at it.

"I also have some cheese and crackers and then maybe later your dad and Luke could run for pizza."

"That sounds good," they both said almost simultaneously.

"Mom, I like your sweater," Taylor said of the blue variegated wool top.

"Thank you. I bought this at the summer church function." Wanting to make sure they were all right she asked, "Are you two warm enough?"

"Oh yes," Luke stated of the temp that was upwards of eighty degrees.

"Yes, very warm," Taylor said.

"I will not let your dad throw any more logs on for a while then, because it is hot," Susan agreed.

Later the boys were out on their drive down to the pizza place. Susan decided to find out how her daughter was doing. "Taylor, Luke hasn't been calling every day, so I was wondering how you are doing."

"It is still a little rough at times, but I am getting over it."

"Do you mind me asking what happened?"

"Actually I do. It was a horrible ordeal, and I wish I could, but I don't want to think about it anymore. I hope you understand!"

Her mother was slow to respond but then gave in by nodding. "Okay, but how are your wounds?"

"They are completely gone. And, Mom, I am sorry, but if I talk about it, it would only get you worked up, and our relaxing visit will be over," Taylor said as she sat there quietly sipping the Chablis in front of her.

"I am so sorry about what happened. It is not easy being a mother, and someday, you will find that out. If they hurt, you hurt worse."

"Mom, I'm okay. Really!" Taylor stated as she saw her mother with tears that were about to overflow. She felt for her daughter who had to go through most of this on her own. She looked at her daughter in the eyes and couldn't hold back any longer.

"Mom, please don't. I am all right." The woman was inconsolable as Taylor moved in to hold her. Taylor, who thought she was beyond the crying part of it, unloaded alongside her. And because of that it was not a pretty sight when the two men entered carrying tonight's dinner.

They both knew what it was about, but they steered clear as the two were part way through the tissue box that sat on the table, with the balled up damp remnants scattered in front of them. After they finished, they were all quiet while they ate. Lucas thought whatever was said at this point was out of his control, but it looked like they got through it unscathed.

Later that night, Luke and Taylor lay in the very creaky full-size bed. He stewed on whether he should ask her if she had said anything. He decided against it, since her parents' bedroom was literally a few feet away, with both doors left open to circulate for the heat. Plus, he knew that because he could hear their bed creak too.

It was going to be very hard having any behind-the-scenes conversation for the rest of the weekend. After all, Lucas didn't want to stop Taylor from saying whatever she needed to say.

They slept eventually, once they pushed the comforter off them and got acclimated to the Naughton hothouse. Susan was unsuccessful on keeping Ken away from adding the wood, that he thought he needed for the evening.

In the middle of the night, Lucas reached down and pulled up the blanket that was down across their knees. The fire had died off, and he thought, maybe he would add some before it got any colder. Luke walked into the living room and opened the screen and added six split pieces. Wanting to warm some he sat in the padded rocker that was much warmer than their bed.

Lucas watched as the flames bounced, expelling more warmth, while the heat incrementally intensified. Sitting there with his eyes closed he felt a tap on his shoulder. Surprised he peered behind him to see Susan, who must be the evening fire tenderer. She must have got cold, just like Lucas had done.

His future mother-in-law parked herself on the sofa just a few feet away from Lucas in front of the now blazing fire. She gazed over at him with him noticing her. "Lucas, I am so glad that you were there for Taylor when she needed you most," Susan whispered.

"Thank you, but I wish I could have been there sooner."

"If it makes you feel any better, she didn't tell me anything."

"It would have been okay if she did," was what he said when he was glad that she didn't know the truth, especially the whole truth.

"You know I went most of that time, without even crying for her. I think I was too scared to," Susan revealed.

"I understand. And again, thank you for being so understanding," Luke whispered and quickly added, "You have your daughter back."

"That is nice to hear," she confessed. Switching to another topic, she added, "You know there is a chance that Kyle and his fiancée might show up tomorrow?"

"Yes, I do, and I will say something to him if I feel I have to," Luke assured.

Susan paused. "You know, we were very close to packing our bags in spite of what you said, but there was only one thing that stopped us!"

"And what's that, Susan?"

"It was the fact that you saved her!"

Lucas was perplexed and almost startled talking about the incident.

Susan finished where she was going with her last comment. "Actually, you saved her twice. Once, when you turned her life around by giving her something to believe in and someone to love. And the second is, and I will never forget, when you brought her to see her grandmother. You didn't do that for yourself, you did it for her."

Lucas didn't know what to say, so he got up and knelt next to the woman who needed someone to comfort her. Lucas hugged her until her tears subsided.

The two heard Taylor as she sleepily entered the room. "Why is everyone up?" she asked.

"We both got up to feed the fire," he stated as Susan wiped her eyes.

"Yeah, I was starting to get a little cold in there," Taylor agreed.

"Well, it is either a hundred or fifty in here. I would like to run the furnace, but your dad likes to burn wood."

"So, Mom, have you heard from Kyle yet?" Taylor asked.

"No, but most of the time, we don't. Kyle pretty much thinks we are home all the time. But I guess in his defense we are," her mom said and then added. "Well, I think I should get to bed. I am cooking a big breakfast in a few hours. Good night," she said as she got up and planted a kiss on her daughter's cheek. She left one for Lucas too before disappearing beyond the light of the fire.

Taylor sat next to Lucas. "Oh, this is nice."

"Yes, it kind of reminds me of the fire at the inn," Luke said, meaning for it to be innocent.

"Not quite, but I know what you mean," she said remembering the size difference and the romantic ambiance. They sat there until they couldn't any longer and moved back to their noisy bed. The blankets and sheets were cold and they figured they would rewarm them before the heat of the fire got to it.

Morning came quickly as the room was toasty for the rest of the wee hours. Taylor was the second to rise as she smelled the coffee brewing. To her it was like an alarm clock for the nostrils. Luke rose twenty minutes later since he reached out for Taylor while he slept and she wasn't there. Ken finally came out of the bedroom and joined the very quiet threesome, but after he of course stoked the fire.

During a lull in the morning dad pulled his daughter aside and closed the door. It was his way of isolating the masses and getting a little one on one time with one of his children. Lucas wasn't worried about what was being said to him.

Ken is a good father, one that is always there for both of his kids' needs, and he had been always there to offer advice if he thought they needed it. If Luke was ever to be a father, he at least had two great role models in Ken and his own father. Going by what they have done and the way they have done it, he couldn't go wrong with what they have accomplished.

# CHAPTER 25

Lucas, while in the living room, saw a car pull into the driveway and sounded off, "Kyle's here." Taylor and her mom perked up. Ken folded his newspaper and placed it on the media rack that Taylor had got him for one of the past Christmases.

Luke and Taylor went out to retrieve the innkeeper and his soon-to-be wife. He shook his friend's hand while Taylor was very bubbly over the fact that her future sister was wearing a nice-looking rock on her ring finger. Even Isla, who was usually reserved, was excited to show off the trinket that Kyle had given to her.

"Good job brother," Taylor said when she realized.

"Why, thanks, sis!"

"That ring looks so beautiful on you, Isla!"

"Mom, did you see this?" Taylor called back.

"I will if you all get your frozen butts in here," her mother said to all four who stood out in the cold. The men grabbed what little luggage they had and headed into the house so they could close the door. Taylor was by Isla's side like they were sisters reuniting after so much time had transpired.

If it was bothering Isla, from Taylor encroaching on her space, she never let on. The six all went to the kitchen, a room that was pretty much maxed out occupancy-wise. "Can I get you two something to drink?" Mom asked her son and future daughter-in-law.

"Yes, hot chocolate for me," Kyle said.

"That sounds good to me too," Isla dittoed.

"So are you going to tell us the story?" Taylor urged.

"Well, I had wanted to tell you, but you never called me back," Kyle said.

"Yeah, I'm sorry about that. I was under the weather for quite a while, but I did text you a few times."

"Just kidding, sis. I am glad to hear you are feeling better, though." Taylor had heard that Kyle had texted her, so Lucas replied while she was unable to get to the phone. "It wasn't anything special because none of you knew, but we have been talking about it for a couple of years. The day she was going to head back home, I proposed to her in the lobby. So instead of her heading home then, we went there and collected the rest of her stuff and brought it back to the inn a couple of weeks ago," Kyle said, concluding the story.

"And now both of our babies are getting married," Mom bragged for just the room to hear.

"Have you picked a date yet?" Taylor said, wanting to be the first to find out.

"We want to get married pretty soon. We want a simple wedding and have it around the end of May or in early September, and the best part is that we both want to have it in Point Hope, at the inn."

"For real? That will be so special," Taylor said showing a few tears of joy. Lucas liked that she was so happy for them. A smile came to Luke's face as he got caught up in the excitement that was oozing out of his fiancée.

Dad took the mic, so to speak, and had them all in stitches, which was rare, with his "the rest had to be tired" banter. The non-stop laughter had Luke's jaws sore. And even though it was not common for Ken, the man rolled it out for his audience of five.

Once the laughter died off, Taylor and Luke were asked the same question. Even though they had talked about it, neither had much to say. They didn't have a date, a venue picked, or anything for that matter. It wasn't that they were not enthusiastic about it, but if they were going to start figuring it out, the past five or six weeks would have been a definite shutdown. The parents understood, but they still hoped that their news would be soon to follow.

The rest of the afternoon flew by. Taylor and Kyle got to catch up, when she wasn't learning more about Isla. Later, the guys moved to the living room where they were talking about sports, while the ladies huddled around the table, talking about girl stuff. Isla, who was fitting in swimmingly, was going to be a great addition to the Naughton clan.

The boys asked if they could go out to play as Ken wanted to take his son and future son-in-law down the road for a beer or two. The ladies stood in the kitchen, making a meal for them all, and Susan said it would be okay if they were home for dinner. The boys threw their jackets on and climbed into Kyle's rental. He backed out to the street and headed the near half mile down to the bar.

The two young ladies cut up vegetables for a salad, while Mom had the oven going for veal shanks. She also had scalloped potatoes browning right next to it. Susan missed cooking for her kids since Taylor was now in Washington, and Kyle was busy with the inn nine months out of the year.

A pail with the first of their dead soldiers remained as a centerpiece between the three men. They each grabbed their last, since they all had to be home soon for dinner. Three caps were dropped into the center of the table, with one bouncing before it fell up against one of the others. "Wow, I can't believe you finally did it," Luke said out loud.

"Yes, I had it planned for the end of our summer. She was still surprised, even though we had talked about it just a few weeks earlier."

"I'm proud of you, man!" Lucas said, lifting the butt of his bottle toward his. Kyle and his father followed suit and clinked their nearly full beer, toasting to the great news that they finally could all share together.

Taylor asked Isla if they had discussed having kids. "Yes, we talked about that a couple of years ago. We both are thinking two." The two Naughton women were glad to hear that. Susan was more than prepared to be a grandmother, while Taylor would be an aunt for the first time. She tried not to think about her circumstances, with her being a few years older than Isla was already.

It was no doubt that this woman, who would be a Naughton soon, was going to make these two ladies very, very happy, when it does happen. She tried to picture how family life would be for them at the inn. It wasn't going to be the first time this has happened with her mom being born there and living there until she was nineteen. It worked for them then, and it would again.

The guys finished their second and last, putting the empties upside down into the icy water. They decided not to go beyond the two, like they had said, because they were not looking to stir up any trouble. And Ken also knew something they didn't. His favorite meal was being cooked right now, and he wanted to be the first one at the table for that.

"Guys, I have a couple of things to run by you," Lucas said.

"Shoot, son," Ken answered with the man not necessarily referring to him in that way.

"I have been thinking about a few things, and I am interested in hearing what you think. One has to do with your wedding." The two men were all ears, especially when Kyle heard it had something to do with his own wedding.

The three walked into the house very joyful, acting like a cat that swallowed the canary. When the eldest female questioned them, her husband just said that they only had two beers. They didn't believe it, but in his case, it was true.

"Nice salad," Kyle proclaimed as he paid notice to his girl that was still throwing it all together.

"Yes, and you said I couldn't cook," Isla blurted out. That comment called for a round of laughter, as it was so well timed and appropriate. She was not as good a cook as she would like to be, but Kyle was slowly teaching her, with his own pretty limited skills. Ken was overtaken by the aroma of the veal, as his wife opened the oven and pulled out the two pans.

"Isla, did you cook that?" Kyle jested. She gave him a loving swat across the chest. It was all meant to be private, but the other four got to see it.

The sleeping arrangements were a little tight with Kyle and Isla having to sleep in the dwarfish den that had to be cleared of all furniture. They said they would be fine since Luke and Taylor would be leaving in two days, and that's when the bed would open up for them.

The fire had to be fed during the evening again, so throughout the weekend, they all got to sit in front of it after everyone had called it a night.

Taylor sat cross legged in the light-blue denim recliner, opposite her brother who comfortably leaned back in the worn brown plaid one a foot away. With brother and sister authoring their own brand of chitchat, Taylor grabbed his robed arm to attest, "I know that we joke all the time, but I don't want this to go unsaid that I am very proud of you! And I can't wait until you make Isla your wife, so I can finally call her my sister."

"I love you too, sis. And you know that you would never be able to find anyone better that Luke either," Kyle answered back noting his sincerity. He closed up the chair, feeling the searing heat that was burning the hair on his legs. He wasn't in a rush to go back to bed but kindly relished in being there with his sister, whom he hardly gets to talk to anymore.

Zipping up the suitcases left Taylor and Lucas bittersweet. The trip had been everything they wanted and needed, as Luke surprised Taylor with a girl's afternoon with Lauren alone. But today they were heading back to Seattle, giving Kyle and his fiancée a real bed to sleep on, hence getting them off that full-size air mattress that they insisted they use.

Luke's phone rang startling her. "Taylor, close the door, please," he asked as he reached down for it.

"Hello, yes, this is Lucas!" he answered to the man on the other end. He had been expecting this call but was astounded that it was this soon.

"Yes, I can call you when we get home. Is tomorrow okay?" Luke said to the attorney. "Okay, we will talk to you tomorrow," Lucas added to conclude their talk. With his phone still in his hand he leaned in seeing she was curious, he didn't want to have her wait until the airport.

"It was your attorney. I won't talk about it if it bothers you."

"No, please tell me," Taylor urged.

"Well, they are moving this case along very quickly, and they want to go to court in another month." She swallowed, trying not to let the details get to her.

"Okay, then I think we should talk about this more when we get home," Taylor said.

While in her padded chair in the living room, she thought about how lucky she was that she hadn't turned out to be the third woman who had vanished without a trace. So because of that, Taylor was going to do whatever she had to, to make sure this woman never walked freely again. The evidence they had so far was mounting, tipping the scales in their favor, except that no bodies had been found to date.

If bodies turned up, there was no possible way the defense would be able to clear her this time. Taylor also knew that the state police were diligent in turning over every last stone to get the proof that left the survivors and the prosecution with nothing to stand on the last time.

Wednesday, Lucas called the law office of Shenley and Cooper. This was to be such a high-profile case that both partners were going to represent all the victims, both living and deceased. "Yes, we can be in later," Lucas said, speaking for Taylor.

"You are not going to be alone through this. The lawyers are going back through the other cases that never advanced due to lack of evidence. The lawyer wants to see you in an hour if you think you can make it. And I will call him if you can't," Lucas said being there for her, no matter what her choice is.

"I will go. I have to do this! All those other women deserve justice. I will be ready when it's time," Taylor said, sadly wondering if the two missing women were going to be found in time.

The lawyer, Robert Cooper, listened to Taylor's entire story, which he looked at to mold it into a rock-solid testimony, since the other evidence had not materialized as of yet. Then his entire team had to sift through the info in hand and see what they could use and what they couldn't.

Cooper heard her words, and after looking at the pictures from the hospital, he thought that another meeting would be in their best interest, with the next being with his partner, Gary. She felt strange having to rehash all the painful memories over again.

Attorney Cooper did not exhibit an ounce of feeling toward her tribulation, except for handing her tissues when she needed it.

Thinking she was all cried out she did manage to break down when it came time to talk about the woman, that she thought was her friend. It was a relative sore spot, and Taylor figured it might always be.

While in the car later she sensed how draining the pretrial made her, as she wished she was home so she could take a nap. It was the longest ninety minutes she had ever spent. Lucas felt so bad that he called Steve last minute yesterday to tell him he would be in on Saturday instead of today.

Lucas had to get back to work, but she wasn't going to be able to do this on her own. He didn't mind the paycheck being short, but he was not there to help with the work that was only getting done by the few that were on this time of year.

Around seven thirty, his father called. It was a call to check in, but he wondered why he hadn't heard from Taylor in some time. Luke only said that she had been busy and she was going to call them this weekend. When they were all talked out, he hung up and figured he would tell Taylor in the morning to call them. He decided not to say anything to his dad, since the court stuff was not information they were going to share with others, besides Lauren.

Taylor and Luke sat with Attorney Gary Shenley this time. The prosecution was brought up to speed on the case, the evidence or lack thereof, and of her story too. But he was there to prep her for court next week.

Shenley observed her to see how she reacted to the questions that the defense was going to ask of her. She did pretty well, although she appeared very dry eyed this time and nervous too. The lawyer did have to calm her several times when she spoke heatedly about the accused, Celeste Harker.

Gary knew that when the time came, she was going to show her true self, as she would have her attacker there in the same room. Toward the end, he could see that Miss Naughton was about as ready as she could be, with him hoping that it would be enough.

At the end of their meeting, Taylor walked from the room, holding the arm of the man that had been there for her the whole time. He had been her friend, her lover, and as of recently, her savior. For without him, she wouldn't be here for any of this.

Lucas, while in the car, told her how proud he was of her. She didn't hear much of it, thinking about the trial, being only eight days away. They were informed that if anything else surfaced that they would be told immediately. She should have been happier knowing this, but this didn't tackle her fear.

The day before the trial, the evidence came in as they had hoped for. With a search that at first proved to be nothing, it seemed the woman had an undisclosed property that in the past went unnoticed. The building, an abandoned warehouse, was found to be purchased through a third party, but the police subsequently traced it back to the missing husband of Celeste Harker.

The search took nearly two full days as Harker had covered her tracks well. But at the end of the day, they found three bodies. The two victims as well as her husband, the man that vanished without a trace.

The news was then passed on to the defense, and they were already talking a plea bargain. But the best part was that Taylor and the other victims and their testimonies were now not needed.

The tapes were deemed as admissible, being that they were there responding to a call, and the rest was found by a search warrant. The bodies were simply the nail in the coffin.

The woman never stood a chance. The case was over basically before Celeste Harker could even change her plea. The forensic evidence, along with the video recordings of the missing women and their deaths, was one that the defense had to bow to.

When they walked away the last time, Taylor was told that all the victims received a call from the lawyers, and he told them of the verdict. She was pleased to hear that she was to serve a sentence of no less than thirty years, and with that, they all would also be receiving a check, which came as a total shock to Taylor.

The firm decided to hit the wealthy Celeste Harker where it hurt, allowing the deal, which only took the death sentence off the

JEFFREY MASTERZ

table, while allowing to spend possibly the rest of her days locked away in prison.

Taylor, after asking him to repeat what he had said, wrote down what Attorney Cooper had quoted her. Staring at the amount, which contained so many zeros, was making her feel uneasy. Will this ever stop, meaning the memories that persisted to this day. She wanted to forget Celeste Harker and the way she was treated. The problem was the check that would always be.

Lucas walked in not knowing what had transpired on what should have been a normal workday for her. Taylor was crying in her chair. He went over to comfort her. She had been a rock lately, and he didn't know what to think. "She is going to jail for at least thirty years," Taylor cried out.

"That's great. So then why are you crying?"

"Did you know they were suing for damages?" she asked.

"Yes, they mentioned it to us," Luke redeclared after remembering that from a week ago.

"She must be very wealthy?"

"I assumed so, why?"

"Because the lawyer called to tell me the amount that we are getting."

"And?" he inquired, bringing her to cry again. "What was the amount, baby?" Lucas urged.

"Well, it is over two million dollars."

"Are you kidding me?" Lucas said, completely stupefied.

"I know what I heard. I even wrote it down."

"So again why are you crying?"

"Well, I almost don't feel like keeping it. I know the money was to reduce her sentence. And I feel funny even having it after what she did. I almost feel like I was paid off, so she could abuse me."

"Oh, honey, no. You mustn't talk like that. We'll talk when we get it, but don't think like that please," Lucas said in a consoling manner as he held her.

Taylor had gone years without flying, and now her miles card was beginning to rack up. This was to be a long flight to Florida, so

344

she decided to try to sleep in the seat that they say reclines. An inch and a half is not reclining!

She felt a hand lightly grasp hers, bringing a minor smile to her face. With the litigation finished, there was that check that they hadn't even started to talk about, still out there.

This time they were off to visit his parents in Florida for Christmas. She closed her eyes while propped up against the window, thrilled that she at least knew that no one was going to be waking her up to go to the bathroom.

Taylor awoke when the captain came back on telling everyone that they were getting ready to descend. Disoriented, she was astonished that she was able to sleep, thinking she only closed her eyes for the first leg into Dallas.

She looked down while descending over the bayside city of St. Petersburg through the small side window. It was a very smooth flight with no snow in sight. Taylor never figured that she would miss the white stuff. But considering what time of year it was, it seemed reasonable that the ground should be covered with at least a little of the powder.

It was six weeks ago when they had done this same routine in Fairbanks, only now it was Luke's parents that were there to greet them. And the Calderone's were donning ugly red Christmas scarves. "What you couldn't find ugly Christmas sweater's down here?" Lucas quipped.

"Are you kidding me? Who do you think knits them all?" his dad said as the two women were commencing with the hugs.

"That makes sense, all the seventy- and eighty-year-olds send them around the country, and now it's a bigger thing than a fruitcake. But I am surprised that you don't have one for…" Tony produced two green scarves and hung them like leis around their necks.

"I'm sorry," Gia said apologetically for the strange and yet typical Christmas gift. All four walked through the exit. The guys even picked out a few of those sweaters. It brought on a subdued round of laughter. The drive out to the parents' condo brought them up the coast so that they could admire the harbors and marinas.

Lucas had seen all this all beofre, but Taylor thought how beautiful it was to see boats and yachts of all different sizes, soaking up the sun. She compared the marina to the one on the sound, but this was much, much larger.

They entered the foyer where Taylor first noticed the Christmas tree in the far corner of the eggshell-hued townhouse. It was a three-foot artificial tree that was centered on an antique round table in the corner, at the far end of the unit. The lights were twinkling red and green, almost to say "It is Christmas," only it was in one of the warmer parts of the world.

Taylor walked her carryon into the living room and remained there waiting to see where Lucas was going to park his bag. Entering through one of the doorways, he entered the den where the two of them put their luggage down in front of the built-in dresser. She looked around the room that appeared to be an office and wondered where they were sleeping.

Maybe it was the open floor, since it did have soft cushy variegated brown carpeting. She also was fascinated by the ceiling to near floor windows covered in sheer curtains. Lucas, who sensed her confusion, walked over and took the two hidden poles and opened the same curtains, only solid, that revealed a Murphy bed from inside the wall.

"That is cool," Taylor said out loud.

"Yes, the unit came with it, but I could picture my dad putting one in if it was his place."

"Me too," Taylor answered.

Lucas pulled at the ring and brought the wall down, so it transformed into a bed. "So do you think you are going to be okay with your accommodations while you're here?" Tony said as he poked his head in the door.

"That is a great idea. When you don't need it, you can put it up, so you don't lose all that floor space. What a grand concept," Taylor said.

Gia called from the other room, "Don't tell me you couldn't smell the stuffed shells?"

"Yes, Mom, I smelled it, but I thought it was a new air freshener." Tony cackled at Luke's response. Gia, not so much. The two of them cleaned up for an old-timer's dinner at four thirty. They didn't traditionally eat at the stereotypical time as many in this complex, but Gia wanted to have food ready for when they finished their cross-country flight. Lucas frankly didn't mind what time of day it was, because he was going to chow down on his mom's Italian tonight.

After unpacking, Taylor took a quick shower to wash away some of the jitters she had since she was confronting Luke's parents for the first time, following her trauma. Lucas agreed with Taylor that it wouldn't do any good to let the parents know unless they were looking for pity, along with all the questions that would follow.

Lucas and his dad lounged out on the balcony, just above the marina's boardwalk. He thoroughly enjoyed the heat of the late afternoon sun when a perky Taylor came out carrying a tray that Gia had given her. Upon the platter sat four mint juleps that Gia had made. She placed them down carefully in the center of the cast iron table.

Gia broke away from her culinary station long enough to join them at the table for a toast of a beautiful Christmas together. Luke's mom was Italian, and of course, where she had always felt the most comfortable, was in the kitchen.

Taylor loved the taste of this cocktail that she had never had before, even though as a bartender, she had made a few. She knew enough of the main ingredient and thought she would watch her intake, so the bourbon didn't sneak up on her.

After they were finished with the juleps, Gia called them to the dining room, where the culinary masterpiece was about to be presented. It was then that Gia had told Taylor that she was going to teach her how to make a real Italian sauce. "Mother, you aren't going to take a whole day of her vacation teaching her how to thicken up sauce are you?" Tony interjected.

Gia looked at Tony. "They are here for a whole week, and I can't teach her one recipe?" she insisted.

Tony conceded, "Now, Mother, let's talk about this tomorrow!"

"Actually, I would love to learn how to cook, I mean Italian meals for Lucas. I know they will never be as good as the ones you cook, but I'd like to try." That was enough to satisfy Gia, who had been wanting to teach her when they were in Seattle last.

Taylor, outside later, took the second drink that was offered but nursed it for the better part of an hour. The bourbon and the mint together, made for a very smooth but potent beverage. She looked down at the illuminated marina, making a mental note that tomorrow it would be nice if she could catch a gulf sunset.

"So what do you think about the bed?" Lucas asked as she mushed in and got herself comfortable on the Murphy bed.

"I don't know. Maybe I wouldn't want one of these." Despite the moving around, they still managed to fall asleep for some much-needed rest.

Taylor awoke moaning as she turned to get to the edge of the bed. Taylor used the walk around the room to stretch and see if she could release the muscles that were giving her trouble.

On her way back to her side, she climbed in and cuddled with Luke. It was easy for him to figure out that she was not going back to sleep. She squirmed until he finally whispered, "You can't sleep?"

She squirmed again and then said, "I need to talk about the check."

"Well, what about it?" Lucas asked.

"I don't think we can keep it." But he knew she meant her.

"Okay, we don't have to keep it, but I do want you to do something good with it. You have an opportunity to take something bad and turn it into something better. We don't have to decide now so it can be for whatever it is that you want."

"Okay, that might be all right. I just don't think I can keep it considering, that's all."

"Then we won't. How's the weather out?" Lucas asked to start a new subject.

"Well, it's not snowing," she said jokingly.

"You miss home, don't you?"

"I do. I think some of it is the snow. I know that it has very low temps, extreme winds, and snow, but I love it."

"Well, what if we started going back to Fairbanks or even the inn, for say a month or so, in the wintertime?" Taylor got excited at that. "And maybe we could watch the inn again, so your brother and sister-in-law can go on a vacation somewhere," Luke added.

"You mean just you and me at the inn like we did last year? Then count me in!"

Without thinking, Taylor remembered their very kinky start, even as Lucas had only mentioned it as a way to get her thinking about the possibilities, in hopes she would forget the money that she kept talking about. He didn't go any further as he was excited that she was in the right frame of mind for all of this.

Luke remembered his introduction of where she was merely putty in his hands. And all he had to do was mold her into something they were both all right with, something that was lasting. Maybe there was still a chance that they would be able to return to the life they had. Lucas thought that if and when it happens, it will be after she tells him she was ready.

"Luke, with all the talk about the other wedding in my family, when do you think we should do it?"

"I wouldn't mind doing it next year, maybe later in the year."

"That early?"

"Yes, I know that we want to have children and I am thirty-five, and you are—"

"Watch it!" she said as she raised her voice.

"You know what I mean? I don't want us being seventy when the kids graduate from high school," he explained.

"Yes, I know. I can hardly believe that we are talking about kids and getting married. It is all becoming so real."

"It is real if you want it to be."

"I do," she answered.

"Then we should set a date, at least for us, when we get home. Why don't we go out and see if my parents are up yet?" The two slinked out in their pajamas to the living room only to receive a good morning from his mother. "Dad's not up yet?"

"He is. He is doing the three Ss!"

"The three Ss, what is that?" Taylor asked.

"Honey, that is military talk for sheet, shower, and shave," Gia answered.

"And my mom didn't mean sheet. I don't think I have ever heard her say a curse word in my entire life and I guess she wasn't about to

349

say shit now," Lucas said telling her the word that it stood for. With Gia in the kitchen, making a batch of peach pancakes for them, Tony emerged, freshly groomed and smelling good.

"Good morning, all," Tony said as he moved in behind his wife and kissed her on her cheek. "Good morning, doll," he added just loud enough for her to hear. She must have heard it because she blushed like a schoolgirl. Lucas saw the display of his parents and only thought of one thing that he couldn't wait to be doing the same thing in another thirty years or so.

"So, Dad, do we have any plans for this week?"

"Yes, tomorrow we are supposed to have great weather, so I didn't know if you wanted to go out for some deep-sea fishing." Taylor beamed at the prospect of possibly going out far into the ocean and catch something big and different.

She had done some in Glacier Bay, when her dad had taken her on a fishing trip, on her sixteenth birthday. But the weather in Florida would make it much more enjoyable. "So what kind of fish are we talking about?" she said as she wanted to know.

"Bluefish! It is catch and release, but I guess they will let you bring one home if you wish at an additional cost. It had a favorable write up in the paper. So I thought that we could either get up early or go later in the afternoon."

"I guess we can figure it out," Lucas said speaking for himself and Taylor. The guests sat and enjoyed their fruited pancakes. Gia still had the syrup, but she added a side mound of fresh whipped cream to dab it in. It was delicious and to their liking.

The next morning the alarm went off as Taylor made her way to the bathroom like she usually did. Taylor was surprised that her back was no longer sore and thought that maybe it was the plane and not necessarily the bed, which made her that way.

With them heading out of port at 6:00 a.m., she got up, with her not wanting to be the one they were waiting on. As she was finishing, she tried to visualize Luke's mom as a fisherman and thought it might be interesting to watch her go through the motions. The woman looked more like the one that cleaned and cooked it, than the one reeling it in.

Yesterday, Taylor had gone online to see what kind of fish the bluefish was. Was it a good eating one and how much of a fight did it give? She was looking forward to all of it. She loved the traveling and the being with Luke time, even though they were in the company of others. She was getting to see how her man spends his off time. He doesn't travel all the time, but she was here with him and she wanted to enjoy every last second of it.

They used the gangway to board onto the thirty-foot fishing vessel. The four were all enthusiastic since the weather report for the day was supposed to be in the high seventies. They first gathered at the stern to get safety information and to be fitted with their gear for the day.

The four all partook, but Gia was happiest just watching. She wanted to be able to see when one of them hooked and pulled in the big one. In between casts, they snacked on what they had brought, along with a couple of bottles of wine.

Taylor couldn't be any happier than she was right now. And that included when she pulled a seventeen-pound, thirty-five-inch blue all by herself. She had a cheering section of the three, as well as nearly a dozen other fishermen who were right alongside her when she hooked it.

When they left the boat, that was the one that Taylor took home for tomorrow's dinner. The charter company had cleaned it and packaged it before they left, saving Gia the first couple of steps.

# CHAPTER 26

Christmas Eve Day, Lucas had sent his parents out on a search and find mission. They were excited that Lucas asked them and graciously ran the errand. When they returned, they were shocked to see that instead of their three-foot scaled down artificial tree that was sitting in the corner, there was now a seven-foot live one. "What happened to our tree?" a shocked Gia asked.

"It is in your bedroom!" Lucas exclaimed while Taylor just stayed back to witness the show, smiling the whole time.

"You went out and bought a Christmas tree the day before Christmas and where did you get the ornaments?" his dad asked.

"No, I rented the tree from a tree farm. They dropped it off with a box of lights and the ornaments too."

"I didn't know they did that. Maybe we should start doing that every year," his equally surprised dad said.

"I wanted this to be a special Christmas for us all. Taylor and I are going to be married next year, and no, we didn't pick a day yet, but I wanted you to know how much I love you all." Gia looked at Taylor, almost to say, I told you so.

Taylor was pleased that she could have just as good a time here as she does with her own family. For her, she was ready to be a Calderone, with her relaxing in their presence. The weekly calls to them helped.

It felt like Christmas, having the tall Sand Pine all decorated, as long as you didn't look outside, with all the people walking around on the boardwalk, as most were wearing shorts. Lucas wrapped his arms around her waist and admired the tree that looked so much better than the web page photo did.

After dinner, the lights were dimmed, and a special toast was made by the head of the household. The four held up tiny fluted drink glasses with an equally distinctive liquor to mark the celebration. "With the new year ringing in soon, it is important that we celebrate not just the future but the past, which has gotten us here," Tony said with his toast. They all clinked glasses before sipping the creamy drink.

"Um, what kind of drink is this? It tastes kind of like eggnog!" Taylor asked.

"It is a drink that we have celebrated with for, I don't know how many years. It is called Italian egg and marsala liquor," Tony answered.

"It's very light and tasty," Taylor said before taking another sip. After, Tony urged Luke to rearrange the furniture so they could all look at the tree. Taylor joyfully pushed Tony aside so that she could help.

The next morning, Taylor was already dreading the flight home. She was having too much fun. Just last night, the Seattle visitors beat Luke's parents in a spirited round of canasta. They had just learned how, but the cards fell their way and they beat them silly.

Lucas stopped Taylor, who was standing unbeknownst under the mistletoe. He caught her by surprise, as he moved in and took what he wanted and then pointed toward the archway as if he needed a reason.

Most of them had different drink choices as one opted for tea, one coffee and two had mulled cider. When they were ready, they all sat around the tree and were prepared to open presents. The first present was from Tony to his loving wife of thirty-seven years.

Gia opened the small gold foil box and teared up. It was a little stained-glass framed piece that had a single red rose with the four digits of the year they met.

"Thank you, dear, roses have always been my favorite," she phrased knowing that he had been going to craft class since they got back after their son's birthday weekend. Gia's present to her husband was for three rounds of golf at the nearby golf course that he frequently played with friends of his.

"Thank you dear," he said. Next Lucas gave Taylor a box roughly the size of eight by eight. She held it on her lap and opened it slowly, not ripping the paper but breaking the tape.

"Where did you find this?"

"I had my parents run out for it yesterday while they brought the tree in." It was a Casa Noble Anejo gift set. A bottle of the tequila and fancy glasses to go with it.

"Oh, baby," she jubilantly stated. Taylor hugged him and then took the present from under the tree and handed it to Lucas. He opened it to find a pro action camera/camcorder along with a mounting bracket.

"You can use it on your boat. And it's waterproof!"

"That will be fun. I can't wait to use it!" Lucas stated following it with a kiss.

Taylor and Lucas got their present from his parents, and then Lucas went into one of the drawers in the coffee table and pulled out a tiny box. It was unwrapped, and she knew for sure that it wasn't an engagement ring, but she looked at him strangely. "You already got me a present."

"Yeah, that was to throw you off. Just open it!" Taylor looked at the box and slowly unwrapped it. Inside it was a pendant on a gold setting with a chain.

"What kind of stone is this? It is beautiful."

"It is amethyst," Luke replied.

"But amethysts are dark purple, aren't they?"

"Yes, but this is a lavender amethyst that was mined in the town of Northway, Alaska," Lucas answered. Her eyes grew as the gift was worth so much more to her than a few seconds ago. It was a beautiful stone, cut to hang down from the setting, displaying its best qualities below. She got up and gave him a kiss and a big hug.

"You know I would be perfectly happy with just the tequila."

"And I know that's true!" Lucas said.

Saving the best for last, Luke reached under the tree skirt and pulled out another present. This one he placed between his mom and dad. They were slow to open it with it maybe being the last one of the day. The paper got torn back slowly to reveal a blue folder, with nothing on its front. They opened it to what they saw was hard to fathom at first. They flipped the pages, containing all the information.

"Luke, we can't except this," claimed his mother.

"No, really son, it is too much," his father agreed.

"Do you know what it is?" Luke asked.

"I think so. It is a cruise from Alaska to Hawaii, but I didn't think they had such a thing," Tony answered.

"It is the first cruise from there to there. Please accept this. Otherwise, the Naughton's will be going by themselves."

"They're going?" Gia and Tony called out synchronized.

Now they were ecstatic. Lucas and Taylor were happy that their homework on this paid off. Taylor hoped that the other part of this would work with Luke being able to get some time off so they could go too. "You see, they are calling it the Wilderness to Paradise Cruise," Taylor piped in.

"How long a cruise is this?" Tony inquired.

"It is twelve nights!" Luke responded.

"Luke, this is too much!" Gia said again.

"So you are going to let them go by themselves?" Luke asked.

"Well, I don't think we should do that. So Ken and Susan are going?" Tony asked.

"No, but this is the line we are going to use on them after you say yes," Lucas replied. "Plus, I am trying hard to figure out if we can make it. I have not been on a cruise, and I think it is time that I do." Taylor nuzzled up behind her fiancé. Tony and Gia talked with only their eyes and then agreed to it.

They all sat and looked at the ports and even talked about how none of them had been to the Alaska locations, and of course, none had yet been to Hawaii. "The cruise sails out of Anchorage, then travels past Glacier Bay to Ketchikan, then to Maui, Oahu, and finally the Big Island. They truly sound wonderful son," Dad said.

The two of them flipped through all the brochures and the catalog that all fit in the pockets of the folder. Lucas and Taylor did well in their find. This was going to be as incredible as when they had cruises that ported in Cuba for the first time. However, this one was unique, with its extreme visiting ports that were so different from each other.

Now before they booked the tickets, Luke had to make sure they were booking the Wilderness to Paradise and not the other way around. Alaska to Hawaii sounded much more exciting. When it simmered down and after the parents had thanked them a million times, Taylor reached under the tree. The last present she handed off was to her future father-in-law. Receiving the gift the man began to ramble on about their little town, just from sheer excitement.

Back in Seattle, Taylor checked off the first few days of the new calendar, shocked that the last year had gone by so fast. It was a year of highs mixed with lows that, as strong as those were, somehow only brought her and Lucas closer together.

And even though the worst moment left her scarred, with her unable to give into sex to this day, she knew that their relationship is unmistakably stronger than ever, with Lucas making sure that he was always there for her. However, Taylor was ready for a new year of only good.

With only one last bump in the road left over from the past year, she thought about the check, dabbling with the thoughts of where the money should go. For her it had to be about her home town, helping its citizens and paying honor to her grandparents in the process. And after clearing this up, she could bury the past knowing that she would never, ever have to see or talk about that woman again.

Lucas and Taylor sat down to what was an early dinner for a worknight. They barely got two bites in, when her phone rang. She looked at the number. "It's my parents!"

She answered the call. "Hi, Mom," Taylor said knowing that it was always mom that made the calls. "Yeah, Luke is home! We were just eating dinner," Taylor said to her question.

"Oh, you got our Christmas present. And what do you think?"

Taylor covered the phone and whispered that they are excited. "No, you are going to have company. The Calderone's will be going, and we are looking into us coming too. He is trying to make it work out." And then she listened.

"Yes, we love our gift. Thank you."

"So do you want to go on the cruise?" Taylor sat there quietly.

"Great. And yes, I will tell Lucas. Talk to you soon, Mom. I love you both," Taylor concluded. After a few seconds, she disconnected the phone.

Lucas sat quietly, waiting for the words he thought he had heard. "The Naughtons and the Calderone's are going on a cruise!"

"Fantastic," Luke responded. He high-fived her from across the table. It was a win.

"Of course, you know that we are going to have to come up with something, just as big next year." Lucas laughed and then thought, *Well, that's next year.*

Today, Lucas started a remodel on a mom and pop convenience store on Mercer Island. It was a quick job since they were to renovate one side and then move on to the other, leaving the owners with no real downtime. Although he did have a large job coming up and for that, he was going to have to travel and most likely stay away during the week to cut down on the commute.

He never had to give it a thought before, traveling whenever or wherever he needed outside their base in Seattle. Well, this time they were packing up the trailers and bringing most of the equipment to Eugene, which was a solid 250 miles away.

Shocked that he won the bid, he called in all of his summer crew for this one. And since he was reactivating them, he looked into keeping them busy until the next slowdown. The guys really loved the travel jobs, although like Lucas most were leaving their loved ones alone during the week. But the upside to that was that after work they all had guys time, with them getting to hang out together, giving them a reason to drink.

A week before Valentine's Day, Taylor made a reservation for dinner at Henri's, per Luke's request. He promised her that he would make it home to spend the weekend with her. For the reservation she called and talked to Henri directly.

They both decided to book for Saturday night instead of on the holiday, Sunday. He had to travel late Sunday, to get back, plus it was a given that most couples would be out in search of Cupid.

Taylor said that they wanted to eat there but only if Henri didn't pay their bill. The restaurateur agreed, but then was handed another stipulation. He was dumbfounded that they would want him to join them on a night that was clearly destined for romance.

The Frenchman finally did give in to that too as Taylor had thought that Henri sounded different somehow. She just pushed it off, thinking maybe it was because he didn't like being backed into a corner over the bill and dining with his guests.

A week later Taylor and Lucas were sitting, doing something they never did, watching TV. The phone rang. It was her brother. Lucas muted the set. "Hi, sis, what's up?"

"Are we really going to play this game again?" she said jokingly.

"Am I bothering you?" Kyle asked.

"No, we were just sitting around, why?"

"Can you put me on speakerphone?" She pressed the button and said, "Go ahead."

"Hey, I just got off the phone with mom and dad and by the way they will not stop talking about the cruise." Taylor was wondering what was going on as Luke was curious too, with them being on speakerphone.

"Well, I just wanted you to know that we have picked a month for our wedding. We are thinking about the beginning of May."

"That's wonderful. You know we will be there!" Taylor said quickly adding, "But weren't you thinking more towards the end of September?"

"Yes, but we had to pick this month," Kyle said happily.

After a brief pause a lightbulb went off. "What do you mean you had to. Oh my God. Are you saying what I think you're saying?" She questioned loud enough for Isla to hear, even if she wasn't in the room.

"Yes, sis, you are going to be an aunt!" Kyle boldly explained.

Taylor and Lucas were joyful as Taylor screeched, "Oh my God!" Pausing, she asked, "How...when did you find out?"

"About two weeks now. And that was part of the call to our parents. They are beside themselves over the news. I wanted you to know, and we hope you can make it."

"We will be there. Oh, Isla will have a baby bump by then. Oh my God." Luke turned to Taylor, who was sitting and then standing and then repeated her moves because of the incredible news.

"Guys I am going to let you two talk, but congratulations. And Kyle I would like to speak to you after you are done speaking with your sister," Luke said to Taylor, before walking from the room.

Luke went to the bathroom and decided to take a shower before bed. He was overjoyed at the turn of events of his future brother and sister-in-law. A baby, what a blessing. Taylor was going to be a great aunt and a fantastic mother someday. Lucas even pictured Taylor holding the little one.

He turned on the shower and thought he should keep it short, in the chance that they didn't talk for long. He climbed in and let the water run down over him as he laughed to himself about Taylor and her marathon calls to family. Lucas rinsed off and stood directly under the flow before finally reaching out and turning the handle off.

After Taylor's talk with Kyle, he just knew that they weren't going to sleep tonight as his girl was going to be a chatterbox, and he welcomed that. Lucas thought somehow, he would make up for it tomorrow night so that he was somewhat rested for their night out with Henri.

Okay, it wasn't exactly romantic, but he needed to talk to the man. Henri was no longer just a client of his, but a friend. Sure, it turned out at first that Henri was a good friend of his father's, but without Luke realizing it, it changed. He felt he needed to tell the man this. But he knew that Henri was not one to sit in one place for more than a few minutes, so he figured that they would only have his company for maybe up to the hors d'oeuvres anyway.

Taylor stepped in sporting a smile. "Do you still want to speak with Kyle?" He reached out and took the phone as he passed her. She went to the nightstand and grabbed the tablet and sat up against the headboard. She had and urge to look at baby stuff, with her wanting to see what she could get for her niece or nephew.

The brunette was so bubbly that she wanted to find the one or two things that would be just right. She went to her fail-safe and went to the online site, which had just about anything you could think of. She got distracted by a thought and wanted to call Lauren, right then and there. Crap, her phone was with Lucas. Taylor would have to do it tomorrow then. Back to her search, she tried baby items.

Lucas and Kyle talked, saying how excited they were. Lucas had no problem with the wedding being stepped up by four months. He thought about how beautiful the weather could be for them by then. He had his fingers crossed for his good friend and fiancée. "I know that we have been talking, and I am going to send you an email, but it is for your eyes only," Lucas said almost in code.

"Gotcha! I will look for it." It was about the conversations they had recently.

"I can't believe you are going to be a father!" Luke stated.

"Why, you don't think I can do it?" he answered jokingly.

"No, you know what I mean. Sometimes you just go through life and think everything is great and then you realize that it was, but something else like a child elevates it to a new level. You are going to be a great father and husband. She will be lucky to have you for both."

"Thanks, buddy," Kyle said, feeling very touched.

Lucas walked back into the bedroom and saw Taylor still on the tablet. "Order anything yet?" She just looked at him as she couldn't curb her enthusiasm.

"Can you believe it?" she asked.

"Yeah, little Isla having a baby."

"So what are you doing online?"

"Nothing, just looking at a few things," Taylor answered.

"Anything, possibly baby related?"

"You know what I'm doing," she replied. Lucas lay down under the covers, and they talked for a little while, as she went through the long list of items that seemed to scroll on forever. Lucas had been asleep for who knows how long before Taylor even realized. She turned off the light, on her side of the bed and thought she should try to get some sleep. After about half an hour, she did too.

For their Valentine's dinner, they sat in the small room Bein-etre, just like the first time they were there together. "I am so sorry. I meant to be with you when you came in," said the frazzled restaurateur. He sat after kissing the hand of the lady at the table. "I hope you don't mind, but I cannot join you for the entire meal tonight. I have some things that I must do."

"That's okay, Henri, I am happy that you could at least join us now," Lucas replied.

"You two look especially handsome and beautiful this evening?" he said in a muted version of the man they have grown to know.

"Oh, Henri, I have great news to tell you! My brother- and sister-in-law are having a baby. We just found out."

"That is wonderful news!" Henri said forcing a smile. "So did you order yet?" Henri inquired as his face turned cold.

"Just appetizers a few minutes ago!" After placing the order he told the man that he felt a growing friendship toward him and was very happy that he had the opportunity to have met him.

A troubled Henri rose from the table. "Excuse me, please." The man bellowed while walking briskly from the table to the door of the courtyard, noticeably in tears. Lucas and Taylor just sat there totally confused by the situation.

"I have to go talk to him," Lucas said as he stood to walk out, with Taylor right behind him. Henri was along the wall in frigid temperatures trying to compose himself.

"Henri, what's the matter?"

"Monsieur Lucas, I have been battling something for a while. I shouldn't have come back to work yet."

"What is it? Can you tell us?"

"I... I... I lost my youngest son, Simon, to a car accident," the man said and then cried out loud.

"Oh, Henri, we didn't know," Taylor said, trying to comfort the man.

Lucas wondered why he hadn't heard anything since his dad and he are such good friends and all. The two of them consoled Henri as he grieved the loss of his boy. Henri was such a family man, and he took it especially hard, having to face the loss of his child.

Taylor couldn't help but wonder if it was her talking about a baby that made him lose it.

After about ten minutes, the three made their way back to the table. Henri went out back to dry his eyes. To the rest of the world, he wanted to appear to be the jovial man he always was. Henri knew that when people came out to dinner, they wanted, no expected and deserved to have a very memorable night. He couldn't destroy that experience just because he had some emotional upheaval in his life.

Arriving back at the table, the three stood surrounding the table as their appetizers had made it there before they had.

"Please excuse me for my outburst. It was not the thing to do," Henri said meekly.

"You don't have to explain Henri. You are human, and there is no reason to apologize. But is there anything we can do?" Luke asked.

He teared up. "Please let your father know. I haven't been able to pick up the phone to tell him."

"I will do that," Lucas said noticing that the man was about to leave again. The restaurateur looked just outside the room to the waitress who was walking in.

"Sophia, please take these away and get them some hot hors d'oeuvres." The woman scooped up the untouched cold appetizers and swiftly left the room. He stood like they kind of felt that he would and said, "I must leave you two to try to enjoy your evening. I am sorry once more, but I cannot join you this time." Henri bowed his head slightly and left them alone in the room. They were there quietly in their thoughts that had changed from news of a wedding and a baby to that of sorrow.

The two walked into the house and hung their jackets up. Henri did not allow them to pay the bill because of what had happened. And how could Luke fight this, however he vowed that they would pay their way next time. Dinner was all right, but they ended up with leftovers this time because neither of them were in the mood to eat.

Lucas went over to his computer to read the emailed reply from Kyle. At the fridge Taylor was silent in the fact that even though she has not had a child yet, she understood the depth of this man's loss.

She put the leftovers in the fridge and went over and opened a new bottle of tequila.

Lucas read the extent of the lengthy email, but was prompted back to the capitalized subject field that displayed, "YES TO ALL!"

Luke shut off the computer and got up to meet Taylor part way across the floor. He took the glass from her, as the ice made a rattling sound. They sipped with no toast and no words. It was all about the man they both still hardly knew, which left them powerless as they both felt for him.

Lucas, when they were through with the two fingers of Casa Noble, said that he had to call his dad, something that he regretted but knew that it had to be done. He put the glass down and retired to the bedroom.

Taylor sat with her balloon of excitement that had a hole pierced through it. Feeling deflated herself, she thought it would be a good time to call Lauren to see if she could talk. When the text went unanswered, she sat in her chair and sipped the water from the ice that melted.

Spring was here, and many things had washed away under the bridge, mostly good. The check she didn't want was sitting in the bank, and the fear did finally subside. They also got to dine with Henri, as he was able to sit through an entire meal with them.

They had talked about things he and Luke's dad had done when they met, some of which they had already heard but enjoyed again. He spoke of his wife Sabine and his living son Ethan. He even spoke of Simon like he was still alive.

He talked about a lot of the good things that they had done together, speaking as though he didn't want to forget him. Henri seemed to be over the pain of it and onto remembering his son for the great man that he was. And Taylor and Luke were glad to see that.

When they left the table at the end of the evening, Luke paid the bill for all three of them, like Henri had agreed the last time. As the two of them were getting up to leave, the waiter brought them a bottle of red wine with a note.

The message said, "May your wine rack never be full and never be empty. Love, your good friend Henri." Taylor, of course, knew what that had meant. Luke was in the dark and didn't find out what it was all about until they were out in the car. Lucas thought it was such a sweet gesture and that the wording as prevailing as it was, deserved to be on a plaque on their wall.

Isla had made many calls in the past weeks to the one she was going to be calling sister soon. She was modestly excited about the wedding that was getting very close now. She had told her that the date, which was a Friday at the end of May was going well, but she was getting scared.

She also mentioned that Kyle and her both opted not for the traditional wedding of tux and gown. Taylor said that was their plans also, for when theirs finally happens.

Isla said she wanted Taylor to be up there with her since she was a little shy to be in front of even a few people, for something this important. She then spoke of picturing the place with small bunches of carnations around for their ceremony. She also added things that told Taylor that she was deeply in love with her brother. If asked years ago, Taylor would have been able to tell her that.

Lucas told Taylor that he was booking the cruises and flights for the six a while back, with Taylor getting pumped as time went on. She even bought a few things to wear, when something caught her eye or was on sale. Luke even had a merry way about him now as he walked in every day with a large smile on his face. The other night he said that he has it all figured out, for getting the time off for Alaska.

The excitement was all around as her parents were calling more often, about all the information they had already heard firsthand. Taylor's dad was growing fond of the girl as of late as he was honored when Isla asked him to walk her down the aisle.

She heard it directly from her mom that he cried after they hung up. Taylor was touched by the request her sister had made, seeing that Isla was probably looking at the man as the father she always wished she had had. Yes, Taylor was going to love this.

They even talked about their wedding, which was getting closer no matter, with the last plan of it being for the end of September.

Taylor even decided on one of the gifts for the baby. She was going to pick it up at a store in Point Hope.

She came up with a dreamcatcher for over the baby's bed. With its hoop, mesh, beads, and feathers, it was believed to give the owner pleasant dreams. The newest Naughton, being part-Indian, should rest well with his or her heritage. With the other gift, she was still undecided on which item to get.

Her mom came up with a beautiful wedding present idea last week. She wanted to make a recipe book that contained all the best recipes of their grandmother and of course herself. Taylor thought that was a perfect gift, and Kyle would love it. Maybe someday, Isla would be able to cook the meals too. Her dad, who was the computer whiz of the household anyway, was going to do the computer part, importing and printing it out.

Taylor started packing a week before their return to the inn, as the idea was getting her bubbly with delight. Luke, who wasn't around much trying to tie up loose ends, still managed that grin when he walked in, no matter what time of night it was.

She knew he was working hard to get whatever he had to do done, as it was peak time for his company. She thought as she made sure to pack up a nice suit and enough clothes to make it for at least a week. For herself, she packed two dresses that she was torn between and could have for the formal cruise nights.

Lucas called during the day, to just say he loved her. Hearing that she knew he was getting stoked about his buddy getting married, and maybe in combination with them being back at the inn for an entire week.

Taylor looked at it as a place where that held so much of her family history. She wondered if he felt the same way that she did, about their start in that very inn. Right now, maybe not as he was too preoccupied.

Lucas sat at the airport trying to remember if he thought of everything. He worked with Steve and John, making sure they would be okay during his absence. Sitting back in the blue plastic chair at the Seattle-Tacoma terminal, he toyed with one of his apps.

Taylor sat calmly conversing with her mother, although she did it at a rapid-fire pace, just as she had for the past six weeks. But it was all in fun, as all she wanted to do was see two people she loved so dearly, married starting a new chapter in their life.

Lucas checked off his completed to-do list. Everything was looking good. Taylor, who asked for the second time, asked Luke what they were doing for the gift for the bride and groom. He just shrugged it off and said it was a surprise. He followed it up with "Do you like surprises?"

She, of course said yes, and thought that she would apparently know when the married couple did. Lucas walked off after waving to her that he was going for some water. Later, he returned with the two largest water bottles he could find.

# CHAPTER 27

Isla rushed into the unfurled arms of Taylor, showering her with a lengthy embrace from the woman, who seemingly emerged into a blossoming extrovert, basically overnight. "Is it too early to call you, my sister?" Isla boldly articulated. Taylor smiled as the men shook hands in the background before finishing with a quick hug.

"You can call me that anytime, but first I have to see your baby bump, sis!" Taylor jubilantly blurted out. After unzipping her jacket in the terminal, Isla took Taylor's hand and lifted it to her bare stomach as she gushed at another person being as giddy as she was.

Not fifteen minutes later, the four rode back to the inn and marched into the kitchen. Stepping in, Taylor noticed a discernible aroma that enveloped her nostrils. She looked about just to be sure. Could it be Gia?

"Taylor, come give me a hug," Gia called out as she walked in from the dining room. Taylor responded but thought even with it being a few busy months, she was sure that she hadn't been filled in on this.

Luke kissed Mom and then leaned back to give Susan a peck on the cheek while he went over to tend to his mom's prize sauce. "How come you guys are here?" Taylor inquired, stating her confusion publicly.

"Because we are going on the cruise together," Susan quickly replied to her daughter's question.

"Oh, I just hadn't heard this before!" Taylor stated as it wasn't sinking in. Still perplexed she poured some wine from the half-empty pitcher of sangria. "But the cruise is next week," Taylor added taking one last stab at it.

"Actually, I ran it by Kyle to see if it was all right. He knows how we all get along so well, and they do have all those rooms upstairs," her mom added.

Taylor shrugged it off for the last time since now it made perfect sense. She partook in a sip of the fruity wine considering that there should be no more questions because their vacation was now at hand. Gia reclaimed her post back at the stove, with a resolute stance that as an Italian woman, no one was going to be hungry tonight. Taylor silently wondered in the background what Luke's mother was going to do with herself when she wasn't cooking for two weeks.

Luke traipsed into the pub to see the two dads sitting at a small table directly in front of the fireplace. And it was the very same location where he and Taylor had shared their first drink and a meal if you call splitting a sandwich a meal.

He walked by and felt the bar top. Adrenaline flowed through him as little flashes made their way from his brain, to be shown again like a filmstrip for only him to relive once more. "So how was your flight, son?"

"Fantastic. And how's your week been?" Lucas asked.

"Great! We got those two things finished you asked for. They came out nice," Luke's dad commented trying not to be heard.

"So did you have fun, Ken?" Lucas asked in reference to their carpentry collaboration.

"I did. I have never done any of that before, but your dad knew that and kept me busy just the same," Ken said appreciatively throwing out his hand and added, "Susan and I want to thank you again, for the cruise!"

"Yes, thanks again, son!" Tony dittoed as Lucas pulled up a chair to join in and watch the fire that jumped erratically as if being controlled by strings. "Oh, and did you see the bar when you came in?"

"Of course! I was here last winter. It still looks wonderful, Dad!"

"Yeah, they kept it in great shape. Hey, get a glass and sit down with us and Johnnie!" His pop exclaimed raising the bottle.

"You don't have to ask me twice," Lucas said as he turned to the bar and clenched a glass and some cubes. While he was there, he looked down at the towel rack, the one that he had used as a makeshift anchor.

The three sat for a few minutes until next week's groom walked in and received a verbal prodding to get himself a holder for his whiskey. "This is going to be a wonderful week for all of us," Luke said.

"You got that right, but you have got to catch up boy as we have been here for a week already," Ken stated, referring to the scotch at their table.

"Lucky you!" Lucas answered.

"No, lucky us," Kyle stated, lifting his newly poured glass for a toast. The toast could have gone without saying as they knew they were all lucky, lucky to have someone in their lives that loved them.

The guys noticed Isla and Taylor as the ladies strolled in, toting their own glasses, with Taylor's being about an inch left of the berry. She was already a bit tipsy as the long flight made that entirely possible. Isla, who was smiling but quiet, handled a nonalcoholic drink of her own. "Boys, the chef said dinner is ready? And they want to know if you want to eat in the dining room?" Taylor questioned.

"No, how about here?" Luke called back.

"Sounds good. Can we have a hand bringing it all in then?" Taylor inquired.

"Sure, but we have to make sure that someone walks Daisy first!" Kyle exclaimed.

"Daisy?" Taylor said as her ears perked up.

"Oh yeah, I meant to tell you that we picked up a dog last week. The breeder got in touch with us because of Chestnut. You knew that Chestnut had a couple litters. Well, Daisy is her granddaughter. I think I said it right. But it sounds strange to me when speaking about dogs."

"So where is she? I will do it," Taylor asked in sheer excitement.

"She's in our room. And you don't mind? She is quite the handful, with her being only nine weeks old."

"I've got this," Taylor stated as she grinned. However, no one knew for sure, because she was already booking it through the lodge to the other side of the inn.

"The lead is hanging up on the back of the door. But remember, we are eating in a few minutes. You have all week to play with her," her brother yelled, even though he knew that his sister was no longer listening.

The dads rose up after the room cleared, giving them ample opportunity to slide four tables together, facing them perpendicularly to the hearth. Then they arranged the chairs so that all eight could sit and talk, with each having a view of the fire if they wanted. Moving to the bar, they grabbed eight wineglasses because wine goes with pasta, as much as bread goes with butter.

In the past week, Tony and Ken worked hard on the project that Lucas had asked them to do, although they were not sure why, except that it was something that Luke requested specifically. They only assumed that it was to be used for the wedding.

A procession of five caravanned into the pub, bearing family style pots of pasta, a meat sauce, a fresh bread, grated parmesan, salad, and the rest of the homemade wine that had been marinating for three days now. Kyle, after placing the sauce down, grabbed a cloth for the modular or makeshift ten-foot table.

With a jubilant Taylor coming out after only the third call, they all hurriedly took their seats as the smell made them quickly realize how hungry they were. The party sat down to loads of laughter, great food, and what was to be for them, newfound memories.

Lucas gazed across to Taylor as she looked back at him endearingly. Even the darkened room couldn't keep them from seeing how they each felt. This was so much better than figuring out what she was going to do like months ago, when boredom had set in, making Taylor feel as though she wanted to be elsewhere at times.

The wine, once the bottle went dry, changed to another that never did, with Kyle opening more so long as there was someone there to drink them. Later the tables were pried apart to clear the floor for those who wanted to dance. With the fire stoked, Tony was put in charge of the digital music choice. He picked his favorite, as the others waited to see what it was going to be.

Anthony placed his arms around Gia, as Nat King Cole's "Unforgettable" began. The ladies were instantly swept away thanks to the men, the alcohol, and the euphoric mystique that enraptured the room, as if cupid had cast a spell by simply firing off a handful of its enchanted arrows.

Deeper into the evening, Taylor held Lucas tight with a commitment of never letting him go. The ambiance whisked her so past the point of becoming drunk, with her now outwardly aroused, if anyone had looked in on them close enough, that is. She melted in his arms, showing Luke that the night for them was over, at least down here anyway.

Following one last song for them anyway, Lucas announced to the masses that they were going to bed, which left the other six bidding a fond adieu in one form or another to the weary Washington travelers.

"Mom, don't do the dishes! I'll do them in the morning," Luke called out loud enough for her to hear. Gia, who had no intention of doing that until the morning, asked her son, "Lucas, can you put the food away, please?"

"Got it," Lucas answered, as the two carried out the plates, leaving them to quickly pack the leftovers away for another day.

Upstairs, Taylor entered their room, room seven, ahead of Lucas. She gazed out over the room, locking in on the area where her first real introduction to kink had occurred. As Lucas wasn't sure how this was all going to go, he just let her have this time to herself.

She gazed up at the beam, where she was strung up like a piece of meat for a man who taught her about the darker side of who he was. She then sat on the bed where she was strapped facedown as she purposely clenched handfuls of the quilt trying to rehash each second of that night.

In the bathroom, where Luke stood in front of her, was where she first got up the nerve to approach him for shower sex and get this all started. This room for her held so many incredible memories that rushed at her like flickering recollections that intervened her conciousness.

In dire need of another BCD moment, Taylor snuck up behind Luke and tugged at his shirt as he rifled through the ditty bag. She continued to yank at him, displaying a wild attempt to not only get his attention but for Lucas to adhere to her beckoning desire.

Leading him to the bed she placed her wrists together, pushing them out in front of her. Even a blind person could see that Taylor was in the mood, so with the man ill prepared, he had to improvise. He wanted to get as into it as Taylor clearly was right now, but it had been six long months since they had had any form of sex and it was all due to her traumatic episode.

She rushed to get naked, and verbally urged him to do the same. Taylor stood there, wondering if he was going to comply with her hint. She made it quite evident, and for the first time in a long time, she needed this and even more than the sex itself.

He moved her near the bed and looked around the room. Lucas pulled away the covers and stacked the pillows in a pile, but not until he pulled the cotton cases free. She became damp just watching him.

With Taylor kneeling upon the bed, he had her bend her top half over the pile of pillows as she began to regain the urge and a sense from her past of where she knew this was going.

Grabbing hold of the pillowcase, he wound the cotton material into what resembled a thickened cord, positioning it along her lower spine. Taking her arms, Lucas slowly coerced them to cross her lower back, where he bound her wrists together, driving the woman insane, in thinking about her naughty bondage predicament.

If she had gone any deeper with it, she would have realized that there are six other people downstairs that might be able to hear them. But Luke knew and didn't much care if they did. He wasn't stopping this for anything.

With Taylor's wrists touching, he constructed the first step of a square knot and drew it tight. Taylor let out a gasp; that was part ooh and part aah. He then completed the knot, locking it in so it didn't slip. "Are you sure?" Lucas asked as he was surprised that she had made it this far.

"Yes! Please!" she answered, almost as if to beg.

The second pillowcase he used to wrap and bind her ankles. When she was unable to move, he slithered cautiously to the luggage, extracting two clean red handkerchiefs. Crafting a tight double ligature in the first, he tied the extremities of the two together, constructing a nearly completed gag.

After the cluster was seated properly within her mouth, he tied the two loose ends. He knew that Taylor wasn't a screamer, but with the alcohol she consumed and with all her pent-up emotions, he knew that it was quite possible tonight.

Taylor lay face down, with her desired need to jumpstart their sexual relations. Trying not to add any unwanted pressure, she appeared fine, even though she was already experiencing negative reservations. As he readied himself for what dramatically could change the flow of the evening and maybe their relationship, he chose not to back out, as he wanted to see this to the end, thinking that this is exactly what she needs.

Luke's cock stood firm as he was now caught up in the sight that he hadn't gazed upon in some time. He brought his first leg over her thighs, straddling her as he bypassed any thought of foreplay. After kissing her between the shoulder blades, he surprisingly slid into her wet vagina, in the first few strokes. That drove her into a suppressed moan as her cavity was filled so suddenly and so completely. Taylor remained as silent as she could because tonight she wanted to be that same novice wide-eyed sub, as a year and a half ago.

He sluggardly advanced back and forth like he wanted this to be his only mission, knowing that this could make or break them. By jerking softly at her hips, Luke found he was satisfying his own repressed emotions. The alcohol, which may have skim coated it, had turned him into an animal, an animal that didn't want to stop until his hunger was quenched.

He pushed and pulled as she groaned internally with satisfaction. The bed, although it was pretty quiet considering, could have been heard downstairs in the kitchen. But no one was around to catch it.

When Taylor was freed, Lucas noticed that she still had been crying, as her eye sockets were damp. He held her tight since even though she was beaming, he knew she had to be working through a lot of this. They lay quietly as her smile softened and deep exhaustion engulfed her. Somewhere between there and falling asleep, she was thrilled that she had finally made it over the mile-high hurdle that had separated them.

The next morning, Taylor went downstairs to see where Lucas was. She found him in the kitchen. "Hi, baby," he whispered.

"Hi yourself. So you really are going to do the dishes?" Taylor questioned as she stepped in carrying the pretty large black-and-white Karakachan puppy.

Luke ran his hand back and forth under Daisy's ear and jawbone. The dog responded by pushing back hard at his fingers and knuckles. "I told my mother I would. I'm a good boy!"

"Oh, so you're a good boy now?" she said raising an eyebrow and the corners of her mouth to the event of hours ago.

"That's me!" he answered. Dialing it down and turning it serious he asked, "So are you all right? I saw you crying after and—"

"I'm great and I mean that!" Taylor interrupted while looking totally refreshed. She picked up a cloth to dry the semi-drip-dried dishes that filled the rack. "Pillowcases, huh? I don't know how you do it, but you keep surprising me," Taylor said.

"And I intend to for the rest of our lives," Luke promised making her beam in adoration.

"The rest should be up soon!" Taylor exclaimed.

"Maybe, but did you see the bottles from last night?" he questioned as he pointed to the box with eight empties in it.

"So I'm guessing that no one heard us then!" Taylor said joyfully.

"Probably not." Luke beamed back.

For lunch Thursday, the pair pulled into the sports bar, with the sole purpose of Lucas surprising his friend Dave, the owner. With the hand written Artic Drift coupon that he brought with him from over two thousand miles away, we awaited the antics.

He had brought it more as a joke than a need for free food. Wanting to see his friends face, he looked around for the tall, portly barkeep.

They propped themselves up at the bar with their first drink in hand, as the man pushed through the swinging door, with a load out in front of him. "Dave," Luke called over to get his attention.

"Lucas! Taylor!" Wheeling a dolly, he uprighted it along with the new keg in tow. He beelined it to see them. "So how is everything?" the man said, shaking their hands.

"Good, very good. We are up here for her brother's wedding," Lucas stated.

"That's right, and did I hear you guys are getting married too?"

"Yes, we are!" she said as he showed him the ring.

"Beautiful, just beautiful. The ring is very nice too," Dave joked and then added. "I am so glad you stopped in to see us. Things are just starting to get busy again with the tourist season already starting. So you two are staying at the inn, I presume?"

"Yes, we are."

"You know I still remember your grandparents. We had moved here, and it was so nice when we got to go to the inn. The inn stood out, so well kept. We almost always got to talk to grandma Tilly or your grandpa Michael, when he wasn't busy. A couple of times, she even brought out a piece of pie for us. They were a great couple!"

"Yes, they were!" Taylor said.

"So have you ordered?"

"Yes, we did, and I have the coupon you gave us," he said jokingly.

"Let me see that. This coupon is expired! Your meal for today is on the house, Mr. and Mrs. Calderone!"

"Thanks, Dave, but I was just joking about the coupon."

"I wasn't," he said in a serious tone as he through it in the trash. "Well, I will let you get back to your meal and thanks again for stopping in. You are welcome here anytime!" Dave walked away and grabbed the empty keg, hauling it away to the backroom.

Sitting in the library, the engaged couples went over the wedding plans, with a near-mute bride-to-be, not adding anything on her own behalf. Taylor was concerned as the woman was much more nervous, even though Kyle did what he could to appease her.

Considering her situation as a foster child, Isla was beginning to doubt what she was going to able to bring to the table as both a wife and mother, and now it was more than a hinderance with it being more like a roadblock.

It got to the point where Ken overheard and took Isla for a drive. He thought since he was walking her down the aisle, that it was only right that he did more than just his fifteen seconds' worth. The two drove away, after a short one-way conversation from her future father-in-law, as Isla looked to relax a little, with her leaning back in her seat.

"I hope she will be all right," Taylor said to Lucas as she was getting nervous for her.

"She'll be fine. He will say the right things I'm sure, and those cold feet she has right now will disappear."

"I hope so."

"Look, if she walks away from this, she walks away from a man who would do anything for her. We are talking a set of parents that even though they are not hers will take her in as if she was and a sister that will always want to call her that and mean it," Lucas said as if reciting a speech.

She thought about it for a few seconds. "Why didn't you talk to Isla? She could follow that."

After a painstaking, long, but relaxed day of rewiring the pub, Luke leered through the front window, as he awaited the surprise he was to spring on the group. It was something he had planned on months ago, and he felt it was highly appropriate for the situation at hand.

The other seven were busy getting prepared for their night out, non-rehearsal, or night before the wedding dinner. Standing by the door, it came around the bend at precisely the time that he had called for it. His dad, who was attaching his watch to his wrist, caught the headlights as it turned into the front lot.

"What is that?" Tony commented as he spryly limped out to check it out, with his wife following a couple of feet behind. Kyle and Isla who heard the commotion, followed loosely about eight feet after them. Throwing on their jackets, they found Luke standing with a huge smirk, next to their mode of transportation for the evening, conversing with the chauffeur.

They all stared with mouths agape, as the cocoa brown limo van, sat in the circular drive, with the bearded driver Merle, awaiting to escort them to the restaurant. The six-foot-five man in a light-gray suit dealt a little small talk with Luke as he casually awaited their departure to the high class but modest Valor Steakhouse.

The general attitude, which was already in overdrive, was that the night was sure to match up with their exuberance and merriment. They were all glad that they were all going to be traveling together in one vehicle, with the plus that they had a designated driver for this important occasion.

Twenty minutes later, everyone boarded the vast lounging chamber of the SUV. Merle looked into the rear view, to check on his clients, before he dropped the limo in drive. The vehicle moved along the strewn access road to another that led them back to town.

It traveled stealthily as the eight gabbed and complimented Lucas on his gift that no one else had thought of. And it was not unrealistic, as they were all too busy thinking about tomorrow, making sure they get home and turn in, for the fireside wedding tomorrow.

Once the drink orders were placed at the restaurant, Ken pulled Lucas aside, to say he would be footing the bill for tonight. Luke who was in a festive mood agreed, as the partygoers convened around the lavish large oval table for eight in the tiny yet quaint private room.

With the waiter away to fetch the drink orders, Lucas extracted a newspaper, waving it about, which hushed all the diners within a period of seconds. "Hey, I brought something I think you would all like to see!" he said.

Sending the folded publication to his left, to his parents first, Taylor grew curious. It lackadaisically made its way around the table further away from her, with each hand off, which made her wonder why she wasn't the first to view it, either here or maybe back at the inn.

Taylor did ask Luke, with him not responding back to her in any way. So she waited impatiently as each read it and passed it on, adding a little comment after they did. Taylor figured it had to be the wedding announcement for Kyle and Isla since they are getting married here in town tomorrow.

The *Point Hope Gazette* moved slowly, as it traveled from person to person in an exasperating clockwise movement. She wondered, *Why aren't they reading faster? Or better yet, why hasn't someone just read it out loud to everyone here?*

The paper eventually made its way to her parents, where Susan kept it folded, concealing its front page, so that Taylor couldn't make out a thing. Placing it down, she proudly looked over to her son and Isla, his future wife. She told the newlyweds that it was an excellent write-up, before she lastly picked up the folded paper and handed it to her daughter, to fully complete the circle.

After rushing through the few highlighted headline of the front page article, she was about to rip into the main article when she froze abruptly, bursting into tears. Five mind-numbing words ultimately halted her from reading any further. Taylor's mom, who was now battling with her own sentiments, assisted her daughter who couldn't help but relinquish the periodical.

Susan wiped a tear away. After the pause to her own water show, she proceeded. "Double wedding at the inn. In what is to be a quite historic event for the town, natives of Point Hope will wed on Saturday, May 22, at the lodge of their grandparents. Michael and Tilly Byrne, the original keepers of the Seaview Inn."

Taylor glanced at Luke who held her hand, while he listened to the article. With her free one she dabbed at her own ongoing water-works. "It says that Kyle Naughton, the innkeeper, will marry Isla Lammis, of Nome, Alaska, while Taylor Naughton, Kyle's younger sister of Fairbanks, will tie the knot with Lucas Calderone of Seattle, Washington. The ceremony, which is scheduled for two o'clock will be a private gathering."

If her mom had said any more and she did, Taylor never heard it. Tears dropped, unable to stop. When Taylor was through, the table sat there quietly awaiting the aftermath from the bombshell that had just been dropped smack dab into her lap. She wiped her eyes somewhat dry as the lack of noise turned her in Luke's direction. "So, Taylor, like I've asked you before, do you like surprises?"

Taylor didn't know what to say. She majorly attempted to reason with the words she had just heard. "I'm getting married tomorrow?" she called out, somewhat quiet, and then it blatantly hit her. "I'm getting married tomorrow!" she exclaimed much louder this time. She kissed her man before finally remembering to answer him. "Yes, I love surprises. I will marry you tomorrow."

The server stood in the background as he waited for the proper time to take their orders. Taylor was the nervous one now, even though Isla was still dealing with not just her own thoughts but her sister in laws too. Taylor caught that as the woman was optically locked on with her.

Taylor decided to try to keep this on the back burner so she could enjoy the celebration that they were all initially here for. But it wasn't easy, as the whole newspaper stunner might have been orchestrated by one, but it was carried out by the seven.

Dinner went very well, with about five pounds of meat being consumed. Tonight, even Isla, who would ordinarily reach for a salad first, ordered one. She told the table that the baby wanted it. Smiles and laughs ensued.

Later, pictures were taken of the couples, after Taylor had done some reapplying of her makeup, that is. The waiter, who was there at every beckoned call, snapped off the photos of the entire group, making the evening an outright success.

# CHAPTER 28

On the return to the lodge, the elongated vehicle rode past all the points in town, showing the older Calderone's how the town had changed and or stayed the same. Tony and Gia were thrilled since they hadn't got to see it last year, when they were here for the funeral. This planned wind-down by Lucas gave everyone the chance to take a breather after the many drinks they had consumed.

At bedtime, Taylor toyed with her hair in the bathroom mirror, giving her time to rehash her thoughts and deal with the fears that had bombarded her earlier. She thought, *What if I had said no?* She had the right to do that, considering the bombshell that was placed in her hands.

But the hardened truth was that she did want to go through with this, no matter how it was presented to her. She just needed time to catch up, since everyone else had been in on this for who knows how long.

If she was to put the words together to explain her state of mind, it would have to be that this was all too rushed. That would accurately describe it in a nutshell, with her being the last to know, with her having less than a day to get onboard with this.

While wiping away the rest of her makeup, Taylor heard a light knock at the open bathroom door. She moved aside, thinking that now she'd get to confront Lucas directly, to discuss this with no prying ears around. However, she was shocked to spy it wasn't her fiancé but Isla. "Is everything all right?" Taylor questioned.

"Yes, I just had to give you a big hug and tell you how excited I am for you two."

Thinking the woman had been clued in on the evenings reveal, Taylor just had to ask. "So how long have you known, you know about us two getting married here too, I mean?"

"I would say probably about three months," Isla answered.

Three months, Taylor ran through her head. She looked at herself in the mirror. "You know, sis, I don't think I can do this," she said, not meaning to make a stink out of it.

"Why what's wrong? Can I help?"

"It's just that I don't know what to wear. And I will be... I don't know, I'm just not ready," Taylor answered in a whirl.

"Well, why don't we check out what you have," Isla inquired. Taylor eventually moved over to the closet and showed her the two dresses that she had brought for their wedding. "I love this! You will look great in this one."

"But I would have brought something different if I had known."

"Like what? You know that I'm not wearing a gown. That is why this would be perfect for you. But if you still have a problem with it, then maybe in the morning we can go to town and find you something."

"No, I guess this will work," Taylor replied. She appreciated that Isla stepped in, but there wouldn't be time for any shopping tomorrow. "I didn't want to dress up for ours either. I just can't believe that tomorrow we will all be married."

Taylor loosened up immensely after the woman explained that her usual male bed partner had been replaced by a much shorter female, such as herself. But that was what Taylor needed the most. She was going to get married, so why did she need to have Luke explain his decision that he surprised her with. He did it, and now it didn't matter.

"I know how special this will be for you tomorrow. You are marrying Luke and in a place that has always meant so much to you." Taylor's eyes opened to that comforting thought, piercing a hole in the fear that blanketed all the good that she needed to come from this union.

The two women remained awake and cackled about everything and how they first met their significant others. Taylor, of course, had two stories, one of when they were very young and the other was a slightly tweaked version, so Isla's eyes didn't pop out of her head. Laughter filled the room and even tears when the story called for it.

Taylor enjoyed these preliminaries of having a sister that she could confide in. Heck, for the rest she still had Lauren. Wondering if there was any more of these so-called surprises, she declined from asking, seeing she wouldn't like it if hers were revealed. The exchange kept the ladies up late into the morning, with both of their nerves subsided by then.

Taylor lumbered into the bathroom to see if her outward demeanor had changed since last night. Seeing the reflection, she spurted out an uncontrollable giggle at what she saw staring back at her. It seemed through the bedtime hours; she had somehow amassed a swirling bird's nest of a hairdo.

Reaching down for a brush to remedy the situation, she went into an unrestrained guffaw, after seeing the follow-up view, which included her future sister in the background, with hair that made even Taylor's hair pale by comparison. It was priceless as Isla caught each of their morning mops, using the reflective quality of the mirror. With not one word being said, the woman performed a duet of unrestrained laughter that rained down through the ceiling and to the early birds below.

As the time drew near, the men worked on the last touches completing the transformation of the pub into a beautiful fireside chapel while the women congregated in the Calderone's room upstairs.

Lucas, in the storage room, studied his father's work, as his dad loomed and glowed in the background. "You did a wonderful job with this! Taylor is going to love it!" Lucas said, referring to the sign he had him carve out of the seasoned Alaskan birch from the garage.

"Yes, I think the gold leaf trim makes it pop," his father stated. "So, are we putting it up now?" Tony asked.

"No, I think we should do it tomorrow," Lucas said as his dad nodded in affirmation.

A half hour before the wedding, Deena, the officiant, was escorted in by Kyle and got the meet and greet with the grooms and the two fathers. They stood with the justice of the peace, talking about their future wives, as Tony and Ken looked on. Lucas and Kyle couldn't hide the fact that each were crazy about the women they intended to marry, as their verbal jubilation engulfed the room.

The guys, who might have been a tad nervous, rambled as maybe subconsciously they knew that their years of being single was quickly coming to an end, and or that it was that they were trekking into something that was unknown for them.

The aroma and sight of the fresh bouquets of flowers around the room was barely noticeable to Luke as his only thoughts were of him wanting to be married to Taylor this very minute. With Susan announcing that they were ready, Kyle scrolled in his phone's library from his preselected list that he and Isla had chosen as their entrance music.

On cue, the mothers strolled in on the arms of their husbands, as each of the men wore their same dapper suits that they sported the evening before. With the women in their seats and Tony by Gia's side, Ken went back to the door to escort the not one but two brides. Kyle turned on the processional music.

As the instrumental version of "Somewhere" over the rainbow began, Ken entered proudly with both the beautiful Isla and his own daughter, Taylor, hanging off each arm. Kyle and Luke's eyes gleamed at the sight of the women looking so gorgeous, as they made the corner bringing the two brides into view.

Taylor sauntered one step closer to her soon-to-be husband, as her trance was suddenly broken by the abundance of bright flowers that illuminated the room. Patches of pink carnations, Isla's favorites, and daisies, which were Taylor's, were everywhere, both on the tables and the mantle too.

She looked forward again to see Lucas looking so handsome there in his dark-gray suit. That along with the dark-blue shirt and belt that she had got him for his birthday made him stand out in an elegant way.

The woman somehow kept it together, grinning as she and Isla joined their fiancés in front of the fire. When the song ended, the four turned toward the woman officiant. She said a few brief words to the couples as she opened her book.

Taylor remained still, except for her knees that shook, that might have emitted a sound had they been much closer. She leaned in a little closer to her intended in her dark-blue knee-length dress, laced around the collar, with her pair of color matching heels. These were the items that she brought to attend her brother's wedding, never thinking in a million years that it would be for her own.

"Today, we are here to join these two couples in marriage and to share in the joy of your special occasion, which will prove to be the most important one in your lives." Isla, who was wavering on the inside and nervous to beat the band, was ready to become a wife, so that she would now be part of a family that she already loved.

With the fire blazing behind Deena the justice, she read on until she got to the part. "Do you, Kyle, take Isla to be your lawfully wedded wife, to honor, to cherish, through sickness and in health, through good times and bad, so long as you both shall live?"

Kyle responded, "I do!"

Next, the other three were asked the same question to which they each answered, "I do!"

A bit quieter, the woman asked the parties if they had the rings. The two fathers came up with their boxes that they were to present to each other. They took the rings for their spouses to be and waited, with Taylor spying the jewelry that Luke had picked out for himself.

"Now place the ring on their finger and repeat after me. With this ring, I thee wed, pledging my devotion!" Deena exclaimed. The four followed suit and copied the woman word for word. The mothers were in the background, crying. But it was more so for Susan, who had both of her children getting married at the same time, there in front of her. Ken even had his hanky out, wiping away a tear before it ran down his face.

His speech, or pep talk, to Isla seemed to have worked as it reminded her how things had changed for her, and all for the better. And it would always remain that way, as long as there was love to carry the two of them through.

The officiant concluded, "You came to me as four single people and you are leaving as two married couples, joined by the binding contract you had all agreed to. I wish the best for you in your futures while you move forward. May your lives be everything you want them to be." She took a little breather.

"Now comes the fun part," she said quietly enough for them alone. "I would like to present Kyle and Isla Naughton and Lucas and Taylor Calderone as the two newly wedded couples!" They all kissed and turned around to clapping by the older generation who were standing and applauding, with a tearful Ken, who was trying to take pictures.

With the service concluded, the parents quickly joined them up front. Lucas pulled Taylor aside to steal his second kiss as husband and wife, preparing himself for the thousands in the years to come.

She admired the ring that he had chosen for her without her knowledge. That and the engagement ring seemed to cradle each other, as they rested comfortably on the finger of her left hand. But even better than that, she liked her newly inherent surname. Taylor treasured how well her name, and her minutes long married one, Taylor Calderone, sounded together.

Getting to the part of where they were to open presents, everyone was surprised as to how many there were considering that the wedding party was so scant. Taylor viewed the bar round that was piled with gifts, as for once she didn't think about her second night at the lodge.

Opening the first that they came across, they opened a card from Lauren and Carl. It said that they were very happy for both of them and that they were sorry that they couldn't be there in person, but they would see them soon.

After Kyle and Isla opened their first, Taylor reached for the next one. It was large and the tiny card stated it was from Henri. Luke brought it down carefully onto a barstool between them to see it better.

They ripped at the paper and then broke the sealed top of the box, pulling at the flaps enough to see an entire case of wine. The card inside said that he had hand-picked these twelve bottles to be added to their own personal rack. After getting to the fourth one, she eyeballed it and instantly began to puddle up, as she recalled the bottle the moment she saw it again. Her hands shook just as Henri's had when he had shown it to her in the wine cellar.

Luke, who never got the full version, waited intently along with the rest of the wedding party while she tried to compose herself. After wiping away most of her tears she tried to reveal it, as if it came straight from their friend's mouth.

"This was the bottle that Henri and his wife Sabine were going to celebrate with on their fiftieth wedding anniversary," she had explained by saying how they had used these wines to remember all the best times in their lives.

The women and even Tony shed tears as they had never heard anything so beautiful. Tony and Gina, who had known the man for over thirty years, were shocked that they had never heard the quote before, thinking that he must have thought Taylor was something special to disclose it to her.

With most of the gifts opened, Lucas handed a present to his brother-in-law and wife, to which Taylor was all eyes, considering she still didn't know what it was that they were giving them. The other newlyweds opened it to show a blue pocketed folder. A prompt bewildering kicked in as she turned back to Lucas, knowing it was the same one that they had given to the parents.

So why didn't he mention that he had picked up another set of tickets? With Isla fiddling through the travel junkets and her husband getting a giddy ear full, she rambled about the news of a honeymoon that she didn't think they would be able to take.

Then from out of the blue, a question popped out, "So what are we doing about the inn? Are we keeping it closed for the first two weeks?" Isla questioned, knowing this was to be an extended trip and they have their first guests of the season booked before they get back.

"No, that is the other part of our wedding gift to you. Taylor and I will run it for you while you're gone," Lucas answered. Taylor was locked into the idea that they were going on the cruise. *What's up with that?* She thought.

"Kyle, then what are we going to do for clothes?" Isla replied knowing that even her summertime best would not work in Hawaii.

Kyle answered, "I picked up a few things. You can try them on, and if not, then we can get some when we get to Anchorage!"

Isla for some reason wasn't worried. She was married and going on a vacation, a cruise with her new family and husband. Taylor was now only mildly put out as she was happy that they were going to benefit from this, and that her sister Isla solely deserved to be indulged. Considering that the woman had never got to see what a real family was like, now she would 24/7.

At dinner, Taylor reached into the case for a bottle, in honor of their first big occasion. It went without saying that this was theirs, and now they had to keep an eye out for the next, making sure it didn't go by without acknowledgment. They all savored the wine, not so much for its taste or the quantity, because of having to be split eight ways, but in the Henri mindset, of the memory it was wrapped around.

At bedtime they basically followed her brother and sister-in-law to get some sleep, as even though they were not leaving tomorrow for the cruise, they still had an inn to open soon. At the room, Taylor told Luke that she had to speak with her brother and would be back in a few.

With some pep in her step, Taylor ran down the stairs and knocked on the innkeeper's door, the home of the newlyweds. Kyle answered. She pulled a bottle of wine that she had hidden behind her back and placed it in his hands. "I want you two to have this."

"But isn't this from your collection? I mean we heard the story, and it is about your special moments," Kyle stated.

"You two are our special moments. We want you to save this for your twenty-fifth!"

"I don't know what to say, but thank you," Kyle said before adding. "And now I feel funny because I was going to ask you if you two wouldn't mind watching Daisy for us while we're gone. But I know that I shouldn't since it looked like you weren't enthused about not going on the cruise."

"It's not that. I just wasn't ready for it, but I am now. I am happy for you two, with the way it turned out, really!" Taylor exclaimed.

"However, you should be worried that I might keep the pup for myself."

"That is a chance that we will have to take."

"I love you, Kyle. Now get back to the missus," she said applying a gratifying smirk.

"I love you too sis!" he said as he closed the door. With what Taylor wanted to do checked off, she turned back in the direction of her own husband.

Taylor returned to the room only to realize that Lucas was gone. Before she even finished reading the short note, he was back in the room behind her. "Sorry, I had to ask my dad something!" Lucas used for cover.

Not sure why she was even bringing this up, the woman finally let it out, "Why didn't you tell me that we were giving our tickets to them?" Taylor asked once she had his full attention.

Lucas just smiled. "Look, I would do anything for you and your family because now they are mine too!"

"But why didn't you tell me? I wouldn't have said no."

"Surprises, baby!" He simply phrased. She stood in wonder, with her eyes flitting about. This was the third time she had heard these words recently, and even though they had all been good, she had trouble keeping up with them. "A better life for us baby, that is what I want!"

She inched her way to the center of his chest, holding her husband close. Taylor couldn't help but wonder if the surprises were finished. Somehow, she thought that wasn't to be the case. Lucas fell asleep with Taylor neatly wrapped in his arm.

She lay there, feeling so safe and happy. The morning would come soon, and they had an inn to prepare. Her mind raced, with the excitement of running her grandparents' business, even though it was only for the two weeks.

Kyle and Isla kept the place quite tidy, but the offseason was about to end, and they have to be ready for those staying the night, and with that, she wanted it to be up to Grandma Tilly's standards. Taylor couldn't turn it off, as the food or menu popped into her head.

In the silence of the place, many suitcases lined the halls, propped against the side of the wall, ready for their move in the morning.

Taylor and Luke already had their own separate hidden agendas. She was going to spiff up the place, while he was going to try to talk her into a nothing day, for their first full day as man and wife. But between them Taylor was going to win.

Lucas, who was the first up, ran into Ken and his dad as they walked down the stairs. "So how does it look?" Tony asked.

"It's perfect, just as I pictured it," Luke said quietly.

The early morning was rushed as the six cruisers were all aflutter, with making sure they didn't forget anything. Luke, who was there to haul luggage, hired the same limo company to bring them all to the airport, giving them one less thing to think about.

The goodbyes were short but sweet, as Tony the military man kept them all on a tight schedule. Kisses and hugs seemed endless until the elders climbed into the rear of the vehicle. Kyle and Isla, who were the last to say their goodbyes, thanked them again for the cruise and taking care of the place.

With them all in the vehicle, the luggage loaded and the chauffeur in his seat, Kyle dropped his window halfway to leave one last comment. "It looks good, Luke. Real good!"

Taylor with the puppy leashed to her right hand sniffed at the ground. She turned back briefly, only to be distracted by her brother closing the window. Kyle and Isla waved as they pulled around the circle and around the field and out of sight.

Lucas stood there in front of Taylor. "Well, I guess it is time to come clean on everything! No more surprises, for now anyway." Taylor thought, finally she was going to be brought up to speed. "First of all, I want you to know that I have no job to go back to. I made the decision not to split up ownership but to sell it off completely to Trent."

Her eyes grew wide from what she had just heard. Not giving her a chance to interrupt he added. "Another thing! I sold the house and the boat. I hope you don't mind!" She didn't understand. Why would he do this? He loved that house. Turning to walk back into the inn, she kept her eyes on him, waiting for the rest. "But because of the stars aligning, there is now a new sign for the inn!" he said, pointing down.

She stared in disbelief. The new routed sign, which the dads had finished before they even arrived, hung as a replacement to the old one. The new one read, "Grandma Tilly's Bed and Breakfast, established 1959," and the last line had her crying: "Proprietors Taylor & Lucas Calderone." She stood there, shaking in the cool morning air in total disbelief.

"But how… What? I mean, what is happening with Kyle and Isla?"

"He has a great-paying job lined up in Anchorage, managing a very fine hotel. He starts a week after they get back."

"I… I just can't believe this," Taylor declared.

"It's true, baby, so I guess I need to know if you want to run this B and B with me?" Luke questioned as she didn't take long to answer.

"Of course, I do!" They walked back into the bar, where Luke poured a couple of mimosas from the leftover ingredients of the mornings bon voyage send-off. It was then that Luke answered all of her questions.

She never knew that Kyle was growing tired of running the family inn and had been thinking about selling it. So Lucas mentioned how it all came into place when Kyle said yes to selling it to another family member, and one that he knew would jump at the chance. Luke even showed her plans for a possible expansion for them and someday their family.

Taylor was so pleased with the way things were going. He is a romantic! She could now see it more and more every day. She looked around, getting excited, as each moment passed.

"Oh, one last thing. Kyle and Isla insisted on coming back for the entire month of November to take care of the inn for us. They want to cover while we go on our honeymoon. And that way we can put a little celebration into your birthday since we weren't able to last year." Luke paused. "But I thought since I have come up with everything else, it would only be right if you decide on where you would like to take it."

"Oh, wow. You are saying it is my choice? Then I think I know exactly where we should go. I would like to spend two of the weeks in Italy, so I can get to meet your parents' families. You need to know who you are and where you came from. For the other two weeks, I would like to be here at the inn, so we can enjoy our niece or nephew. We are not going to see them much, and that is what I really want. I hope that's all right with you?"

"I would have been shocked if you hadn't said that as I knew that you would want to be with family. And thanks to you, I know it's time to reunite with mine too," Lucas stated.

"Oh, and I wouldn't be opposed to your mom and dad going too, if they want," Taylor commented.

"We can run it by them when they get back."

"Lucas I want to thank you for everything. This is more than I could have ever asked for!" she said holding eye contact with her husband. "I also have to let you know what I have been doing, concerning the check that we received. I knew that I couldn't keep it, so I talked to several of the town council members, and with their okay, I have pledged to rebuild the memorial library into a library, senior center, and affordable day care." Taylor paused.

"I put a lot of thought into this since you mentioned that I should do something good with it. However, it was the council's recommendation that we memorialize it to people that have made such strides at bettering the town and the way people feel about it. The entire council voted, and it was unanimous that they chose my grandparents," she stated as she brought her cheeks up high to a grin.

"That is a fantastic idea," Lucas proclaimed before adding, "Mick and Tilly would be happy, with them still able to assist the town."

"I think so, and they would also be pleased that the inn will continue to be run by family, with a chance of maybe their great grandchildren taking over someday."

"Well, that brings up something that I wanted to discuss, knowing that we both want children. I'm not sure how soon we are talking, but parts of our life will have to change. So I'm thinking that maybe we can continue our BCD moments until we can't."

"I'm game for that!" she inferred with a grin just to get his goat.

"Oh, I almost forgot. I got a voice mail from Kyle that I think you will want to hear," Lucas said as he handed the phone to his wife.

Taylor pulled the phone tight to her ear. "Hey Taylor, I want to let you in on something since I didn't do it last night. Isla and I didn't give you your wedding present, but I know you will get over it, when I tell you. When I said we picked up Daisy last week, that was true. But I think you thought she was our dog. I have got to apologize, but she's not, she is yours. I hope you will love her as much as you did Chestnut. Well, enjoy each other and we will see you in a few weeks and thank you for everything."

Taylor, whom thought she had not one more tear left from crying over all the happy that had crossed her plate, bawled again. Daisy scampered into the room and around Taylor's legs as the dog wasn't sure what the strange sound was that was coming from her new owner.

She bent over to hug her pooch until her ducts went dry. Luke waited for a few minutes since Taylor was stuck in the puppy zone. When she finally stood up to look her hubby in the eyes, she did it with glassy ones.

Luke, who couldn't verbally hit her with one more thing, turned on the new light that he installed, allowing it to beam down over the granite mantle and the new addition above that. Her eyes were drawn to the lit thick wooden panel, peering at it, studying the words that she now knew so well.

The professionally routed medium-stained piece was centered for anyone who visited the room. The new mantra, whose letters were painted in gold leaf, scrolled across the four-foot piece. "May your wine rack never be full and never be empty."

Showing no tears, her head bobbed gracefully with unspoken words that seemed to say that she could work with this. When he thought she was back with him and was all right with all the new changes, he kissed her. "So what do you think? Are you ready to do this?" Lucas said as he held out the unlocked stainless-steel bracelet.

"Oh yes, sir!" Taylor enthusiastically answered by placing her wrist across the jewelry. Then with them both displaying a pair of broad smirks, he locked it.

# ABOUT
# THE AUTHOR

Jeffrey Masterz is a husband and father of two grown children. He lives in a small town in Western Massachusetts with his wife of over thirty years. Since the age of seven, Jeffrey has sought to express his creative side through various forms of art from drawing and sketches to poems and short stories. Over those years, his wife has encouraged his imagination and played the role as his muse, audience, and critic.

Jeffrey originally developed this book's narrative in the form of a two-chapter short story that he presented as a birthday gift to his spouse. After she first read it, his wife persuaded him that his work deserved to be expanded upon and shared with the world. So with her as his inspiration, he poured his heart, soul, and countless hours into creating something she would be proud of.

CPSIA information can be obtained
at www.ICGtesting.com
Printed in the USA
BVHW092354180222
629164BV00001B/2